PRAISE FOR W.A. KELLY

"A gripping page-turner! I loved the return of Mickey Blake in this superb crime thriller."

LAUREN NORTH - BEST-SELLING THRILLER AUTHOR

"The Call Back reads like Guy Ritchie and Antti Tuomainen got together to create a masterpiece. There's action, there are questionable decisions, and there's a black humour that runs through it."

CHRIS McDONALD - BEST-SELLING CRIME AUTHOR

"The Mickey Blake series is that rarest of beasts... thrillers that thrill, while packing humour and heart into every chapter."

DAN HOWARTH - AUTHOR OF 'LAST NIGHT OF FREEDOM'

THE CALL BACK

A MICKEY BLAKE THRILLER

W A KELLY

First published in the UK by Pick Lock Publishing

ISBN 978-1-0683379-0-1

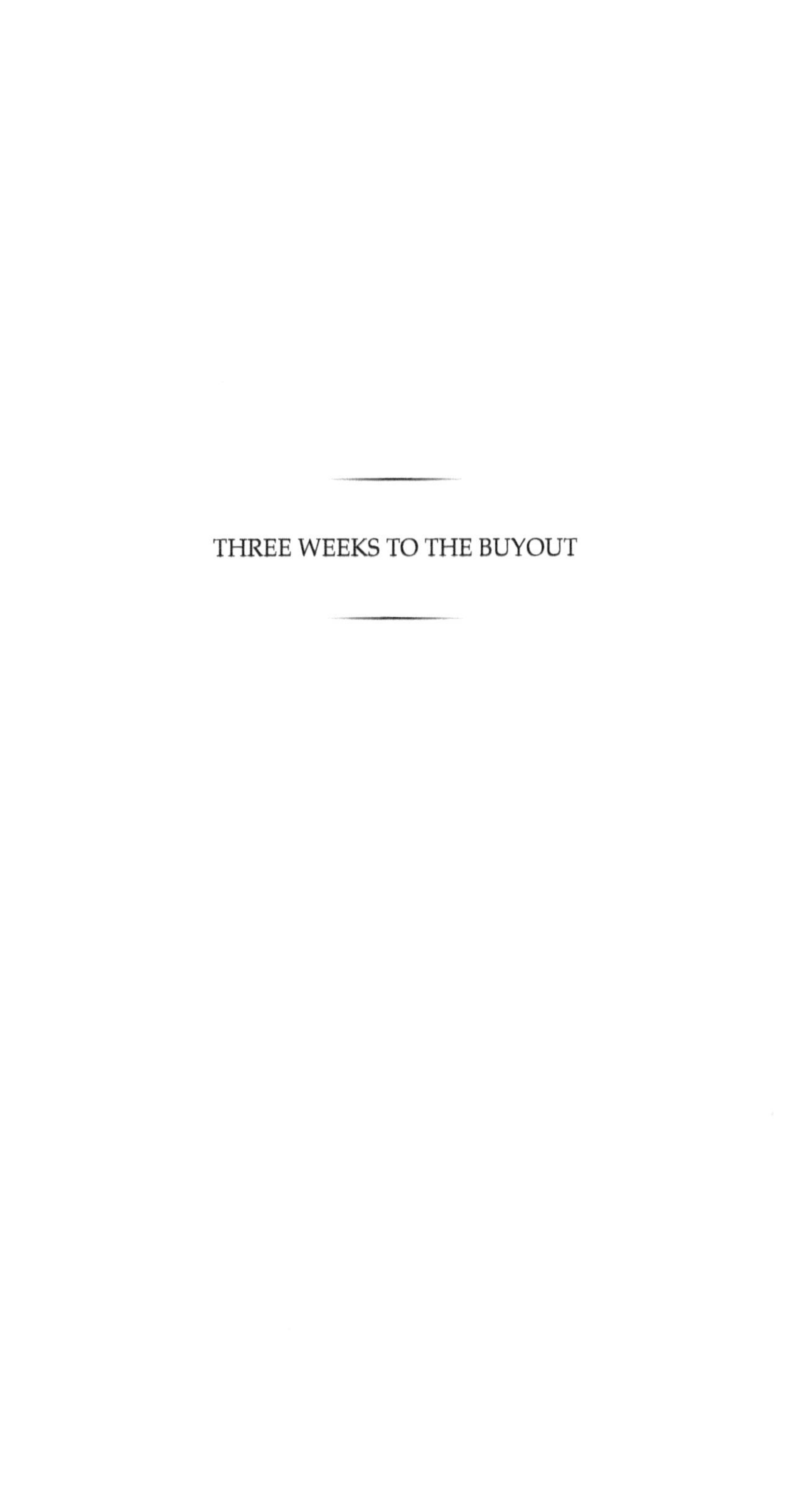

THREE WEEKS TO THE BUYOUT

CHAPTER 1
MICKEY

I SUPPOSE I should be turned on, but the look on her face and the cuffs confirm something I've been wondering about all night; she knows who I am. Who I *really* am, I mean.

I've cracked impenetrable vaults and stood toe-to-toe with men who wanted to kill me, but I would've taken any of that over what faced me tonight: my first date with a woman in decades. *Date.* Even my terminology is off. Apparently, you don't call them that anymore. Not since the advent of Tinder and all the other apps I've been forced to look at over the past couple of months. Warren, my twenty-one-year-old apprentice and pain in the arse, has been assuring me it's all about 'hook-ups' now and that I 'need to put it about a bit, bro'. Keeps telling me to 'see the light and swipe right'. Daft sod.

Anyway, turns out all my fears were justified. Tonight has been a total shit-show and to top it off, I come out of the bathroom now to find she's handcuffed herself to the bed.

Teeth bared, she says, 'Fuck me now, you fucking… fucker.'

Not the most articulate woman I've ever met.

She's attractive, late-fifties, auburn hair with a great figure. Tasteful matching burgundy underwear and, until ten minutes ago, a perfectly polite divorcee who surprised me by insisting I came in for a coffee. We'd barely made it over the threshold before she'd pinned me to the wall in the hallway and was trying to get her hand into my jeans while pushing her tongue down my throat. I suggested we take it upstairs. At sixty-two years of age, my days of shagging on the stair carpet are well and truly behind me.

Don't get me wrong. I'm no prude. But any lust I felt for her left the building when I looked into her now crazed eyes. She's biting her lip in a way she must think is sexy, but all I'm getting is *Exorcist* vibes, expecting her head to do a three-sixty any second. Where's my holy water? I'm wearing a pair of boxers, but the semi I was nursing when I stepped back into the bedroom has disappeared faster than Road Runner legging it from Wile E. Coyote. Aside from all that, blokes who get off on role-playing rape are weirdos.

'Come on. What are you waiting for, Mickey Blake?'

And there it is. Proof she's rumbled me. I don't use my real name on those apps. Found out pretty soon after I came back home that if I wanted to truly leave my old life behind, I'd need to be selective about when I used Mickey Blake. For strangers and clients and anyone else I need to keep at arm's length, I go by 'Michael' these days.

'Come on,' she says again now. 'Thought you could open anything?'

'Some things are better left shut, love,' I tell her. 'And you can start by closing your legs and telling me where the key to those cuffs is, so I can make sure you're free before I get out of here.'

'What?' She looks crestfallen, but quickly recovers. 'You telling me you don't want *this*?'

I'm guessing she's trying to gesture to her admittedly great body, but seeing as both her hands are cuffed to the metal struts of the bed-head, all she can do is use her chin to point out what I'm missing. Looks like she's having a minor stroke. Either way, I need to tread carefully. Have to let her down gently. I don't need this erratic shit in my life right now and a woman that pulls this kind of stunt with someone she must assume is some edgy criminal, is to be avoided at all costs. I step closer, scanning around the bed for the key, and she stretches out to stroke my leg with her foot. Makes me jump and she laughs. Get a grip, Mickey.

'What's the matter with you?' she asks, in between lip-bites, shag-me-eyes and pouting. 'You can do what you want to me. I don't care.'

'That's all very well, Jeanette. But all I want to do right now is unlock those cuffs, get dressed and head home.'

Her face hardens. 'Are you serious? I can't tell whether you're being serious with all your sarcasm. Been doing my head in all night.'

It's called dry humour. It's not my fault you're about as funny as a migraine. 'Yeah, I'm an acquired taste.'

'What you on about now?'

Christ. I force a smile. 'I can be a smart-arsed twat at times.'

'Why didn't you just say that then?'

'Anyway. Obvious we're not well-suited. You're not into smart-arses and I'm not a fan of tie-sie-up-sies. So why don't you tell me where the key is so we can call it a night?'

She thinks for a few seconds, then blurts out, 'I swallowed it.'

'You did what?'

'The key. Swallowed it. Wanted to make sure you'd have to do it.'

'Do what?' I ask, trying to keep the anger out of my voice.

'You know. Show me what you can do with those magic hands.'

'That's exactly what we'd be doing right now. I'd be using these magic hands on your amazing body. But you're crackers and instead you've pulled this crap.'

There's a pause. The pout returns before she says, 'So you think I've got an amazing body, do you?'

For fuck's sake. This is pointless.

'Right,' I tell her, as I retrieve my jeans and the rest of my clothes from the bedroom floor. 'If you want to carry on role-playing *Basic Instinct*, that's up to you but—'

'*Basic Instinct?*'

'Doesn't matter. Forget I said that.' I pull on my jeans and sit on a pink stool she's got in front of her mirror. I put on my socks, look her in the eye and speak slowly. 'Point is, I'm leaving. If you tell me where the key is, I'll unlock the cuffs before I go. If you don't, I'm gone, and you can work it out yourself.'

'I told you,' she says, 'I swallowed it.'

I take a deep breath, hold it for a few seconds and let it out slowly through my nose. Why is nothing ever straightforward in my life? Millions of people using these apps, getting their end away or starting relationships easier than ordering a pizza, and my first time out, I pull an absolute psycho.

I go to her now, reach out to touch her face. She turns her head, trying to manoeuvre my fingers into her open mouth. Wouldn't surprise me if she tries to bite me, so I stay away from her lips and gently run my thumb across her skin, tracing her eyeline until my hand is in her hair. She groans and it's one of those contrived, breathy sounds all the women seem to make in every porno I've ever seen.

'Just relax, will you,' I tell her. 'Take it down a couple of notches.'

She bites her lip again and arches her back until her left nipple almost crests the edge of her bra. Something stirs in my boxer shorts and for a few seconds I consider throwing caution to the wind, giving her what she says she wants and worrying about the consequences later. But the stakes are too high. Barely been eighteen months since I came back from exile and whilst it looks like most of my legal issues are in the rearview mirror, the last thing I need is some trumped-up sexual assault charge or a bullshit tabloid story about how 'Mickey Blake got hands-on with a fifty-eight-year-old stunner'. And what about Hazel? What would she have to say about this? Will this be a funny anecdote I can share with her, now we're 'just good friends'?

'What are you thinking about, you bad boy?' Jeanette asks now.

Not you, love. 'I'm thinking your hair would look better down.'

'Yeah?'

'Yes.' I pull out one of the hair pins she has in the bun behind her head, then immediately take a step back away from the bed.

Slack-jawed, she asks, 'What're you doing?'

I ignore her, already working on the thin metal pin, bending it until it's straight, then folding one end into a right-angle. Taking it between my teeth, I remove the tiny plastic-coated tip and spit it out on to the carpet.

'You're doing it, aren't you?' she asks. 'Working your magic.'

She looks like she's getting off on all this and I hate that I'm performing for her, like some prancing bear dancing for scraps of food. Still, the sooner I unlock the cuffs, the sooner I can get out of here and put this night, and Crazy Jeanette behind me.

I step up to the bed again, close enough to smell her perfume and the wine on her breath. 'Don't do anything stupid or the only magic I'll be working is a disappearing act.'

'At least talk me through it. Tell me how you do it,' she says.

'Google it.'

And with that, I get to work. The cuffs are old, probably police issue and the kind you used to see back in the eighties. They're double lock but no plastic shielding like the modern restraints. Nothing to stop me getting at the mechanism with my improvised pick. I push the tip of the pin into the lock cut-out and put another kink into it by twisting it to the left. Now I've got a small s-shaped tool and can get to work on releasing the first lock. I move the pick to the upper part of the keyhole, and using my thumb and forefinger, make tiny movements, mentally mapping out the internal mechanism, as if drawing a minuscule maze in my mind. Compared to a safe, this is a piece of piss and within a few seconds I've sussed out the direction of travel for the key. A sharp, anti-clockwise turn releases the double lock, leaving the way open to tackle the remaining mechanism. That takes even less time than the first one and the cuff pops open with a satisfying click. Jeanette moans like this is foreplay. She runs her hand through my hair.

'What did I just tell you?' I ask, sounding like a parent cautioning a child. 'Keep your hands to yourself and let me work.'

She frowns, sticks out her bottom lip but takes her hand away.

I move to the other cuff. 'Are you going to let me leave with some dignity when I've done this?'

Like a scolded kid, she looks away and gives me a little nod. I've barely got the pick in the lock when the cuff pops open – it wasn't locked! Takes me less than a second to realise I've been a dozy twat. Without being a contortionist, of course she couldn't have locked both of them. While I'm figuring that out, her other hand rears up like a rattle snake, to grab me, or God-knows-what. I catch it with my left hand but I'm not quick enough to stop her punching me – closed fist! – with a good solid left hook. I spring up and take a couple of steps back from the bed. She bares her teeth, leaning forward on her hands and knees, like a cat poised to attack. A nervous laugh escapes before I can stop it and when I touch my throbbing lip, there's blood on my fingertips. I should be fuming, but I'm struggling not to find the whole thing funny. Not to mention the fact I'm embarrassed I couldn't avoid the punch. To think I used to be a boxer.

She's breathing heavily and clearly waiting for me to have a go back. Instead, I laugh again, harder this time, which only seems to annoy her more.

'Listen,' I warn her, my hand raised to show her the blood, 'you clearly have some issues you're working through, but I'm not the kind of bloke you obviously think I am. And if you want my relationship advice, I'd find a different type to go for.'

She deflates, shakes her head. 'What a let-down you've turned out to be.'

'You're not the first person to tell me that. Doubt you'll be the last.' Keeping a wary eye on her, I look for my shoes and spot them over near the dressing table. I snatch them up and start backing out of the room, but the sexy siren act is already fading away to be replaced by resignation and disappoint-ment. She sits back and slowly pulls up the sheet to cover herself. Closing-up shop. I take one last longing look at what I could've won, until I remember my fat lip and realise I've dodged a bullet. I turn and leave.

When I'm halfway down the stairs, I call back up to her. 'Tell you something, Jeanette. That's some left hook you've got.'

'Fuck you!'

You wish, love. You wish.

CHAPTER 2
LIAM

LIAM CHECKS HIS PHONE AGAIN, partly wondering how his dad's date is going but mainly using it to justify stepping away from the dreary conversation he finds himself in. Or rather, the conversation he finds himself standing on the outside of, nodding occasionally and smiling at what seem like the right moments. On the face of it, it's a welcome party for his agency's latest signing: ex-banker and supposedly reformed white-collar criminal, Asa Harrington. But it's much more than that. The fact it's taking place not in Liam's shabby-chic building half a dozen tube stops further up the Northern Line, but here at the offices of LimeLight International Entertainment, means he's taken another step closer to the buyout he seems to be sleepwalking into. Everyone tells him it's the smart move.

Take the money, Liam.

His eyes drift over the shoulder of the twenty-something playwright who's boring the arse off everyone, complaining that nobody wants serious work anymore, to the twenty-foot high, plate glass windows. It's dark outside, the window becoming a black mirror, reflecting back the scene. Christ, he thinks. It's like a warped Hopper painting. This is only Lime-

Light's foyer, but it's a huge space: marble floors, low-backed sofas and angular minimalist furniture. Fifty or so people are dotted about in little groups. Everyone selling themselves hard, waiting for another gap in the conversation to talk at their audience. All of them on TRANSMIT, nobody really listening. Liam wonders if his eyes look as empty as they appear in the glass, or if it's just him projecting.

It's at times like this, surrounded by middle-class stuffed shirts, society girls and fame-hungry wannabes, who all seem to be from the same side of the tracks, Liam feels like a stranger in the company he co-founded more than a decade ago. If the deal goes through, will he just be the company mascot? The working-class type they roll out to show how diverse and modern they are?

He mutters an apology to the group he's found himself attached to and pretends he has something to do on the other side of the room. Neither of the two people he was supposedly conversing with seem to hear him, or care, as he makes his way to a quiet corner and stares at his phone screen, pretending to answer some important emails. What he's actually doing is scrolling through a bunch of photographs of his two girls, Isobel and Grace, and counting the hours until he can get back home to see them. Still, it's why he's worked so hard to build the agency in the first place, to give the girls and his wife, Claire, the life they deserve. When the buyout goes through, Claire will finally be able to get her PT business off the ground. After what he put her through with the fallout from Kendrick going to prison, not to mention what happened with his dad in Skegness, he's lucky she's stuck around.

He puts away the phone again. It's making him sad, and he needs to be smiling and 'on', working the room and scouting for any new talent he can poach from his rivals. He forces himself upright and pushes his shoulders back in the tailor-made, dark blue suit that cost more than his dad would've paid for a car back in the day. *Project what you want the world to see.* One of his dad's better mottos, something Liam has taken through his life, from his younger days on the stage to his time working the business side of the game. As he looks around the room, he wonders what projections and fakery half this lot are trying to pull. He focuses for a few moments, tunes in and uses the natural abilities he's honed over the years.

Two of his youngest actors, fresh out of drama school, are off to the right, talking the head off a bored-looking TV exec. To be fair, the exec is doing a good job of feigning interest, but Liam spots the subtle flick of her wrist, freeing the cuff of her jacket so she can glance at her watch. She's counting the minutes until she can leave.

The man of the hour, Asa, is in the corner, surrounded by some friendly members of the press and a few long-standing clients, like Martin Chalmers, who is graciously introducing Asa to everyone and pretending he's not jealous or bitter. It's one of the best performances he's put on for a while, but Liam registers one of Martin's many tells, the way he's talking out of the side of his mouth, pretending to take Asa into his confidence. Subconsciously shutting out the other members of the circle, a transparent attempt to be part of Asa's gang. Even though Liam knows Martin will be back on the phone again tomorrow, moaning about 'the lack of decent roles for old white blokes'. Liam wonders what Asa, an erudite, privately-educated black man, would make of some of Martin's comments about 'political correctness gone mad' and 'those wokey twats at the BBC'. He reckons Martin is maybe two glasses of red away from letting the mask slip. He makes a note to intervene before that and sighs. Sometimes, being so tuned in to human behaviour can be exhausting.

Half a dozen of his office staff are letting their hair down, without getting too drunk. Smiling, being attentive to the right people at LimeLight and making sure Flick's champagne glass stays topped up. Felicity 'Flick' Graves, the woman who gave Liam the financial backing he needed to set up his little agency more than a decade ago. In truth, despite Liam's mum's maiden name being over the door, it was Flick's family money that bankrolled those early years. Liam's hard work was what built their roster of clients. Things changed a few years in, when young talent seemed to be made up entirely of rich kids. The children of those who had the money and the contacts to allow their little darlings to take unpaid internships at TV companies or spend months attending auditions. All without ever having to slum it or sign on, like most of Liam's generation had had to do. It's why the industry is now awash with upper-middle class actors and presenters that went to the best schools money can buy. 'Cookie-cutter cunts' is how Martin Chalmers had described them after one too many sherries at the agency Christmas do.

Liam's phone vibrates in his pocket and he's glad of the excuse to take it out and look at it again. Until he reads the message from an unknown number:

HOW GOES IT, JEFE?

A breath catches in the back of Liam's throat. Only one person has ever called him Jefé, *boss*. Despite being certain who he's talking to, he taps out a reply:

WHO IS THIS?

Three ghostly dots on the screen undulate in time to Liam's elevated heart rate, a reply being typed.

LET'S NOT PLAY GAMES. WE NEED TO TALK.

Liam stares at the message whilst nervously tapping his knuckle against the side of his head.

'Trying to tap some sense into it?' He jumps at the sound of Flick's voice. She laughs. 'What could possibly be troubling you? Talking to that rogue of a father of yours?' She glances at Liam's phone and he slips it into his inside pocket and forces a smile.

'Not this time.'

'Well, why the fuck not?' she asks, her words slow and full of mischief.

'We've had this conversation, Flick. You know this really isn't his thing. Anyway, he's busy tonight. Shall we start inviting *your* dad to things?'

She gives Liam a look. Evidently, she can bring up his father, but he can't mention hers, the ruthless businessman, Robert Graves. 'He's boring. I told Asa the great Mickey Blake, safe-cracker *du jour* would be here.'

Liam tries to remain calm but can't bring himself to hold her eyes as he speaks. 'I told you. Those days are long behind him. He's a locksmith.'

She really lets go with the laughter now, her long blonde hair tumbling over her face as she leans forward and puts her hand on his chest. Ever the flirt. She's beautiful, if high-cheek boned, willow-thin women in nice clothes are your bag, but she isn't Liam's type and, anyway, he would never cheat on Claire.

'Of course. I forgot. A locksmith,' she mocks now. 'The absolute balls of the man! I love it. Does he get any work?'

'Yeah. He does actually,' Liam says, suddenly feeling protective, despite himself. 'He's got his own business. All above board and doing well. He's trying to put all that other stuff behind him.'

All that other stuff, he thinks. Four little words trying to sum up his dad's life of crime, a twenty-year estrangement between father and son, a kidnap, a reconciliation and the death of Liam's mother from cancer. In Spain, Liam and Mickey had cared for his mum in her final weeks, coming together for her sake so she could die happy. Afterwards, Mickey had made the surprising decision to come out of exile, return to the UK to face his legal troubles and try to build some kind of relationship with Liam, Claire and the kids. Since then, the peace between Liam and Mickey is a fragile one, but in the main it has held. Part of the reason for that is that Mickey's desire to change seems real. He's mellowed, softened and has spent quality time with Claire and the kids, trying to get to know them and finally accept the role of grandad. For his part, Liam has tried to make good on the things he said to his dad when they stood bleeding and broken after the trouble in Skegness. He meant what he said then, about letting go and moving forward but saying something and living it, are two very different things. With that thought, Liam's unfinished text message conversation pops back into his head. He wants to delete the messages, block the caller and ignore any further communication, but has a feeling that approach won't work.

'...think you can do that?' Flick is asking another question Liam has missed.

'Hmm?' he asks.

'What on earth is wrong with you tonight, Liam? You're away with the fairies again.' She takes another sip of champagne, juts out her bottom lip in mock disappointment. 'I said, how about arranging a more discreet meeting between your father and Asa? Do you think you can manage that?'

'Is that wise?' he asks. 'I'd have thought you'd want to play it safe until we get the buyout over the line.'

'Nonsense. Making sure Asa signs some juicy book deals is going to be one of the things that gets us over the line. A couple of pics of him and your notorious father and the offers will be coming in before you can say "six-way auction". It's bad enough you couldn't persuade Trent to leave his little creative retreat to come tonight. He's one of the main reasons LimeLight have stayed the course.'

Liam is about to respond, when his phone jerks to life inside his pocket. Keen to escape Flick's questions, he takes it out and answers the call.

Before Liam can speak, a low bass-filled voice says, 'You ghostin' me, Jefé?'

'No. It's just that—'

'Yeah, you're playing nice with all those posh fuckers. I hear ya. Shall I come in and say hi?'

Liam tenses, his eyes flick to the large plate glass window just as headlights flash twice on to the dark street outside. Liam can't see the vehicle through the glare of the interior lights, but it's out there, waiting. 'You're here?'

'Of course. Figured my invite was lost in the post. Maybe the email got stuck in the spam filter, yeah?'

Liam clears his throat. Flick eyes him with curiosity. He needs to front this out. He makes his voice cold, professional. 'Look. I'm afraid this isn't a good time. Let's do lunch or something? I can ask my assistant to call you and sort a—'

'You really want me to come in there? Make a show?'

Liam's eyes automatically flit to Asa in the corner, holding court with the journos and a photographer. The LimeLight CEO beaming, no doubt rubbing her hands together at the thought of getting access to Liam's roster of clients. 'No,' he says into the phone. 'That wouldn't work for me. Maybe a quick chat now would be OK, providing it's only a few minutes.'

'If you're not out here in one minute, Jefé, I'm coming in.'

The line goes dead. The call Liam's been dreading for four long years has finally come. He needs to leave now. Kendrick Locke waits for no one.

CHAPTER 3
LIAM

THE SECOND LIAM had closed the car door, the Range Rover had taken off down the street, wheel spinning and throwing him back into his seat beside the man who has called this impromptu meeting: Kendrick Locke. Now late thirties and sporting a new fade on his sharp haircut. Dark, predator eyes, pinpricks of light staring straight ahead. A slim-fit jacket over a designer T-shirt that probably cost more than Liam's entire suit. All packaged in a heady cologne that fills the small space; the man even smells expensive. Which is a surprise, given his career effectively ended around four years ago and he's spent some of that time in jail.

The three of them – Liam, Kendrick, and Danny 'Titch' Titchener, the young woman behind the wheel – are winding through London streets, vaguely North, Liam thinks. Titch has slowed to the legal limit and other than Liam saying hello when he got in the car, no one seems eager to speak. Back in the day, Titch was always chatty and warm, so her silence unsettles Liam the most.

He assumes they're heading to a particular destination, but for what reason, who knows? It's making him nervous, so he decides to look out of his window and try to work out where they are. Although, if he needs to make a run for it, he's not sure how far he'd get. Titch is small but athletic, and isn't afraid to use violence when she needs to. She used to carry a can of pepper spray, but Liam's pretty sure she ended up being arrested for causing some handsy nightclub bouncer to have an epileptic fit. Add that to the fact Kendrick was a gifted runner in his youth, and Liam realises he isn't going anywhere. Nowadays Kendrick looks stronger, fitter; his time in prison giving him the build of a middleweight boxer. Liam is lean, works out two or three times a week, but spends most of his time doing cardio. Sitting beside Kendrick, he feels weak, but maybe that's just because of the atmosphere Kendrick's created in the car. As if reading Liam's mind, Kendrick finally speaks.

'OK,' he says, drawing his gaze away from the car window. 'That's enough of the intimidating silence.' He must see something in Liam's face, and smiles. 'Yeah? It worked? Powerplay 101, innit? You know who taught me that?'

For the first time since he got in the car, Liam feels his tension ease a little. He forces a smile, but says nothing.

Kendrick's grin widens. 'That's right, Jefé. You! That's why I called you The Boss.'

No, it isn't, thinks Liam. It's because you watched too many episodes of *Narcos*. But he says nothing.

'Yeah. You still got it, Jefé.' Kendrick laughs, then goes serious. 'Unless, of course, you're shit-scared and trying to hide it.' He leans in, quick enough to make Liam flinch, his face inches from Liam's. 'Yeah. Thought so. Never did have the stomach for a fight, despite all the working-class, "I worked my way up" bullshit.' He leans back, stares ahead, thinking.

Liam clears his throat. 'Ken, I get that you're pissed off, but—'

'Pissed off? You think I'm pissed off? No. That doesn't cover it. I spent nearly three years inside, never once tried to bring you into it. I took my medicine, the public shaming, the usual "successful black man falls from grace" and "once a street kid, always a street kid" narrative they're always itching to pull out. I took all of that, and more, on the condition that when I got clear of it, you and me, we'd be straight, and you'd put me back where I belong.' He turns away again, looks out of the window, shakes his head.

Liam's mind is racing, trying to keep up with Kendrick's tirade, trying to think through the angles and consider his options. Trying to draw on the skills he's honed over years of negotiations with powerful men and women, people who run multi-million-pound businesses and head up huge media empires. But Kendrick is a totally different animal. From a young age, he's had to negotiate his way through the world and knows how to keep his emotions in check. He had a terrible start. He was born on a tough estate in Leicester, to a mother with a drug problem and no father in the picture. By the age of three he was put into care, tossed into the system like someone might throw an old pair of trainers into the washing machine; maybe he'd come out clean, maybe he'd be torn to shreds. As with most things in life, it was somewhere in between. By his teens, he was getting into trouble, picking fights and dealing drugs. Making friends with the wrong people. At fifteen, he narrowly avoided having to do time in a youth offenders' institution when he was accused of fatally stabbing a rival gang member. An older boy went down for it, but one drunken night many years ago, Kendrick had tearfully admitted he had been responsible. He said he had never told anyone else, and Liam had believed him.

Escaping conviction had been enough to wake something in Kendrick. He started spending time at the youth centre, using their computer to make music, instead of roaming the streets. That's when Ronnie Pope, ex-footballer turned youth worker, had come into the picture. Kendrick always said, without Ronnie, he'd have been dead before he became an adult. He didn't take to football, but he could write, rap and act. Throw in his natural charisma and intelligence and Ronnie's belief in him, and good things began to happen. Liam had met Kendrick early in his journey and they seemed to form a bond, both of them outsiders in their own way. Liam took a chance on him when no one else would.

In the early years of the agency, Liam had liked to lean into the notion that he too was a working-class boy overcoming a traumatic upbringing. The son of a criminal. Liked to think it gave him an edge, made him stand out. And it had. But, deep down, he knew there wasn't much substance to it. As Mickey always liked to remind him, Liam's childhood was very different to his. Liam's upbringing was safe, with a decent standard of living in a nice area with both parents (just about) managing to stay together. Dangerously close to being described as 'middle class'. Still, he thinks now, he's the only one who really knows Kendrick's full origin story. It's not exactly leverage, but it's something.

'Look,' Liam says now, trying to find his feet in the conversation. 'You're right. I probably should have reached out before now—'

'You think?' Kendrick asks, still looking out of the window.

'But to be honest, I wasn't sure you'd want to talk to me again. I knew you were out and I did follow what bits and pieces I saw online. From all accounts, you're doing OK? I just assumed you'd want to put me and all this shit behind you.'

Kendrick, slow and deliberate, turns to face Liam again. 'Oh, you did, did you?'

'Yes, I honestly did.'

Kendrick winces. 'Oh Jefé. Using the word "honest" in a negotiation? You been slippin' without me around, haven't you?'

Liam sighs. It's true, he had once told Kendrick using that word when you're trying to convince someone of your sincerity, usually backfires. Why? Because until you mentioned honesty, the client wasn't even questioning your integrity. Now they're wondering why you brought it up.

'Thing is,' Kendrick continues, 'you're right. Financially speaking, I'm alright. But since when has making bread been what drives me, Jefé?'

Since forever, thinks Liam, but he decides to say nothing. Kendrick seems to read his mind anyway.

'Ha,' he says, the smile appearing again. 'OK, I'll admit, it feels good to make a few quid. Captain of industry and all that. Money is power, for sure. But you know what lights my candle, don't you, Jefé?'

Liam frowns, starting to understand where all this might be going. 'Fame?'

'Fuck no!' Kendrick slaps the back of the driver's seat. 'You hear that, Titch? Man tainting me with that *fame* shit. Thinks I wanna be some no-mark YouTuber, some fuckin' influencer prick! You believe this shit?'

Titch raises her eyebrows in the rearview mirror, shrugs, but says nothing.

'Well what the fuck do you want then, Kendrick?' Liam snaps. 'Because you've dragged me out of an important work event, driving me God-knows-where, just to give me some long drawn out speech, like you're still playing Bolt.' Bolt, the young maverick TV detective Kendrick was best known for, before he blew up his career.

Kendrick is still. He's staring at Liam, jaw clenched in the passing orange half-light of the street. Eventually, he blinks slowly. When he speaks, his voice is ice. 'I'd consider your tone, if I was you. I'm about as close to that two-dimensional cop character as you are to Dirty Harry.' Satisfied he's put Liam in his place, he leans back in his seat again. 'But you have brought me nicely to the issue at hand, yeah? That stereotypical bullshit you had me in back then? That's what we need to avoid going forward.'

'Going forward?' Liam asks. 'And *we*?'

'Yes, Jefé. The dream team back together. Yeah, you got faults, sure. But you know me. And, more importantly…' Kendrick turns, waits until he's sure Liam is properly tuned in to what he's saying, '…you *owe* me.'

Liam feels a pressure building, like there's a fat man sitting on his chest. 'Look, Kendrick,' he says, trying to keep his voice reasonable, 'You're right. I definitely owe you a favour and maybe I can put in a couple of calls behind the scenes, see if there's a smaller independent agency that might want to take you on, build a name for themselves—'

'Palm me off to some tinpot chancers?! You think that's gonna make us square?' Kendrick unbuckles his seat belt, slides over and gets in Liam's face. Liam jerks away, the back of his head bumping against the window behind him. The seatbelt alarm pulses away in the background, as Kendrick speaks through gritted teeth. 'I did time for you and kept my fucking mouth shut. All that gear I was bringing in? Most of it was to keep your clients, and people like them, fucking happy, yeah?' With each hissed word, comes the smell of chewing gum on Kendrick's breath. 'You asked me if I could score and I came through. Every. Fucking. Time.' He slides back to his side of the car and clicks in the seatbelt. The alarm stops wailing. The ringing in Liam's head doesn't. His mouth is dry and he has to work hard to stop his left leg shaking. He chances a glance out of his window, tries to work out where they are, but before he can process anything Kendrick picks up again, his voice calm now.

'And why did you ask *me* for the drugs, Liam?' He doesn't wait for an answer. 'Could it be because I was the only black man you knew and so I just had to be a dealer, or know someone who was?'

But you were *dealing drugs*, Liam thinks. Despite that, he does hate himself for the fact there's something in what Kendrick's saying. Although it's less about the fact Kendrick was black. It was because he was the most 'street' person Liam knew. Truth be told, at that time anyway, Kendrick was the *only* person Liam knew like that. But saying any of that out loud seems unwise.

'You're probably justifying it by thinking you didn't know anyone with my connections, yeah? But that's total horse shit. Old golden boy, Trent, the kid who stepped into my shoes before I'd even been fitted for my prison Crocs. You ever ask him to score for you?' He doesn't wait for Liam to answer. 'No. Didn't think so. Because he's white.'

Trent Williams. Council-estate kid from Nottingham. Grime artist, producer and now fledgling actor. Once in awe of Kendrick, looking up to him like a younger brother, Trent was now poised to become Liam's most lucrative, high-profile client. It was true, Trent had picked up the ball left behind by Kendrick and run with it.

'No. I'm not having that. It's got nothing to do with the colour of his skin.' Liam softens his tone. 'Fact is, I was wrong back then. I was young, hungry, trying to build a business, doing anything to keep these people happy. It's what an agent does, or so I thought back then.' Kendrick is giving him the side-eye, waiting to see if that's all Liam is going to say. He doesn't look satisfied, so Liam keeps talking. 'But, despite what you say, I didn't know the full extent of what was going on and—'

'Ah-ah-ah,' Kendrick says, wagging his finger, 'let's not be telling porkies now. I've got dozens of emails between us that say different. I was supplying in bulk and you were distributing.'

'Come on,' Liam says, raising a finger of his own. 'You make it sound like I was slinging dope for you or something. You sold me a couple of packets for some industry parties I threw. And only because I was getting pressure from Maria and Jonny-Dee.'

'Yeah, those posh fucking influencers were hoovering it up

like Pacino in Scarface. Call it what you like, but you were pushing product.' Kendrick cranes his neck to look out of the front window, then taps Titch on the shoulder. 'Yeah, that's it. Take a left up here.'

For the first time since they got into the car, Liam takes a proper look out of his window. Now he recognises the neighbourhood and realises where they're going. They're driving back to Liam's house.

CHAPTER 4

MICKEY

DESPITE THE TIME, I'm wide awake. Reckon I'll need an Ovaltine, a proper old man's drink, to help me sleep. I'm still wired from the run-in with Crazy Jeanette. On the way to the kitchen, I stop in front of a gold-framed mirror to assess the damage done by Jeanette's left hook. My top lip is split, angry red and swollen but it's not too bad. It'll heal. Unlike the rest of my ageing face, the grey, almost white hair, crow's feet bracketing tired eyes. The little birthmark near my mouth, the one everyone always says is shaped like a heart, just visible through the day-old stubble. Getting old, Mickey. No. You *are* old. Sixty-two isn't exactly prime of life is it? Even if those Saga adverts try to tell you different. Yes, people in their sixties might look and act younger than the same generation did when I was growing up, but the aches and pains are just the same. Still, I've tried to keep myself in good nick. Still run five or six miles most days and workout out on the punchbag when I can. I'm not too bad for an old bastard.

I make my drink, settle back in the lounge and check my phone again. Still no reply from Liam. It's getting late now and I thought his party would have finished, but I'm guessing he's busy or just too knackered to text back. Jesus. Listen to me, talking about him like he's still a kid. He's thirty-seven, a grown man, and I'm expecting him to check in with me.

I'm sitting in the lounge of Auntie Barbs' house, where I've lived since I came back. I stare at the white stucco ceilings and black painted beams. The brass ornaments hanging on the exposed brick wall above the fireplace. The dated Axminster carpet. It's all so different to the Spanish villa I was living in only a couple of years ago. Still, the weather might be shit here, the ceilings too low and the winters too dark, but it's home. Leicestershire, the place I grew up. And now I'm living in a house opposite one of my favourite places in the whole world: Bradgate Park. And coming back was only ever about rebuilding my relationship with Liam and being a better grandfather than I was a father. Well, be honest, Mickey. It might have had something to do with Hazel as well. I tap out a text.

AREN'T YOU GOING TO ASK HOW DATE WENT?

What am I doing, texting her at this time? I doubt she's even awake, probably in bed with that pompous prick she's shacked up with now. Except, she's not shacked up with him, is she? Not really. They've been together over a year and I know for a fact Craig – a copper, of all things! – is keen to move in, but Hazel keeps putting him off. Why is that? Don't know, but it's my only chink of light. I know I shouldn't be bothering her now she's with someone else, but I can't help but feel like there's still something between us. Just seems like the timing is off. By the time I got back to the UK, I was still officially mourning Maggie and Hazel was already in a steady relationship with Craig. Can't blame her. She deserves some happiness. I need to let her get on with her life. But then my phone vibrates with her reply and all bets are off again.

GO ON THEN. TELL ALL.

I type out a few different beginnings to a message, trying to work out how to begin, but then decide to chance my arm and send this instead:

YOU UP? FREE TO CHAT? SHIT AT TXTING

I know the misspelling is a bit obvious, but it seems to do the trick and after a few seconds she calls me.

'Ay up,' I answer, in my best Leicester accent, which has definitely come back stronger since my return.

'Come on then,' she says now, the smile in her voice. 'Spill the beans.'

So I do, laying it all out with as much deadpan, self-effacing delivery as I can muster. She giggles, then stifles a full-blown laugh, like she's trying to be quiet. Which must mean Craig is staying over. She never stays at his.

'She actually punched you?' she asks.

'Yep. Gave me a fat lip.'

'Well,' she says, laughing again, 'at least you got a good anecdote out of it.'

'Oh, I'm glad my pain is entertaining for you.'

'So. What's the plan now?' she asks. 'Get straight back onto the horse? Or, in your case, back on the app?'

'I think I'll give it a while before I listen to your son again, thanks.'

'Oh, bless him. He's only trying to help.'

'Is he? Or is he like his mum and just wants a good laugh? Please, do me a favour and don't give him any details. I'll never hear the end of it.'

'Well, I hope the next one, whenever it is, goes better than tonight,' she says.

For some reason, that deflates me and even though I don't reply, she seems to sense it. There's a few seconds of awkward silence, before she fills it.

'Anyway,' she says, 'have you heard anything from Liam? Didn't he have some big party tonight?'

'I've just text him actually but not heard back. Bet he's busy.'

'Is this the one he asked you if you wanted to go to?'

I sniff, stalling. 'Well, he did ask me, yeah, but I could tell he didn't really want me to go.'

'What makes you say that?'

'Trust me. I know Liam. When I said I'd got something on but could change it, he jumped on it. All relieved. Said not to worry and maybe I could go down for a visit another time. I know he's got a lot on with this big buyout stuff as well. He won't want me showing him up.'

'I think you might be projecting a bit there, Mickey. Be honest. Did you really want to go?'

Damn. Even when she's not here in person, extracting the truth with those gorgeous eyes of hers, she can still see right through me.

'Well… no,' I say, trying and failing not to sound defensive. 'But that's not the point. I knew he didn't want me there either.'

'I doubt that's the case. You two have been getting on so much better this last year. He's probably ready to introduce you to his work colleagues and show you what he does.'

'Hazel, bless you for saying that, but let's be real. He isn't going to want to introduce his ex-criminal dad to his London pals is he? And I don't want to make him feel any more awkward than he probably already does. My focus now is trying to be a good dad and grandad to those little 'uns.'

That's true as well. I've loved taking them to Bradgate Park, showing them the deer, the ducks and the ruins. But the last time we all went, what really made it was Hazel being there, seeing how the kids took to her as much as they they've accepted me as their new grandad. Kids don't tend to hold onto stuff in the same way adults do. An ice cream and a sense of fun can do wonders. If only it was that easy with Liam.

'Fair enough,' Hazel says. 'But don't keep trying to second-guess him and assuming he always thinks the worst of you. I can see he's trying to build bridges as much as you are. He wouldn't have bought that house if he wasn't serious about being able to spend more time with you.'

Liam recently bought a huge rundown manor house on the outskirts of Swithland Woods and Bradgate Park. It's currently being renovated, but the plan is for Liam, Claire and the kids to be able to spend extended weekends and holidays there.

'Depends if he ever takes a break,' I say. 'He's a workaholic. It's a wonder Claire puts up with it to be honest. Could be even worse after this buyout. He puts everything into that job and there's not a lot left over for anyone else.'

Hazel laughs incredulously.

'What?' I ask.

'Does what you're saying not sound a bit familiar? Didn't you say you spent most of your twenties and thirties working?'

Working. That's an interesting way of putting it, considering I was out knocking off safes and casing places to rob, but I suppose she's right.

'Well, either way, I thought he might've learned from my mistakes. At least he's not chosen the same career path as me. He's always flown straight and he's built himself a great business down there. I'm proud of him.'

'And now you're trying to do the same,' she says, pausing before adding, 'and I'm proud of you too.'

'Yeah. Well…' That wrong-foots me a bit. Never have been good at taking a compliment. 'I'm giving it my best shot. Looks like everything is settling down now and all I need to do is stay out of trouble. And how hard can that be, round here?'

CHAPTER 5
LIAM

KENDRICK CLOCKS LIAM'S FACE. 'What are you worried about? Just dropping you off at home, safe and sound.' A little grin surfaces, like he's enjoying Liam's discomfort. 'You've moved since we last met. Nice area. Looks like *you've* come up in the world.'

Liam leans forward and says to Titch, 'You can pull over anywhere. I can walk from here.'

'Nah,' Kendrick says. 'Be nice to see your new digs. Will Claire still be up? Haven't seen her for years.'

'No, she's out.'

'Really?' Kendrick asks. 'At this time on a Thursday night? Who's looking after Izzy and Grace, then?'

Liam clenches his fists, stays quiet, scared of what he might say or do.

'Chill, Liam,' Kendrick says. 'I'm just making what-do-you-call-it? Polite conversation.' The car pulls to a stop, just down from Liam's house, a modernised Victorian semi in a leafy street. Kendrick peers out, appraising the house. Liam tunes in, watches Kendrick, who squints and leans closer to the window. It's obvious this isn't the first time Kendrick has seen the house.

'Listen,' Liam says, trying to keep a lid on the anger and fear rising in his chest like heartburn. 'Whatever it is you think I need to pay for or make up to you, my family have nothing to do with it. Whatever all of this has been about tonight… I'm not having you bringing them into it. They're off-limits. OK?'

Kendrick sits statue-still, those dark eyes pinpricked with light. Liam tries to slow his breathing, to look for Kendrick's tells, get ahead of the conversation for the first time all night. But he's wasting his time. When Kendrick shuts you out, you're out. All Liam can do is mirror the body language and hold his nerve.

After a few seconds, Kendrick leans forward, just enough to bring his face into the light. He narrows his eyes, playing a part again, and makes a show of assessing Liam. He nods and claps, slow and sarcastic. 'Well bra-fucking-vo, Jefé! Finally trying to show some cajonés. I mean, you still look like you're gonna shit yourself, but at least you gave it a go.'

'Fuck you,' Liam says. 'If you think threatening my family is going to get you anywhere, you obviously don't know me at all.'

Kendrick puts his hands to his chest, mock-wounded. 'What? Liam, I'm hurt. I didn't bring you here to threaten your family. We're here to see just how well you've done since I've been off the scene. The cosy vanilla world you've built on the back of my success.'

'Your success?' Liam asks. 'When you did what you did, I lost all those contracts, just the same as you. I've had to shake off the association, rebuild my reputation. This success, as you call it, is in spite of you, not because of you!'

'Rebuild your reputation?! I've done fucking time. You wanna talk about what I've had to shake off? I'm poison in this industry and to top it all I've had to watch from the side-lines while Trent Williams rises to the top in the lift I built.'

Ah, and there it is, thinks Liam. The second time he's

brought up Trent tonight. Finally, Kendrick is giving him something he can work with, some idea of where this negotiation might be going. Whatever it is, Kendrick's protégé, Trent Williams, is at the heart of it. He pretends Trent's name isn't still hanging between them, takes a beat and tries again.

'What, exactly, is it you're asking from me? I can't represent you, Kendrick. And anyway, I think you need a fresh start. Re-establish yourself.'

'I only want one thing from you.'

'Yeah?' Liam asks, playing dumb.

Kendrick nods. 'Set up a one-to-one between me and old golden bollocks, Trent.'

'Why?'

'The fuck you mean, why? Does the genie ask why? Your wish is my command, Jefé! Grant me this, and me and you are done.'

'I can't just set up a meeting like that, not without having a good reason. Especially right now. He's not taking any meetings or doing any public-facing stuff. He's writing.'

'Fucking hell,' Kendrick says and now Liam sees genuine hurt in his eyes. 'Is there anything he didn't steal from me? Now he's using my process, as well? And you reckon he's not riding my coat tails?'

It's true, to an extent. But if Trent is using Kendrick's blueprint for success, it's because Kendrick willingly gave it to him.

'I get it,' Liam says now. 'I might feel the same in your position, especially after he went off the scene during your trial and everything.'

'Off the scene? Little prick ghosted me.'

He's right. Trent pretty much disappeared for months after Kendrick was arrested. At the time, Trent had said his mum was ill and he needed to take care of her, but the timing had seemed too perfect. And only a few months after Kendrick went down,

Trent had called Liam and asked for a meeting. Since then, he'd been busy, writing and producing three albums in two years, pitching a TV series of his own and now trying to put himself in the frame for a part in the new Larson Wainwright film. Liam can understand why Kendrick might feel a little hard done to, but he doesn't want to be any part of a reconciliation, and he's fairly confident Trent won't want that either.

'Why don't you approach him yourself?' Liam asks. 'It will mean more coming from you.'

'You think I haven't tried? Different number. Bounce-backs on his old email address. I don't know where he's living now and even if I did, not sure how he'd react to me just turning up. Probably scared of me stinking up his new wonder boy rep and all that. Little pussy would probably call the police.' He pauses, clasps his hands, and Liam knows he's finally going to lay out what he has in mind. 'So we'll need to keep it under the radar. Come up with something he'll go for, a meeting at a location out of the way. Then he doesn't have to worry about being seen with me.'

'Well, I don't think it's that—'

'You don't?' Kendrick snaps. 'I'm not stupid, Jefé.' He lets out a long sigh and with it, most of his anger. 'Maybe I'd be the same in his position, I don't know. But I just want a chance to talk, that's all.'

'About what?'

'Pitch him a couple of ideas.'

'Great. Pitch them to me and maybe I can pass them on.'

'Come on, Liam. You know how it works. You don't pitch to the middleman, the gatekeeper. What's the point?'

Liam almost smiles at that, yet again hearing his own wisdom used against him. 'No,' he says. 'I don't like it. I'm not arranging anything unless you at least give me some idea about what you want to discuss.'

Kendrick stares into the footwell. 'Look. I know he's not

shouting it from the rooftops these days, but me and Trent genuinely were close for half a minute back there.'

'I know you were.'

When Trent had arrived all those years ago, a rough-around-the-edges skinny white kid from the St Anne's Estate, he and Kendrick had bonded pretty quick. Kendrick had clearly spotted something and took Trent under his wing – even when most of his friends took an instant dislike to the younger man. Much of that had to do with the fact Trent was from Nottingham, and to add insult to injury, a Forest fan. Leicester lads don't take too well to that, but Kendrick was never into football and didn't care. Liam thinks the connection came from the fact they were both working-class men, desperate to express themselves and escape their backgrounds. Trent is five years younger than Kendrick and, in truth, a more gentle soul than Kendrick ever was. Kendrick may be complaining about it now but back then, he treated Trent like an apprentice, keen to show him the way. He also protected him from the other side of his world: the violence, the drugs.

'I know he's doing fine on his own, but this project I want to talk to him about, it's big. Something that's gonna take him to the next level and maybe let me at least get my foot back in the door.'

'If that's what you're looking to do, maybe I can make some calls, behind the scenes, pull in some favours and get you a couple of meetings and—'

'No!' Kendrick punches the back of the driver's seat. Titch flinches, glances behind and clears her throat, but knows enough to stay silent. Kendrick pinches the bridge of his nose, takes a breath and starts again, calmer this time. 'Look. I just want to make amends and start the rebuild, Liam. Know what I'm saying? If Trent says no, fine. I'll deal with it. But I have to hear it from him personally. That means getting me in the room with him, somewhere we won't be disturbed and he won't be embarrassed.'

'If I ask him for the meeting, Ken, he's going to say no. Regardless of where it is.' It sounds harsh and Liam wonders how Kendrick will react, but he seems calm, resigned even.

'I know that,' he says, like he's speaking to a child. 'Which is why all you've got to do is get him in the room and I'll do the rest. Tell him it's for something else. Don't give him a heads up, otherwise he'll be prepared with all his bullshit excuses.' He pauses, leans in, makes sure Liam is paying attention. 'And I will know if you've tipped him off.' Another pause, then, 'But if he says no to me off the cuff? We can all move on and you and me are square.'

Liam hesitates, then asks, 'And if I don't?'

Kendrick gives a sad smile, gestures over Liam's shoulder to the house. 'That's why we're here, Jefé. Not to threaten you, but to remind you of the stakes. If you don't play along? For starters, all those emails I've got saved are gonna come out.' He tilts his head. 'And then what use will you be to Trent or anybody else down there at that fancy agency? And that buyout of yours will be dead in the water as well, won't it?'

Liam tries and fails to hide his surprise.

Kendrick grins. 'Yeah. You think I don't still read the trades? You'll be finished, won't you? And what will Claire and the kids think of daddy then?'

Liam stomach rolls over, acid rises in his throat. 'Can I think about it?'

'If it makes you feel better, but...' He looks at his watch. 'You've got one week to make the meeting happen. After that, I think I'm gonna have to start clearing my inbox.'

CHAPTER 6
LIAM

IT'S BEEN a restless night and Liam feels bad about not calling his dad. But he knows if he spends any time speaking to Mickey in this frame of mind, he will sense something's wrong and start asking questions. Liam's on edge, wound tighter than one of the strings of the acoustic guitar he finds himself staring at now. It hangs from a bracket on the wall of his home office, where he's been hunkered down since before dawn. The curtains behind him are parted a few inches, a line of sunlight slicing the room neatly in two. He's at his desk, an A4 refill pad in front of him, its pages creased and decorated with a combination of scrawled handwriting and looping doodles. The concentric circles and flower-like drawings remind him of more care-free times, being a kid, laid out on his belly with his Spirograph set. Then, it was fun to try to create a coherent picture from a series of unrelated shapes and ideas. Now, all he sees is a chaotic mess of ink and an accurate picture of where his head's at right now.

He lays it out again in his mind. Kendrick wants a favour. Simple enough. Except that 'favour' involves blindsiding Liam's best client, someone who has become a friend. And what happens if somehow Liam can arrange this meeting?

When Kendrick gets his one-to-one and Trent, inevitably, declines whatever project he's pitched, what then? Kendrick just says, 'Oh well, never mind, thanks for trying, Jefé'? No. He'll be asking for the next favour, and the next until he gets what he feels he's owed. Liam knows that once you give a blackmailer what they want, they're unlikely to stop.

Unless they're made to stop.

OK, tough guy, he thinks to himself, as he scribbles the word 'PROACTIVE' down on the pad. Like he's Jason Statham, and not some mild-mannered entertainment agent. So maybe Liam isn't the one to get Kendrick off his back, but who? He can't go to the police, not with all the emails Kendrick says he has. He sits back in his chair. With thumb and finger, he tries to rub away the gritty tiredness in his eyes. What he's really trying to rub away is the obvious solution forming in his mind. The idea that's been there from the moment he woke up and tiptoed down the stairs to his study this morning. *Ask Dad for help*. There, now he's admitted it. But the idea of telling Mickey about Kendrick, the emails and admitting he's not the man his dad thinks he is, makes Liam feel physically sick. He can already see the look of disappointment, the sadness in his eyes when he realises his 'perfect' son is flawed after all.

No. He can't do it. He won't do it. That's why he had held Mickey at arm's length on the phone this morning. Although reluctant to admit it, recently he's felt the returning pull of the strong bond he once had with his dad. He has resisted it, still is resisting it, but alone, to himself, he has to admit things began to positively change after what went down in Skegness. Yes, his dad had been a career criminal, but by risking the legal consequences and moving back here to try to build a new life – a legitimate one – and spending time with Liam, Claire and the kids, Mickey has shown he's serious about wanting to change. Even if Liam still isn't ready to accept this new version of his dad, it would be wrong, and hypocritical, of him to ask Mickey to risk all that now.

Which leaves what? Perhaps he should take Kendrick at his word? Trust him to do the right thing and move on, once this Trent favour has been done. He instinctively knows that's a non-starter. Liam can't quite explain it, but even from their short meeting in the car, he can tell Kendrick has changed – and not for the better. It was there in his eyes, a lingering darkness; cold, hard. Kendrick has always had that in his locker, but Liam has spent enough time with him to know that was a façade, the humanity lurking just beneath the surface. But something is broken now, Liam can feel it. This version of Kendrick Locke feels somehow desperate. He's out to take back what he feels was stolen from him, and he isn't going to stop until he's back at the top. And what exactly will Kendrick do if he gets some face time with Trent? Because Liam had seen something else in Kendrick's eyes too: violence.

An hour later, Liam hears the toilet flush upstairs and then what sounds like Claire going back to bed. It's a rare morning off for her. She's a personal trainer. Most days she either runs an early class at the gym or meets one of her pre-work one-to-one clients. She'll be getting up soon to start sorting things out, but they have an unspoken agreement that when Liam hears her stir and he's already up, tea in bed is required, sharpish.

When he takes it up a few minutes later, she's on her side, pretending to be asleep. Liam plays along, as he always does, whispering and tiptoeing into the room like she's a timid kitten he doesn't want to scare away.

'Babe. I've brought you a tea.'

She forces out a syllable which might be, 'Thanks.'

Liam smiles, trying not to laugh as he puts the cup down on the bedside table and perches beside her on the bed. He begins his usual shtick.

'Did you sleep OK?'

Another muffled sound that Liam takes as a yes. Despite her chosen profession, Claire is not a morning person. He smiles, adding an even more cheerful tone to his voice.

'What have you got on today?'

No reply.

'Didn't you say you had a one-to-one but it's not until ten?'

No reply.

He reaches out, strokes her back. 'Much on in the afternoon? Do you still need me to pick Isobel up from gymnastics at four?'

No reply.

'Come on, babe,' he says, struggling to keep a chuckle out of his words. 'Let's have a big conversation.'

'Noooo!' Finally, Claire forms coherent words. 'Shut up.'

Liam laughs. 'What? I'm just having a chat with my wife.'

'Nob head,' she says, but there's no malice in it.

'Rude word, rude word!' Isobel bursts into the room, her long hair messy with the kind of heavy sleep only little kids seem to have. She's eight, wearing her Bluey pyjamas and bursting with energy. She runs, jumps and deliberately face plants on to the bed beside her mum. There's a pause, before she turns her head and says, 'Mummy. What's a nob head?'

'Yes, Mummy,' Liam says, playing along. 'What is that?'

Claire rolls over, gives him the side-eye. 'Like Izzy just said, *Daddy*. It's a rude word, that sometimes adults use when they get cross.' She rolls back to face Izzy, gently parting her daughter's hair to reveal her inquisitive eyes staring back up at her. 'But I think you know that, little lady. And I don't want to hear it come out of your mouth. OK?'

'What was the word?' Grace has appeared in the doorway,

ten years old, going on twenty. She already has most of her school uniform on and has probably been reading in her room. She pushes her glasses back up her nose and waits.

'Nob head!' Isobel shouts and giggles.

'Izzy! What did I just say?!' Claire grabs Isobel, tickling her and pretending to be angry, which only makes Isobel laugh harder.

Grace sighs. 'Oh. I've heard that before.' She turns and leaves without further comment.

Claire sends Isobel away with instructions to brush her teeth and have a wash and they're alone again. She sits up, just enough to be able to drink her tea, which Liam hands to her.

She takes a sip and eyes him over the brim of the cup. 'Well? Why were you up so early today? You were tossing and turning in the night as well.'

'Sorry. Did I wake you?'

'Briefly, but that's OK. What's bothering you? The buyout again?'

'Yes,' he says, getting up and opening the curtains. Bright sunshine pours in and Claire cowers away from it like a vampire. 'Beautiful day,' Liam says, hoping it's enough to distract her.

'Come here,' she says, patting the space beside her. He does as he's told, lying on top of the duvet, back against the headboard. 'What's wrong? Really, I mean?'

'Like you say, it's the buyout. Just a lot going on, that's all.'

'Did it go OK last night? The party and everything?'

'Yeah, fine. Very corporate, bunch of stuffed shirts. You know the drill.'

'A bunch of stuffed shirts who are going to make us a lot better off,' she says and takes another sip of tea.

'Hopefully,' he says, trying to sound more positive than he feels.

Claire is staring into the middle distance. 'I was thinking about it last night. The first thing I want to do is get my own space. I'm sick of having to pay the gym their cut and I know there's at least half a dozen clients who'll come with me straight away. That's before I do any kind of marketing.'

'Yeah. It's going to be great, babe.'

Despite his reservations about the deal, he is genuinely looking forward to watching Claire build something for herself, in the same way he had with his agency all those years ago.

'So,' Claire says, turning to face him again, her dark blue eyes bright with curiosity. 'If it's not the buyout, what is bothering you?'

'What? No, like I said. It is the buyout. Just a lot to sort out to get it over the line.'

'Liam. Are you sure that's all it is? You'd tell me, right?'

He gets the urge to swallow and somehow manages to keep his face neutral. He hopes. 'Of course I would.'

'Because after everything that happened with your dad and then, you know the stuff with Kendrick before that. You can't keep everything bottled up.'

The stuff with Kendrick. As far as Claire is concerned, that was just another case of the damage drugs can cause, but she still has no idea of the extent of Liam's involvement in it. She can't ever know. Not after what happened to her brother, Luca.

He forces a smile, reaches out and touches her cheek. 'I don't like to pass my cares on to you, that's all. You've got enough on your plate, trying to get your own business off the ground and being an incredible mum and all-round great wife.'

Her eyes narrow. 'Alright, alright. Let's not gild the lily there, Hugh Grant.' She finishes her tea and puts down the mug. She cups his cheek, gets close to his face. She's warm, cosy bed vibes coming off her in waves. 'But seriously, if there's stuff on your mind, things happening or whatever. I need to know. No more secrets, Liam. I know you do it to protect me, but we're a team. Yes?'

He nods, leans in and kisses her on lips still hot from tea. She raises an eyebrow.

'Mmm. It's like that is it?' she says before kissing him back, pulling him close and running a hand through his hair.

'Give me my hairbrush, nob head!' Isobel, shouting at her sister in the bedroom next door.

Claire freezes, opens her eyes and they both laugh and roll on to their backs. A pre-school roll-in-the-hay? What were they thinking? But for a few seconds, Liam was distracted enough to forget the buyout, Kendrick's visit and his impossible dilemma. Now, as he lies in the warm embrace of his wife, listening to her dreams of a new life and the giggles of his bickering children, he realises just how much he has to lose. He must find a way to give Kendrick what he wants. But how?

CHAPTER 7
MICKEY

'CHERELLE SAYS she wants a man that respects her career ambitions. She's well-clever, yeah. Doing Psychology at De Montfort Uni.'

'I know, Warren,' I say, trying to keep the edge out of my voice. 'You told me.'

He's been chatting my head off for the entire half an hour's journey. Thankfully, he's so excited about his date on Friday, my grilling about last night was fairly short-lived, and I've been happy to grunt and nod in the right places. He continues to blurt out a series of statements about why this new girl in his life is so great and how he wants to impress her and how his YouTube channel is ready to go to the next level and something I didn't even understand about Twitch streaming or something. I'm knackered listening to it.

Despite that, I'm genuinely pleased he's found a reason to stay on the straight and narrow and focus on something positive. When I first suggested he be my apprentice, it was just another attempt to impress his mum, but he's surprised me with his enthusiasm and commitment.

'I defo reckon I'm gonna hit ten thousand subs in the next few weeks,' Warren says, but I can't for the life of me work out what he's on about or how we got on to it. Clearly not paying enough attention.

'Subs?' I ask.

He looks at me like I'm recovering from a brain injury. 'Subscribers? For my YouTube channel?'

'Oh, right. That's… impressive.'

I think I managed to salvage some enthusiasm by the end of the sentence. Either way, at last he pipes down, taking time out to scroll through his phone. No doubt checking his stats, or whatever he calls them. Good. I can get five minutes of peace before we arrive at the first job of the day. We're heading up the ring road, approaching what the locals call 'Pork Pie Island', because of the big, round library building that overlooks it. There's an old dear in Wigston who's forgotten the combination to her document safe apparently.

Most people laughed when I told them I was going to start a legitimate business. They laughed even harder when I told them I was going to be a locksmith. Mickey Blake, infamous safe-cracker, widely believed to have been behind one of the biggest safe deposit robberies of the past fifty years, thought people were going to trust him to change their locks, check their alarms and have access to their homes and vaults? *Deluded*, seemed to be the consensus. But what was I supposed to do? Get a part-time job at Tesco? Work in an office? My CV isn't exactly diverse. My skillset is specialised. I can lay my hands on a cold steel door to coax out its code, find its secrets and trace its history. My fingers find life and memory in everything I touch. It's how I've always felt my way through the world. From the warm plastic of the steering wheel I'm holding now, to the smooth skin on the back of Hazel's neck, it's all there, a map of my past and future.

Fact is, in the beginning, the notoriety helped. Random phone calls asking if I was *that* Mickey Blake and could I 'really open a safe with just your hands'? I was a novelty, and people would pay me to open their safe, just to witness it.

Like it was some magic trick. I suppose, as far as they're concerned, it *is* a magic trick. But it's nothing more than me having a natural ability that's been honed through practice over the many decades since my grandad first introduced me to it. It's dexterity and a heightened sense of touch. End of. Like having an aerial that's tuned in to a very specific frequency.

When the novelty wore off and the calls slowed, I took the opportunity for some reinvention. I stopped introducing myself to strangers as Mickey, adopted the more middle-of-the-road 'Michael' and gave the business a nice generic trading name: SAFE HANDS. Once I stopped being news and being mentioned in *The Leicester Mercury*, I could get out from under the burden of being *that* Mickey Blake. I'm trying to build a normal life and a successful business, in the hope that my grandkids only ever know this version of me. Well, I can dream can't I? Not sure I'll ever change Liam's opinion of me though. Every time I think I'm making headway, there's a bump in the road – like this morning's call with him. He was short with me, business-like and I could tell he was pissed off. Once again, I've misread him. I tried to second-guess him with the invite to attend his event, thinking I was doing him a favour by not going, and now he thinks I don't give a shit. Truth is, the thought of going down there, with all of those middle-class London types, did fill me with dread, but I would've done it if I thought he really wanted me there. Not sure I'll ever fully understand him now. I thought we bonded when his mum passed, but it feels like he's becoming distant again. I'll keep trying.

But should I keep trying with Hazel? Is that what I'm doing, trying? With all the phone calls and texts and seeing her whenever I can? We had to drop in there this morning so Warren could grab his suit and that five minute conversation we had, even with all the shit with Liam hanging over me, has lifted my spirits. She always knows what to say and just seeing her smile at me in the way she does is enough to take twenty years off me. Jesus, Mickey, you soft sod. One thing's for sure; I'm not imagining this cooling of things between her and Craig The Copper. He called when I was there this morning. I made out I wasn't listening, but it was obvious he'd worked out I was there and got shitty with her about it. She called him a prick, under her breath just after he'd rung off. She had given me a look and I thought for a minute she was going to talk about it, but then old dozy bollock Warren came bumbling back into the room and that was that. It's so obvious Craig's not right for her. Even so, that doesn't mean she wants to be with me. Auntie Barbs would tell me we need our heads banging together.

We pull up outside the address for the job. It's a red brick, council estate terraced house, in front of an island of overgrown, muddy grass that maybe once an idealistic young town planner called 'a green'. Now, there's a half-flat, yellow football in the centre of it and a load of empty HSL cans dotted about the place, like a sprinkling of despair. That said, the place we're going to has been well looked after. I tell Warren to start unpacking the tools, while I go and give the front door a knock. The garden gate still works and there's a window box full of red and yellow flowers. There's a telly on inside, volume cranked up in the way old folks often do. There's no reaction after my first knock, so I try again a bit harder. This time, the TV goes silent and I can hear someone making their way to the front. Eventually, there's a muffled voice from the other side of the door.

'Lewis? That you?'

'Hello,' I reply, checking my paperwork. 'Is that Mrs Gardner? It's Michael, from Safe Hands, the locksmith?'

A couple of seconds, before she says, 'Locksmith? Oh.

Sorry, me duck, I think you've got the wrong house. I haven't called a locksmith.'

'That's strange. Definitely got a call for number twenty-two. Are you Mrs Gardner?'

There's a rattle and a scrape, as she puts the security chain on and opens the door a few inches. She's skinny, with wild but thinning white hair so sparse that I can see the psoriasis on her scalp.

'Well… yes, but I'm sure I didn't call a locksmith…' She's sounding less certain with each word. 'I'd have remembered. I know I would.'

I check the paperwork again. 'Ah. Looks like your nephew made the call? Is he here, Mrs Gardner? Says here you have a small document safe you've lost the combination to?'

'Nephew? Now, I know that can't be right. Nicky, my sister's boy, he lives abroad in erm… whatdyacallit? The place with the dancing rugby players… tut. Hang on. It'll come to me…'

'Dancing rugby – oh, you mean New Zealand?' She's talking about the All Blacks doing The Haka, bless her. Normal for someone of her age to forget the odd word like that, but she seems more confused than the usual forgetfulness. I'm starting to sense she probably has some dementia. Last thing I want to do is stress her out. I remember when my grandad started to go that way. It was heartbreaking.

'New Zealand!' she says now. 'Yes, that's it. Moved there years ago. Still sends a Christmas card, but last time I spoke to him was at our Janet's funeral. Three years ago.'

'So,' I say, making a real effort not to patronise her, 'is there anyone else at home? Maybe they made the call?'

'No,' she says, closing the door another inch so that all I can see is a single beady eye. 'I'm on my own but I've got a Lifeline button if I need anything and I definitely didn't call a locksmith. I'd remember. I know I would.'

It's obvious she's trying to convince herself, as much as

me, but this is pointless. Whoever made the call isn't here and now I'm just scaring a confused old woman.

'Of course you would,' I tell her as I take a couple of steps back from the door step. 'Must be a mistake back at my office. But if you do need anything, you can call back—'

'I didn't call in the first place,' she says, more confidently now.

'Right you are. Anyway, we'll leave you in peace and—'

From the street, there's a loud double-tap of a car horn. I turn to see a silver BMW pulling up behind our van. Warren, large holdall over his shoulder and a rolling tool box behind him, turns to admire the car. A slim white bloke, early-thirties with a shaved head and sunglasses gets out of the car. He's wearing a shiny grey suit, flashy purple tie popping against his crisp white shirt. He's holding his keys in one hand, big iPhone in the other as he skips around the car, only giving Warren a cursory glance, before he hurries up the garden path towards me.

He stuffs his phone in his inside pocket and holds out his hand. 'Sorry mate. Got caught up in a meeting. I'm Nick. I called about the safe.'

I briefly shake his hand. It's limp, hot and moist – the worst trilogy since they remade those *Star Wars* films. There's something about his weak handshake and the sensation of his soft sweaty mitts, that makes my memory flick back to when I met a man who was calling himself Snell a couple of years ago. That didn't turn out well and I take an instant dislike to whoever this Nick bloke says he is. He seems to sense my distrust and lifts his sunglasses, resting them on his head to reveal his small but alert eyes. He's trying to weigh me up.

'Who's that?' the old lady asks from behind me.

'Good question,' I call back over my shoulder, then lower my voice to speak to the bloke. 'What did you say your name is?'

'Nick. Nick Hughes.' He points to the clipboard I'm deliberately keeping close to my chest. 'I made the call about the safe. You should have my details on there.' He points over my shoulder towards the front door. 'That's my auntie, Mrs Gardner.'

I check the paperwork again. 'What's your auntie's name?' I ask him, quietly. 'Her first name, I mean?'

He shakes his head, rolls his eyes. 'What's that got to do with anything? Not being funny. I'm pretty busy. Can we just crack on? You've got the details there.'

I take a step closer to him and give him *the look*. He doesn't back away, but his Adam's apple bobs up and down twice in quick succession, a little yo-yo giving away his nerves. 'This lady is elderly and vulnerable. So why don't you just answer my question so I can make sure this is all above board.'

He opens his mouth, like he's about to shoot back with something, then seems to think better of it. He licks his lips and quietly says. '*My* aunt's name is Eileen.' The heavy emphasis is him trying to regain some kind of high ground.

'Wait there… *please*,' I tell him. Jumped up little prick. Mrs Gardiner has opened the door a little wider to see what's going on, but has wisely kept the door-chain in place. I approach her again and keep my voice light. 'Mrs Gardiner. It's Eileen isn't it?'

'Yes. How did you know that?'

Knowing her first name doesn't exactly prove the bloke is on the level, but before he turned up, I did get the sense the woman wasn't quite with it.

I smile and gesture over my shoulder. 'This gentleman says he's your nephew, Nick? The one you said you thought was still away? Could it be you were just getting a bit mixed up?'

She squints, trying to get a glimpse of the bloke behind me. I step back so she can get a better look.

'Well… I suppose he does look a bit like our Nicky,' she says, and I feel a little twinge of emotion, remembering the first time my grandad didn't recognise me. Even when you know it's coming, nothing really prepares you for it.

'Of course it's me, Auntie Eileen,' the Nick bloke says, giving her his 'favourite nephew' grin.

If he is experiencing the same feelings I felt when I was losing my grandad, he's doing a good job of hiding it. Something's off. I can feel it. But maybe it's just my Dickhead Alarm being tripped again.

Something occurs to me, and I lower my voice. 'Mrs Gardner. Is he right about you having problems with your safe? Is that bit true?'

She brightens up, like she's back on solid ground. 'Oh yes. I used to have the combination written down in my little telephone book but my friend, Brenda, said she'd seen something on *Crimestoppers* about not doing that, so I scribbled it out.' She laughs and slaps the back of the door. 'Well, I'll be blowed if I can remember it!'

'Easy done,' I tell her. 'But can you remember what was in there? Anything important?'

'Well… there's my bonds, bit of rainy-day money and all me other personal bits I s'pose.'

'And do you want me to open it for you?'

'Well, yes, I s'pose I do really. Not likely to remember it any time soon, am I?' She laughs.

I give her one more chance, hooking a thumb back over my shoulder. 'And now you've had a better look, do you recognise your nephew?' I step back again.

She has another good look, hesitates and then nods. 'You know what, I can see it now. I think he's had a hair cut, you know.' She bites her lip and looks down for a few seconds. 'You must think I'm awful, forgetting my own flesh and blood. It's just…' She taps the side of her head. 'Sometimes I go a bit foggy, you know? Old age?'

'Don't you worry about it,' I tell her. 'We all get a bit foggy sometimes.'

She frowns again, looks past me. 'Is the, er… coloured lad with you as well?' There's no malice or racism there. I can tell she was trying to remember the right word.

Warren's appeared next to me. 'Everything alright, Mickey?'

'It's fine,' I say, then, to Mrs Gardner, 'This is Warren, Eileen. Works for me.' I give her a wink. 'I'm training him up. Got to show these young 'uns how it's done.'

She smiles and takes the chain off the door. 'Too right,' she says. 'Cuppa tea?'

Before I can answer, her nephew calls, 'Yes please, auntie. Two sugars.'

There goes that Dickhead Alarm again. Something is definitely off here. I can feel it.

CHAPTER 8
LIAM

LIAM SITS IN HIS OFFICE, glad to be back in the more cosy surroundings of his own agency, Harris Entertainments. Rather than the minimalist marble and polished chrome of LimeLight, the vibe at Harris is more traditional. Dark wood desks and bookcases. Piles of scripts and contracts with pink and yellow Post-it notes protruding from them. Liam's Apple Mac laptop is open, with another larger, stand-alone monitor beside it. In front of him is the note book, a page covered in curling doodles, all surrounding three large words Liam has scratched into the centre of the page in black Biro.

The Call Back.

The words every auditioning actor pins their hopes on. Most of the time, these hopefuls, young and old are trudging from one open casting call to the next. They wait with dozens of other desperate people, trying to memorise the 'sides', or script fragments they've often just been handed. All while attempting to ignore the competition. They are eventually summoned to 'The Room' to have a cursory chat with the casting director and a couple of junior staff. Depending on the level of the role, perhaps even the producer or actual director is present too, all of them looking the talent up and down, assessing their look, their demeanour, already deciding if the person in front of them has 'it'. Whatever 'it' is. With pleasantries out of the way, lines are read, parts acted and before the actor realises it, they're back outside the room without a single real clue of how they did or if they'll get the role. Only the most confident performer would ever dare to hope the part was theirs already. There are rare occasions where an actor does so well and the director is so decisive, they're offered the part there and then. But for most jobbing actors, the best they can hope for at that stage is the hallowed 'Call Back'. The casting director saw potential and now they want to see more. In the words of TV talent shows… they're through to the next round. Every day, Liam has to field several requests from his roster of artists, all asking variations of, 'did I get the call back?'. All of which gets Liam thinking about a way he might be able to make this meeting between Trent and Kendrick happen.

His train of thought is interrupted by a series of light taps on the office door, before Flick pushes it open and steps inside. Despite feeling the urge to quickly shove it in a drawer, like a teenager hiding a porn magazine, Liam closes his notebook slowly and deliberately. His forced nonchalance doesn't fool Flick.

'Ooh, is that a diary?' she asks. 'Am I in it?'

Liam smiles. 'You'd be disappointed if you weren't.'

She has on her coat and a fresh layer of make-up. Her favourite woven Bottega Veneta bag is draped over her shoulder.

'Got a meeting?' he asks. 'Or a hot date?'

'Meeting, unfortunately. One of the LimeLight bods.' She gestures to Liam's notebook. 'And you and I both know your life would be pretty fucking dull without me in it.'

Flick swears in that way only posh people can; it's somehow lighter, less offensive than when someone like Liam's dad uses profanity.

'I agree,' Liam says. 'But probably less complicated as well.'

'Bullshit, young man, and you know it. I'm fucking fabulous at all the paperwork. Speaking of which, just over two weeks to go and this is where they start to try to throw in all kinds of last-minute shit.'

'Like what?'

She puffs out her cheeks. 'Where do I start? They want one of their smaller subsidiary companies in the mix now, so they can sub-contract production contracts or something. I've got more due diligence to do on that one. But then they want to put a cash value on every piece of talent in the agency.'

'We OK with that?' Liam asks.

'It's fine but I'm negotiating bonuses for each of them for when the deal is done – Trent being at the top of the pile and, let's be honest…' she lowers her voice, '…that clown Chalmers at the bottom.'

Liam laughs. 'He's not that bad. Just a bit behind the times.'

'Behind the times? At the social last week, he drunkenly referred to Lorraine Kelly as "that Scottish bint on ITV". Luckily, he said it to Asa, who thought it was funny.'

'Jesus,' Liam says.

'Indeed. Anyway, I'm just giving you a heads up that the contract revisions are going to come in thick and fast. I'll keep you in the loop.'

Liam makes a crucifix with his forefingers and holds it up like he's trying to ward off vampires. 'You know I don't do paperwork.'

She rolls her eyes. 'You can't avoid this stuff, you big baby. It will require reading and signing, that's all. Your only other job is to keep that young stud, Trent, onside and help me get this deal over the line.'

Liam pulls a face. 'Young stud? Yuk. Stop flirting with him. It's creepy. You could be his mother.'

She gasps theatrically, clutches her wounded heart. 'How dare you. I'm barely fifteen years his senior. Another crack like that and I'll be prodding you with the Violator 3000.'

Liam laughs. 'Fucking hell. Please tell me you're not still carrying that around? You know tasers are illegal, right?'

'It's not a taser. It's a stun gun.' She pats her handbag. 'But, yes, damn straight I'm carrying it around. You try being a woman walking the streets of London these days. Fucking terrifying.'

Liam could say, but doesn't, that Flick rarely walks anywhere. She takes black cabs when in London and drives her Mercedes everywhere else. The truth is the Violator 3000 – if that's even its real title – was a gift from Flick's father, when they were still on speaking terms. Liam suspects she only carries it around as some kind of good luck charm, a symbol of her hope he will one day get back in touch and tell her he's proud of her or something. Highly unlikely, in Liam's opinion. The ruthless old bastard. Liam knows it's what's driving Flick's determination to complete the buyout, more than the financial rewards. It's going to make a big splash, one that's bound to get back to Robert Graves eventually. Liam has told Flick, more than once over a late-night glass of wine, that trying to impress her father is a fool's errand. Men like him only care about themselves. Liam feels a pang of guilt. Mickey has his faults, but at least he isn't Robert Graves.

'Anyway,' Flick says now, as she takes out a small mirror and checks her lipstick. 'I'm off. Keep all our little starlets happy and I'll see you later.'

She leaves before he can answer, her words still hanging in the air. One of the most basic requirements of an agent is to keep the talent happy. In the short term, Liam can make Trent very happy by giving him the news he so desperately wants to hear. But what happens after that?

CHAPTER 9

MICKEY

'WHY YOU STILL STARING AT it, Mickey?'

Warren's voice makes me jump. He's standing behind me in Eileen's bedroom. He's got a point. Why am I just gawping at the safe? I want to tell him it's because these hands of mine bring up memories, good and bad, in the same way an old photograph or song on the radio does for other people. Sometimes, it's hard to resist, especially as I've gotten older. Touching this little document safe transported me back to the first time I showed Liam how I do what I do. I had let him have a go and we were both shocked to find he had a gift for it. Must be in the genes or something.

'I'm not staring,' I tell Warren. 'I'm assessing. And waiting for you to come back from the bog. I hope you haven't dropped any friends off at the pool in this nice old lady's toilet?'

He grunts a single laugh. 'I'm not an animal, man.'

'Come on. Let's crack on before that shady nephew makes an appearance with the tea.' I step aside so that Warren can get in front of the safe. He clasps his hands and cracks his knuckles.

'Woah. Be careful,' I tell him. 'Why are you doing that? It's like bending a screwdriver before a job. Those mitts are the best tool you've got in this game. You need to treat them with care. Not act out some crap you've seen in a heist film.'

'Shit,' he says, raising his hands, showing me that he's rubbing his forefingers across the tips of his thumbs. It's a gentle circling motion like I've shown him. It increases the sensitivity, like a singer doing vocal warm ups. 'My bad. I'm ready to feel the force.'

I stifle a sigh. Warren's a good kid these days and he's taken to being an apprentice much more seriously than I thought he would, but it's becoming obvious I'm flogging a dead horse when it comes to trying to show him how to use his hands like this. After more than a dozen attempts, on all kinds of safes, he hasn't shown even the slightest sign that he'll be able to pick it up. I even tried to show him the ring-roll trick, threading a ring over and under all the fingers of your hand, in one smooth motion, and he just can't do it. I used to do the trick all the time with Liam's old ring, but since I managed to return it to him in Skegness, I've gone back to using my wedding ring. Something else that would annoy Maggie if she were still alive. She couldn't get me to wear it while we were married.

Like I said, it's not the first time I've tried to pass the torch. Liam had been about twelve, sitting with me in the back office of Greasy Tony's garage. Tony was outside, underneath my car, changing the brake pads, while me and Liam waited in the tiny room, kept warm by the Calor Gas heater in the corner. There was a small green cash safe. We had half an hour to kill, so I thought *why not*? Just a way to pass the time. So I called Liam over to sit beside me in front of the safe. Gave him the same spiel my grandad had given me the summer after I'd hung up the boxing gloves for the last time. I told him to rest his fingertips on the safe door, to close his eyes and wait. He was always a bright lad and, back then, eager to please. He did what I asked without question. I can still see the flicker of his eyelids, tiny movements like unseen fish in a pond, as he sensed those first little sensations when he turned the dial. It blew my mind to see he had a natural aptitude for it, straight off the bat. He didn't get that first one open on his own, but he found one of the numbers and was buzzing about it. I had to quieten him down and swear him to secrecy. I knew his mum would've gone nuts if she'd found out. Despite his enthusiasm and obvious natural ability, I came to my senses a few days later and made him promise never to do it again. I think it was the start of him realising what I did for a job. Thinking about it now, how easily it had seemed to come to him, and how Warren is yet to find a single number, makes me wonder if there really is some genetic skill to it. Something I've passed down in the blood. If that's the case, I'm wasting my time persevering with Warren.

Despite all that, I push on and go through the motions. I give Warren the same spiel I gave Liam all those years ago, try to get him to block out everything and really feel what's going on in the tips of his fingers and inside the workings of the little safe. But within a minute or two, I can see it's futile. His eyes are closed and he's making all the right faces, but I can tell there's nothing happening.

There's a creak on the stairs and a second later, Nephew Nick appears in the doorway holding two mugs. 'Alright gents? How's it going?' He raises one of the mugs. 'Who has the poison?'

You, if I had anything to do with it, I think. You slimy prick. Cyanide, preferably. 'Warren's the one who takes sugar,' I tell him and gesture to the bedside table. 'Just pop them on there, ta. Shouldn't take much longer.' He puts the cups down and just stands there, looking at us. I give it a few seconds to see if he shows any sign of leaving. He doesn't.

'You can go back down to keep your aunt company if you like.'

'She's fine. Watching *Homes Under the Hammer* or some other shite.' He looks past me, to the safe in the wardrobe. 'Anyway, probably be best if I'm here when you get it open. Thought you'd have done it by now.'

I fold my arms. 'Why would it be best you're here? What are you trying to suggest?'

'Come on,' he says, giving me a wink that makes my skin crawl. 'We both know you lads must pick up the odd trinket when you're doing these kind of jobs, especially when you're dealing with the likes of Eileen.'

I give him my 'Resting Bastard' expression and the cold, dead eyes I've had to use to survive many situations over the years. It can work as a deterrent with hard cases or scare the shit out of chancers like our Nick here.

'She's just Eileen now, is she? Not your auntie? You might think like a thief, but me and him?' I point at Warren. 'We're not like you. Wanna know why?'

He swallows, then lifts his chin, trying to front it out. 'Not really. But I've got a feeling you're gonna say it anyway.'

'Because you're a cunt,' I tell him and take a step closer. Not exactly Oscar Wilde and I'm not a big fan of that word, but it works a treat when you need to flush out a scumbag like this.

His mouth drops open, but when the surprise wears off, he's seething. 'Who d'you think you're fucking talking to, you old bastard?'

'And there he is,' I say to Warren, pointing at Nick. 'There's who we're really dealing with. Even if you really are her nephew, it's obvious you're only after whatever's in this safe. Your mum… Beryl, isn't it?'

There's a split-second pause before he answers. 'Yeah? What of it.'

'She must be rolling in her grave at the way you're treating her sister. Especially seeing as…' I close the gap between us, get in his face, '…her name isn't Beryl. It's Janet. So who the fuck are you?' I poke him in the chest to emphasise each word of my question. He takes it, face reddening by the second.

'Mickey…' Warren says, like he's trying to stop a Doberman from ripping out the throat of the postman. 'Come on. He's not worth it.'

'Wait a minute,' Nick says, as he takes a couple of steps backwards and almost falls onto the bed. 'Mickey? As in, Mickey Blake? The gangster?'

Gangster? Nobody that knows me would ever describe me as that, but this is what you get when the media gets hold of something. Anyway, on this occasion, I'm happy to roll with it, if it gets rid of this jumped-up con artist without having to get physical.

I straighten up, push my shoulders back. 'Yeah. That's right. I'm Mickey Fucking Blake. And I've met enough pond life in my time, to know you're down there with the kiddie-fiddlers and rapists. Preying on the old and vulnerable and bragging to your mates about it down the pub. Scumbag.'

'No. That's not true. I'm—'

'Save it.' I take another step forward. Pretty sure I could still deal with him if he does try to throw his weight around, but he's probably thirty years younger than me so if I can avoid it, I will. 'Here's what's going to happen. We're going to go downstairs and tell Eileen you've made a mistake. You've come to the wrong house and you're not "Nicky" after all.' I whip my phone out and take a photo of his startled face. 'And now I've got your picture which, if I need to, I'll be sharing with a few pals of mine. The kind of blokes that'll break your leg just to hear it snap.'

The colour drains from his face. There's a sheen of sweat

on his top lip. He opens his mouth to speak, but all that comes out is a tiny croak.

'Warren,' I say over my shoulder, without taking my eyes off the greasy conman. 'Have a look out of the window, will you. Make a note of his reg.' Warren does as I ask, taps it into his phone. I glance past 'Nick' and clock Warren's little smile of… what? Pride? I maintain my game face. 'So, Fake Nicky, if I see you, your car or even somebody else like you, that I think you might have sent back round? I'll be making calls. And we work this area all the time, so if I see that wanker-mobile of yours anywhere else on the estate? Well… I think you get the idea now.'

He does. He's grey-faced; eyes wide and looking like he wants to sprint out of the front door and not come back. And once we've squared it with Eileen downstairs, that's exactly what he does. Then we speak to her neighbour, a nice woman in her late sixties who looks out for Eileen. I give her a heads up on what's happened and she even comes to watch us open the safe. There was a few hundred quid in there and the neighbour is going to make sure it gets deposited in Eileen's post office account.

So, I've stopped him from ripping off one old lady this week. Big whoop. No doubt he'll be straight on to the next one. And what's to stop him coming back to have another crack at Eileen? To try his luck with another locksmith, or even take it out on her some other way?

Let it go, Mickey.

That's what I keep telling myself for the next few hours, while I quietly seethe, thinking about the next vulnerable person he decides to go after. It's not my problem. Shit like this has been going on forever and I can't save every defence-less old man or woman that comes across spineless twats like him. For every one you dig up, another one takes its place, like weeds that grow up through the cracks in the pavement. There's probably a hundred similar characters stalking the city streets right now, at least. All of them looking for the next defenceless target to prey on.

Let it go, Mickey.

It's the sensible thing to do – the *only* thing to do. Which is why, when we pull up on to the drive of the next job, I ask Warren to text me Nick's car reg. I've never been a sensible man. No point in trying to start now.

CHAPTER 10
LIAM

UP UNTIL RECENTLY, 'THE CALL BACK' didn't loom large in Trent Williams' world. Just like his one-time friend and idol, Kendrick, his main focus had originally been on music. That was a tough act to follow. But with Kendrick out of the picture, it seemed like there was a vacuum Trent has been more than willing to fill. He changed his image, grew the beard and worked hard in the studio. Things eventually took off with the second album, with a sell-out tour and an explosion in Trent's social media following. It was only a matter of time before casting directors would want to jump on the band wagon.

Trent began to have scripts sent to him to consider, no audition required. Despite that, all he was being offered were street thugs and dealers. Parts that every urban working-class actor gets sent. With the occasional 'detective's sidekick' thrown in for good measure. Trent turned them all down and surprised Liam by pitching his own TV series about a grieving father who goes undercover to find out who killed his son. It's been picked up and is in pre-production now. He's writing a film script. Expectations for the next album are massive – which is why Trent is currently hunkered down on one of his writing retreats. Even Liam doesn't know where he goes. Trent describes it as 'Going to my Bat Cave, mate.' Liam doesn't care, as long as he keeps developing and delivering.

So Trent is hot right now, up and coming, but he wants more. Unlike most of Liam's clients, 'more' for Trent isn't more fame or celebrity. No, Trent wants more challenges, more avenues for his seemingly never-ending creativity. He wants to do it all. And right now, top of that list, is being seen as a serious actor. Which is why he's so desperate to get a part in the latest Larson Wainwright project.

Wainwright is one of the most reclusive, renowned film directors of the past twenty years. He hasn't made a film for almost a decade. He's rarely seen in public and doesn't do interviews but is often described as this generation's answer to Stanley Kubrick. Three months ago, it was quietly announced that he had another script in production. He's the quintessential 'auteur' and every A-lister on the planet wants to work with him. Trent isn't deluded. He knows he doesn't stand a chance of a lead role, but there's a scene-stealing part in Wainwright's latest project he's sure he could pull off, so when Liam managed to get him an audition a couple of months back, Trent was over the moon. Wainwright wasn't at that casting call – he has a trusted team he leaves to whittle down a shortlist – but Trent came back saying he felt he'd really clicked with the casting director. So now he wants the same as every other aspiring actor: the call back. That second chance to shine, a sign you're at least in the mix. Since Trent's audition, he checks in every couple of days asking Liam if he's heard anything. Up until now, it's been silent. Liam suspects the chance has passed, but the fact there still haven't been any official announcements and that no one else in the industry seems to know anything either, has kept the hope alive. It also presents Liam with an opportunity.

In any other circumstance, with a different project and a less eccentric director, Liam wouldn't even be able to attempt what he has in mind. It isn't without risk. To dangle this opportunity and then snatch it away from Trent is like showing your kid a new bike on Christmas morning, then sending it back to the shop. Tears and tantrums will undoubtedly follow. For Trent, that could mean firing Liam, and Liam wouldn't blame him. What he's contemplating is beyond unprofessional. It's cold, calculating and totally out of order. He classes himself as a friend of Trent's as well as his agent. They've built a real rapport. Trent can be fragile and flighty but trusts Liam implicitly. Does Liam really expect to be able to rebuild that trust after a stunt like this?

But what's the alternative? If Kendrick's emails come to light, Liam's professional reputation will be destroyed and there's every chance he will face charges. Not only will the acquisition be dead in the water, his own agency will be in jeopardy. If Flick can't pick up the pieces, almost twenty members of staff will lose their jobs. All of that stuff is true, but it isn't what's driving Liam's thought process. That's all just money and business. All that really matters is Claire and the kids. Aside from the fact he won't be able to provide for them, how will he be able to look his little girls in the eye when they're old enough to understand what he's done? And what about Kendrick's vague, but all too possible, physical threat to them? Is Kendrick really capable of that now? But Liam keeps coming back to the look in Kendrick's eyes as they sat outside Liam's house the other night. Hard, flat and full of darkness. Prison has changed him, no doubt about that.

No. This is the only way forward now. If he loses Trent as a client, so be it. It will be difficult professionally and on a human level, but the acquisition would still likely go through. Then Claire can go it alone with her business and his girls will be safe from the knowledge of what he's done.

He makes the call before he can lose his nerve.

Trent picks up on the second ring. 'My agent actually

calling *me*? And when I'm in the Bat Cave? Can only mean one thing.'

'I call you all the time, you cheeky sod, but I know better than to bother you when you're writing.'

'Which must mean you've got some good news for me then?'

Liam takes a deep breath. 'Maybe,' he says, still teetering on the precipice.

'What's that supposed to mean? Have I got the call back or not?'

Liam stares at the notebook again, his looping ink scribbles blurring, seeming to thrash about like the tentacles of an octopus.

'Liam? You still there?' Trent asks.

'Yes, sorry.' A pause, while Liam forms the lie. 'All I know is I've had a call, from one of Larson's usual associates, and they're asking for a one-to-one meeting to chat things through. They've asked me to choose the location and insisted it's totally private. If there's even a hint of it being leaked, they'll call the whole thing off.'

'Standard practice for him,' Trent says, and Liam can hear the excitement building in his voice.

'You can't mention it to anyone, OK?'

'It's a call back, I can feel it. The secrecy, all that shit? Got Wainwright all over it.'

It hurts Liam to hear the excitement in Trent's voice. He closes his eyes, drops his head. 'Let's try not to get our hopes up. Do the meeting and see what happens.'

'When is it?' Trent asks, before immediately adding, 'Doesn't matter. Whenever it is, I'll be ready.'

'Next Tuesday,' Liam says. 'We can meet at my new place up in Leicester. It's in a bit of a state, ready for the decorators to come in, but it's secluded and who knows? Maybe I can sell Larson on using it as a location? The views of Bradgate Park are amazing.' He feels like he's watching a film now, someone else playing the role of Talent Agent, Liam. Lies trip off his tongue as he sells the idea to Trent and himself.

'Sounds perfect,' Trent says, 'and I've been wanting to take a look at your new pad since you bought it.'

'Great,' Liam says, hoping the soul-crushing disappointment he feels with himself doesn't seep into his voice. 'I'll finalise the arrangements and confirm everything tomorrow. And Trent?'

'Yeah?'

'I know this seems big, but don't get too excited yet and remember, you cannot tell a soul. If word gets out, he'll walk. That's if he even attends in person.'

'No dramas. I'll take it to my grave, mate. It's him, for real. I can feel it. Let's just make it happen.'

The say their goodbyes and Liam ends the call, putting his phone on the desk then pushing it away like it's toxic. But it's not the phone that's poisonous. It's him, poisoning his relationship with his best client. His eyes settle on the framed photograph on his desk – Claire and the girls, chocolate cake on their hands and faces as they laugh in the kitchen. That's why you're doing this, he reminds himself. Now make it happen.

TWO WEEKS TO THE BUYOUT

CHAPTER 11
LIAM

LIAM DRIVES beneath the red brick arches of Leicester Train Station and pulls into the only vacant pick-up and drop-off space. It's almost eight o'clock at night and the last of the London day commuters are getting in. They're easy to spot, with their drawn faces, rumpled suits and skirts creased from a day in the capital and hours on a no-doubt packed train. Business men and women dragging brief-cases on wheels, the occasional 'creative-type' hugging their faux leather satchels like their life depended on it. All of them carrying their baggage and trying to get home. Home. Where Liam wishes he was right now, putting the girls to bed, maybe opening a bottle of wine with Claire and winding down for the night. Instead, he's wound up, legs tight, hands clenched on the steering wheel.

You could still back out, he thinks. Call Kendrick and tell him Trent's had some urgent meeting to go to, maybe a family emergency. But then what? Even if Kendrick bought Liam's excuse, he would simply demand they reschedule, and the torture would begin all over again. No. Liam has to see it through, watch how it plays out and deal with the conse-quences.

'It will be OK,' he says again, his voice sounding shaky and nervous in the empty car.

Get a grip, Liam. That seems to have been his mantra for the past week since he came up with this ridiculous plan. Thank God for the well-known eccentricities of auteur, Larson Wainwright. He's infamously private and secretive. The idea he would want to meet somewhere off-grid fits well with his public image. But all Liam cares about is making sure Kendrick and Trent aren't spotted together or that Trent is in anyway associated with the now toxic Kendrick Locke. He could have booked a hotel room somewhere in London or borrowed an office, called in a favour, but the entertainment industry runs on gossip and rumours. Even your most trusted confidante can sell you out for the right price or the promise of a favour from a producer or powerful agent. Just a whiff of a write-up in a gossip column or, more likely these days, a social media post could derail Trent's career. And some proof, like a photograph or video clip? With barely a week to go until the acquisition, the shit would well and truly hit the fan. For Liam, the solution had been obvious: use his newly-purchased house up here, in the no-man's-land of The Midlands. Leicester – the place *Eastenders* characters are sent to when their storyline is put on hold. This unassuming little city that people might know thanks to a dead king found under a car park and an underdog footballing achievement, but even then, it's unlikely they've actually visited the place. Up here, people think a paparazzi is a type of pizza. Truth is, Liam isn't a fan of the city itself, or at least what it's become. A hotchpotch of new development and abandoned heritage. The shiny Highcross shopping centre, rubbing shoulders with an increasingly rundown city centre, like the private school pupil made to sit next to the council estate kid. Liam remembers it from his summer visits as a child. The vibrant clock tower, meeting place for everyone before the advent of mobile phones. The famous Golden Mile of Leicester's Asian community. The market, a cacophony of 'three for a pound!' and 'come-and-get-your-juicy-apples!' and a dozen other calls from the traders standing out there in all weathers. On Liam's recent visit, the centre seemed to be dying. The historic market has been flattened while the council decide whether to rebuild it or sell it to the highest bidder. Despite all that, Liam can't bring himself to hate it. He still has too much affection for the little town that's always punched above its weight. And the wider county is as beautiful as it ever was.

There's a bang on the car roof and Liam flinches so hard he bumps his elbow on the door handle. Trent comes into view at the passenger window, smiling through his thick beard, as he tries to open the door, which is locked. Liam swears under his breath and presses the button to disengage the central locking.

'Liam! Sorry mate,' Trent says, laughing and sliding into the passenger seat. 'Looked like you were going to fill your pants!'

'Yeah,' Liam says, trying to keep his voice light. 'It was touch and go for a minute there. Where did you come from? I didn't see you leave the main entrance.'

'Got in a bit early, mate. Went to the shop to grab a pack of Extra Strongs. Last thing I need is Larson turning me down for bad breath.'

Mate. Trent uses that word a lot, always infused with a broad Nottingham accent, making Liam feel like he's in a Shane Meadows film. But it's also another reminder of the rapport the two men have built up over the last couple of years. They've become more than agent and client and now Liam is betraying that trust. He realises Trent is staring at him now, eyebrows raised.

'What are we waiting for?' He rubs his hands together, beams. 'Don't want to be late for the big man.'

Liam doesn't get to see this excitable side of Trent as much these days. He usually plays it cool and keeps his emotions in check but it's obvious he's buzzing. Liam backs the car out of the space, glancing again at his passenger. As usual, Trent's dressed immaculately. Fitted dark grey trousers, box-fresh white trainers and a crisp white T-shirt. A Flannels black jacket. He's clearly had a trip to the barbers for the occasion too, his dark brown hair cut short with a precision-tooled fade, his full beard shaped to within an inch of his life. He grew that not long after joining Kendrick's clique. In the beginning, the crew laughed at him, but now it seems every young man is rocking some form of facial hair. It's hard to remember what Trent even looks like under there.

Trent has clearly made a big effort for tonight, which turns Liam's stomach with guilt. He's going to have to come clean, but should he do it now or wait until they arrive at the meeting? He opens his mouth, trying to form the words, but Trent starts up again.

'So. Have they sent over any more sides, mate? Any more hints which role they've got in mind?'

'No,' Liam says as he drives away from the station. 'Thing is, Liam. I don't think—'

'I know, I know. I shouldn't push it. Don't try too hard and all that.'

'Well, yeah, but, not just that.'

Trent stares at Liam. 'You OK, mate? You don't look so good.'

'Me?' Liam forces another smile. 'I'm fine.'

Trent keeps staring, then sighs. 'Liam. Why can't you just be straight with me?'

'What do you mean?' Liam asks. Trent's looking at him now, disappointment etched on his face. He knows, Liam thinks. His hands tighten on the wheel.

Trent says, 'I know you've been lying to me.'

CHAPTER 12
MICKEY

IT'S BEEN a few days since we bumped into that sly shitbag who was trying to rip off the poor old woman in Wigston. In a way, I'm quite proud of myself. For all that time I've had his car reg on my phone and have resisted taking things any further. That's progress, in my book. Personal growth, I suppose the younger generation would call it. It's a stupid thing to do, to escalate what could be a one-off. I already did the sensible thing by not actually getting violent with him and warning him off with threats. Chances are, that's done the trick. He did look shit-scared when he scarpered from Eileen's house. And yet, every night since, right before I go to sleep, I see his shiny grey suit and Eileen's look of confusion. The thought of him going back there and doing it again, or moving on to the next weak person he can find, is driving me mad. Also, let's be straight about it, my delay has less to do with self-control and more to do with the phone call I need to make, if I'm serious about taking it further. The thought of talking to a certain man again and asking for a favour is only slightly better than knowing that conman is still out there. But it's the lesser of two evils, so I make the call.

He's probably going to flip his wig when he sees my number pop up on his phone. That's if he hasn't blocked me – although that wasn't part of our deal, when we parted ways after that nightmare in Skegness. After two rings, it goes to voicemail. I don't leave a message, not yet. I can't think exactly what message I would leave and I'm going to give him the benefit of the doubt and assume he's just busy right now. Less than a minute later, he calls me back.

'DI Harper,' I answer, feeling weird and realising it's the first time I've said his real name out loud. Long story. He was undercover when we first crossed paths.

'Why are you calling? What's happened?' Predictably, he's speaking in hushed tones, the words sounding like they're being forced through gritted teeth. He always was an uptight twat.

'I'm doing well,' I say. 'Thanks for asking. How's your little 'un? Not so little these days, I suppose? What is he? Coming up on three now?' It's a genuine question, but when I hear it out loud, I worry it might sound like some veiled threat, what with me being an ex-criminal and all that. 'They grow fast. Can't believe how much my grandkids have changed since I came back.'

That seems to take his tension down a couple of notches. 'Yeah. I heard you were back and by all accounts actually trying to go straight?'

'No need to sound so surprised,' I say. 'I've got my own business and everything now.'

'Locksmith? Beggars belief.'

So, he has been keeping tabs on me after all.

'Well, we all have to work with the skills we have, Andrew. I'm good at unlocking stuff and you're... what exactly are you good at?'

'Ha fucking ha,' he says. 'I'm guessing you're in the shit or are about to dump some shit at my door, so get on with it. Why did you call?'

The level of self-righteousness with this dick is off the charts. He seems to have totally forgotten I pretty much saved his career and kept him out of prison. When I don't speak for a few seconds, he finally seems to read the room and moderates his tone.

'Sorry,' he says. 'But I'm seriously busy and I've had to step out of the office to take this call. Only reason I did, was because we agreed you would only call if it was desperate or if that mad bastard, Southey, ever pops up again.'

'Not likely, is it? Southey, I mean. Thought he was doing a ten stretch, at least?'

'Twelve. But he's throwing a fortune at his appeal and we both know things weren't exactly done by the book. Anyway, we'll worry about that if and when it happens. Maybe if he does get out early, he'll be a reformed character.'

He tries to inject some humour into that last statement, a bit of sarcasm, but we both know firsthand how dangerous and unhinged Graham Southey is. Hazel knows more than anyone. I dread to think how she would cope if he is released. I push on, before Harper can give me any more bad news. He always was a fucking Jonah. Maybe calling him for a favour wasn't such a good idea.

'I'm not calling about any of that and I'm not here to piss on your promotion parade. Just wanted a simple favour. I think we can both agree you owe me that.'

'Depends. What is it?'

Jesus. How could I forget how annoying this prick was? I swallow down any smart-arse comments I'd like to make and say, 'Just to run a plate for me, tell me who it is and where he lives.'

'Why?'

'Someone's crashed into the side of my van and driven off. Been caught on camera.'

'Have you not reported it?'

'Strangely enough, Andrew, the boys in blue up here aren't that fussed what happens to me or my property.'

'And what will you do if I get this info?'

'Politely ask for them to contribute to the bill for repairs, of course,' I say, all sweetness and light. 'It's a BMW, Andrew. You know what those bastards are like.'

'I drive a BMW,' he says.

'I rest my case.'

He lets me hang for a good few seconds, sighs and eventually says, 'OK. Give it to me. But this is the last time I do anything like this for you. And I don't want to read about any Mickey Blake road rage incidents.'

'Not my style, Andrew.'

I give him the details and hang up, actually shivering after the call ends, like someone's just walked over my grave. Can't stand the bloke, but since the only other copper I know, Ron, just had another stroke, he's my only option.

Half an hour later, Harper texts me a name and address, somewhere over near Coalville, in a village called Ravenstone. I'm busy with work tomorrow, but looks like I'll be making a trip to North Leicestershire at some point on Thursday.

I can't let it stand. I just can't.

CHAPTER 13

LIAM

'HOW DO YOU KNOW?' Liam asks, trying not to panic.

'It's obvious,' Trent says. 'Just wish you'd been able to be honest with me, that's all.'

Liam racks his brains as to how Trent could have worked it out. Has Kendrick already reached out to him, tipped him off? But why? He's about to speak, when Trent holds up a hand and goes on.

'Don't look so crestfallen, mate. I know you're the master when it comes to picking up body language and all that, but maybe I've learned a few tricks along the way. I've seen the strain it's been having on you.'

'Well… yes, but—'

'The buyout, mate. It's made you more cautious. You've not been yourself. You think I'm wasting my time with this Wainwright part. Am I right?'

Like the after-glow of a good whisky, relief spreads through Liam. 'No, Trent. I don't think that at all,' he says. 'You're a natural when it comes to the acting and you're getting better with every part you pick up. Getting the Wainwright role, regardless of how small it might be, would be massive for your confidence and development.'

'Oh,' Trent says, 'so you do get it?'

'Of course I do.'

'Then what's going on, mate? Because I'm definitely smelling funny vibes. And to be honest, it's not filling me with confidence, and you know I need to be on it tonight, yeah?'

Now is the time. This is Liam's opening. Just say it, he thinks.

Trent lays a hand on Liam's shoulder. 'But more than that, I'm worried about you. You look exhausted, mate.'

It's more than Liam can take. He's never felt more duplicitous in his life. 'Right. Listen,' he says and when Trent tries to interrupt again, waves him off. 'Please. Let me talk and when I'm finished, I'll totally understand if you want me to turn around and drive back to the station.'

'Fucking hell, mate,' Trent says, stretching the words out, voice full of concern, not anger. 'What's occurring?'

They roll up to another set of traffic lights in front of what was once the Leicester Mercury building, but now houses a call centre and a kids' trampolining place. Liam stares at the red light, lets out a slow breath and lowers his voice again.

'I'm really sorry, Trent. I'm in a lot of shit, and I thought this might've been a way out. But seeing you now, how up for the meeting you are, well-prepared as usual… I just can't. This was a mistake.' The light turns green. Behind them, an impatient car honks. Liam moves forward again and says, 'Kendrick is back.'

Trent's face goes slack, he leans back in his seat and stares ahead as Liam lays it all out. Kendrick turning up last week, the drugs, the threats of blackmail and everything else. Throughout it all, Trent says nothing, just keeps his head back, letting it sway with the movement of the car, his energy and enthusiasm seeping out like air from a slow puncture. When Liam is done, they're out of the main city, driving out through the suburbs towards the outer villages. On the left is the large Catholic school, English Martyrs. There's a lay-by for buses and Trent motions towards it.

'Pull over,' he says, speaking for the first time since Liam began his confession.

Liam does as he asks. When Trent doesn't make a move to get out, just sits there, staring out of the window and thinking, Liam turns off the engine and waits.

After a few minutes, Trent says, 'I should've known.'

Liam can't think of anything to say to that, despite wondering how it could be true.

'I think I might've spotted him, well, maybe his car, from a distance, a few weeks back. I was coming out of the studio, late, with Zac, Ben and a few of the lads. There was a Range Rover parked on the corner. Pretty sure Titch was driving – remember her? Little hard nut Ken kept around back in the day. Couldn't see Kendrick, but seemed too much of a coincidence. Drove off sharpish once I think they'd clocked me looking over.' He changes position in his seat to get a look in his wing mirror. 'Been on edge ever since, to be honest. Wondering when he might show up.'

'Why didn't you tell me, Trent?'

Trent looks at Liam for a few seconds, then says, 'You serious, mate? Why didn't I tell *you*? Why didn't you tell *me*?'

'Well, yeah. Fair enough, but I just mean if it was a few weeks ago, I could have been prepared, maybe taken out an injunction or something.'

Now Trent laughs. 'Firstly, how do you think that would pan out if he's holding all this shit over you. And secondly… I'm not scared of him.'

The pause tells Liam otherwise. 'Maybe you should be, though. You didn't see him last week. He seems… different. I know he was goaded into some stupid bar fights back in the day, but he was never truly violent. Not really.' He pauses, thinking of Kendrick's tearful late-night confession to the stabbing of that poor kid from his estate. 'Either way. If he's already been watching you, waiting… I don't know. Just feels like he's been building up to something and now I'm delivering you to him on a plate. I'm sorry, Trent. I really am.'

Trent is looking away now, staring up at the big imposing school beside them. 'Reminds me of where I went. Full of cunts, no doubt.'

It's a weird gear change and Liam doubts Trent's comprehensive bore much similarity to English Martyrs, but he says nothing. He remembers his dad telling him it was where the posh kids went, when he was growing up.

Trent snaps out of his reverie. 'So, hang on. Does that mean I haven't got the call back from Wainwright? Has the part gone?'

'The part hasn't gone, not as far as I'm aware. I've been asking around and no one has heard any announcements yet.'

'So I'm still in the mix?'

'Definitely,' Liam says, desperate to placate Trent and salvage what might be left of their relationship.

Trent sighs. 'That's something I suppose.' He doesn't say anything for a long minute or so. The occasional car blurs past. An old man shuffles up the road with his dog, a whippet that stands taller than the old man's waist. The dog keeps looking around at his owner, as if to say 'Come on, mate. Let's get a move on'. Despite the tension in the car, Liam almost laughs, imagining the dog taking off and dragging the old man down the street. He wishes someone or something could pull him out of the situation he's created for himself.

Eventually, Trent sits up straight and points ahead. 'Fuck it. Let's do this. Get it over with. Rip off the Band-Aid and all that.'

'You can't mean…'

'Yes, mate. The meeting. Let him say what he's got to say and we can move on.'

Liam shakes his head. 'No. Absolutely not. I'll put him off.'

'What, and have him trash your career? Mine as well? Ruin everything with LimeLight and all that? Everything you've built?'

'Maybe we can arrange a call or something?' Liam asks, getting desperate now.

'No, mate. Chances are he wants me to apologise. You know, for disappearing when all the shit went down with the trial and everything. I can see how it might look. The timing of it. And now he sees me doing well, probably even thinks I've stolen his career or something.' He catches the look on Liam's face. 'He's said as much, has he? Thought so. Fair enough. Let him say his piece, I'll say sorry. I don't want it hanging over me. Who knows, maybe we can find something for him? A writing job somewhere? Bit part in an indie film? As long as I'm not associated with it?'

'I just think the whole thing is an unnecessary risk. Let me call it off and we can come up with another idea.'

'Nope,' Trent says, clicking in his seatbelt. 'This ends tonight. Hurry up, or I'll be late.'

Liam is frozen, every muscle in his body resisting what Trent is telling him to do. He realises he's slowly shaking his head. He turns to Trent, ready to plead with him again.

Trent seems to react to Liam's fear and breaks out into a huge smile, the one he likes to use to disarm music journalists and producers. He rubs his thumb and forefinger together, doing his impression of David Brent from *The Office*.

'And what about the bunce?' he asks. 'Bunsen burner, nice little earner.'

Liam manages a smile. 'For the part? We haven't even got to the money side of things yet. We won't until they offer you the role.'

'I'm not talking about the role, mate. My bonus from the buyout, remember! And all the money you stand to make when it goes through in a couple of weeks. We can't let Kendrick ruin all that, can we?'

'Well… no, but—'

'But nothing, mate. Let's go.' Trent gets serious again. 'I want to get there before he does.'

Leg shaking, Liam starts the car and drives on, into the dying light of the day.

CHAPTER 14

LIAM

BY THE TIME they reach the turning for Liam's house, it's almost dark. Either side of the entrance to the driveway are the huge trees that provided the name for the property: Twin Oaks. Their massive trunks mean they've been here for centuries. They lean across the drive, branches intertwining high above, like two doomed lovers clasping hands. Skinny, tall pine trees line the gravel track, creating a dark path towards the house. It's only fifty metres or so, but the surface needs attention and Liam has to drive slowly to avoid the potholes. It's dimly lit by a series of pole-mounted solar lights, each giving a weak orange glow. Some lights flicker or don't come on at all. Yet another thing Liam will need to fix before he can start bringing the family up here more regularly. But right now, bouncing and swaying in his seat, he feels like he's on a slow, uncomfortable train ride to an unwanted destination.

Beside him, Trent rocks with the motion. His face is hard-set, focussed, like he's preparing to go on stage or wait for the director to call 'Action!'. Liam is about to apologise again, when up ahead a security flood light comes on. The house, in silhouette, appears through the trees off to the right. It's a large, grey stone, lodge-style place that always reminds Liam of Michael Corleone's compound in *The Godfather Part II*. Imposing floodlights cast shadows through the surrounding pine trees. In front of the house there's a car, a figure beside it.

'He's early,' Liam says, frustration in his voice.

Trent is calm. 'Of course he is. This is *his* call back.'

'Trent. I really am sorry. I—'

'Save it. Let's just get through it and see how it shakes out. He probably just wants to say his piece and get his pound of flesh with some kind of apology.' He pauses, never taking his eyes off Kendrick, who is now picked out by their headlights as Liam swings the car around to park beside Kendrick's Range Rover. 'Or, you know… he's just trying to make a few quid.'

Liam hopes it's the latter, but doubts it. If money is all Kendrick wants, why isn't he blackmailing Liam for cash? Not for the first time since Kendrick demanded this meeting, Liam feels a horrible dread hardening in his veins, making his arms feel heavy and tired. What if Liam isn't just risking his relationship with Trent and putting the man's career at risk? What if the *pound of flesh* Kendrick is seeking is literal?

Trent opens his car door and Liam grabs his arm. 'Trent. Wait. This is a mistake.'

'You think? Mate.'

Trent's tone is bitter and sarcastic. Even if they come out of this physically unscathed, Liam realises it's going to take a lot to regain Trent's trust. 'Please. Be careful, that's all.'

Trent snatches his arm away, irritated. 'I can handle myself if I need to, Liam. I'm not the green little kid I was when he went inside. Be cool and let's get it over with.'

Before Liam can argue, Trent steps out and slams the door shut. Liam scrambles to follow him, fumbling with his seatbelt, turning off the headlights and eventually stepping out into the cooling, late-Autumn air. He catches the faint smell of woodsmoke, which must be from the nearest house, almost half a mile further down the hill. Trent stands a good ten feet away from Kendrick. Both of them still and unsmiling. The two men stay like that for a few seconds, like the peace before the shootout in a Western. Liam waits, unsure what to do or say, then flinches when Kendrick bursts into laughter, and strides towards Trent.

Arms outstretched and welcoming, Kendrick says, 'Look at you, bro. Dressed all gangsta and shit! And what's with the beard? Who you hiding from?' It's playful and warm and Trent seems to take it in the spirit it was meant. They embrace. Liam tenses.

Trent smiles. 'You're looking pretty sharp yourself, Ken! Good to see you.'

Watching the two men slip back into practised rhythms, in the way only old friends can, Liam finds himself taken in by Trent's performance. The smile, the glint in his eye, the way his hands linger on Kendrick's arms as he takes him in. Seconds ago, Trent was talking about 'getting through it' but now you'd think it was a heartfelt reunion. Trent has never been physically tough in the way Kendrick is and has always avoided confrontation where he can. In the past, he always deferred to Kendrick when things got heated. Maybe there is a chance this could all turn out for the best. Perhaps there's a way Liam could spin it into some positive story about two working-class lads, one white, one black, putting their differences aside to take on an increasingly middle-class industry. Once the acquisition has been completed, obviously. Liam allows himself to fantasise about this silver lining for a few seconds before reminding himself why they're here: because an ex-convict has blackmailed him to arrange a meeting in the middle of nowhere. A blackmailer, with a history of violence.

Liam sharpens up, slips back into Agent Mode. 'Can't tell you how good it is to see you two together again.' The words come out smoothly, and Liam is surprised how sincere they sound, even to his own ears.

Kendrick and Trent share a look and then Kendrick says, 'If you say so, Jefé,' and they both laugh. 'Let's go in. Getting cold out here, man.'

It isn't much warmer inside and Liam realises he should have put on the heating before he left earlier. He leads them through the wide wood-panelled hallway and is about to take them into the cosy-sized lounge when Kendrick strides past him into the larger sitting room at the back of the house. Looks like they'll be taking the meeting there. Liam hurries around the room, switching on different lamps until there are several pools of warm yellow light. There is a large bay window, with a sill so deep, you can lie on it. Liam thinks back to when he and Claire had a long weekend up here back in June. He pictures her, cushion beneath her head reading in the sunshine. Now the glass is a black mirror, the room and the three men reflected.

'Have a seat,' Liam says, gesturing to the two ox-blood red Chesterfield sofas which face each other in the centre of the room, a glass-topped dark wood coffee table between them. 'Sorry it's so bloody old fashioned in here. We bought it in an auction and it came fully furnished. Not really our taste, but it's Claire's project for next year apparently.'

Trent sits down, crosses his legs and projects calm and control. This, Liam can see is an act. The tiny up and down movement of his Adam's apple, the way he pretends to pick a piece of fluff from his trousers. Kendrick, on the other hand is still circling the sofa opposite, studying the room. He goes to the window, cupping his hands on the glass and trying to see out.

'Bit overgrown at the minute,' Liam says and flicks a switch on the wall by the window. Light floods the garden, revealing a landscaped but currently wild-looking plot. There are multiple flower beds either side of a winding moss-covered stone path which leads down to a small, ancient-looking grey stone structure, with wooden boards across it. Beyond that is a drystone wall with a gate set into it.

Kendrick points at the structure. 'Is that a wishing well or something?'

Liam smiles. 'Not sure there's any wishes left in it, but yes, it's a well. Natural spring under there. It's listed. We're going to get it properly renovated at some stage.'

'And what's the other side of the gate? Braggy?'

Braggy. The local nickname for Bradgate Park. 'Yep. We can walk straight out into the middle of the park. In the daytime you can see the monument over the wall.'

Kendrick whistles and switches off the floodlight. 'Some serious cheese to buy this place then.' He doesn't wait for Liam to answer, instead wandering over to the mantelpiece to pick up a framed photograph of Claire and the kids. Liam feels edgy, like his privacy is being violated. It's why he'd wanted to do it in the other room.

'Wow,' Kendrick says, studying the photograph. 'This recent? Kids are growing up fast, yeah?'

Liam looks for hints of some kind of subtle threat, but Kendrick's smile seems genuine as he nods and carefully puts the picture back onto the mantelpiece.

'Too fast,' Liam says. 'Izzy's new favourite word is nob head.'

Behind them, Trent laughs. 'Ha. You must be so proud.' He gestures to the seat opposite. 'Hey, Ken. You going to take a seat or what mate? Don't forget you called the meeting. Although, maybe just ask me yourself next time?'

A dark cloud passes over Kendrick's face. 'Would you have answered the phone?'

Trent pauses, his confidence fading, then says, 'No. Probably not.'

'Then don't talk shit, yeah?'

One-nil to Kendrick, Liam thinks. He offers them a drink, which they both turn down with a silent shake of the head. Kendrick continues to stare at Trent with hard, cold eyes for another few seconds, then seems to will himself out of it. His shoulders loosen again, and he takes a seat opposite Trent.

'So, Kendrick,' Liam says, 'you said you had a pitch for Trent. Was that genuine?'

'Course it was fucking genuine,' Kendrick says.

'OK. Just checking, that's all.' Liam gives a gesture that says the floor is open. He drags a small wooden chair over from beside the bureau and sits at the end of the coffee table between them. As soon as he sits down, he realises he looks like a tennis umpire, ready to adjudicate the game.

Maybe he is.

CHAPTER 15
LIAM

EVENTUALLY, Kendrick gives the smallest of nods and seems to make a decision. 'Fair enough. Brass tacks, let's not fuck about. I'll give you the pitch.' He claps his hands, then opens them slowly, a magician laying out his trick. It's slick, rehearsed. 'At the centre of it, there's two kids. One of them is black. Let's say the other is mixed, but passes as white.'

'Why does that matter?' Trent asks.

'It doesn't.' Kendrick gives the faintest of smiles Liam can't read. 'OK. Let's not worry about ethnicity. One of them is a black kid from the streets – the real streets – and the other kid isn't from that world at all. But he wants to be. Thinks there's some kind of glamour in it.'

Trent seems to be paying more attention now, the smile fading. 'Are they friends? These two kids?'

'Yeah. They're tight. At least when the story starts.'

'Ah, but let me guess. Things don't work out?'

'Wouldn't be drama without conflict, would it?' Kendrick asks, and now he's smiling, like he can tell he's reeling Trent in.

'Screenwriting 101.'

Kendrick winks. 'Knew you'd get it. Anyway, I know what you're thinking. The usual crime story, doomed friendship, *City of God*-type deal? But it's not. Been done too many times. Neither of these two will end up being crims, at least not like most of the shit on TV right now. *Top Boy* did it well, but I think it's time we told a different story.'

'We're in total agreement there,' Trent says, and Liam notices the mask is firmly back in place. Either that, or he's genuinely interested. Liam can't quite work out which yet. 'But how is it going to be different?'

'That's up to you, really,' Kendrick says. 'I've got some ideas, like wanting this story to be about business, not more crime bullshit. But I'm after true collaboration.'

'Oh,' Trent says. 'So you're not just looking for some option money? Sell me the idea and walk away?'

Kendrick slowly shakes his head. 'Would I have gone through all this if all I wanted was option money? No. After what I've been through these past few years, I need to… reinvent myself, yeah?' He pauses, seems to weigh his next words. 'You, of all people, must understand that?'

Liam feels like he's missing something here.

Trent's face is frozen, like he's holding for the end of a take, waiting for the director to call 'CUT!' Eventually, a wide smile spreads across his face. 'I see where you're going with it,' he says. 'And I've definitely got some ideas forming in the old back brain.' He gestures with both hands, his voice suddenly bright with enthusiasm. 'You've got my neurones firing, mate!'

Liam watches Kendrick, sees how Trent's words are landing. Kendrick isn't beaming, but he's trying not to smile. Liam realises he's trying to play it cool.

'So you're interested?' Kendrick asks. 'For real?'

'Definitely, mate,' Trent says.

'You sure? Because we both know what it's like to have

one of those bullshit pitch meetings where everyone's blowing smoke up your ass and then they ghost you and move on. So if this isn't real, if you don't want to work with me, you need to say. Now.'

'What?' Trent asks. 'Are you joking? This could be great. Us two as producer-writers? Your redemption? An original story that ditches all the usual stereotypes? Could be massive.'

Kendrick frowns. 'And you'd be happy to be seen working with me? Not worried about all the shit you're going to take?'

'Oh, there'll be work to do on the optics, for sure. But that's where our agent comes in.' Trent gestures to the end of the table. 'I know we've got to let this LimeLight stuff play out, but after that, you can sort it, right, Liam?'

Liam hopes his look of surprise isn't too obvious, but once he's picked his jaw off the floor, he manages to say, 'Yeah. I'm sure we could. There would still be things I—'

'See?' Trent says to Kendrick. His excitement is palpable now. Liam hasn't seen him this enthusiastic since he found out about the Larson audition. 'And fuck all that shit from the press. They're always going to be looking for the negatives.'

Kendrick jumps to his feet. He smiles and offers his hand to Trent. Trent tries to hide it, but Liam senses the tiniest hesitation, before he too stands and the two men shake on it. Except Kendrick doesn't let go straight away.

Liam tenses, leans forward, ready to intervene if he has to. Something is off. He looks past them to the reflection in the huge window, sees the two men shaking hands and the scared-looking version of himself in between.

Kendrick is smiling but still hasn't released Trent's hand. 'There was one other thing, though.'

'What's that, mate?' If Trent senses something is wrong, he doesn't show it.

Kendrick finally lets go of Trent's hand, smiles and sits

down. He seems casual and friendly again. 'Just wanted to chat about reviving an old project too. Goes way back. Not even sure if you'll remember it.'

'Try me,' Trent says, taking his own seat again.

'More of a documentary really. Remember Lady Jane?'

'Lady Jane!' Trent says, clicking his fingers and pointing at Kendrick. 'Wow… now that is a blast from the past. You're going to need to remind me of the details. But before you do…' He turns his attention to Liam. 'How about you get us that drink after all, mate? Have you got a nice bottle of something out there we can celebrate with? And maybe a few snacks? I don't know about you, Ken, but I could murder a cheese and onion sarnie right now?'

'Yeah, I could eat,' Kendrick says.

'Well, we haven't got any bread—'

'Stick a frozen pizza in then, or something. Few bags of crisps. Whatever you've got, mate.'

Liam hesitates. What's happening? 'You sure you don't want me to hang about to give my input on this other project or—'

Trent waves it away. 'No, mate. I'll fill you in when you come back.' He glances at Kendrick. 'Looking forward to hearing more myself, to be honest.'

Liam looks from Trent to Kendrick and back again. 'Trent. You sure you don't want me to stay? Just to hear the details.'

'I'll be fine.' There's the same edge Liam heard back in the car. It's a warning: back off.

'Not being funny, Jefé,' Kendrick says. 'You're beginning to hurt my feelings. You think I'm gonna rip your boy off or something? We're making plans for the future. It's all good. Relax.'

Liam's beginning to feel like the gooseberry on a best mate's date, like he's killing the romance. But is that what this is? Two old friends wanting to get intimate and share their secrets? Or is there something else hanging in the air between them? Liam still doesn't move, desperately trying to find an excuse to stay in the room.

'Liam,' Trent says, this time with some fake levity. 'Will you fuck off and sort the food and drink?' Liam can't argue any longer. He plays the dutiful agent, nods stoically and leaves the room.

CHAPTER 16
LIAM

LIAM THINKS about lingering outside the room in the hallway and trying to catch some details of what the two men might be discussing. Either that or waiting for any sign something is amiss. He really didn't like the vibe when he left the room and Kendrick had told Liam to make sure he closed the door on the way out. Like a doctor has the Hippocratic Oath, Liam likes to think agents have their own version, a duty to always put the needs of their client before anything else. He often feels like he's in a minority, especially the more time he's spent with the team at LimeLight. As far as they're concerned, if it's good for the agency, it's good for the client. He shuffles closer to the door again, hearing only low, mumbled voices. His phone begins to vibrate in his jacket pocket. He takes it out. It's his dad. Shit. Liam forgot to tell him he wouldn't make it to movie night tonight.

As quietly as possible, he backs away, answering the call as he gets to the kitchen.

'Dad. You're wondering where I am. I've cocked up.'

'Took the wrong exit off the M1 again? I told you, it's twenty-two when you're coming here and twenty-one A when you're heading into the city.'

Liam smiles. 'Thanks, but there's nothing wrong with my satnav. I've ballsed up and forgotten I'd got an important meeting tonight. Meant to call you to cancel and completely forgot.' There's a couple of seconds of silence, so Liam adds, 'Sorry.'

'No, no. Don't be sorry. No big deal. Would've been nice to see you, but maybe we can sort another night?'

'For sure. I'll check my work diary tomorrow and give you a call?'

'Yeah, definitely.' Mickey pauses and Liam waits, knowing he wants to say something else. 'Liam?'

'Yes, Dad?'

'Everything alright?'

'Yeah, yeah,' Liam answers too quickly. 'You know what it's like. Just a bit crazy at the minute with this buyout and everything.'

'I know. Claire was telling me what a big deal it is for you. Sounds like it's going to help out on the money side of things too.'

When has Mickey spoken to Claire?

'Yep,' Liam says. 'You know what she's like. Spent the money before I've even got it.' He feels a pang of guilt. Claire isn't like that at all, but he wants to get off the phone as quickly as possible and thinks it's the kind of thing his dad would agree with.

'Well, to be fair, Liam, I think she's been a bit worried about you.' Another pause, then, 'We both have.'

'Have you? Why?' Liam feels an irritation he struggles to keep out of his voice. He goes to the fridge and takes out a bottle of Prosecco Claire must have left in there. He puts it on the side and goes to the cupboard to find some glasses. 'Been talking about me, have you?'

'Hey, come on. Don't get defensive. I FaceTimed her on Friday to talk to the kiddies, like I always do, and we had a little chat afterwards. I asked her if I'd offended you by not going to that do last week.'

'Do? You mean the launch event at LimeLight? No. You had plans. I told you it was fine at the time.'

There's another brief pause and Liam half-expects Mickey to snap back at him. But he doesn't do that as much these days, and now Liam feels the guilt rising up again.

'No worries,' Mickey says now. 'I can tell you're stressed out and I'm not surprised. You've got a lot going on. All I'm saying is that when you want to talk… well, I'm here.'

Liam feels awkward. It always freaks him out on the rare occasion his dad shows any kind of sensitivity. He forces a laugh. 'I'm fine, Dad. Honestly. I am sorry about tonight though. I'll definitely—'

There's the smash of glass from the other room, raised voices.

'Dad,' Liam says quickly. 'Got to go. Call you later.'

He hurries through the hallway, tries to open the sitting room door. It's stiff, wood swollen in the frame, but eventually gives way and Liam bursts into the room. The two men are on top of the broken remnants of the coffee table, its glass top shattered into tiny fragments spread across the floor. Trent is on his back, Kendrick on top of him. They're locked in a struggle. Trent is screaming through gritted teeth, Kendrick making low guttural sounds. There's blood. Lots of it. Liam runs over, grabs Kendrick, pulls him off Trent. He tenses expecting Kendrick to resist, to lunge at him, something. But Kendrick just flops onto his back. He lies there, blinking slowly. There's a black-handled knife stuck in his chest, his once-white shirt now soaked crimson with blood. His lips open and close, like he's silently spilling his secrets.

Liam drops to his knees between Trent and Kendrick. He picks up random details. Blood. The knife. Trent's terrified face. Kendrick's leg twitching, mouth moving. The sliced flesh between Trent's thumb and forefinger.

'Liam… Liam… LIAM!' Trent's rasping voice finally cuts through. 'He had a fucking… knife. He came at me. He—'

'Wh-what? What should I…' But Liam can't finish the sentence, can't yet put it all together. Can't make sense of anything. 'Are you OK?' he eventually asks Trent, as he scans the man for any other injuries. There's blood. Blood soaked into his T-shirt, blood splattered on his chin and his cheek. Blood from the wound on his hand. But no other injuries, as far as he can see.

Through rapid breaths, Trent whimpers, 'He came at me. The knife. He had a knife. He had a fucking… Liam. He had a knife. He…' His words dry up, replaced by heaving wheezes of breath. He's in shock, Liam thinks.

Liam's eyes fall again on the knife in Kendrick's chest, blood seeping with every faltering breath Kendrick tries to make. Finally, something switches on inside him: *Kendrick is dying. Do something.* He reaches out for the knife, stops. What is he going to do? Pull it out? Isn't that supposed to be dangerous? Terror fills his head, like steam trapped in a kettle. The realisation he has no first aider training, no idea what to do for the best. Wanting to do something – anything – he scrabbles closer to Kendrick.

Pulse, he thinks.

Check the pulse.

But why? He doesn't know, only that he must do SOME-THING. He presses his fingers to Kendrick's neck. It's cold, clammy with sweat. There's something there, weak, but now he notices Kendrick's eyes are fully open, his face relaxing, no longer wincing with every breath. In fact, the breathing has slowed, become less erratic. A regular snatch of breath every couple of seconds. He locks eyes with Liam and with a single slow blink, Liam knows he's being summoned. There's just something about it. Using his thumb, Liam wipes away a tear on Kendrick's cheek and leans closer.

'Why?' Liam whispers. 'Why did you do it, Ken?'

Kendrick's lips move again and there's a distant sound that might be words but Liam can't make them out. He leans closer still, until his ear is less than an inch from Kendrick's mouth. He feels one last hot breath and with it, a single word.

'Bro.'

No more breaths.

No more movement.

Liam screams, 'No!' but it comes out as nothing more than an anguished cry. Kendrick's eyes are still open, but he's gone and not coming back.

CHAPTER 17
LIAM

ALL THREE OF them are on the floor. Liam sitting with his back against the bookshelf, legs splayed, chin on his chest. Trent is beside the sofa, holding a bloodied tea towel to the wound on his hand and crying. Kendrick lies dead between them, eyes still open, the pool of blood congealing around him.

Liam has stopped weeping. There's nothing left in the tank twenty minutes, or however long it's been, since he burst into this surreal nightmare. In between stifled sobs, Trent has been muttering the word 'why' over and over again. Neither of them has been able to hold anything like a conversation yet, but Liam can tell it's imminent. They've been coming down off a drug, adrenalin, the weird high of shock thinning out like morning fog in the sunshine.

After another couple of minutes or so, Liam asks, 'What happened?'

'What?' Trent has been staring again at Kendrick, but looks up at the sound of Liam's voice, like he's seeing him for the first time. 'He had a knife. He had. A fucking knife.' His voice is small, eyes still wide and glistening with tears.

'But what happened?' Liam asks again, his voice giving

out on the last word. He clears his throat. 'Seemed like you were on good terms when I left the room.' You lying piece of shit, he thinks to himself. He'd known something wasn't right and still he'd left Trent alone.

'We were. Just wanted some privacy, that's all. I thought Kendrick was going to apologise or something, and I knew he wouldn't want you around for that.'

Liam thinks about this, or tries to, but he's struggling to make anything add up. He has questions forming but Trent goes back to staring at Kendrick and speaks again.

'As soon as you left the room, he started on me, saying I'd deserted him. That he thought I'd genuinely liked him, that we were cut from the same cloth and all that. Said he'd treated me like… well, like a member of the family or what- ever and that I'd just fucked off without a word.' He drags his gaze away from Kendrick, to look at the window and the negative mirror image of the room reflecting back on the dark glass. 'He was right about that,' he says quietly. 'But I told him the truth, Liam. I was scared and my mum was poorly.'

'And that's when he got angry?' Liam asks. 'Why did he pull the knife?'

'The knife?' Trent asks, looking at it sticking out of Kendrick's chest. 'Don't know, to be honest. It just seemed to be there. And he came at me.' He raises his hands, towel still held firm. 'I somehow grabbed it, or tried to. He forced me back. We fell. When you pulled him off me… it was there…' He gestures to Kendrick.

'So, it was an accident?'

'An accident?' Trent shouts. 'A fucking accident? He tried to kill me, Liam!'

'I don't mean—'

'You don't mean what?' he screams. 'He tried to kill me. Kill me! Kill! You understand?'

He's losing it, Liam thinks, and fights to keep his own

voice calm. It feels like he's teetering on the edge, heart racing again. 'All I'm saying is, you didn't mean to kill him.'

'Of course not!' Trent says then seems to try to mirror Liam's quiet voice. 'I was trying to survive, that's all. If I hadn't fallen over the table... well. I'm guessing it'd be me lying there.' He pauses, then says, 'And maybe you lying right beside me.'

'Me? Why would he want to kill me?'

'I don't fucking know! I still don't know why he wanted to kill *me*, but he obviously did. And do you think he'd just let you go? The whole thing, Liam. Coming out here, in the middle of nowhere, on our own, no witnesses. It's obvious what he had planned.' Trent's mood has shifted again, the sea of shock tossing them both around like dinghies in a storm. 'Fuck him.'

Maybe he has a point? Hadn't Liam as good as told Trent he thought Kendrick might be dangerous? But you didn't stop it, did you, Liam? he thinks. It's a moot point now. Everything is over. His life, his career, everything he's built and will ever build in the future. All gone because he thought he could somehow escape his past. He digs into his pocket and retrieves his phone.

'What are you doing?' Trent asks.

'Calling the police, obviously.'

Trent scratches at his beard, leaving traces of blood high on his cheek bone. 'Well. Hang on. Is that the right thing to do?'

'What else is there? The longer we wait, the worse it looks.'

'Worse it looks?' Trent asks, lifting himself up to perch on the edge of the sofa. 'How can it look any worse than it already does?'

'What?' Liam asks, genuinely puzzled. 'It's clearly self-defence. You were attacked.'

'We know that, but what will it look like to the police? You think they'll buy this? Meeting in secret? Up here? Him just out of prison?' He stands, getting more agitated. 'And what about you? You ready for all the drug stuff to come back out, the blackmail and everything else? You think they're not going to find out about that? We've given them an oven-ready motive.'

'Motive? For what? For...' The pieces tumble down and lock into place. 'Murder? Like I lured him out here or something?'

'Yes, murder.' Trent strides over and snatches Liam's phone. 'Fuck's sake. You make that call and it's over. Everything. You want your daughters visiting you in prison?'

'But, I haven't done—'

'You set all this up, Liam!' he shouts. 'I was coming here for a call back, remember?'

Liam drops his head, like a chastised child. 'I told you I was sorry about that.'

Trent crouches beside Liam. 'And I told you I'd get over it, mate. But that doesn't change the fact you put me in a room with a violent man, yeah? Because of shit he had on you, not me.'

Liam cannot deny the logic. He was trying to save his own skin. And Trent is right. It could have been them lying there, instead of Kendrick.

'You're right,' Liam says. 'It's all my fault and thank God you're OK. But, Trent, we don't have any other option than to come clean about this. I'll back you all the way. I saw what happened. You were attacked. We'll get our stories straight. But the longer we leave it, the worse it looks. Please.' He holds out his hand for the phone. 'Let me make the call.'

Trent shakes his head, stands up and takes a couple of steps back. 'No, Liam. I can't let you do that. You're in shock and not thinking straight. If we get the police involved, there's only one outcome. Me and you go down for it.' He hooks a thumb towards Kendrick. 'And that piece of shit gets away with what he tried to pull tonight. You think people will remember what he did before? No. He'll become the martyr and I'll be the bitter protégé jealous of him trying to make a comeback. My legacy will be gone, your life and career in tatters.' He pauses and Liam can sense he's waiting to land the fatal blow. 'You know people will be quick to say you're just like your dad after all.'

That hurts Liam all the more because it's almost word-for-word the argument Kendrick had used to manipulate him. Despite that, he can feel his resolve crumbling.

'But… how?' he asks.

'No one else knew he was coming here, right?'

'Not from my side of things. I didn't put anything in the diary and kept it as vague as possible. I didn't give Ken the address until tonight and insisted he kept it secret and came alone. But, how can we be sure he didn't tell someone?'

'It's unlikely,' Trent says, stepping over the body to take a seat on the sofa again. 'Especially with him bringing the knife and doing what he did. Obviously planned it. Why would he risk telling anyone else?'

Liam concedes that's a good point. And a reminder that Kendrick was prepared to kill them both. Why should his life be over because some psycho was warped by revenge? But, still, he can't take his eyes off the corpse. There's a queasy roll in his stomach, a bitter taste in his mouth. You can't just make a body disappear. And what about Kendrick's family? Is there any family? Liam knows Kendrick was in care by the time he was three, foster homes and all the rest of it. But he can't ever remember Kendrick mentioning any other relatives he stayed in contact with. And, apart from Titch, most of his friends and hangers-on faded away once he went inside.

'But then what are we supposed to do?' he asks. 'I don't have the first idea of how to deal with anything like…' He gestures again to Kendrick, '…this. Do you?'

Trent is on the verge of tears again, hand shaking as he

raises his phone. 'No. But I know someone that can help. They owe me.'

'Is it wise, involving someone else? Who is it?'

'You don't need to know.'

No, Liam thinks. I don't. If he had to guess, he assumes it would be someone from Trent's previous life, back from the dark days in Nottingham.

Liam shakes his head again. 'No. We can't do that. I won't do it. We have to—'

'Life over!' Trent makes a throat cutting gesture. 'Life. Over. Yours and mine. Claire. The kids. All gone. Or…' He raises the phone again. '…you let me make this call and maybe, just maybe, it goes away.'

It, Liam thinks. Like they aren't talking about an actual human being laying dead between them. But what's worse? Somehow dealing with what's in this room, or seeing the look on the faces of Claire, the kids, his dad, when they discover the truth? All at once, the fight leaves him, his head slumps and all he wants is to go to sleep and not wake up.

Seeing Liam's body language, accepting it as an agreement, Trent steps out into the hallway, closing the door behind him. A mumbled telephone call ensues, but Liam can't make it out and doesn't really want to. He stares at his own reflection in the window, face empty and lost, but can't resist looking again at Kendrick's body.

Trent comes back into the room. 'Don't keep thinking about him, mate. He's gone.' He waggles his phone. 'I know what we need to do now. First, we clean this place up and then you'll need to dump his car somewhere. If you think you can handle that, I can deal with…' He glances again at Kendrick. '…I can sort the other stuff out.'

'But, how?'

'It's sorted. Less you know about it, the better. Yeah?'

Liam knows this is it. His last chance to get out, make the call and deal with the consequences. He shifts his gaze, past

Trent, to the picture on the mantlepiece. Claire and the girls. The laughter, the innocence. The hope. All of it gone once they find out what he's a part of. The police, the interviews, the press, the courtroom, the slam of the cell door… he sees it all play out and it takes all his strength not to curl up on his side and weep. He won't just destroy his life, but theirs too.

He locks eyes with Trent, nods and they get to work. Neither of them hears the scrape of the rusting bolt on the gate at the bottom of the garden, or sees the small figure slipping out, into the darkness of the park beyond.

CHAPTER 18
MICKEY

WHEN HAZEL DOESN'T PICK up, I think about leaving her a message, but I'll only end up stuttering out some load of old nonsense like I always do on those things and she'll know why I was calling from the text conversation we've been having. Maybe she's in the shower. Or she's gone out. Or she's watching the telly with that cocky twat she's seeing. Or maybe she doesn't want to talk to me right now and she's been humouring me with the texts. I need to remember she's in a relationship. Maybe Barbs is right and I'm overstepping. It might feel like there's more between us sometimes, but at the end of the day she's with someone else and I need to accept it.

But when the shit hits the fan or I'm struggling with stuff, she's always the one I want to talk to about it. Come to think of it, even when things go right, it's her I want to share it with. I should probably get some actual friends. Sad bastard. In any case, I'm probably blowing all this stuff with Liam out of proportion, but tonight's conversation was the weirdest yet and what was that noise just before he cut me off? And he *did* cut me off. Blurted something and just hung up. I don't like it. I've sent him a few follow-up texts and he hasn't replied. Not even sure he's seen them. I'm really tempted to call him back – that's what I wanted to ask Hazel about – but I feel like I'm getting on his nerves, bothering him. Claire assures me he's happy I'm back and she seems genuinely chuffed the kids can have a grandad in their life, as her dad passed away a few years ago. Still, maybe I am stepping on his toes? Fucking hell, I don't know. I'm annoying myself going round in circles, so there's no doubt I'll be pissing him off.

What if I give Claire a call? Ask her how he's been doing and tell her I'm a bit worried? Yeah, great idea, Mickey. Taint her with your anxiety. I'm sure she's got enough on her plate now with doing the prep for her own business and the second house up here and all the rest of it. Not to mention the time of night it is now. I can't be phoning her out of the blue and telling her what, exactly? Liam's missed our silly film night, and he sounded a bit stressed on the phone? Oh, and I think I might have heard a glass smash in the background? No. I need to get a grip. He'll no doubt drop me a line as and when he sees my messages. I'll give him some space. All I can do is tell him I'm here if he needs me. I'm not sure if I have anything to offer to him now, but as Hazel likes to remind me, sometimes, being ready to be needed by your kids, is the best you can do. I just hope Liam knows I'm ready.

CHAPTER 19
TITCH

SHE'S RUNNING, as fast as she can, on uneven ground that feels spongy and wet and dangerous. More than once, her foot catches on one of the small rocks that jut out at weird angles. She stumbles, gets her footing, runs on. Her heart pounds, like it's trying to punch its way out of her chest. She squints in the blue-black darkness, trying to make out the terrain. She's heading up hill – towards the monument? Maybe. She came here once as a kid, on a school trip, but all she remembers is eating a fish paste sandwich in the car park. Not having any money for an ice cream.

She keeps running. Legs burning now, hair dank with sweat beneath her hoody. She picks out features in the distance, a bigger outcrop of rocks to her right, trees silhouetted somewhere above her. She tries to concentrate, not to fall, but it's hard when all she can think about is what she's just seen through that window. It happened in seconds and yet it had been like slow motion. Hadn't seemed real. Like it was some weird internet video. Like she could watch it, leave a comment and move on. She'd stood there transfixed, hadn't done anything to stop it. But how could she? What could she have done, a tiny woman, standing out there in the cold behind a pane of double-glazed glass? Kendrick. Oh Jesus. Poor Ken. Watching him go down like that had been a kick in the gut. But hadn't she told him it was a bad idea? Hadn't she said he was making a mistake?

These past few months with Kendrick, before he got that letter, have been great. She's felt different, lighter somehow. Useful. He reached out to her as a friend, offered her genuine work, nothing shady. Before tonight, all she's done is drive him around and help him in the studio. She might only have been there to make the tea, fetch his lunch and keep the place tidy, but Ken insisted she give him her honest feedback on the album too. She felt privileged, special.

He told her he didn't want anyone else around from the old days and said she was the only one he still trusted. The only one who hadn't used him and then thrown away their friendship like one of those cheap plastic vapes you see littering the streets these days. She had stuck by him through everything, sent him letters while he was inside and even managed a couple of visits, when she had the money to make the trip. It hadn't gone unnoticed. But even before that, back in the old days, when Titch had been lurching from one crisis to the next, he treated her like a human being. And it was never about sex, either. He knew Titch wasn't into blokes – not that that stopped some men – but he always treated her with respect. She never really understood why he kept her around back then, but since he got out, with seemingly no one else around, she's been keen to repay his faith. He's been paying her, cash in hand, when he has it and recently, she had begun to allow a little hope back into her life. Had begun to consider some kind of positive future, with money, a job, self-respect and her own place to live. Even so, she had sensed a shift in Kendrick a few weeks ago and felt her chances of a better life somehow slipping away, like a sinkhole opening up at her feet. She wasn't sure what was happening, or why, but instinct told her things were turning for the worse.

She still doesn't know the real reason Kendrick wanted the meeting. She knew there was beef between him and Trent, but he'd been cagey about telling her the full story and she didn't want to ask. She knows she talks too much sometimes. She doesn't like silence and the bad shit that often follows it, but the vibes Kendrick was giving out about this Trent thing, had been next-level and she wasn't sure she wanted any part of it. But, she thinks now, you agreed to go with him tonight. She'd had a bad feeling, but even with that... the knife! What the fuck? That had shocked her as much as anyone. Titch has seen a lot in her short twenty-nine years on the planet, witnessed a lot of violence and, when she's needed to, dished it out too. But nothing like this. And now Kendrick's dead.

Kendrick is dead.

That thought is finally enough to make her stop. She turns. She's on higher ground now and can just about make out the light from Liam's house in the distance. She's panting hard, gripping the phone in her pocket. She still can't take it in, doesn't want to believe it, but she knows what she saw. The knife in Kendrick's chest, him not moving, the sound Liam had made. Kendrick had to be dead, didn't he? Maybe he's just badly hurt, she thinks. Maybe they called an ambulance or patched him up. Maybe he'll call me in the morning and ask where I am?

Bullshit. He's dead, Titch, she thinks. He's dead and you let it happen. And that fucker, Trent will cover it up, she's certain. But Liam isn't like that. Kendrick told her the ins and outs of the drug stuff and though it suited Ken to put some dirt on Liam, she knows Liam isn't cut from the same cloth as people like Kendrick and her and Trent. She'd seen Liam's reaction when he burst into the room, had heard him scream, even from outside the window. So will he go along with everything, if Trent does decide to bury it? Bury it. That image makes her lightheaded and sick. She sees Kendrick, lying in a shallow grave somewhere, animals feasting on what's left of him. She leans forward, hands on knees, and dry heaves. Nothing comes and she spits on the ground before straightening up again.

Got to think this through, Titch, she thinks. Got to look at it like anything else you've seen go down over the years. Being soft only brings you more pain and suffering. No one knows she was there, except Kendrick. If they'd seen or heard her in the garden, they would already have followed her into the park. But no one's coming, so she has to assume she got out clean. What she should do is pretend none of it happened and get the fuck out of Leicester. Except she can't move away. Not while she's still on licence for the shit with the pepper spray. Not to mention the fact she's stony fucking broke. There's work going in town, if she wants to throw her lot in with one of the gangs doing street rips or shoplifting, but she's getting too old for that shit now. And besides, if she gets caught again, especially while on probation, she'll go away for some proper time. She promised herself she'd get sorted this time, finally put all the crime behind her. Live a 'normal' life like most people do. Proper job, steady girlfriend. Maybe do that catering course she always talked about. But she's going from a standing start, less than zero. Living in sheltered accommodation when she can get a bed, and sofa-surfing when she can't. She's halfway through a two-week stint at a place near Belgrave but they lock the door at eleven and she knows she won't make it back there in time tonight. That doesn't worry her. If she can get back to the city centre, she'll mooch about until she finds some of the old crew she used to hang about with round the back of Sainsbury's. Half of them off their face or blind drunk, but familiar faces who'll let her bed down with them for the night, keep warm and talk bollocks. They'll give her shit, back at the accommodation tomorrow, but she knows she can talk them round. She always does. Then she can get her head down for a few hours, charge her phone and work out what to do next.

By tomorrow, or the next day, she'll know whether Liam did the right thing. Or – she suddenly thinks – if Trent *lets* him do the right thing. And what if Trent can't talk Liam around? What will he do then? That's not your problem, Titch. Wait. See what happens. People like her don't get many opportunities for escape. Yes, she got away tonight, but if she really wants to get out, to something better, she is probably going to have to take a risk to do it.

She turns and trudges on up the hill, plotting a course out of the park towards the dull lights of the city.

CHAPTER 20
LIAM

SOMEHOW, on autopilot and in a daze, Liam has spent the last hour and a half helping Trent deal with the body and clean the room. Liam had pulled a bundle of polythene out of the recycling – left over from when his and Claire's new bed had been delivered – and they'd wrapped Kendrick in that. Trent didn't mention doing anything else with the body and Liam didn't ask. Even rolling Kendrick in the plastic had been horrible, grisly work and Liam had only managed to get through it by pretending it was a mannequin, or some kind of prop. He had to keep going somewhere else in his mind, trying to control the convulsions in his arms and legs, the acid in his chest. He kept thinking of the Guy he and his dad had made for Bonfire Night when he was a kid. At first, every time he touched Kendrick, he flinched and had to swallow down the retch in his throat. But then he pictured that Guy flopping about in the wheelbarrow all those years ago, its lopsided head and crooked smile. Somehow it helped him do what was necessary. The rest was a blur. The congealed blood on the floor, the scrubbing, the cleaning. The cloying stench of bleach burning in his nose until it was all he could smell.

Now the two of them, Liam and Trent, stand behind

Liam's car. They're lit by the rear lights, everything bathed in red. The engine is running, plumes of exhaust smoke swirling about their legs like dry ice. Both breathing heavily from the effort of getting the body into the boot.

Trent taps the boot lid. 'OK. I'll sort this and then bring the car back here.'

'Right,' Liam says, still trying and failing to apply logic to any of this. 'And what am I doing again?'

'You're going to park his car, somewhere near the city centre. Stick to the outskirts, away from anywhere there might be cameras. But somewhere it's not going to be spotted for a while.' Trent drums his fingers on the boot again, thinking. 'Maybe a car park? A shitty one where you pay on exit? That way it could be in there for ages and no one's going to notice.'

'And then what?'

'Liam, mate,' Trent says, laying a hand on Liam's shoulder. 'Come on. I'm struggling with this as well, but if this is gonna work, you've got to switch on and start thinking straight. Let's do it like my contact said and—'

'But who was that on the phone? Did you tell them everything? Was that wise? How do you know they'll keep—'

'I only told them the basics. They're sound. Trust me. Neither of us is cut out for this, mate. OK?'

Liam nods, swallows and looks again at the red-tinged gravel behind the car, watches the breath-like fumes from the exhaust pipe.

'So,' Trent goes on. 'Once you've parked the car, you walk into town and get a taxi – black cab, not Uber – back to the village. We'll spend the night here and then we can always say you invited me up for a meeting and it turned into a bit of a social and I stayed over. Right?'

'Right,' Liam says, realising how far away his voice sounds. He says it again, louder this time and tries to sound confident.

Trent, on the surface at least, seems to accept it. 'Good man. Let's get it sorted and put it behind us.' He glances back at the car. 'That bastard can't hurt us anymore, mate. It's for the best.'

'It's for the best.' Liam says it without conviction and turns to go.

'And Liam? Don't do anything stupid, like call the police or drive to the station, yeah?' He looks at his watch. 'It's just gone nine. Be back here by eleven. Or I'll have to assume you've had second thoughts.'

Is there a threat there? Liam's too disorientated to decode it and anyway, he's glad Trent has come round from his earlier hysterics and is taking control, because Liam is in no fit state now. It's like they're taking it in turns to deal with the shock and trauma, passing the baton between them so they can somehow get to the finish line of this horrible nightmare. So he nods and heads to Kendrick's car.

Trent calls after him, 'And don't forget to dump the keys.'

It's a tight timescale, but Liam makes it back to Twin Oaks at five to eleven. Just to be safe, he'd been dropped off by the taxi a good ten minutes' walk away. He makes his way down the drive and eventually sees his car is already parked outside. Without realising why he's doing it, Liam touches the car bonnet. It's cool to the touch, which probably means Trent has been back for a while. He lets his hand linger there and wonders where Trent might have left Kendrick. Wonders too if his car has been caught on camera anywhere. Why had it seemed like a good idea to put Kendrick in Liam's car? Doesn't that seem stupid and reckless now? More grim paranoia sets in, and Liam becomes convinced Kendrick is still in the boot of the car, that Trent has left him to deal with it. Panic surges up and he's on the verge of running to the back to check the boot, when he hears the front door of the house open.

'Liam? That you?' Trent asks. 'What you doing standing there? You look like a broken toy, mate. You coming in or what?'

How can Trent be so calm? It's unnerving and Liam finds himself unable to walk out of the shadows and towards the house.

'Liam?' Trent asks again, before he softens his voice. 'Come on, mate. It's sorted now. Let's have a drink and a chat.'

But still Liam is welded to the spot. Trent steps out and slowly approaches. He's glancing left and right, trying to be casual, but to Liam, he looks like a cautious animal, a fox or something, checking the trees for signs of predators.

'I'm on my own,' Liam finds himself saying.

Trent reaches him, stops and smiles. He lays a hand on Liam's arm. 'Of course you're on your own, mate. Never doubted it.'

But Liam spots the tight smile, the wary eyes. There's doubt there, the remnants of adrenalin. Maybe fear? He can tell Trent wasn't sure Liam would come back at all and something about that comforts him. He's not struggling any less than I am, Liam thinks.

Without saying it, neither of them wants to go back into the now disinfectant-stinking room they were in earlier. Liam doesn't want to stare at the bare space in the middle of the room, where the glass coffee table used to be. Where Kendrick breathed his last.

So they go to the smaller sitting room at the front of the house. There's an old gas fire, one of the ones with fake coal and after a few attempts, Liam gets it going. He turns on the tall uplighter lamp in the corner and they sit in the orange half-light and sip their whisky. Liam watches the flames reflected in his drink and eventually becomes aware of Trent staring at him from where he sits a few feet away in an armchair.

'It's bad, mate. No denying that,' Trent says. 'But it's done now. It's over. He was on a bad path, I can see that now. Probably the time inside tipped him over the edge, but we both know he had that side to him.'

Liam makes a non-committal grunt, which Trent seems to take as agreement, but Liam isn't sure he agrees. True, he'd seen Kendrick get physical, pulled him off a particularly offensive photographer who had tried to pap him coming out of a club at three in the morning. Liam had paid off the man for the broken camera and black eye. He had once witnessed Kendrick having to front it out with some coked-up chancers who tried to goad him into a fight at an awards after-party, seeing Kendrick bare his teeth and scare them off with genuine malevolence. But still... serious violence? And carrying a knife? Now, that *was* new. But Liam had sensed Kendrick was a changed man, damaged in some way, on that first night in the car with Titch.

Titch.

Seemingly the only person from the old days still willing to hang out with Kendrick, the one who had stayed with him throughout it all. Liam wonders if Kendrick had told her where he was going tonight. How will she feel when she realises he isn't coming back? Liam flinches, his guilt a stab in the kidneys. The thought of Kendrick lying out there somewhere in the damp and the cold, already rotting and being forgotten. The idea of Titch or anyone else who might still care about Kendrick, losing their friend because of Liam's actions makes him shiver, in spite of the warmth of the fire and the whisky.

'Unless he made some new friends in prison,' Trent says

now, again seeming to read Liam's thoughts, 'there isn't going to be anybody missing him anytime soon, mate. No good to dwell on it.'

When Liam doesn't reply, Trent says, 'Look, mate. You think this isn't breaking me up inside? I loved him back in the day.' He becomes hoarse on the last word, puts his head in his hands. 'Why did he do it? It's fucked up, mate.'

He's shaking, crying, leaning forward and hiding his face. Liam wants to cry as well, but he can't. Too numb, too exhausted.

'Come on, Trent,' he says now. 'We'll get through it. Like you said, it's done.'

CHAPTER 21
TITCH

A COUPLE of days have passed, and Titch has heard nothing. Nothing from Kendrick, nothing on the news. To anyone looking from the outside, her life is just as shit as it was before the meeting at Liam's house. She managed to talk her way back into the accommodation. She gave Grant, her support worker, a bar of Cadbury's Caramel, his favourite. Had told him she'd been looking after a mate who was having a relapse. Grant had looked at her long and hard but had eventually relented.

'I know you're not being straight with me, Titch,' he'd said, 'but I also know you're still sober. That's the only reason I'm giving you another chance, OK?'

Another chance. Her whole life had been littered with that phrase, or different versions of it. We're giving you another chance. Don't mess it up again. We're trusting you. Titch had heard all the clichés. But, to her mind, she never had a chance at all. No real opportunity to get out, to break the patterns and start afresh. It's difficult to overcome a bad beginning and Titch had the worst. She was born into care, a baby with heroin withdrawal symptoms. Never got to meet her biological mother, an addict who died before Titch could speak. A child with 'complex needs' is a tough sell for most adoptive parents, so Titch was raised in foster care until she was four. When she was finally adopted, everything seemed to settle down, her rage calmed by a caring mum and a nursery school she loved. Titch still remembers the joy she felt, walking to school, with her own lunchbox, a book bag and a friend to meet at the gates. Then her adopted parents split up and Titch's new step dad was a real charmer. After a drink he'd hit Titch's mum. When he was sober and alone with Titch, he laid his hands on her too. But Titch didn't have black eyes or broken bones like her mum. Her wounds were invisible and would likely never heal, especially as her mum refused to believe what was happening. Titch didn't think that relationship would heal anytime soon either. The rest is a blur of petty theft and super-strength lager, punctuated by pockets of mindless violence.

She needs money, real money and she needs to be somewhere else. Which is why she sits on her bed back at the centre now, turning over the phone in her hands, weighing it like a bag of gold. She been holding it so long it's warm on her palm, but she knows it's also hot in the same way stolen jewellery is. The longer she holds on to it, the more danger she's in. Or at least, the longer she holds on to what's actually on the phone. She can feel it. She rolls it over again, thinking. But... the longer she leaves it, the less valuable it becomes. Niamh comes into the room, tosses a big packet of Cheetos onto Titch's bed. Titch flinches and stuffs the phone into her hoodie pocket, like she's been caught watching porn.

'Eeyar! Have these if you want,' Niamh says as she collapses onto her own bed, opposite Titch. 'Some religious do-gooder gave me them when she came out the station. Sooner have had the money, but beggars can't be choosers and all that.'

Titch smiles at Niamh's unintentional irony. *Irony.* Kendrick had taught her that word, when he'd been going on about a script idea he had. He'd started doing that with her, pitching her ideas and stuff. She wasn't stupid enough to think it was for any other reason than he didn't have anyone else to tell, but still… it had made her feel important. And she'd loved learning new stuff. Kendrick had been a good teacher. No, she thinks now. He'd been more than that. He'd been a good friend. One of the few real ones she's had. And now he's gone. Tears tingle at the edge of her vision and she blinks them away before Niamh can notice. It's clear now Kendrick isn't coming back and all Titch has is a bed in a hostel and a big bag of crisps to her name.

She takes out the phone again and this time she searches for a number and heads outside to make a call.

CHAPTER 22

LIAM

LIAM IS WARMING down on the treadmill, walking off the steady five miles he's just run. It's the first time he's managed any proper exercise since what happened at Twin Oaks a couple of days ago and this is the best he's felt in all that time. He's in the basement of his three-storey, semi-detached London house. Converting the basement into a gym was one of the first things Liam and Claire had done when they got the place. It wasn't huge and the ceiling was too low to do a full HIIT workout, but it was fine for the free weights, treadmill and cross trainer they had down here. There's a large, flat-screen TV mounted on the wall between the treadmill and the cross trainer and Liam has had it tuned to the BBC News channel, sound down, for his entire workout. Subtitles on, him scanning every word spoken, every bit of rolling news scrolling across the bottom of the screen. Convinced he's going to see something, anything, about a body being found or a missing person's callout for Kendrick. Some revelation waiting to stab him in the foot like a shard of broken glass in the sand. Part of him, the self-destructive part, wants it to happen. Wants it all to be over so he can confess and deal with whatever comes next. Like being a kid again, being sent to the headmaster's office. The wait outside was always worse than the punishment itself. Except, if what happened to Kendrick ever comes out, he won't be getting a detention, won't be given one hundred lines to do at lunchtime. No. He'll be going to prison and his life and the lives of everyone he cares about will be ruined as well.

He takes another pull on his water bottle and keeps walking as his mind drifts back to his dad again. *He knows*, Liam thinks. *He knows something is wrong.* Mickey had bombarded him with texts on the night everything had happened. He'd heard the smash of glass, picked up on the edge in Liam's voice. Ever since, he's been asking if Liam is OK. It took Liam all his time to finally reply the following day, and even then, not until he'd dropped Trent at the station. Trent, sharp as ever, had picked up on it, of course. Had noticed the missed calls and text messages coming through.

'You've got to carry on like nothing has happened, mate,' Trent had said. 'If that's Claire, or your dad, a client, whatever. You don't want any of them sensing something's up, yeah?'

Liam knows Trent is right. But putting on a game face with clients and in business meetings is one thing, hiding your feelings from those closest to you, is another. Liam doesn't feel equipped to do it just yet. So he's thrown himself into work, stayed at the office late and got out early both days so he can minimise his contact with Claire. So far, she seems to be going with it. She knows he's been a little on edge with the buyout and Liam is leaning into that, but unless he can get his head straight, the dam is going to burst at some point. So this morning, Claire had an early session booked in and Liam had volunteered to drop off the kids at school. Then he'd headed back for a quick blow out on the treadmill. He'll shower, grab some breakfast and head to the office before Claire returns for lunch. Exercise has always been a help during times of stress, and, despite everything, Liam is feeling better for the run. His head is clearing. Even with all the furtive looks at the television and doom-scrolling local newsfeeds, he is starting to feel a shift in his mood.

Thoughts aren't facts. He remembers reading that somewhere and tries to focus on it now. Just because Liam is convinced Kendrick's death will come to light, it doesn't make it inevitable. Also, thinking more about his long-term mental health, he's starting to accept Trent's point of view. Kendrick, for reasons best known to him, attacked Trent, wanted to kill him, in fact. If he'd been successful, would he have let Liam walk off into the sunset? Unlikely. At best, he would be using it as another bargaining tool for Liam to do his bidding. At worst… Liam would also be rotting out in the wilderness somewhere. He shudders, turns off the treadmill and is about to step off it, when his phone rings. It's a blocked number, probably a cold call, and he considers bouncing it straight to voicemail, but changes his mind at the last second.

'Liam?' says the voice. 'That you? It's Titch.'

Shit. Theres only one reason Titch would be calling him. He forces a smile into his voice.

'Hey Titch. Kendrick got you making his calls now, has he?'

There's a long pause, before she says, 'Why d'you say that?'

'Well, I'm struggling to think why else you'd be calling me.'

'You sure about that?'

Liam doesn't like the edge in her voice. 'I'm not with you, Titch. Are you saying he didn't ask you to call me?'

'No. He didn't.' Another pause, like she's leaving a gap for Liam to fill. When he stays quiet, she says, 'I haven't seen him since Tuesday. Have you?'

'Me? Last time I saw him in person was that night in the car. With you?'

'Really?' she asks, with a coldness Liam hasn't heard from her before. Kendrick must have told her about the meeting. Shit. Should he carry on feigning ignorance and just front it out?

'Yes,' he says, 'I'm sure. He was blackmailing me, Titch. Remember? I'm not likely to forget that.'

'He wasn't blackmailing you, Liam. He was reminding you what was owed, that's all. And I'm pretty sure he was going to a meeting with you on Tuesday night.'

Fuck. Liam tries to mirror her calm, cold tone. 'Ah, right. Yeah, that was one of the dates we were looking at, but I had to move it. Had something come up with another client. Anyway, Titch. I'm busy, so unless there's anything else—'

'Stop it, Liam,' she says, sounding on the verge of tears. 'Just stop it. Now. I honestly didn't think you'd go along with it.'

'Go along with what?' He steps off the treadmill and sits down on the edge. The sweat on his chest suddenly feels cold. Goose flesh prickles his arms.

'You fucking piece of shit, Liam.' Tears turning to anger. 'Did Trent threaten you? Is that what it is?'

'I don't know what you're talking about,' he says, hoarsely. 'But I really have got to go now, Titch. Bye.'

'I know—'

He kills the call before she can finish her sentence, tosses the phone onto his towel on the floor, like it's about to burst into flames.

She knows? She knows what? That Kendrick went to the meeting and that he didn't come back? That's bad, but is he really surprised Kendrick confided in her? And does it matter? What can Titch actually do with that information? Nothing, he tells himself now, snatching up his phone and getting back to his feet on shaky legs. She can't do anything. Something about that makes him sad, though. He knows how hard Titch has had it most of her life and he's now taken away one of her only friends.

No, he reminds himself. You didn't take him away. It was Trent and it was an accident. Self-defence, actually. No choice. He does feel bad for Titch and her words had stung him, but that's all they are: words. People like Titch don't go to the police and even if she considered it as an option, she has nothing other than the fact Kendrick is missing.

Liam's phone chirps with a message. It's from Titch.

I WAS THERE. I KNOW WHAT YOU DID.

CHAPTER 23
MICKEY

IT'S EARLY. Half-six. I've just put the kettle on when the lounge door opens and Tilly comes trotting in, her collar jingling, tail wagging, always happy to see me. A few seconds later, Auntie Barbs appears, old fashioned cream-coloured nightdress down to her ankles, arms folded against the night time chill. She makes her way to the kitchen.

'Bleddy hell,' she says, tucking a strand of white hair behind her ear and pushing her thick glasses up her nose. 'Did you mess the bed?'

'I'm always up early, you cheeky bleeder.'

Auntie Barbs, isn't actually my auntie and, in fact, she's only seven years older than me. She was my mum's best mate from work and was always there when I was growing up. We're not blood relations, but we may as well be.

'You didn't go to bed until God-knows-what time,' she says, hustling me away from the kettle and taking charge of the tea-making. 'And by how many times you went to the toilet, you've either got a dodgy prostate, or you've got some-thing on your mind.' Without asking, she puts the pan on and makes me a bacon sarnie. 'Which one is it?' she asks.

I frown. 'What do you mean? I always have brown bread. You know that.'

'Not the bread, you silly sod. Who was on your mind. Hazel? Or Liam?'

'Maybe a bit of both?'

We're back in the lounge now, me munching on my sandwich and Barbs curled up on the chair opposite. Tilly sits in front of me, tilting her head and whining every couple of minutes, hoping I'll throw a piece of bacon her way.

'Look at you,' Barbs says. 'I only have to mention her name and you've got that sloppy grin on your face.'

I hold up what's left of my sandwich. 'That'll be the bacon.'

'Hmm. If you say so. But watch my lips,' she says, pointing at her mouth to help me out. It's sort of her trademark move. 'You had your chance with her. She's settled and you need to leave her alone.'

'You make it sound like I'm stalking her, or something. We're just friends, that's all.' I give my last piece of bacon to a grateful Tilly. 'I know it's difficult for your generation to understand.'

'My generation is your generation, you cheeky so-and-so.'

'Joking aside, we're just mates, Barbs,' I lie. 'I'd never do anything to mess with her relationship.'

'I should hope not, my lad.' She pats her leg and Tilly jumps into her lap and settles down for a post-bacon ear-rub. 'And what's bothering you about the boy?'

I tell her about him standing me up the other night and then the weird phone call, with him hanging up.

'You should've gone to his soirée, you know. It was obvious he wanted you there. He's probably just a bit mardy about that.'

'You think?' I ask. 'That wasn't the vibe I was getting.'

She tuts, shakes her head. 'Vibes. That's half the problem with you two. You need your heads bashing together. Instead of all this guesswork, why don't you have a proper conversation every now and then?'

I sigh, sip my tea. 'We do talk. Almost every day.'

'About nothing. Leicester City, which he's not really interested in anyway, how his agency is doing or your business or whatever. Small talk. Life is short, Mickey.'

'So you think we should be sharing our feelings twenty-four-seven?'

She stands and Tilly jumps down, recognising the signal that it's time to go back upstairs. 'Just once every six months would be a start.' She looks down on me, eye brows raised, lips pursed and I feel like a little kid again.

'Alright, alright. Give it a rest,' I tell her. 'Hopefully he'll come up next week for our film night. Maybe *Godfather Part II* will stir some powerful family emotions.'

She frowns, thinking for a few seconds and then says, 'Isn't that the one where Michael kills his brother and alienates himself from everyone?'

I laugh. 'Knew I shouldn't have introduced you to my DVD collection. It's coming back to haunt me. Get yourself back to bed, you silly old woman. Oh, by the way. Any chance I can borrow your car for a couple of hours this morning?'

'You hear that, Tilly? Calling me a silly old woman. Made him a bacon butty as well.' She lowers her head to give me a look over the top of her glasses. 'Why do you need my car? What's wrong with the van?'

'Got to pop into town for a few bits, that's all. Easier to park when I'm not in the van.'

She narrows her eyes. 'Rubbish. You're up to something. Best not be getting yourself back into bother, my lad. Fat lip last week and now you've got that look on your face again.'

'What look?'

'Mischief!' she says. She points at her mouth and starts to speak but I cut her off.

'Yes, I know,' I say. 'Watch your lips.'

'Less of your cheek. Just don't be bringing trouble to my door. OK?'

I can see I've genuinely pissed her off, but she turns and leaves before I can apologise, Tilly trotting after her.

———

I'm out of the house by seven-thirty and on my way up the A50, to Ravenstone, a nice little village just outside Coalville. Part of me knows heading over there so early is pointless. I've only met this bloke once and instinct tells me he isn't an early riser. Eventually I'm off the dual carriageway and driving through the centre of Coalville, a place that's always been the punchline to a bunch of jokes from the locals. Every city or county has at least one area, town or estate that seems to be the whipping boy for everyone else. All the same clichés get trotted out…

You live in Coalville? Have you got webbed feet?

A Coalville man, seen here with his wife and sister… why is there only one woman in the photograph?

My nan's knitted me gloves with six fingers… she must think I live in Coalville.

Coalville? Don't you mean 'Dole-ville'?

The last of those tells you everything you need to know. Local snobbery, looking down on a community that's seen better days. Once a bustling mining town, Coalville's been on its arse for decades. Working-class people that suddenly had their main source of income snatched away. Once the mine closed, what did everyone think would happen? Other factories closed, the centre became more run-down, and the town's reputation was forged. A reputation pushed by other working-class people, because even we like to look down on someone if we can. *We're poor,* we'd say when I was growing up, *but at least we don't live in Coalville.*

Truth is, it's never been that bad here. We're all fucking snobs. The long-term residents might come across a bit rough around the edges and Coalville does have its own particular accent – seeming to pull in more of Derby and Nottingham, than Leicester – but they're mostly friendly and no-nonsense. And looking around now, I can see signs of reinvestment. More shops and takeaways on the high street, a craft beer place and even the bikers' pub, The Vic, looks like it's been done up since I was last here. There are new housing estates being built as well, like the one I drive past as I take a left and push on towards Ravenstone.

According to the info Harper sent me, this bloke's name is Josh Sanders and by the looks of it, he's doing alright. His house is a decent-sized, three-bed detached in an estate that only looks about twenty years old. I park up the road a bit, making sure I'm not directly outside anyone else's house. That always attracts the wrong kind of attention. As long as you're not blocking a drive or outside their house, most people ignore you. I make sure the car is facing in the opposite direction and use the wing mirror to keep my eye on the place. It's barely eight o'clock and, sure enough, his silver Beemer is still on the drive. I settle in. Can't see him appearing much before nine.

Over the next half an hour, the locals leave their houses, one by one. The knackered-looking bald bloke in what looks like a bank uniform. A young dad, herding a couple of kids into an SUV and losing his shit when his daughter realises she's forgotten her lunch. A young plumber climbs into her van, massive thermos tucked under her arm, waving at an old dear she passes a few doors down. None of them seem to notice me, all of them wrapped up in the daily grind of their morning routine. It's like some well-rehearsed scene in a play, all of them hitting their cues and crossing the stage of the street. It's mesmerising and I almost miss someone coming out of Josh's house behind me. I put a hand on the keys in the ignition, ready to make a move, but relax when I see it's a young woman, clearly doing the walk of shame wearing last night's make-up, a short skirt and high heels, as she totters down the driveway, clutching her phone and a small handbag. A few seconds later, an Uber turns up. I try to snatch a glance at her as the car whizzes past, but it's hard to make out any detail. I get another chance a few seconds later, when the taxi does a U-turn in the cul-de-sac and drives back in the direction he came from. The woman has her head down, and even with the smudged eyeliner and remnants of lipstick, I can see she's barely twenty. If I had to guess, I'd say Josh swipes right most nights. Clearly not the settling-down type yet. Suppose he's throwing around all the money he gets from ripping off old ladies. Fucking scumbag. Maybe now his one-night stand has left, he'll follow soon.

CHAPTER 24
MICKEY

IN FACT, it's nearly half-nine when the lazy prick finally shambles out of his door. He's puffing on a vape, stopping to cough out a lungful of whatever shit is in those things. He's tapping on his phone, oblivious to me or anything else going on around him, as he unlocks the car and gets in. I key the ignition and slowly drive up to the top of the cul-de-sac to spin the car around and manage to time it so that Sanders has already backed off his drive and is heading out of the estate. I don't want to get close, but the lad isn't hanging around, so I have to put my foot down enough to at least keep him within sight. The country roads leading out of the village and back to Coalville are easy enough. I can keep a good distance, and it looks like he's winding his way to the A50, no doubt to head towards Leicester. I also like to keep at least one car between me and anyone I'm following and that happens naturally when we turn on to the main drag in Coalville. He pulls out on someone at the junction – typical BMW driver – and I play it safe and let two cars pass before following. His silver twat-mobile is still easy enough to pick out ahead as we make our way back through the town centre. The problem comes when the road becomes a dual carriageway, and the two cars in front both drift into the right-hand lane, leaving me no other option than to tuck in directly behind Sanders. He doesn't make the lights and for a second I think he's going to go through a red, leaving me stranded, but he must remember there are cameras on this stretch and jumps on the brakes at the last minute. I'm close enough now that I can see his face in the mirror, his mouth going ten-to-the-dozen as he either chats to someone on the phone or sings along to some music. Difficult to tell which, but either way he looks totally absorbed in it. Despite that, it occurs to me, too late, that I should put my sun visor down to at least obscure some of my face on the off-chance he checks his mirror. Shit. It's probably the movement of me pulling it down that draws his attention, because his beady eyes snap to the left and I'm pretty sure he's clocked me. I sit as straight as I can, trying to get as much of my face as I can behind the sun visor. After a few seconds, I sneak a peak around it and see he's squinting into his mirror and definitely trying to get a proper look at me. I'm going to have to abandon what I now realise was a bloody stupid thing to be trying in the first place. What's the plan? Follow him around all day and then punch him if he goes near any old people? Duff him up if he visits his grandma? No, this was silly. I'll drop it and think of something else.

But when the lights change and he sticks his hand out of the car window to give me the middle finger and shouts words I can't hear, something snaps. The light turns green, but I see red. He floors it, a small wheel-spin as he takes off towards the roundabout and down the next stretch of the dual carriageway. I try to do the same but Barbs' car is designed for comfort, not speed and it seems to take an age before I can get it in second. The engine screams as I take the revs as high as I can before slamming in the next gear. He's got a decent start on me, but I know he's got to slow down again after half a mile or so, because there's another round-about to negotiate. I drive like a mad man, overtaking a delivery van and getting back behind Sanders, who is still a few hundred feet ahead but now having to slam the anchors on to slow down for the roundabout. For the sake of speed, I'm guessing he'll try to go straight over so I take a gamble and leave my braking as late as I can, gaining as much ground as possible. In fact, he slows down so much I realise, too late, I'm going to smash into the back of him. I swerve right. He takes a sharp left. I brake and feel my back end start to drift out. On instinct, I pull hard right. The whole car judders and weaves, like a wild horse trying to throw me out of the saddle. Still I'm braking, turning, expecting the car to flip over at any second.

Engine stalls, the car still drifting in a wide arc until I'm halfway around the roundabout and facing back in the direction I came from. The delivery man honks his horn. A woman driving a little Ford, manoeuvres around me, open mouthed at what she's just witnessed. Smell of burned rubber, hands shaking, as I go on autopilot and restart the car. Stall it the first time, then try again, before edging my way back around the roundabout. Sanders is going to be long gone by now.

Except he isn't. The sharp left turn he made was into the car park of a pub called The Oak. Why the fuck hasn't he just driven off? More to the point, why don't I just drive away now? I've made a right twat of myself. No. Fuck that. Use the adrenalin, get this done. He's clearly intimidated or he wouldn't have floored it in the first place. I take a few deep breaths, get full control of myself again and drive to the car park. I pull in right next to Sanders' Beemer. It's empty. It's not even ten yet, so there's no way the pub's open but unless he's gone hitchhiking down the A50, that must be where he is. I kill the engine and chew my lip, thinking. Use your brain, Mickey. What the fuck are you doing? Chasing about after some no-mark criminal, like you're fucking Batman or something. Wasting time and energy and risking life and limb for what? You think you're going to make him change his ways? See the light? Get a grip. Drive home and forget about it.

My hands have stopped shaking and my heart is no longer trying to punch its way out of my chest. I start the car again, glad that I've seen sense, when someone emerges from the side door of the pub. A bloke, in his sixties, shaved bald head, white drop-handlebar moustache. A familiar face it takes me a few seconds to place. He lowers his head, squinting in my direction then giving me a smile and a thumbs up. It's Frank East, better known as Yeasty back in the day. Used to work on the door of Joker's Nightclub in town. Haven't seen him for maybe thirty years. He used to be a formidable character, but we always got on well. He gestures me over. I sigh and get out.

'As I live and breathe, mate,' Yeasty says, giving me a firm handshake with his oversized mitts. He's still in good nick, proudly showing off his physique in a tight white T-shirt. 'The lad said it was you, but I didn't believe him. Come on in, mate. We'll have a coffee.'

I frown, look back at Sanders' car.

'Oh, don't worry about him,' Yeasty says. 'He'll be gone in a minute. I've told him to fuck off, pal, while me and you have a chat. Come on.'

If it was anyone else but him, I doubt I'd follow, but unless he's completely changed, Yeasty has always been a straight shooter. What you see is what you get. So we go inside and he slams the fire door closed behind us. I follow him down a narrow, tiled-floor corridor, lined with a bunch of cleaning stuff. A mop and bucket, Henry Hoover and a load of old menu holders. From somewhere deeper inside the pub comes the sound of another door slamming.

'That'll be him legging it,' Yeasty says over his shoulder. 'Trust me. It's for the best.'

We emerge into the main bar, acidic smell of old beer, laced with Bac Spray and floor cleaner. A scent I always think of as *Pub at Opening Time*. I got used to it when I was a kid, following my old man down to the club and being the first ones in there. Yeasty gestures for me to take a stool and heads behind the bar.

'You don't need to worry about me, Yeasty,' I tell him. 'I'd already decided to let the little shit go. Don't know what I was thinking.' I turn around at the sound of Sanders' car starting up and see him disappear out of the car park.

'Frothy coffee, pal?' Yeasty asks.

'Cheers.'

'Yeah, I was surprised when he said it was you after him, to be honest. Not really your style is it?'

I give him a run down of how I met Sanders, while he sets about making the coffees on a big, automated machine. When I've finished, he puts a cappuccino down in front of me, tutting and shaking his head.

'Absolute shithouse, mate. But then most of these young 'uns are. He gets away with it because of his uncle.'

'His uncle? Who's that?'

'Ripper Bates? You not heard of him? Don't suppose you have, what with being away all that time. Anyway, he pretty much runs everything in this neck of the woods. Owns this pub. That's why that little coward ran in here. Knew I'd have to sort it out.'

'So, you work for this Ripper bloke then?' I ask.

'Not in the way you're probably thinking, pal.' He takes a sip of his coffee, his little finger sticking out in a dainty gesture that makes me smile. 'Them days are long behind me. No. I've been running pubs for years now. Used to be with a brewery but since Ripper bought the place, he's my landlord.'

'Sorry to hear that.'

'Nah. It's fine. The man's always been alright with me and I can still make a good living. Got some good regulars and I live upstairs. I've told him I don't want any drugs or owt coming through here and I think that's how he wants it anyway. It's become his local and he likes to do his business lunches down here every so often.' He starts laying out the drip mats across the bar. 'Still wouldn't want to get on the wrong side of him, mind. And neither should you. Which is why I'm telling you to stay clear of that little twat.'

I give him a little salute. 'No worries there, mate. Came to my senses outside.' I neck half my coffee and wipe the foam from my top lip. 'Just pisses me off, you know? The idea of him out there, right now, ripping off old biddies.'

'I know mate. If it was up to me, I'd string him up by his bollocks, but then I'd have to answer to his uncle. He's supposed to be selling windows and fascias, but he's always doing stuff on the side. Slimy fucker knows he's protected – even though Ripper would go nuts if he knew that's what he was up to.'

I finish my coffee, swirl the last suds around in the bottom of the cup, like I'm trying to read tea leaves. 'Why's he called Ripper?'

Yeasty chuckles. 'No one really knows mate. I've heard half a dozen stories over the years. Gruesome shit, like he ripped someone's face off in a fight, to it's just because he used to be a used car salesman flogging death traps for loads of money. Who knows? But he can handle himself if he has to. I've seen him deal with three drunks in here, before I could even get round the bar.'

'Fair dues. Moot point anyway. I'll not be bothering Joshy again.'

'Wise man. I've told him to keep his trap shut with his uncle and I'll do the same. He won't want Ripper knowing he's been robbing old ladies. Trust me.'

As Yeasty waves me off in the car park, I'm torn between feeling like I've dodged a bullet and that I've just let a total shitbag off the hook. What's that saying about bad things happen when good men do nothing? Well, who says I'm a good man? I should get down off my high horse and let it go. That said, if I catch him at it again, it can't go unpunished. It just can't.

No sooner am I driving away, my phone pings with a text from Hazel and it's like I'm being rewarded for making the right decision.

GOT YOUR TEXTS. FANCY MEETING FOR A DRINK AND A CATCH-UP TONIGHT?

And just like that, my day gets a whole lot better.

CHAPTER 25
LIAM

WHEN LIAM CALLS TRENT, he's looking for some reassurance. He's overreacting, right? There's no way Titch was actually there that night and if she was, where? And what would she really have seen? But it takes Trent about five seconds to realise what should have been obvious to Liam.

'The window. That fucking big window,' he says.

'The one on the back? No, no,' Liam says, even as he knows it has to be true. 'We'd have seen her. And Kendrick came alone. There was no one else in the car. We'd have seen.'

All this comes tumbling out, a torrent of nervous energy. Liam's been in the shower, necked a smoothie and is walking to the tube. He's had time to try to get all this straight in his head and now Trent pops his balloon within seconds.

'No, mate,' Trent says. 'We wouldn't have seen shit. He was already there when we arrived, which, thinking about it, should've tipped us off. We were early and he was there, waiting.'

Liam stops outside a church, steps off the busy pavement and heads into the graveyard to find somewhere to sit. Despite the shower, he's already sweating again, heart going ten-to-the-dozen.

When Liam doesn't reply, Trent asks, 'Do you see it now, Liam? He made sure he was there before us and that he had backup. It was all pre-meditated. When Titch saw it didn't go to plan, she bolted.'

Liam can't think of anything useful to say. He plonks himself on a bench and stares up at the dirt-covered stained-glass window, criss-crossed with protective mesh. He can't make out the scene depicted, but thinks he can see a sad-looking woman, hands clasped and head down. He's not religious, never has been, but right now he feels like praying for a miracle.

'You still there, Liam?' Trent asks.

'Yeah. Still here. What the fuck are we going to do, Trent?'

'Has she sent you anything else since that last text?'

'No. I tried calling but she didn't pick up. Should I text her back?'

'No, mate. Absolutely not. Don't say or send anything that could link us back to it.'

'Then what?' Liam asks.

There's a pause, Trent obviously thinking. Eventually he says, 'We need to find her. Sharpish.' When Liam doesn't answer, he adds, 'Just to talk to her, obviously. Find out what she thinks she knows and to see what she wants.'

'What she wants?'

'Yes, mate. What she wants. Don't be naive. I don't know Titch well, but she's a survivor and she's just going to want to get what she can out of this.'

'She was his friend, Trent.'

'Maybe. But she's also a realist, mate. If you're worried about her going to the police, forget it. No chance. She might be upset, mad, or whatever, but she's got no right. She must have known what Kendrick had in mind. Either way, when she calms down, she'll just want a few quid and to disappear. Trust me. I know the type.'

Not for the first time, Liam marvels at how calm Trent is.

Trent has always been laid back, able to side-step confrontation, but other than his initial shock and hysteria, his composure has been impressive. The agent part of Liam's brain knows this is another reason Trent will eventually find massive success in the industry. He's made for it. Liam tries to match Trent's energy, but despite his steady voice, he's now leaning forward, looking at the ground and watching a beetle crawl along the path. He lifts his shoe to allow the insect to pass underneath it. As it does, Liam thinks about bringing his foot down to crush it, then changes his mind and watches it scuttle away. Poor little bastard isn't bothering anybody, after all.

He sighs, then says, 'So what? We just wait?'

'For now, yes. Let's give it a day or two and see what happens. Do you know if she's sober at the minute?'

'She was straight when I saw her last week,' Liam says. 'She was driving the car and seemed sharp to me.'

'Fair enough. Maybe she's sorted herself out then. Probably in sheltered accommodation or something. Unless she's actually got herself a real job, but I can't see that.'

Liam needs time to think independently, away from that maddeningly calm voice of Trent's. So he agrees with the plan and says he'll keep Trent up to date if anything should happen.

'Great,' Trent says. 'If you can, find out what number will make her happy and let's pay her off. And Liam?'

'Yes.'

'Don't forget. Keep going about your business as normal. Don't start acting weird. Focus on that buyout. Gonna be massive for us.'

He hangs up and Liam leans back, looks up at the window, just as the sun comes out from a cloud and hits the glass, lighting up reds and greens and yellows. He can see the figure more clearly now. A woman in light blue clothes, eyes closed and head down. Above her, Jesus on the cross, crown of thorns, nails and blood. The whole deal. An ironic smile settles on Liam's face. As signs go, it's a bit on the nose, he thinks. If one of his writers put it in a script, he'd tell them to take it out. But there's something about it, the woman – Mary? – crying and her son in pain, that makes him think of his own mum. In a few months it will be two years since she died. What would she think if she was here now? Would she be crying? Or would she be telling him to sort things out? Somewhere in between, probably. But he knows what her first piece of advice would be. She would tell him to stop ignoring those texts and calls from his dad and let him in on what's going on. Once again, he hates to admit it, but this is sort of his dad's area of expertise. Liam has to tell someone, has to get some help from somewhere and it can't be Claire. Trent may be confidently telling him it's all under control, but the more Liam thinks about it, the more Trent's cold attitude begins to unnerve him. It's weird.

He looks at his phone again and thinks about calling Mickey, but this isn't a bombshell he can casually drop on the phone. No. He needs to see him, face-to-face and get his take. He's going to be devastated, no doubt, but after seeing first-hand in Skegness just how tough his old man can be, Liam knows it's the right thing to do. Probably the *only* thing to do. He types out a text and, after several drafts, eventually gets something he thinks will do the job. Vague enough not to cause alarm and yet serious enough his dad will know it's important. Now he needs to get into the office, pretend every-thing is OK and come up with reasonable excuse to clear his schedule tomorrow for a trip back to Leicestershire.

CHAPTER 26

MICKEY

'IT SAYS "DAD, are you around tomorrow morning? Can I pop up and see you for a couple of hours? Need to chat about something." What do you think?' I ask Hazel.

We're sitting in The Linford, a little club-cum-pub within walking distance of Barbs' place. I was surprised when Hazel suggested we meet for a drink and a catch-up. I assumed PC Plod would put the kibosh on it, but I think she feels guilty for ignoring my call and texts last night. So here we are. Just good friends, and all that.

'I think it's great that whatever it is, he wants to talk to you about it.' She smiles, and without taking those big brown eyes off me, uses her lips to adjust her straw to take another sip of her gin and Slimline. 'It might be some good news he wants to share face-to-face, or it might be something more serious, but whatever it is, you have to be ready to listen to it without judgement. And if it's some achievement or whatever, then make sure you tell him you're proud of him.'

This last statement is delivered as a playful warning. She knows I haven't always been great at telling him that stuff.

'Duly noted,' I say with a mock salute.

I'm about to tell her what happened today, the drama this

morning with following Josh and all that, when I see sense and realise it's a bad idea. I don't want Hazel to get even a hint I'm falling back into my old ways. So instead, we settle in to a comfortable silence for a minute or so, sipping our drinks and taking in the atmos. There's probably only a dozen people in here tonight, but it's the middle of the month and there's still a nice little buzz about the place. It's geared towards the older crowd and the locals who don't want to use the more touristy pub down the road, but the staff are friendly and if you're a member, like me, the drinks are cheap.

'So,' I say, putting my pint back on the table, 'are things back on track with you and young Craig? Was he alright about you coming out with me tonight?'

She narrows her eyes. 'Why wouldn't he be? And don't call him that. Makes me feel old and he's not that young anyway.'

'Question still stands. Are you getting on better now?'

She takes another sip, stalling? Deciding something? Eventually she says, 'It's… fine.'

I wince. 'Fine? Fine? Talk about damning with faint praise and all that.'

'Hey!' She laughs, shakes her head. 'I didn't mean it like that.'

But we both know she did mean it like that and I find myself leaning forward, eager to hear more. 'So, what is it then? Amazing?'

'Now you're just taking the piss,' she says. I bring my pint up to try to hide my smile, but it's too late. 'Yeah, I can see your face, you cheeky shit.'

I have a drink, then wipe the foam and the smile from my lips. 'You know what I mean, though.' I pause, thinking. Maybe I'm buoyed by the news Liam is coming to see me tomorrow or maybe it's that she seems different tonight, more relaxed, open. But I decide to say what's on my mind. 'We both know you don't feel the same way about him as… he does about you.' Fucking hell. For a split-second there, I almost said 'as you feel about me'. That could've been awkward. Still, there's a light in her eyes and something in the way she's playing with her silver pendant, that suggests I may not have been too wide of the mark. Easy, Mickey. Don't get carried away.

'He's just a bit ahead of where I want to be at the minute, that's all,' she says, unconvincingly. 'I mean, wanting to live together full time and all that. I'm older than him and I like my independence.'

He still stays round most nights anyway, I think. So that doesn't really add up. She doesn't want him selling his place, making things formal. Doesn't want to commit. She wants a way out. I don't say any of this out loud, but yet again she reads me with those truth magnets she calls 'eyes'.

'I know what you're thinking,' she says. 'It's a commitment thing.'

'Isn't it?'

She looks out of the window, at the autumn sunshine dipping behind the huge thatched roof of the cottage opposite. After a few seconds, she turns back and says, 'Yeah. Probably.'

'So what are you going to do about it?' I ask, feeling only slightly guilty, like I'm frog-marching poor old Craig towards the guillotine. I can't help thinking his days are numbered.

She drains her gin in one long noisy suck and giggles at the snorkelling sound the straw makes in the empty glass. 'I don't know. Let's have another drink and talk about something else.' She nods towards my glass. 'Same again?'

A couple of lovely hours, and several drinks later and we're the last two in here. We've gone from serious – her nightmares have been getting worse – to emotional – her wishing her mum was still around and me telling stories about my grandad. But we've ended the night laughing about the time Warren came home and caught me wearing nothing except his kimono, and his mum half-undressed. Both of us jumping up from the sofa like a couple of randy teenagers. That was back in Skegness and the night I discovered Warren was her son. Only been a couple of years and yet it seems like we've known each other forever. Sometimes you just click with someone, man or woman, and you know it's going to work. Like when I find that first number of the combination on a safe, that flash of excitement, me knowing I can open the door. Alright, Mickey, I think to my half-drunk self. Let's not get all poetic and soppy. You just fancy her, and who can blame you? Her smooth chestnut skin, her legs in those slim-fit jeans and the way she rests her hand in the nape of her neck as she takes me in with those eyes. But it's more than that. It's her warmth, the way her face seems to crack open when she laughs, like the sun coming out from behind a cloud. Fuck's sake, Mickey. Thought we agreed to rein it in with the poetry.

'It's time,' she says now.

'Huh?'

She holds up her phone. 'Uber's nearly here. Five minutes. Shall we wait outside?'

We go out, arm in arm, like an old married couple, but she's swinging her hips, playfully bumping against me and trying to make me laugh.

'Come on, you daft sod,' I tell her and say goodnight to the woman behind the bar as we step out into the fresh night air. 'You want my jacket while we wait?'

'Ner,' she says and slips her arm around my waist to pull herself in close. 'I'll just use you as a windbreak.'

Her arm is inside my jacket, her hand warm against my back. She gently rakes her fingernails along the side of my ribs. It tickles through my shirt, but I don't want to move in case she stops. I'm looking straight ahead, pretending not to notice her looking up at me as she gets even closer. If Craig was to turn up, what would he make of it? Difficult to dismiss it as a couple of mates waiting outside the pub. The thought makes me tense, just a little and she senses it.

'Hey,' she says, softly. I finally meet her eyes, half-mast with the booze and lust and God knows what. 'You're right, you know. I'm going to end it with him. It's not fair.'

I nod. 'That's the right thing to do. Regardless of… us, this, or whatever.'

'No. Not regardless of this. I want you, Mickey.'

'You sure?' I ask, bolstered by the beer and her hand that's now found its way underneath my shirt. 'Because I want you too, you know?'

'I do know. I've always known. But I'm talking about, now, tonight.' She stands on her tiptoes and moves in to kiss me.

CHAPTER 27
MICKEY

PAP-PAP!

The fucking Uber has arrived. I thought that shit only happened in films, saved by the bell and all that, but it's a wake-up call and the spell is broken. What am I doing? She's still with Craig. I don't like the bloke, with all the passive aggressive shit he uses on Hazel, but taking her back to mine would be totally out of order. Young Mickey occasionally pulled that kind of move, but I'm done with all that shit. I acknowledge the driver but Hazel hasn't moved, still inches from my face and staring at me, waiting for me to say something.

'Come on,' I tell her, gently pulling away. 'You'll be getting a bad rating.'

'Fuck that,' she says. 'I'll pay him. But let's go back to yours.' When she sees I'm already shaking my head, she adds, 'You know. Just to talk, I mean.'

I laugh. 'Yeah, right. We both know if we go back to mine like this, half-pissed and randy, the only talking we'll do is pillow-talk.'

I expect her to be angry, but she laughs. 'Pillow-talk. Again, how old?'

'Old enough to know it wouldn't be fair on Craig, not while you're still officially together.'

'You can't stand him!' she laughs, then leans in again. 'Anyway, I told you. It's over.'

'I hope that's true. But you're saying it after six G&Ts and you might feel differently tomorrow.'

'Not sure I can take you being all mature and gentleman-ly.' She sighs and takes a step back. 'But I suppose you're right.'

'I am.'

'But Mickey,' she says, coming in for one more embrace. 'I'm serious about ending it with him. And I've had a lovely night. Chat tomorrow?'

'Definitely,' I say.

'Good luck with Liam in the morning.' She plants a kiss on me, lips hot on my cheek, and skips off towards the waiting Uber. 'And I mean it,' she calls. 'I'm doing it tomorrow!'

We'll see, I think, but I can't stop the rush of joy it brings me to think we might actually have passed some invisible barrier and can finally have something close to a real relation-ship. I stand there, grinning like a loon as she looks out of the back window and blows me a kiss. The car drives away and I wait for a full minute, listening to the night. I snap out of it when I hear the clack of the bolt on the Linford door behind me. A few seconds later, the main pub lights go out and I take that as my signal to start my short stroll back to Barbs'. I zip up my jacket and get going. I've barely got more than a couple of houses away from the pub when the road lights up, car headlights clicked on somewhere behind me. The sound of an engine starting, no doubt the barmaid leaving for the night. Tyres on gravel as the car pulls away but it seems to be crawling along towards me, getting closer like some creeping death. I don't want to look back, not yet. I'm no doubt being paranoid and the woman from the pub is just sorting her stereo or putting on her seatbelt before she puts her foot down and gets going. Despite that, I pick up my pace and push on. I'm only minutes away from home and it's probably just the rush of being with Hazel and the beer sloshing about in my system that's making me all dramatic. But still… the car isn't getting any quicker and now it's right behind me. I'm about to chance a glance over my shoulder when the bright white of the headlights is bathed in a new blue tinge. There's no siren, thank fuck.

Now I turn to see the police car that pulls to a stop. Where the fuck did that come from? It must have been parked just up the road, out of sight. Waiting. Shit. I stop and turn around, squinting to see past the headlights. Looks like there's only one of them in the car. The door opens and it's a woman copper, high-vis, radio clipped on and all the works, who climbs out and puts on her cap. She's familiar in a way I can't fully process yet. But I've definitely seen her before.

'Good evening, Mr Blake,' she says as she strides towards me and, again, I recognise the voice, but it's deeper than last time I heard it. More authoritative. It can't be her, can it?

I stand, slack-jawed and wait for her to reach me. My worst fears are confirmed. It's Crazy Jeanette. The last time I saw her she was handcuffed to a bed and writhing around like some demented ghost.

She steps up to me and I stand taller, push my shoulders back. She managed to split my lip when I was sober, so God knows what she could do when I've had a few.

'Had a nice night, have you?' she asks, close enough that I can smell her Red Bull-soaked breath.

'Lovely thanks, Jeanette.'

'When I'm in uniform it's PC Crane.' She leans even closer to whisper in my ear. 'But you can call me Jeanette when we're on our own. I'll even keep the uniform on for you, if that's your thing.'

I carefully take a step back. 'I thought you might have got the message before. None of that shit is my thing.'

'You looked like you were getting pretty cosy with Ms Cooper back there.' She looks over my shoulder, and pronounces 'Ms' like she's spitting out poison.

'Oh, right,' I say, taking another step back – just in case. 'So now you're stalking me and checking up on who my friends are?'

'Friends! You must think I'm blind. Fucking bitch was all over you.' She takes a step forward again and I relax my knees, getting ready to move quick if I have to. It's bad enough she's deranged, but what am I supposed to do now I know she's police?

'We're mates,' I tell her. 'End of.'

'I'm sure Craig will agree when he sees the picture on my phone.'

Jesus fucking Christ.

'Know him well, do you?' I ask. 'If you did, you'd know he's fine with me and Hazel being friends.'

'He's at HQ in Enderby and I'm based in Beaumont Leys but we're all brothers and sisters in blue.'

I have to laugh at this ridiculous statement. I can't help it. Jeanette doesn't take it well. She clenches and unclenches her jaw, anger coming off her in waves. I stop smiling and get ready to face that left hook of hers again.

'I'm arresting you,' she says.

'What for?'

'Criminal damage.'

'To what?' I ask. 'Your fucking ego? Grow up, woman.'

She moves fast and throws out a heavy kick to the garden wall of the little thatched cottage we're standing in front of. Her steel toe boot connects hard with the loose Bradgate slate and a big section of the wall collapses. The house itself remains dark. The owner is either asleep or out.

'Mindless vandalism, if you ask me,' she says, already grabbing the cuffs from her belt. When I tense and step back, she says, 'And I'd be happy to add "resisting arrest" to the charge sheet if you like? You know I like to play rough.'

This is only going to get worse. I need to get to the station and call my solicitor. So I bite my tongue and do as she says, turning around with my hands behind me to let her put the cuffs on – standard issue this time. She pinches my arse and marches me to the car. All I can hope is that I'm out before Liam gets here in the morning.

CHAPTER 28
LIAM

LIAM IS TURNING INTO BARBS' courtyard when his dashboard lights up with a call from Barbs herself. He's almost an hour earlier than he said he was going to be and hopes he isn't stepping on anybody's toes, but he had to get out of the house early again to avoid any long chats with Claire.

'Hey Barbs. You must be psychic. I've just arrived.'

'Arrived? Here? What, now?'

Her voice is different, strained somehow.

'Yeah, just pulled in. You OK?'

'Tut. Oh, Liam. I'm so sorry. I bleddy told him he should've called you!'

She abruptly hangs up and a couple of seconds later, opens the front door. She looks dishevelled, still in her floral pyjamas and clutching her phone. Tilly barks good-naturedly and runs out to meet Liam as he gets out of the car. He scoops up the little dog, leaning away as she tries to lick his face. After a quick hug from Barbs on the doorstep, he follows her inside.

In the kitchen, she busies herself, filling the kettle, pulling mugs out of the cupboard, a plate and some digestive biscuits. She looks manic and distracted in a way Liam has never seen. It's freaking him out.

'Never mind all that, Barbs,' he says as gently as he can. 'Come and sit down and tell me what's going on.'

Unusually, for Barbs, she does as she's told and takes a seat at the kitchen table. She keeps checking her phone.

'He said he'd call when he gets out.' She runs a hand through her hair, sighs and tuts again. 'I was hoping he'd be back before you got here. This is why I said he should've called you. Told me I'm not supposed to say anything but… bugger it. I'm not telling lies!'

Liam struggles to keep up. 'Get's out? Is he in hospital or something? Is he OK?'

'Hospital? What? No!'

'But you said something about him getting out?'

'I did, didn't I,' she says. 'Well… I don't know the full details and he assures me it's some kind of misunderstanding, so don't shoot the bleddy messenger, but he was arrested last night.'

So much for him turning over a new leaf, Liam thinks. Barbs tells him what she knows so far, which isn't much. Mickey has said it's some kind of personal vendetta, apparently, and it happened when he was walking back from the pub in the village. Liam can't imagine what major drama or crime could have taken place in Newtown Linford on a Thursday night, but then this is Mickey Blake we're talking about. Liam doesn't get a chance to react, before they hear the sound of a car outside. They both go to the kitchen window to see Mickey climbing out of an Uber. His coat looks creased and his hair is wild. When he sees Barbs and Liam looking at him from the window he stops for a moment. His shoulders sag and he looks at the ground for a few seconds before carrying on to the house.

Mickey closes the front door quietly and Liam can almost hear his mood in the sound of the footsteps coming through the hallway. When Mickey stands in the doorway, bloodshot eyes and pale skin, he looks every one of his sixty-two years and a few more besides. Liam's never seen him look so old.

'You're early,' Mickey says to Liam. His voice is flat, emotionless.

Liam wants to be angry, to tell Mickey how out of order he is starting this conversation by somehow trying to blame him for being arrested. But he can't. Partly because his dad looks so fragile and also because he knows, deep down, Mickey wasn't accusing him of anything. It was more a statement of fact.

'Yeah. I'm early,' Liam replies, matching his dad's energy.

They stand like this for another few seconds, both of them regarding each other like they're staring into a mirror. Neither of them seems to expect the reflection to talk back.

'Hello?' Barbs cuts in. 'Anybody there? What have you got to say for yourself?' She goes to Mickey, who doesn't take his eyes off Liam. Barbs finally seems to realise how delicate Mickey is and softens her tone. 'Come on. Give me that jacket and go and sit down in the lounge.' She turns to Liam. 'Both of you. Go on. I'll make that cup of tea.'

Mickey nods and trudges through to the other room. Liam lingers for a moment, until he feels Barbs' hand on his arm. 'Don't be too hard on him,' she says.

When Liam reaches the lounge, Mickey is sitting in an armchair, rubbing his eyes with his thumbs. Liam takes a seat on the sofa, angling his body towards Mickey.

'You OK?' Liam asks.

'Exhausted. Pissed off... but I'll live.' He shakes his head. 'I'm really sorry, Liam. About not phoning you, I mean. Honestly thought I'd be able to get back before you arrived and—'

'And what? Hide the fact you were arrested?' Liam doesn't mean to put so much venom into the words, but he can see they sting.

'No. I'm done with keeping secrets,' Mickey says, quietly. 'But I wanted to get showered and sorted and tell you what happened without you seeing me come back like this.' He opens his hands, gestures to himself. 'I feel as bad as I look. And what I look like is a bloke who's spent the night in the cells.'

'So what happened? Really, I mean?'

Mickey tells him about coming out of the pub, about some supposedly deranged female police officer and her kicking a wall down. To Liam, it sounds made up. Yet he knows it's true. It's too outlandish to be a work of fiction.

'And you met this woman on Tinder or something?' Liam asks, feeling all kinds of weird for even contemplating the idea of his dad out on the dating scene.

'Not Tinder, but yeah. One of those apps. Would you believe it was my first date since... well, you know. Since your mum.'

'Right,' is all Liam can think to say.

'I didn't sleep with her or anything,' Mickey says, seeming to read Liam's tone as 'disapproving'.

Liam waves it off. 'None of my business.'

'But I didn't,' Mickey says and then goes on to talk about the woman handcuffing herself to a bed or something. Liam only half-listens and Mickey eventually seems to realise his son doesn't want a blow-by-blow account.

'Anyway,' Mickey says, 'point is, she was crackers. Even punched me and split my lip. Thought that was the last I'd see of her and the next thing I know, she's nicking me because she saw me kiss Hazel.' He stops, abruptly, like he's said something he shouldn't.

'You and Hazel? I thought she was with someone?'

'She was, well she is, I suppose. But she's finishing it with him.'

'Not really appropriate then, is it?' Liam says, realising he sounds like a disappointed parent. But he can feel the irritation and anger building in him, and knows it's somehow made worse by the fact it's Hazel. 'Shouldn't you at least wait until she's single again?'

'Hey,' Mickey says, leaning forward. 'That's exactly what I told her when she said she wanted… well, when she said she wanted to stay over.'

'Oh, fucking great,' Liam says. 'More imagery of your sexual exploits. Just what I need.'

'Fuck off, Liam,' Mickey says, quietly.

'Fuck off? Fuck off?' Liam says. 'You get arrested and you're messing around with a married woman and you're telling me to fuck off?'

Mickey shuffles forward to perch on the edge of his seat and points at Liam. 'First off, she's not married. Right? Secondly, I just told you the arrest was a load of bollocks.'

'So you say.' Why did Liam say that? He doesn't mean it and believes Mickey's story. He also knows, without his dad explicitly saying it, that Mickey has real feelings for Hazel. And from the couple of times he's seen them together, Liam thinks Hazel probably feels the same. Maybe that's why he's giving Mickey such a hard time, which he knows is messed up.

You're a piece of shit, he thinks to himself now. You're punishing him because you've done something much worse and you don't know how to get out of it. Because you came here for help and the one time you reach out to your dad, he gets himself arrested.

'Now. Watch my bleddy lips!' says Barbs, who has probably been standing outside waiting for the perfect moment to enter. She's carrying a tray, with two cups of tea and a little plate of digestive biscuits. She puts it down on the coffee table and points at her mouth, in the trademark style Liam has become accustomed to. 'You. Two. Will. Not. Bleddy. Argue. I won't have it in my house and there's no need for it. Right?' When neither of them says anything, she asks again. 'Right?'

This time they both nod and mumble.

'Good,' she says, moving to leave again. 'Liam, I know your dad can be a bloody idiot at times—'

'Thanks,' Mickey says.

'—but he's been trying really hard since he came back and it does sound like he's just stepped into something nasty with this daft policewoman. And as for the carry-on with Hazel…' She glances at Mickey. '…he knows how I feel about that. It's obvious they should be together and they've been playing silly-buggers for far too long. So if things are moving in that direction, Liam, you should be pleased for him.'

Under the pressure of her stare, Liam gives a begrudging nod.

'Right. That's my two penn'orth,' she says. 'I'll leave you to it. Liam, why don't you talk to your dad about whatever it is you wanted to ask him about and I'll go and do my washing.'

'We both know you're going straight to the utility room to listen in at your nosey grate,' Mickey says, and points up to a metallic grate high up on the living room wall.

'Hey! Cheeky! Don't flatter yourself. I'm too busy to listen to your prattle.' She gives a half-smile. 'And maybe you'll tell me all about it later.' She winks at Liam and leaves the room.

CHAPTER 29
LIAM

THERE'S A PREGNANT PAUSE, which Mickey eventually breaks by saying, 'She doesn't change, does she?'

'No. She doesn't, bless her.'

Liam's anger has gone now, replaced by anxiety and the realisation he can't tell Mickey about the Kendrick situation. How can he? His dad now has to deal with the fallout from his arrest and it sounds like he's on the verge of things finally coming good with Hazel. And what? Liam's going to casually toss his problems onto the pile? That look he'd seen in his dad's eyes, standing there on the driveway when he'd realised Liam was watching him, was haunting. It had been almost as bad as seeing Mickey staring down a gun back in Skegness. The disappointment, the longing to have done better, the sense he'd failed his son yet again. Except it was Liam who had let *him* down, this time. Him the one who'd failed to live up to the unrealistic expectation Mickey had set for him.

No, he can't do it.

'So, what did you want to tell me or get advice on?' Mickey asks.

Liam's mind is blank, but this isn't the first time he's had to reply to a question he doesn't know the answer to. In meetings with clients and studio heads, casting agents and directors, it happens all the time. So he does what he always does in those situations. He switches his mind to autopilot and simply begins to talk.

'It was about work, actually,' he says.

Mickey frowns. 'Work?'

'Yeah. You know, you've heard me mention the acquisition, the buyout? Claire's probably told you it's been a bit intense.'

Mickey looks surprised that Liam is talking to him about this stuff, which Liam finds somehow sad.

'Yeah,' Mickey says. 'It sounds like it's been really busy and stressful.'

'It has.'

'It'll all be over soon though, won't it? Couple of weeks or something?'

Liam nods. 'Less than, if it goes to plan.'

'But... you're unsure about it.' It's not a question and in that moment, Liam realises it's the truth. He is uncertain about it. Mickey adds, 'That's understandable.'

'Is it?' Liam asks. 'It's loads of money and it will change our lives. Claire can finally get her business going properly.'

'Isn't that going to happen anyway though? Claire's all over it. I know it might take a bit longer without the big windfall, but seems to me like she's not the type to quit now.'

'She isn't. But she's already sacrificed a lot for my career and kept everything running with the girls and the house and everything else. She deserves this.'

'I'm pretty sure she'd be willing to wait a bit longer if it meant not pushing you into something you're clearly having doubts about.'

Who is this person? Liam asks himself. Where is Mickey Blake, the man he grew up with? The bloke who didn't really do *feelings*?

'And,' Mickey continues, 'I'm pretty sure this other firm will be run by a bunch of corporate cunts.'

Ah, thinks Liam. There's the man I recognise.

'I probably wouldn't put it quite like that,' Liam says, 'but yeah. They're definitely more corporate and structured.'

'And you think your personality and all the other stuff you've poured into that business of yours will get washed away, or at least diluted.'

'Maybe. But I think it's more than that. Right now, the agency is mine, something I built up on my own. I know I needed money in the beginning from Flick and I've definitely used a few of her contacts when I've needed to, but she deals with all the paperwork, the business side of things and leaves all the client stuff to me. Everyone knows it's my agency, my name above the door.'

'Well, your mum's maiden name,' Mickey says, and smiles to let Liam know he's not having a dig.

'Yeah, well, even so. You know what I mean.'

'I do. It's your baby. So what are your options?'

'Options?'

'Yeah. Can you kill the deal?'

Liam's breath catches in the back of his throat at Mickey's turn of phrase. He swallows and then says, 'We're less than two weeks away.'

'And?'

'And? There have been lawyers hammering out the details for months now. It's not the kind of thing where I can just turn around and say I've changed my mind, Dad.'

Mickey shrugs. 'What do I know? I'm just an old bloke who's never been near a boardroom in his life.'

'I wasn't having a go.'

'I know you weren't. I can understand why you might think I'm over-simplifying it. But, the grey hair should tell you I've been around long enough to know only two things are inevitable. Death—'

'And taxes,' Liam adds.

'Depends who you talk to about that. But everything else is negotiable and saying no is always an option. Even when you think it isn't. I learned that the hard way after everything that happened in Skeggy.'

There is an appealing logic to what Mickey says, but Liam cannot fathom a situation in which he could possibly hold back the buyout at this point. It's like a runaway train and nothing is going to stop it now – even throwing himself on the tracks. But he doesn't want to make his dad think he's ignoring his advice, especially since Mickey assumes it's the reason he's driven all the way up here.

Liam nods. 'Hmm. I know what you're saying. I need to think about it.'

'You do. But if you want my opinion, you need to include Claire. Tell her how you're feeling. She'll understand and I'm sure she'll support you, no matter what you decide.'

Yeah, thinks Liam. That's not going to happen.

'I will do,' he says now. 'But do me a favour, dad. Don't say anything to her, will you? Let me do it in my own time.'

'No problem. But, son, everything can be sorted out. Don't suffer in silence and keep stuff bottled up. I'm really chuffed you came up to talk to me about this. Means a lot to me.'

Liam swallows down a wave of emotion. 'No worries. Thanks for your advice.'

'I hope you know you can always talk to me and I'll always do my best to help. You sure there's nothing else bothering you?'

Liam licks his dry lips, takes in this new version of his dad, someone closer to the man he remembers fondly from his childhood. Before everything soured in his teens and beyond. He's older now, but wiser too, his eyes searching his son's face for signs something else might be wrong. If he asks the question again, Liam isn't sure he will be able to resist telling him the truth.

He forces a smile. 'No. That was all. Thanks for listening. I appreciate it.'

They fill the next hour with small talk, all the time Liam's mind racing as to what his next move should be, before he makes his excuses and says his goodbyes. As he drives away, one thought taps at his skull, like a woodpecker on a tree; he has to find Titch. He doesn't know where to start looking, but as he passes the sign to the next village along, Anstey, an idea begins to form. It seems he won't be driving straight back to London after all.

CHAPTER 30

LIAM

'THERE'S something I wanted your advice about.' Liam is parked up on a side street.

'OK,' says the voice on the other end of the phone. 'Shoot.'

'Well, you're not going to believe this, but I'm literally just around the corner. I've been visiting my dad in Newtown Linford. Be good to see you again anyway.'

'Erm… OK,' the voice says. 'If you give me ten minutes or so, I could meet you at a cafe or something?'

'What I wanted to chat to you about is a bit… well, I'd just sooner talk about it in private, that's all. Maybe I could drop by your house?'

Five minutes later, Liam is pulling up outside the house of once award-winning filmmaker, Eddie Vaulter. Liam isn't sure what he expected, but Eddie's place is a cookie-cutter detached home, in a well-established estate full of the same style of house. They all have caramel-coloured brickwork, double garages and a square lawn out front. Eddie's grass could do with a mow, dandelions dotted about it like the floral version of measles. Eddie opens the front door before Liam reaches the end of the path. He's put on a little more weight since Liam last saw him a few years ago, the middle-aged paunch straining against the brown belt holding up his jeans, but he's chubby, rather than fat. His shirt is creased, and he seems flustered. It was presumptuous of Liam to think he could drop in unannounced. Still, Eddie manages a smile and makes a good show of pretending he's glad to have a visitor.

'Come in, Liam. Long time no see,' Eddie says as Liam steps inside and closes the door behind him. 'Probably around four years ago? Wasn't that when you got me to do the profile piece on Leona?'

Liam follows him through the hallway to the kitchen. On the way, he glances into what must be Eddie's office and gets glimpses of a messy desk and a laptop covered in Post-it notes.

'Yes,' Liam says. 'You did a great job there. Made her seem a lot more interesting than she actually was.'

Eddie chuckles and flicks on the kettle. 'Bit harsh. She had big artistic aspirations, from what I remember.'

'Yeah, maybe she did once. Now she's just chasing fame and fortune, like so many of them do. That's why she moved to a different agency. Last I heard, she was doing a pop week-ender at Butlins with Little Mix and Bewitched.' Even Liam is surprised at how bitter he sounds and tries to wave it away. 'Sorry, sorry. She's a lovely woman and I wish her all the best.'

Eddie bursts out laughing. 'I think you just made it even worse, Liam!'

They shoot the breeze like this while Eddie makes them a coffee and then leads them through to the lounge. The curtains are drawn and the room smells a little fusty and stale. There's an empty packet of pickled onion Monster Munch on the floor and several DVD cases. One of the films is Eddie's feature-length documentary, *Dot On The Landscape*.

Eddie, clearly embarrassed at the state of the room, rushes to open the curtains, scoop up the crisp packet and nudge the cases closer to the TV unit.

'Reliving your glory days?' Liam asks, trying to smooth over Eddie's obvious discomfort.

'Something like that,' Eddie says. 'Sorry about the mess. Wasn't expecting visitors.' He raises a hand, closes his eyes briefly. 'Apologies. That came out wrong. Didn't mean to be rude.'

'No, don't worry. You're right. I should have given you some more notice.'

'Ignore me,' Eddie says as he crams the crisp packet into his pocket and takes a seat. He motions for Liam to do the same. 'I've been shutting myself away for a few months, trying to come up with the idea for whatever will be my next film.'

'How's it going?'

Eddie pats his paunch. 'I'm binging Monster Munch with the curtains closed in the middle of the day, Liam. What do you think?'

'Struggling for inspiration?'

'Oh, I've had loads of ideas, but they all seem to be too niche, not commercial enough. I'm trying to come up with something that will actually sell. Passion projects don't pay the bills.'

Liam nods to the DVD case still poking out from the bottom of Eddie's TV unit. 'That one did, didn't it?'

The film in question, *Dot On The Landscape*, was centred around a traditional boot and shoe factory threatened with a foreign buyout. It was a mixture of heartfelt interviews with veteran staff members and undercover filming of the new American bosses who were trying to destroy hundreds of years of history. Liam had loved the film and it had gone on to win a BAFTA, amongst loads of other awards. It even had a limited run on Netflix.

Eddie sighs. 'It did OK, but not as well as people assume. And don't forget I made that with someone else, so everything was halved anyway.'

'Great film, though,' Liam says. 'Powerful. The secret filming, all the undercover stuff, was amazing. And I bet you didn't start out making it for the money.'

'Far from it. Cost us money and only made it back when we got lucky and it found an audience.' There's a few seconds of silence while they both seem to process this, then Eddie adds, 'Anyway. You didn't drop by to hear my woes. You said you needed advice about something? You're not going into filmmaking, are you? The last thing I need is more competition.'

'No, you're safe on that score. I struggle to use my phone camera. It sort of links back to one of your older films, actually. *Home Sick*?'

'The thing I made for the homeless charity?' Eddie asks. 'One of the only films I've done that actually did well on social media. More than a million views on YouTube and counting.'

'Yeah. If you remember, that's the reason I chose you for Leona's film. She was a big fan of it.'

Eddie clicks his fingers and nods. 'Right you are. Remember now. So, what did you want to know?'

'You followed the story of the same three homeless kids over a year, or whatever. Really powerful.'

'Thanks.'

'But how did you do it?' Liam asks. 'How did you manage to stick with them for that period of time? Keep track of them and know where they were at any given time, I mean?'

Eddie narrows his eyes. 'What's this about, Liam?'

Liam runs his thumb over the material on the arm of the sofa, back and forth. 'Well, I can't say too much about it right now, but I might need to find someone... who's in a similar situation.'

'Living on the streets?'

'I think so, yeah.'

'In London? That's going to be tricky unless the person tends to return to the same area lots of time. Or if they've got a regular place they get their head down.'

'It's in Leicester, actually,' Liam says.

Eddie is surprised. Leicester is not Liam's regular turf. 'In that case, it's a lot easier, but it still depends on whether this person wants to be found. When I made *Home Sick,* as you know, it was set in Nottingham, but I did a lot of research and made a few contacts in Leicester. I can give you some places to try, people you can reach out to. Young or old?'

'Sorry?' Liam asks.

'The person you're looking for. Are they young or old?'

'In their twenties. Does that make a difference?'

'Yes. Different schemes and facilities are available. Are there alcohol or drug dependencies going on?'

Liam considers for a moment, then says, 'Maybe. Definitely in the past, but I think she's been clean for a while.'

'So it's a woman? Again. That can make a difference.' Eddie pauses, then says, 'Don't suppose you want to tell me what this is about?'

Liam slowly shakes his head. 'Not right now, Ed. I can't. I'm sorry.'

'Fair enough. You can't blame me for asking though, can you? My story-senses are tingling for the first time in months. I'd offer to help, but I can see you need to keep things to yourself right now, so I'll email a list of places to try.'

'Will they talk to me?'

'They will do if I tell them a friend is going to get in touch. But Liam...' Eddie pauses, becomes serious, '...if I do this, you have to assure me you're not trying to find this young woman for the wrong reasons—'

'Wrong reasons? What makes you—'

'I'm taking that as a given.' Eddie raises a hand to silence Liam. 'But also, if there is a story to be had here and you do think a film could help the situation in some way…'

Liam points at Eddie. 'Then you're the man, obviously. Goes without saying.' He smiles, hating himself for how easy the charm and the lies come. What possible opportunities for a film could be here? 'Either way, if it's a money project you need to keep you ticking over, I'm sure I could get you involved in some of the promo work for one of the latest batch of posh-kid actors we've just taken on?'

Eddie pretends to retch. 'I wish I had their money – then I could have some principles again. But, sure, in the meantime I might have to take you up on that.'

Liam chuckles then makes it clear there's a time-critical element to all this. Eddie agrees to send him the contacts later today. He gets in the car and heads back to the motorway. Claire has a busy weekend coming up and he's hoping he'll get time to do some research. But finding Titch isn't the only thing on his mind. Two words keep resurfacing from the night Kendrick died… Lady Jane.

CHAPTER 31
MICKEY

SOMETHING STILL ISN'T SITTING RIGHT with me about Liam's visit this morning. I know I didn't exactly do myself any favours trudging in from a night in the cells, but still. There was something else in his eyes, right when I asked him to tell me why he'd come to see me. It was the same look he used to give me when he was a little kid, just before he told some silly lie. To be fair to the lad, it didn't happen much when he was growing up. He was generally pretty honest. I think I went totally overboard the first time I caught him at it, told him it was the worst thing he could do and that he would always be better off giving me the truth. It had seemed to keep him honest, most of the time.

There were a few other times when I knew he wasn't being straight with me, but I let it go to spare both our blushes. Like when I came home unexpectedly in the middle of the day and heard him scrabbling around in my wardrobe, where I was pretty sure he'd found some soft porn mag I'd left in there. He was fourteen and when I'd asked what he'd been doing upstairs, I gratefully accepted the bullshit that he'd been doing his homework. But the fact he's been honest most of the time, means it's easier for me to spot when he's not. And I definitely sensed he wasn't giving me the full picture with all that stuff about the buyout. I don't doubt he's stressed out about all that, but there was a moment, before he started talking about it, where he looked like he was about to say something else. If I didn't know better, I'd say he opened up about the business stuff to avoid telling me something else. Something bad. I can feel it. If I had to guess, I'd say it's an affair or something. He's the right age for the mid-life crisis and Claire has confided he's not been himself. I hope he's not going to mess up everything with her and the kids. Don't want him to repeat my mistakes.

Either way, thanks to Crazy Jeanette, I've had to put Liam's woes on the back-burner for now. Fortunately, Barbs knows Marjorie, the woman whose wall Jeanette demolished last night. As soon as Liam left, we both headed round with a bunch of flowers and a posh bottle of wine. She was perfectly happy to accept my version of events. Ever since they refused to come out after a break-in, Marjorie isn't a fan of our local constabulary. Add that to the fact one of them issued her a ticket for parking on double yellows outside the local shop on a bank holiday a few years back, and it's safe to say she won't be pressing charges against me anytime soon. In fact, I've had to talk her down from making a complaint herself. Last thing I need is anyone else stirring up the hornet's nest that is Jeanette, AKA 'PC Crackers'. I've already booked a drystone wall specialist to come and sort the damage for Marjorie this week, so my solicitor is pretty confident it's all going to fade away. I hope so, but I'm not sure Jeanette is going to be warned off so easily. Especially seeing as she's already texted me again today:

NOT OVER. I'LL BE WATCHING.

I should just take that straight back to the police, but I'll keep hold of it and save it with any others she decides to send.

I've also had a difficult phone conversation with Hazel.

Craig is based in Enderby, but clearly the copper grapevine works pretty quick because he broke his neck to tell her all about my troubles. The bloke makes out he's a good guy, but I could tell even Hazel was pissed off at how desperate he seemed to tell her about it. Apparently, they had a row and he went off like some mardy kid. I know it's all fuelled by jealousy and normally I might say he was being insecure, but after last night and what nearly happened? I'd be a lying twat, wouldn't I? At least Jeanette doesn't seem to have told Craig she saw me and Hazel together. I did my best to smooth things over, but I'm hardly in a position now to push her on her promise to end things with Craig. The subject just sat there, hanging around in the background of our conversation like a fart in a space suit. I suppose the arrest has given her an excuse to delay things again. Or maybe, Mickey, I think, it's brought her to her senses, and she realises you'll only ever be trouble?

Fuck off with your negative comments. I'm not in the mood for them today. So instead, I've cancelled the day off I was going to give myself and I've taken a last-minute call-out job that's just come in. Warren thought I was going to make him come along but I could hear the smile in his voice when I rang and told him he could go back to prepping his next streaming session, or whatever he calls it. This is only a quote job anyway. Some big empty warehouse place over near Coalville. A new business is moving in, and they want a cost for me to do a full alarm system and fortify all the existing locks and shutters. If they go for it, it could be a good payer.

The whole time I've been driving over here, I've found myself checking my mirror, half-expecting to see Jeanette stuck to my bumper, crazy eyes glaring at me through the windscreen. I'm going to get whiplash turning my head to look behind me so often. I pull into the industrial estate just after three. The first few units near the entrance are a mixture of car parts companies, office supplies and couriers but as the estate has only been built a few months, the rest of the place is pretty deserted. The warehouse I'm looking for is on the outskirts and surrounded by as-yet unfilled units. There's some garish bright green SUV parked at the end of the road – presumably the bloke I'm meeting – so I pull up in front of it and get out. The road is a dead end, but it doesn't seem right calling it that. There's a wrought iron fence, but beyond it is a big swathe of rolling North West Leicestershire countryside. It's beautiful and from where I'm standing, I can only just make out a thin grey strip of the M1 in the distance. I hear a car door close behind me and see a big bloke wearing a tight-fitting, light brown blazer and black polo neck sweater. His skinny jeans and pointy shoes make him look like a fridge on sticks. He's probably late forties, with close-cropped receding hair. I suppose it's racist if I say he looks Eastern European, but he's got that vibe about him with the high cheek bones and a serious expression. So I'm surprised when he starts talking with a high-pitched Coalville accent.

'Alright me ode? Mickey, is it?' he asks, holding out a meaty hand to shake.

'Michael,' I say, doing a fairly good job of hiding my irritation and accepting the handshake.

'Right you are, Michael. I'm Ralph. Thanks for coming out.'

He witters on about his business – something to do with plastic manufacturing and windows – while leading me to the main entrance: a uPVC door with a standard Euro cylinder lock. Beside it, there's a big, steel rolling shutter, high enough to drive a decent-sized truck through. Motorised and remote controlled by the look of it. I'm taking all this in and jotting a few things down on my clipboard as we step inside. He gives me a quick tour of some empty offices and I clock the windows and do a rough calculation of how many sensors they're going to need. Ralph has stopped talking now, which is a bit weird considering how much he was waffling on outside, but I suppose that could be down to me being a bit distant. I'm struggling to concentrate, so it helps to focus on the job in hand and to keep making my notes. I can feel Ralph watching, taking it all in and probably wondering how much this is all going to cost. That's usually all a customer's bothered about, which is why I don't throw a load of sales talk at them while I'm doing a site visit. Once we've looked at the whole place, I'll ask a few more questions and give him some different options.

'OK,' I say, gesturing for him to lead me to the next area.

'Right you are,' he says.

We head out into a passageway that has a windowless kitchen off it, a store room and another door at the end. We make our way down to the door, which presumably leads to the factory floor, or whatever he's using the main area for. I hear muffled voices the other side. Ralph reacts, taking a split-second to glance at me before he continues towards the door.

'Thought the place was empty?' I ask.

Without turning around, he says, 'Yeah. Me too. I bet a few of my lads have come down to measure up for some of the machines.'

Something doesn't feel right.

I pause in the passageway and Ralph stops with his hand on the door handle. 'You alright, me ode? Something else you need to check?'

That lilting voice of his seems full of friendly concern but, like when I sense the combination in a vault door, there's definitely something else behind it. He's on edge and impatient for me to follow him.

'Yeah,' I tell him, tapping the clipboard with my pen. 'The main entrance back there… did you say you wanted a standard mortice or was it Euro cylinder?'

'I've got no idea, me ode. You're the expert.'

'No worries,' I say. 'I'll just have another look at it.' I head back up the passageway, past the offices to the main door. I try the handle, which doesn't move. There's a jangle behind me.

Ralph is holding up the bunch of keys. 'I locked it, remember?'

But the truth is, I don't remember. I was so wrapped up in pretending I was paying attention, I didn't even notice him locking the door behind us. Why would he do that? I suck in a deep breath, instinctively pushing out my chest and trying to look bigger and stronger than I feel. I take another look at this Ralph character and know two things: One, he's a lot younger and fitter than me and two, he knows I've rumbled him. Still, I've got to try to play the game.

'Well, no worries,' I say, as casually as I can manage. 'Just open it up a sec, will you? And I can check the mechanism.'

He tilts his head and gives me the kind of smile a caring headmaster might give you, right before he pulls out the cane. 'Come on, Mickey. Sooner we get it over with, the sooner you can get back for your chippy tea. Fish 'n' chips Friday, innit? It is in my house anyway.'

'Get what over with?'

He pushes open the door. The voices beyond it stop abruptly. 'Just a quick chat, that's all. By the way, most people call me Ripper.'

CHAPTER 32
MICKEY

THE MAIN FACTORY FLOOR, or warehouse space, or whatever it will be when a real business takes it over, is empty, except for a red metal table in the middle of the room and two battered office chairs. Standing around that are two stocky gym rats – an Asian bloke with a ponytail and a pasty ginger fella with freckles. Both of them look late-twenties and desperate for their next protein shake. The main source of illumination is from three skylights, a pool of light on the concrete beneath each one. I can smell new timber and fresh paint.

'This him?' Ponytail says, gently shifting on the balls of his feet. 'Old.'

'Experienced is the word you're looking for, sonny,' I say. 'But I wouldn't expect you to know that word… what with it having more than one syllable.'

'Cheeky cunt,' Freckles pipes up.

I give him a single nod, like I'm proud of his assessment. There's a noise in the pitch-black office behind them, but when no one appears, I keep talking. Pretty sure I know who's in there, but best to play dumb for now.

'Anybody want to tell me what this is about then? Are you

starting a new self-help group? Twats Anonymous? Must be easier ways to recruit new members.'

I somehow keep my voice even. I need a piss and my mouth's drier than a bag of self-raising, but I'll be fucked if I'm going to let any of this lot know that. They're sharks and any fear I show now will be like a drop of blood in the water.

Ralph, or Ripper as I now know him, is standing a few feet off to my left and laughs. 'Funny in't he, lads? But don't be fooled, me odes. He about shit his sen when he knew I'd locked the front door.'

Freckles rolls one shoulder, then the other. Warming up. Ponytail's eyes seem to get even closer together.

'Look,' I say, turning to Ripper, 'I think you lot have been watching too much telly. You've managed to lure an old locksmith to an empty warehouse. Well done. And now you're all standing about trying to look menacing. You're more *Brookside* than *Breaking Bad*.'

'What's Brookside?' asks Ponytail.

It's a fair question. A soap opera that hasn't been on for twenty-odd years isn't exactly a topical reference, but it's the best I could come up with.

'Alright, let's stop mucking about,' Ripper says. 'You're here because you hit one of my staff.'

'Hit? As in punched?' I ask. 'Do I look like the fighting type to you? And at my age?'

Ripper makes a show of looking me up and down. 'Matter of fact, me ode, you do look like you've got it in you, old boy or not. I've spent a bit of time on the cobbles over the years and I know a fighting man when I see one.'

He's got a good instinct. I was a boxer in my youth, and I keep myself in shape, but those days are long gone. Still, takes one to know one, which only confirms I was right to be wary of him.

'Maybe as a kid, but now the only scrapping I do is to get to the front of the queue at the Wetherspoon's.' Total bullshit, of course. I hate Wetherspoon's pubs, but I can see it lands well with him. Know your audience and all that. I project my voice back over my shoulder, to whoever's hiding out in the office. 'Only person I've had any kind of bother with lately is a slimy piss-ant who I caught ripping off an old woman. Ugly twat, shiny suit and no bottle.'

'Josh!' Ripper shouts. 'Get your arse out here!'

'Oh,' I say. 'You know him, do you?'

There's the scrape of a chair inside the dark office and out walks Josh, shaved head and horrible shiny suit still both present.

I hook a thumb at him and say to Ripper, 'He's the reason I'm here? Fuck's sake. The lad was trying to rob an elderly woman with dementia.' My fear starts to turn into anger, now wishing I hadn't let him get away that day I followed him. 'That's the kind of outfit you're running, is it?'

'He didn't say owt about her losing her marbles.' Ripper narrows his eyes at Josh.

'No, Unc'. She was all there. Honest.'

'That why you told her you were her nephew? And why she believed you?' I ask.

Josh starts to come back at me, but Ripper cuts him dead. 'Doesn't matter right now. We'll be having words about it later, mind.' He turns his attention back to me. 'But either way, Mickey old son, you're putting your nose in my business, and I can't have you laying your hands on any of my employees – but especially when it's family.'

I sense movement behind me. The two lunkheads come closer.

'Like I just said: didn't put a glove on him. Seem to remember I took a step towards him and he fell over.'

Ripper flashes a disgusted look to Josh. 'If that's true, that's… very disappointing me ode. But even so, I heard you went to his house, followed him and tried to run him off the road.'

I laugh, remembering my shit attempt at following him. 'I nearly ran myself off the road. The lad's painting me like Clint Eastwood.'

But Ripper doesn't laugh, or even crack a smile. I wonder if I can make a run for it, back to the door I've just come through, but he takes a small step to his right. There's no way I'm getting past him. The rolling shutter at the other end of the space is firmly shut and, in any case, I wouldn't fancy trying to outrun the Thick Twins.

'Listen,' I begin to say, but Ponytail and Freckles each grab one of my arms and drag me backwards. It's all I can do to stay on my feet but I manage it until the back of my legs connect with the chair and the heavies plonk me down on to it. They hold me in place as Ripper makes his way over. Josh appears to my left. I see his punch coming and do my best to ride it. It connects with my jaw but it's obvious the lad doesn't know how to punch and it hurts him more than it does me.

'Fuuuuck!' he screams, clutching his hand.

'Never mind,' I tell him. 'Looks like you broke it.'

'You fucking—' He swings a kick at me and misses.

'Oi!' Ripper shouts at Josh. 'Step away, you daft bastard!'

I've stopped struggling against the weight of Ponytail and Freckles. It's a waste of energy.

Ripper levels a look at me. 'You must think I'm running a right bleddy amateur outfit.'

'I've seen worse, believe me,' I tell him.

'Well, either way. It's a bit embarrassing to be honest.' Ripper winces when Josh howls in pain again. 'Fuck's sake, man! Get a bleddy grip. You're showing yourself up.'

Josh does as he's told and continues to walk around, breathing heavily. He splits his time between looking up at the ceiling and giving me daggers.

Ripper scratches his chin, steps closer and lowers his

voice. 'Sorry about this, Mickey. Yeasty tells me you're a decent bloke. You can see me dilemma though, can't you?'

'Not really,' I tell him. 'The kid has spun you a yarn, trying to save his blushes and he's family, so you're bound to believe him. But you know I didn't touch him at that woman's house.' I flick my head towards Josh. 'Look at him. Didn't need to.'

Ripper purses his lips, nods and makes his decision. He gestures to Ponytail. 'His hand. On the table.'

I flinch but it's too late. Ponytail grabs my right forearm and forces my hand onto the table. He pushes down, one hand on my arm, the other on my wrist. Fucking hell. I've been here before. The cold dimpled steel of the table stings with a memory of that vault in Skegness, an image of my hand waiting to be crushed in the door.

'Don't,' I say, my eyes darting from Ripper to the table, and back again. But the warning carries no weight.

Ripper sighs, clenching and unclenching his fist. He leans down close enough that I can almost taste the tang of his aftershave, and whispers in my ear. 'I'll pull the punch, but it's still gonna hurt me ode. Got to do somat, though. With the lads here and that.' He stands up again and I try to clench my fist on the table. He shakes his head. 'You do that, and I'll break your fingers me ode. Lay it flat and let's get it over with.'

After a couple of seconds, I relent, accept my fate. Reminds me of when I had some stitches taken out of my hand in my twenties. Nurse telling me it might be a bit sore. It was probably the worst pain I've ever had and after the first stitch, I had to relax, accept it and go somewhere else. I do the same now. Let out a long slow breath, raise my chin and stare past Ripper. Josh is standing there, still holding his own hand, with a sickly little smile on his face now. I stare back and give him nothing.

Ripper slams his fist into the back of my hand hard

enough that the table moves a couple of inches. I bite down against the intense pain and just about stop myself from crying out. The only sound I make is a deep grunt. Hot pain blossoms in the centre of my hand and flows into my fingers. I imagine molten ore being poured into a mould of my hand, filling up each digit until it sets into one aching block. Cold sweat runs down my back. I close my eyes for a couple of seconds, then open them before they start to water. I won't give these fuckers any satisfaction.

I shrug off Ponytail and Freckles, who both let go at the same time. I was never really any threat to them to begin with, but now I'm just an old bloke with a bust-up hand. Freckles strides away, walking on the balls of his feet towards the shutter at the other end of the room. Few seconds later, he's raising the shutter and the late afternoon sunshine is pouring in.

I stand on up on legs that feel like marshmallows and walk in a straight-ish line towards the open shutter. I daren't let my hand swing down, scared of what fresh hell that might bring, but do manage to resist cradling it.

'Sorry about that, me ode!' Ripper calls to me. 'Had to be done. Pop into The Oak some time and I'll buy you a pint.'

I clench my jaw even harder against the 'FUCK YOU' that's bursting to get out and comfort myself with distant fantasies of what I'm going to do to Josh if I ever see him again. But even now, flooded with anger and pain, I know that's all it is – a fantasy. I'd be stupid to escalate things any further but, more than that, comes the realisation I couldn't do anything even if I wanted to. As I trudge back to the van and somehow drive away, I've never felt older or weaker than I do right now.

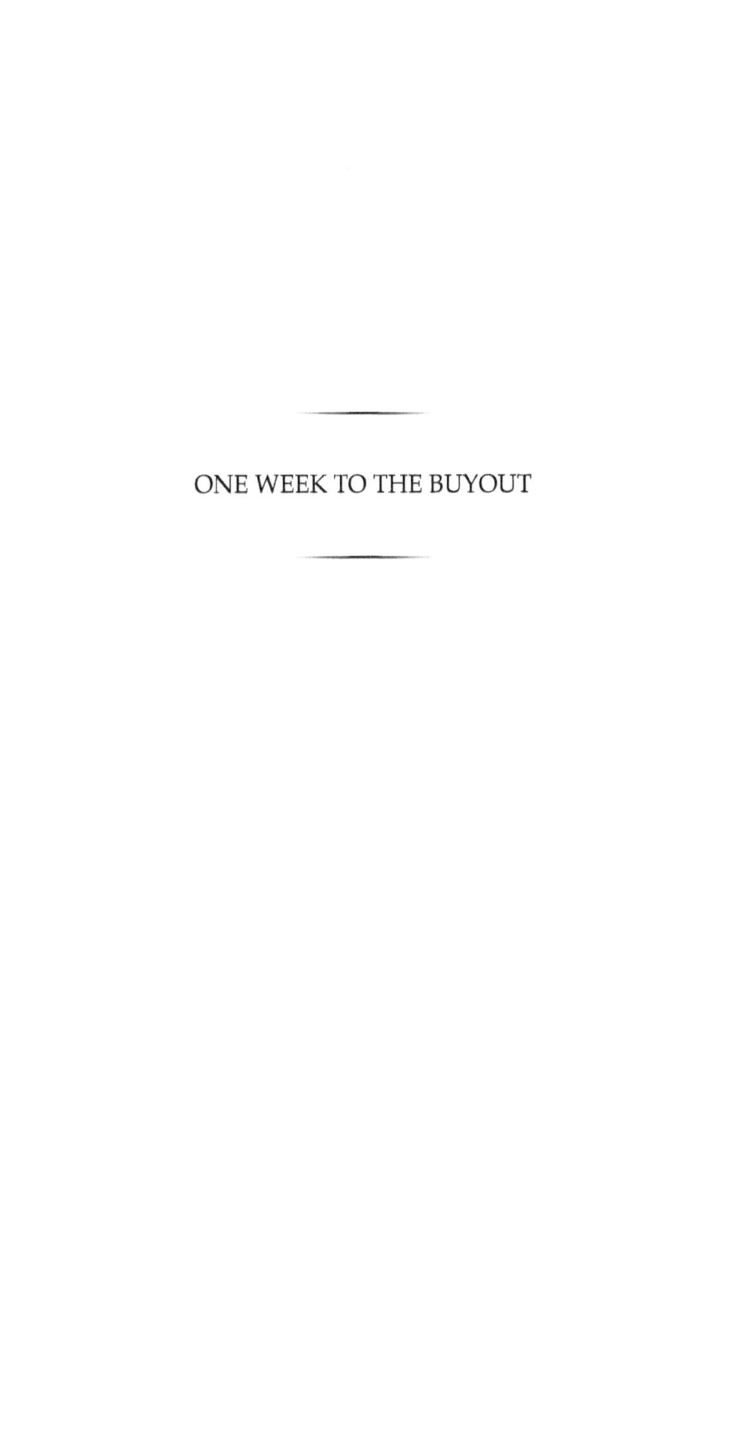

ONE WEEK TO THE BUYOUT

LIAM

LIAM IS BACK in the car, coming off the M1, heading to Leicester city centre. It's been a weird weekend. Claire had a few Saturday clients booked in and Liam had been glad to spend some quality time with the girls. They went ice skating in the day, and he even let them watch Frozen (again) on Saturday night. It was great to see their little gleeful faces, when he'd told them it was going to be one of their special Daddy-Daughter Days. Claire was out with friends on Saturday night and had come in so drunk that she'd passed out within seconds of coming to bed. Predictably, she hadn't been at her best on Sunday, which meant he had an excuse to sneak off to his office to follow up on some of the leads Eddie had sent him. But even when Claire is busy or not firing on all cylinders, she doesn't miss a trick and there had been some gentle probing as to whether Liam was OK and if he had anything he wanted to tell her. He's been vague, apologising for being distant, blaming the buyout and hoping she will drop it. Even so, he made sure to leave early this morning.

He's called the office and laid it on thick about his dad not being too well and wanting to spend some time up in Leicester, while making it clear he's still available for calls and anything urgent that might come up. If Trent finds out Liam's breaking with routine, he will no doubt call to berate him for it. But for now, he hasn't heard from him since last week. Flick has been sending a flurry of emails, full of business-speak and contract amendments for the buyout. All bog-standard and routine, Flick assures Liam. He'll take her word for it. Trying to sift through all the small print makes him go cross-eyed or sends him to sleep. He's told her, more than once, he's happy for her to take care of all that stuff but, he supposes, it's good of her to keep him in the loop.

Eddie has sent through the first couple of places to speak to about Titch, and Liam is glad of the excuse to take action, move forward, to do *something*. He could have called the facilities, or sent an email but instinct tells him it would be better if there's no paper trail to Titch. But why is that? He keeps asking himself that question and others... like what is the Lady Jane project Trent and Kendrick were talking about? Post-modern historical romps are all the rage these days but try as he might, Liam can't imagine Trent and Kendrick writing or producing something like that. Whatever it was, it seemed to change the mood in the room when Kendrick brought it up. And hadn't Trent asked Liam to go and get the drinks just after that? Was Lady Jane code for something else? Drugs?

He's going over this incessantly in his mind, like trying to complete a Rubik's cube using only trial and error – shifting the sides into a new configuration, looking at it and trying again. But he's no closer to solving the puzzle. He's heading over the Burley Flyover when a call comes in. It's Claire. Shit. He thinks about avoiding it, but realises that will only make things worse. He forces a big smile into his voice and answers it.

'Hi babe. You OK?' he says.

'Yeah, I'm good. But you're not. I can tell. Where are you?'

He winces. 'In the car at the minute.'

'Obviously. But where? You left at the crack of dawn again.'

'Leicester,' he tells her. 'Forgot to tell you. Rescheduled film night with dad. I cancelled on him last week and felt guilty.'

'OK.' Two syllables, loaded with doubt. 'So, you're staying over or driving back late?'

He's thinking so hard about what to say, he misses his exit on St George's island and has to go round again. 'Well, actually, I was thinking about staying up here for a couple of days. If that's alright with you?'

'To spend time with your dad, you mean?' she says, and Liam pounces on the unexpected hope he hears in her voice.

'Yes, thought I could work remotely from our house. I'll get more done away from the office and be good to catch up with Dad properly.'

'He'll love that.'

'You sure you don't mind?' He knows she won't. Since he and Mickey reconnected, Claire has been desperate for the relationship to work. She lost her own dad a few years ago and doesn't want Liam to have the same regrets. She wants the kids to have a grandad in their life too.

'No, I don't mind at all.' After a beat, she adds, 'But I do want a proper talk when you come back. I know you're keeping things from me again, Liam. I can take anything but dishonesty. I warned you what would happen after last time, with Kendrick and all the rest of it.'

'I'm sorry. I know I've been a bit distant. Just with the buyout and everything else… it's a lot, you know?'

'I do, but you can talk to me about it anytime. And it will all be sorted next week, won't it?'

'Fingers crossed.'

'Great. And then maybe we can take a long weekend, and

all go up to Leicester? Spend some time in the house together? Get it sorted?'

Liam swallows hard at the thought of Claire coming to the house, smelling the bleach, somehow sensing something has changed. He's not sure the place will ever be the same again for him. 'Sure,' he says. 'Right, I've got to go as I've been roped into going to Tesco's to get some supplies for Barbs before I arrive.'

Claire chuckles. 'She doesn't change. Say hello to her and Tilly for me. Love you.'

'Love you too.'

He ends the call and squeezes the steering wheel hard, as if he can push out all of the lies and guilt building up inside. It doesn't work, so he focuses on the satnav, following the blue line to his first stop, a hostel on a side street near Victoria Park.

Having eventually found a parking space, Liam is now walking along a row of what would once have been grand, three-storey Edwardian villas. Now, almost all of them have jungle-like front gardens, over-flowing bins and rusting broken gates. The panels beside each door confirm what the multiple 'TO LET' signs were hinting at – that all of the houses have now been carved up into cheap flats. Less space for the tenants and more cash for the landlords.

Further down, on the corner, Liam spots the place he's looking for. It looks like it was once a small hosiery factory. There's a series of windows, high up and criss-crossed with a protective mesh. Half a dozen steps lead up to an alcove, discreet and set back from the road. There's a security door with a buzzer for visitors. It's now, as he stands at the bottom of the steps, looking up at the entrance, Liam realises he's totally out of his depth. What was he planning to do? Knock on the front door and expect some random stranger to let him in. Eddie had offered to see if he could get access, or at least a point of contact for each one, but again, something about that felt dangerous and wrong to Liam. Despite this, something compels him to go up the steps. He stands in front of the battered and once-white security door for almost a full minute, willing himself to press the buzzer. He's made a mistake. What the hell is he doing? He turns to walk away when a scratchy voice comes through the intercom.

'Hello? Are you OK?'

The voice is female, friendly and sounds like the person at the other end is used to unexpected and confused-looking visitors. The thought makes Liam glance down at himself, to consider what he's wearing. Smart jeans, polo shirt and a jacket. He doesn't look homeless, does he? That thought makes him feel guilty, like some kind of self-entitled snob.

'Are you looking for someone?' asks the voice, clearly reading Liam's body language.

'Erm… no. Don't worry. I think I've got the wrong…' He tries to think how to finish the sentence and comes up blank.

'The wrong what? Temporary housing project?' Despite the sarcasm, there's a warmth to the voice. 'Give me a sec and I'll come down. Hate talking through this thing.'

Right, Liam thinks. This is my chance to leave before I say or do anything else stupid. He jogs down the steps and gets to the bottom, just as the door buzzes and opens behind him.

'Thought you had the look of a runner,' the woman standing at the top of the steps says, as she pulls the door closed behind her and looks down at Liam.

She's late forties, large glasses and dark hair. Around her neck is an orange lanyard with her ID and door pass. She folds her arms in a relaxed way that's neither threatening nor defensive. Despite himself, Liam immediately feels more at ease than he had five seconds before.

'Be honest,' she says now with a smile, 'you were going to leg it weren't you?'

Liam can't hide a sheepish grin. 'I was. I didn't want to waste your time.'

'You're not wasting my time. I usually come out for a vape about now anyway.' She produces a sparkly purple vape from her pocket and descends the steps.

CHAPTER 34
MICKEY

DRIVING HOME. No good. Thought I could act all manly and do some work, despite the injury to my hand, but it turns out I was only getting in the way on this morning's job. So I've left Warren to it, upgrading the window locks at a leisure centre over in Loughborough. I was convinced my hand was broken, but after a trip to the walk-in centre on Friday, they told me it's just a very bad bruise. So it's heavily bandaged and I'm keeping an ice pack on it when I can. Which is exactly what I plan to do when I get back.

My phone pings with a text message, which pops up on the screen in the van. It's Claire.

FINALLY GET TO HAVE YOUR FILM NIGHT TONIGHT! ENJOY. SO GLAD LIAM IS MAKING AN EFFORT. SEE, MY NAGGING DOES WORK SOMETIMES!

She's signed off with a winking face, tongue sticking out. A film night? Tonight? News to me. Unless Liam is about to call me to arrange it.

No. Who am I trying to fool? I knew he wasn't giving me the full picture last week and here's the proof. It has to be an affair.

'You idiot!' I shout in the empty van.

Why is he risking what he's got there with Claire and those lovely kids? Still… who am I to judge? I wasn't much better. Even so, I'm surprised at Liam. It seems so out of character, but people change and me and Liam were near-strangers for the best part of two decades. How do I really know what he's like now?

A thought pops into my head. Well, more of an image. The bunch of keys I've got hanging up back at Barbs' place. The spare set to Twin Oaks that Liam gave me so I could check on the place from time to time and sort deliveries or whatever when they were down in London. Yeah, and he didn't give you those so you can go snooping around his stuff, Mickey.

Yes but… wouldn't it be better if I can get a bead on where his head's at? Intervene and get him to put an end to it before Claire finds out? There's only one way it ends if he keeps going down the infidelity road. It might already be too late. Yes. Decision made. I'll go home and grab the keys, pop up to Twin Oaks and see what's what. I can always say I was just checking on the place anyway.

Yeah, you keep telling yourself that, Mickey.

I try sneaking into Barbs' house, but of course, it's no good. Barbs doesn't miss a trick and when I come in as quietly as I can through the front door, she calls down from upstairs.

'Why are you creeping about? I just heard your van pull up. Wait there.'

I think about racing into the kitchen, whipping the keys off the hook and doing a runner but what's the point? Knowing Barbs, she'd probably chase me out onto the drive. Instead, I amble into the kitchen, pour myself a glass of water and lean with my back against the sink. My injured hand is down at my side, but it makes no difference.

'What the bleddy hell have you done now? It's that hand

isn't it?' Barbs asks, with barely a foot through the doorway. She points at my bandage. 'Told you not to go to work. Bleddy stupid.'

She comes at me, like some kind of caring bird, flapping about the place and trying to get a look at my hand.

'Calm down, woman,' I say, trying to sidle out of her orbit. 'I'm fine.'

'It's broken, I've told you. And you still haven't told me how you did it.'

'It's not broken. And I told you, I trapped it in the van door.'

She takes a step back. 'Mickey Blake. Watch my lips!' She does the usual gesture. 'You've been repeating this silly story all weekend. Since when do we lie to each other?'

I think about doubling-down on it and repeating the van story, but she's right. We're always honest with each other. It's our thing.

'I know. I'm sorry. Just didn't want to worry you.'

'Never mind all that flannel. What's happened now?'

I give her a quick run down of what went down at the warehouse and why.

'Cowardly bastards,' she says, with so much bitterness, for a second I think she's going to spit on the kitchen floor. 'So why are you creeping about now? You're not going to do anything stupid are you?'

'If you mean trying to get back at that lot, no,' I tell her. 'Too old to be messing about with people like that again. Them days are gone.'

'Glad to hear it. But…'

'But, I might be doing something else on the silly side.' I tell her about Liam lying to Claire and all the rest of it and wait for the inevitable dressing-down about me invading his privacy and probably getting the wrong end of the stick.

After a few seconds, she says, 'You best get up there and see if you can find anything.'

'Really?' I ask.

'Yes. I'd come with you but I'm meeting Joan for a coffee in a minute. Tell me what you find.'

I nod, neck the rest of my water and reach for Liam's spare keys from the hook on the wall.

Barbs huffs. 'If he's been dipping his wick somewhere else, I'll be giving him what-for when I see him.'

'Well, let's not jump to any conclusions, eh?'

But as I head out the front door, ready to get into the van, I can't help but feel I'm driving into trouble. By the time you get to my age, you can almost smell it. Maybe that's why I decide to pocket the van keys and walk up there instead. I need to clear my head.

CHAPTER 35
LIAM

'RIGHT,' Liam says. Why can't he just summon the words he needs to politely leave? There's something about the woman that reminds him of a younger version of Auntie Barbs. Not in the looks or the way she talks, but something about her demeanour. Kind, but no nonsense. You'd have to have some balls or be a bad person to give this woman shit, Liam thinks.

She extends a hand to shake, exhales a plume of vapour which smells like Parma Violet sweets and says, 'I'm Bez. What do they call you?'

'Liam,' he says, without thinking about it. So much for keeping a low profile.

She nods. 'So. What is it? A brother? A sister? Friend?' When Liam frowns, she adds, 'Who you're looking for? I'd say you're too young for it to be one of your kids. You've got the look of a big brother.' She winks at him and takes another huge drag on the vape.

He gives a non-committal smile which Bez seems to take as confirmation she's right. She continues to vape and turns to look away down the street, like she doesn't want to pressure him, but he can tell she's willing him to say more. He's torn. It seems reckless to be making enquiries like this, in person, but what else had he planned to do? Did he think he was going to drive aimlessly around homeless haunts until he found her? Chances are, Titch has already left town. She had sounded scared on their call. But where could she feasibly go, without money and a place to stay? Did homeless people just move to a new town and be homeless there? All of these thoughts bloom in his mind and then pop, one after another, like bubbles in his head.

'You look troubled,' Bez says.

'I'm worried about her, that's all.' Again, the words form without him being able to stop them. Bez seems to have a talent for getting people to talk.

'Ah,' she says, smiling. 'So it's a *she* you're looking for. How old? What does she look like?' She chuckles, sucks on the vape and speaks again as she exhales. 'Ha. Sound like I'm playing Guess Who, don't I? Remember that game? I used to love clacking down the faces, getting nearer to the answer.'

Liam smiles. He used to play that game with his mum. He's pretty sure he never played it with his dad. He can't imagine Mickey having the time or patience for it.

'She's quite young,' he says now. 'Mid-to-late-twenties.'

'That's not as young as you'd think. Not out here.' She motions to the street, like it's a wilderness.

Maybe it is, Liam thinks.

'Is she loud? Quiet? What colour hair? Build?' Bez fires out the questions in quick succession now. It's like she's been fishing, waiting patiently until she had Liam on the hook. Now she's frenetically trying to reel him in. It's working.

'She's small, very small. But tough. Red hair.'

Bez's eyes widen as she lets out another plume of confectionery-tinged vapour. 'You're looking for Titch? Why didn't you say that at the beginning?'

'You know her?' Liam asks, feeling his spirits lift.

'Loads of us know Titch. She's one of the good ones,' she says, eyes hardening. 'But you're not her brother. Not unless you're long-lost and you've come to claim her like some character out of a Dickens book.'

The sarcasm is sudden and cutting, but Liam knows it's driven by Bez's desire to protect. It takes him a moment to recover, but he straightens up and tries to get his game face on.

'I never said I was her brother,' he says, evenly.

'Didn't correct me though, did you?' she asks, taking a half-step backwards and now openly looking him up and down. 'So who are you?'

'I'm a friend.'

Bez pushes her glasses up her nose and narrows her eyes, considering his words. 'Hmm. That might be true. She does have one or two friends on the outside.'

The outside, Liam thinks. Which would make Titch's life on the streets a prison. Liam supposes it's as good a metaphor as any. He could apply it to certain aspects of his own life.

'Well,' he says, deciding only the truth, or at least some version of it, will satisfy Bez now, 'one of those friends…' He trails away, realising he was about to use the past tense, and starts again. 'One of those friends is Kendrick Locke. I'm guessing you've heard of him?'

'Yes, obviously.' She holds the vape in the corner of her mouth and takes three quick puffs on it, like she's Sherlock Holmes with his pipe. 'And I did know Titch was pals with him. Isn't he in prison, though?'

'He was released recently,' Liam says, now realising what his play should be. 'And he wants to reconnect with Titch. Says she was one of the few people who didn't disown him when he got into trouble.'

'Hmm. She's fiercely loyal, that one. As long as you don't cross her, of course.' The smile is back, defences lowering. A little. 'But what has that got to do with you?'

'I'm his agent.'

She gives Liam another quick look up and down. 'That checks out. You look the type.'

'Not sure how to take that,' Liam says, suppressing a laugh. 'Get lots of agents round here, do you?'

'I've met plenty of salesmen in my time. Anyway, why isn't he here himself if he cares that much about her? Too big for Leicester now, is he?'

'He wanted to come. I convinced him not to. He needs to keep a low profile right now, take time to rebuild his image.' The lie comes easily. Maybe 'salesmen' is a fair description of what he does after all. Say what you need to, to get the deal done. Either way, Bez seems to accept it.

'I can't be giving out details of where she's currently registered. It wouldn't be right,' she says. When Liam tries to interject, she adds, 'But... I can tell you she's not here. Last time I spoke to her was a few weeks ago at the Job Start project. I was leaving and she was going in – which I was really pleased about. Means she's got herself straight again and thinking about the future. She looked good too.'

Liam sees an opening and goes for it. 'Well, that's kind of what I want to talk to her about, or should I say, Kendrick wants to talk to her about. He's thinking of starting a youth project, based at his studio over in Syston?' Bez shrugs, like she's never heard of it, so he goes on. 'Anyway. He thinks Titch would be good to have around the studio, help him reach more of the right kids.'

'So, it's a job he's offering?'

'Exactly. All above board and I've been helping him with the grant applications and all that stuff. He's really serious about it and, me being the cynical agent – sorry, salesman – thinks it could be a great way to rebuild his public image.' He flashes her a smile that he hopes reinforces her assumptions about him.

Bez sighs. She has the vape at her lips, but doesn't take a drag. She's looking at him differently now. There's a sharp edge she clearly keeps hidden and ready to use when the need arises. Liam's admiration for her goes up a notch; she would be a great person to have in your corner, he thinks.

'I just hate the idea of her missing out on an opportunity, that's all,' Liam says now. It does the trick and he sees something unlock in her, the same look he's seen in hundreds of client meetings over the years. It never fails to give him a spark of exhilaration and he wonders if this is how his dad feels when he opens a safe.

Now Bez sucks long and hard on the vape, stuffs it back into the pocket of her jeans, and lets out the vapour in a steady prolonged plume. Her last hit for a while, Liam assumes. She takes out her phone and starts tapping away. When Liam tries to ask what she's doing, she holds up a finger, telling him to wait.

'So,' she says, reading from her phone. 'You're Liam Blake. And this is your agency.' She flashes the phone at him, and he sees the agency website briefly. 'Chances are, she's either over at St Luke's off Conduit Street or Bright Futures, the women's-only place near Belgrave Boulevard. Best bet would probably be Bright Futures.'

'Thanks that's—'

'But,' she says, taking a step closer, 'if I hear either you or Kendrick what's-his-face has harassed her or done anything to mess up the progress she's been making... well, I know where to find you now, don't I?'

CHAPTER 36

LIAM

LIAM FINDS himself picking at the leather stitching on the steering wheel. He's parked twenty metres or so down the road from the large, double-fronted detached house that has been converted into a base for the Bright Futures project. According to the website, it's a small facility that can house up to six women at a time, offering addiction recovery services and a safe place to sleep for up to six weeks at a time. He's been here for over an hour, just sitting, waiting and worrying. Whilst he's pleased to have got a solid lead from Bez, it came at the expense of his anonymity. She not only knows who Liam is, she knows Kendrick is involved too. She isn't the type of person to forget a conversation like that. At the same time, what's done is done. He needed to find Titch and even if he had got around all of the places on Eddie's list, he wouldn't have known about this one. That's if she's here, of course. So far, Liam has seen two women come and go and one of them looked like they worked at the project. He needs to speak to Titch, that's all. See her face, hear in person what she has to say and make his mind up about what she says she saw. It's how he's wired. It's why he's good at what he does, working in a business where the face-to-face meeting is everything.

His stomach grumbles and he checks his watch: almost two o'clock. He's hungry and stressed and starting to get a headache. Maybe a quick stretch of his legs and a look around the area wouldn't be such a bad idea. He remembers seeing a shop on the next road over. He gets out, locks the car and walks in the direction of the project building. He's on the opposite side of the road and snatches a couple of glances towards it as he passes. Through the large bay window downstairs, he sees someone in what he assumes is the lounge. She's an older woman in a blue tabard. She's dusting photo frames on the windowsill and looks up, momentarily catching his eye. He turns away as casually as he can and doesn't look back.

In the corner shop. There's very little natural light, every-thing bathed in a washed-out apricot hue. There's a strong smell of Indian spices that make Liam even hungrier than he was when he stepped in here. He grabs one of the large, what look like, homemade vegetable samosas and a bottle of sparkling water then heads to the counter. The young Asian woman serving is polite, but isn't subtle about looking him up and down, taking in his smart-casual appearance and unfamiliar face. He pays for the items and with a beaming smile, manages to coax a shy grin out of the assistant.

He holds up the bag with the samosa inside. 'These look lovely. Do you make them here?'

Before the woman can answer, the electronic door sensor chimes behind him. Instinctively, he looks over his shoulder and there, holding open the door and staring right at him is Titch. There's a pause – perhaps less than two seconds where they're both stuck, unsure what to do. Liam, frightened of scaring her away, Titch already in fight-or-flight mode. A breeze blows her copper-red hair across her forehead and it's like a starting pistol.

She turns and runs.

'Shit! No, Titch!' he calls. 'Wait!'

But she's gone and if he doesn't move now, she will be out of sight. Without thinking, he drops the samosa and water back on the counter and sprints out of the shop. Titch went left, feet pounding the pavement, already a good ten metres ahead of him. He follows, calls her again but knows that only makes him sound more threatening and desperate. Better to save his breath for the run. He closes a lot of the distance, before she darts right, across the road and into an alleyway that runs behind a row of houses. He pushes on, wishing he'd skipped the treadmill this morning. Shin splints radiate up his legs. His flat deck shoes aren't made for this kind of abuse or terrain. He reaches the alleyway, an uneven cobbled surface, littered with broken glass. Black wheelie bins stand on either side of the alley, lining the route like soldiers on parade. The alley bends off to the left and Titch must already have rounded it, because she's out of sight now. Liam finds another gear, picks up pace and a few strides later feels a wobbly cobble give way beneath his foot. He's going too fast, tumbles forward, left ankle twisting. He brings up his arm and turns, tries to roll. His elbow connects hard with the ground, stops him dead.

It doesn't hurt straight away, but he knows the pain is in the post and sure enough, a hot flare pulses up his arm and into his hand. His jacket is ripped and he's pretty sure his elbow is bleeding. He sits up, gingerly stretching out his back, slowly moving his head. Doing a quick systems check before he tries to get up. He catches some movement in the corner of his eye and looks up to see Titch. She's standing five or six metres away, back in the direction he's just come from. Breathing heavily, head down, hair hanging low as she watches him and waits. For a moment, he's confused. Then he realises she must have been hiding behind one of the black bins – she's easily small enough. Either that or she must have ducked into one of the gardens. Her plan had obviously been to double-back on him. It was a good bet. She should already be on her way. Yet still she waits.

'You OK?' she asks, through ragged breaths.

'Bruised ego, maybe a twisted ankle. Probably a few cuts and grazes, but I'll live.' In truth, he feels hot and sick and the ache in his ankle seems to grow with each breath he takes.

'You look pale. Like you're gonna puke.'

He swallows and nods. 'Fair assessment. But I'll be OK in a minute.'

'What are you doing here. How'd you find me?'

She's still primed to run. Liam can see it in the bend of her knees and the way she rocks on the balls of her feet. He's mindful of spooking her again and is careful not to show any signs of getting to his feet.

'I know someone who's familiar with…' He tries to find the right words. '…your world. They gave me some places to try.'

'Bullshit. You been tracking my phone?'

He wants to laugh, but manages to rein it in to a smile. 'No, Titch. I don't work for MI5. Only the police and people on the telly can do stuff like that. I really did have a list of places to try. But at one of them, I got lucky and found someone who knew you. Said I should try here.'

She gives him a slow blink, says nothing. She still looks like a frightened deer ready to disappear into the forest.

'Either way,' Liam says, trying to keep her talking, 'I just wanted to talk to you face-to-face.'

Something occurs to her and she looks over her shoulder, back up the alley. 'Is he here? You bring him with you?' The words are short, sharp and edged with fear.

'Trent? No. Absolutely not.' He levels a look at her. 'I haven't told him and don't want to. Right now, he's in London.'

'You believe me, don't you.' It isn't a question.

'Honestly? I wasn't sure, Titch. That's why I wanted to see you.'

'And now?' she says, like it's a challenge.

He considers this, sees the look of fear in Titch, the desperation. 'I believe that you believe it. For now, that's all that matters. And yes, I have had a strange feeling about Trent since it happened. I can't explain it, but something feels off.'

She lets out a single hollow laugh. 'Wait until you see the video. Then you'll see how *off* he is.'

'A video?' he asks, the desire to be sick now back with a vengeance. 'Can I see it?'

She hesitates, then says, 'Yes. But my phone's flat. And I'm starving. Missed breakfast at Futures this morning and you can't just hang around there in the middle of the day.'

'We could find a cafe somewhere?'

'No.' She takes a breath to say something, changes her mind and then blurts out, 'That house. Where it… happened. That your place?'

Liam nods.

'Can we go there?'

'Well, yes, but—'

'I want to see it again. Tell you what I saw. How it went down.'

'OK. Then that's what we'll do.'

CHAPTER 37

MICKEY

THE FIRST THING that hits me when I walk through Liam's front door is the smell of bleach. Standing in the hallway, I sniff again. No, it's not exactly bleach. There's other stuff going on. Pine disinfectant, maybe? Smells fresh. That wouldn't be strange, except I didn't think Liam had been up here for a while. At least, if he has, he's kept it quiet from me. I give my head a wobble, remind myself Liam's pushing forty and doesn't have to tell me everything he does. Still, the idea he's been making trips up here and actively avoiding me stings a bit. Why would he do that?

An affair, Mickey. Obviously.

No. Pack it in. Got to look at this with an open mind. I wander through the house, poking my head in various downstairs rooms, seeing if anything obvious hits me, but also realising I've got no bloody idea what I'm looking for. He's got two big lounge-type rooms downstairs – I think he calls one the study, or something. Jesus, if that's not a sign he's lived a different life to me, what is? *The study.* What would my old man make of that? He'd shit on it, like he did on everything else. He told me I was getting up myself when I bought a new car, back in the eighties. Said I'd got ideas above my station and that I'd only brought it round to show him what a big shot I was. Told me I was rubbing his face in it. He liked to say that, did my old man. Bitter old twat.

Anyway, the normal living room, lounge, whatever he's calling it, looks as old-fashioned and neglected as when I was last up here, so I head over to the study. Linger in the doorway, left hand on the rough, once-varnished door. A spark flares in my mind, remembering the same style of door in that shithole of a casino back in Skegness. It had once been an old bank, all fancy carved oak doors and brass handles everywhere, long since past their best when I got there. I know that feeling. I give the room another cursory look and I'm about to head upstairs when I turn back.

Something isn't right. I sniff again. The smell of the bleach or whatever it is, is stronger in here. That doesn't mean much on its own. Maybe someone spilled something and it needed to be cleaned up. I keep breathing in through my nose, trying to get a better hold on the various scents. If only my sense of smell was as good as my sense of touch. Bleach, disinfectant and something else tangy, sour… fruity? Wine, maybe? I tour the room, trying to work out what else it is that's bothering me. I've only been up here a couple of times and I'm not really one for taking much notice of decor and the like, but it still feels as if something has changed in here. My eyes keep being drawn back to the centre of the room, but I still can't put my finger on it, so I head to the window and look out down the long garden. It's a bit wild, but it's better than when I last saw it. I think Liam said he's had a gardener up here a couple of times to clear it. He's got that old boarded-up well at the end of the garden, a swarm of midges or bees – can't tell which – buzzing around it. Got to watch the midges at this time of the year in the park. Get eaten alive if you're not careful.

The table. That's it. I turn back to look at the middle of the room. That's what was bothering me. There used to be a coffee table there. Dark wood, maybe? Definitely had glass in it. Wonder when he decided to get rid of it. And why? It was probably Claire's idea. Liam doesn't strike me as the type to give a shit about stuff like that. At least I'm not going nuts in my old age. Still got some powers of observation. Speaking of which, I need to check upstairs. Hope to God I'm not going to see any kinky sex shit. Not sure I'll be able to look Liam and Claire in the face again if I do. That's why you shouldn't be snooping about the place, Mickey, I tell myself. Yeah, yeah. Save it. Anyway, I'm not snooping. I'm investigating and trying to protect their marriage.

Nothing out of place up here and it doesn't look like any of the beds have been slept in recently. Not sure what I expected to find, really. If Liam is having an affair, is he really going to be stupid enough to bring them here, their family home? Wouldn't he go to a hotel or something? Or her place, whoever this mystery woman might be. Of course, this could all just be in my mind. Maybe he wanted a night of peace and quiet on his own and he's used me as his excuse. Only wish he'd told me, that's all.

I'm looking out of the main bedroom window, the one on the back of the house, with the amazing views of the park, when I hear the sound of a car coming up the drive.

Shit.

Could be a delivery or something? The gardener? I dart across the landing to one of the kids' bedrooms on the front of the house. Just as I reach the window, I spot Liam's car pulling up. I take a quick side-step out of view. Standing next to the window, I peek out, careful not to get too close. The car pulls to a stop and a few seconds later Liam's door opens. Fuck it, I'll just announce myself when he comes in and tell him I was out for a walk and decided to swing by to check on the place. No need to be creeping about. Embarrassing, but then again, he didn't tell me he was sticking around up here, so neither of us is being entirely straight, are we? I'm about to move away from the window when the passenger door of Liam's car opens and out steps a young woman – red hair, jeans and a baggy sweater. Not exactly glamorous and, at least from this distance, she looks way too young for Liam. Oh, did you hear that, Mickey? That was your Hypocrite Alarm going off again. How much older than Hazel am I?

Either way, if I was worried about it being awkward before, what the hell am I going to do now? Just greet them at the front door, like he's a teenager getting in past his curfew? Too late for me to get downstairs and out the back door as well. No, I'm better off trying to wait it out. Please, please, Liam, I'm begging you. Don't bring her up here, and if you do, don't do it in one of the kids' rooms. I close the bedroom door but leave it ajar. Enough to hide me if they do come up to the main bedroom, but not completely closed so it looks weird. I wait behind the door, hear them enter the house, and once again question my timing and life choices.

CHAPTER 38
LIAM

IT HAD BEEN an awkward car ride over. Liam had tried several times to start up some conversation. He had asked about how Titch had been doing since he'd last seen her properly, which, he had worked out, was probably shortly before Kendrick's sentence hearing. He tried getting her to chat about what she had been doing, the places she had been staying, what her plans were going forward. Anything to lift the tension and get her talking but she had been monosyllabic and nervous, sitting low in her seat, hand up to her face. Once out of the city, she had relaxed a little, but it was clear she didn't want to do small talk and wasn't going to open up – maybe – until they were safely back at Twin Oaks. So Liam had put on the radio and turned it up in an attempt to at least dampen some of the fear coming off both of them in waves.

They arrive at the house and Liam asks, 'You OK?'

Titch licks her dry lips and gives the smallest of nods. Liam moves to get out when she asks, 'Where's his car? Kendrick's, I mean.'

Liam takes a deep breath then says, 'I moved it on the night, while Trent—'

He pulls up short, realising what he was going to say, but Titch knows anyway.

'While Trent got rid of Ken,' she says. Her voice is flat, eyes glassy. 'Do you know where he is?'

Liam can't speak for fear his voice will break, but manages to shake his head. He gets out and closes the door. He sucks in a deep lungful of fresh air, and is relieved when Titch unclips her seatbelt and gets out of the car. For a few seconds, he had wondered if she would change her mind, run away again or demand he drive her back.

Inside the house he limps to the kitchen and offers her a drink. She follows him, watching while he grabs her a can of Coke from the fridge. The whole time, her eyes are wide, taking in what must seem like strange surroundings to her. She stands near the door and sips at the drink, looking from one thing to another; the old clock on the wall, the novelty Bradgate Park tea-towel on the draining board, Izzy's drawing on the fridge. It's like she's ticking off items, each one alien to her and the upbringing she undoubtedly had. At least, that's how Liam interprets it. Maybe, he realises, she's just scared out of her wits and unsure what to do. He has to put her at ease, let her know he means her no harm.

He points at the picture on the fridge. 'Not bad for an eight-year-old, is it? I can't draw for toffee, so she must get it from Claire.'

Titch stares at the drawing, then says, 'That's Braggy, isn't it?'

Braggy. What most of the locals call Bradgate Park around here. Liam smiles, remembering it's how his dad and grandad always referred to it.

'Yes,' he says. 'The ruins. Have you spent much time in the park?'

She gives Liam a look. 'What do you think? Didn't exactly get to do many day trips when I was growing up.'

'No. S'pose not.'

The clock chimes for quarter to the hour and Titch almost jumps out of her skin. She's terrified and for a second Liam thinks she will run straight out of the front door and not come back.

'It's OK, Titch,' he tells her. 'He's not here and you're safe.'

'Yeah?' she asks, slamming down the Coke can on the table and taking a step towards him. 'And how do I know I can trust you?'

'You don't. And yet you suggested we come back here, knowing it would be easier for me to…' He struggles to find the right words.

'What? Get rid of me?' She grins and looks him up and down. She reminds Liam of a terrier, small but determined and ready to bite to protect herself. 'Like to see you try.'

He laughs and raises his hands in surrender. 'You're absolutely right. I haven't got it in me and I would back you in a street fight with most people. Even so… it was a strange decision to come back here.' She's about to snap back when he adds, 'Don't get me wrong. I'm not complaining. Surprised, that's all. And I think it shows that you do trust me on some level.'

'I saw it in your eyes. Back there in that alleyway. You know what he is, deep down. But you don't want to believe it. That's the only reason I'm here.'

Liam nods.

She relaxes, goes back to the can of Coke, picks it up and heads out of the kitchen. She calls back over her shoulder, 'Come on then. Let's do it.'

They're in the study. Titch is over by the window, pointing.

'I was out there, literally just the other side of the glass, only a couple of feet from the window, but I knew none of you could see out.'

'It was bright in here and dark out there,' Liam says, remembering how the three of them – him, Trent and Kendrick – had been reflected in the glass.

'Yeah. Like one of those, what-do-you-call-it? Two-way mirrors they have in some of the police interview rooms.' She turns back to look at Liam, who's standing in the middle of the room, watching her relive it for him. 'Once I realised you couldn't see out, I could get close, see everything. I couldn't hear what was being said, but I stood right there with my phone and just kept filming.'

'And what did you see?' Liam asks.

'Not a lot, at first. Me and Ken got here way before you two, had a quick look around and thought this would be the best room for me to get a picture, a video, whatever I could, really. Ken said he was going to try to meet in here.'

Liam thinks back to that night, tries to remember how things played out when they came into the house. He does have a vague recollection of Kendrick leading the way, getting himself comfortable in here.

'Fair enough,' he says now. 'But why?'

'Why what?'

'Why did he tell you to get a picture or whatever?'

She shrugs. 'I assumed he was going to put it on his Insta. You know, stir up some shit or try to get some buzz going. Rebuild his rep? Dunno.'

'So he didn't explain to you what his beef with Trent was at all?'

'All he said was that Trent had fucked him over and owed him a payday. It was something to do with the letter he got a few weeks ago. I know that, because I was there when he opened it.'

'What letter?'

'Dunno but you know that look people get sometimes? All pale, funny looking? Looked like he was going to pass out or lose it. To be honest, I thought it was a doctor's letter or some-thing from the hospital.'

'What makes you say that?'

'There was a logo and stuff I couldn't make out, but it looked official. And once he'd read it, he went all weird.'

'And he wouldn't tell you what it was?'

'No. Folded it up, put it back in the envelope and then – this sort of freaked me out – he went straight to the safe in his studio and locked it inside. With his demos and whatever else he keeps in there. You remember his safe?'

Liam does. A retro-looking fire safe with a combination lock. About the size of a small beer fridge, tucked into the corner of the control room, usually with a bottle of Jack Daniels sat on top of it.

'Yeah,' Titch continues. 'Put it in there and then told me I needed to go. Proper cut the day short. Sent me back to town in a taxi. Said he needed time to think. Then the next time I saw him he was different.'

'How?' Liam asks.

'Just… dunno. Hard to explain. But he was pretty positive when he first got out. Talking about getting back to the music again and keeping it more real and stuff. Then, he got that letter and changed. Sort of bitter? You know what I mean?'

Liam nods. Kendrick had definitely seemed darker, harder somehow that night he called him out to his car. He had assumed it was prison that had brought on the change.

'So he hadn't mentioned Trent before that?' he asks.

'Oh yeah. Loads of times. Making digs at him and stuff, but he just seemed more angry, upset even, after he got that letter. Then he started talking about a payday and needing to set up a meeting. I suggested you might be able to help.'

'Oh, thanks for that, Titch,' Liam says, managing to keep his voice light.

'I know,' she says, worrying at a thumbnail and staring again at the spot on the floor where Kendrick died. 'I feel like shit about it. If I hadn't said anything, maybe they wouldn't have met. Maybe he'd still be alive.' Her eyes go glassy, but she resists crying, forcing back the emotion, holding it in check.

'No,' Liam says gently. 'Would only have delayed the inevitable. It was obvious Kendrick was going to make that meeting happen one way or another. You can't blame yourself for that.' Like he blames himself.

'Easier said than done,' she says, looking up at him as she digs in her pocket and produces the phone. 'You want to see?'

No, Liam thinks. I don't want to see. Not really. But it's why Titch is here, and he has to know for sure if his gut feeling about Trent is based on anything more than intuition.

'OK.'

Titch scrolls through her phone, finds the clip and hands Liam the handset. 'Just press play.'

CHAPTER 39
LIAM

THE FOOTAGE IS SHAKY, initially emerging from one of the bushes outside the window. Some rapid zoom in, zoom out camera angles before Titch settles on a wide shot and moves closer to the window. It's been shot portrait, rather than landscape and there are a couple of moments in the footage where Titch swings the camera left, then right, as if she is checking her surroundings.

'Just before that someone turned on the garden light,' Titch says. 'Shit me up. I hid in the bushes until it went off again.'

Liam remembers that now. Hadn't he been the one to turn it on? He concentrates again on the footage. Eventually, Titch is at the window and Liam sees himself, Trent and Kendrick in the room. It's like having some strange out-of-body experience, watching himself in a dream or something. Like the three of them are in a play. Wind blows across the phone's microphone, giving an eerie soundtrack to the footage.

He watches on, sees the tension seem to dissipate between Kendrick and Trent and the way they embrace and look directly at the camera, the two of them regarding their reflection. Liam now realises Kendrick was actually giving Titch the best chance to get a clean shot of them together. Did Kendrick feel any genuine emotion at that moment? Liam wonders. Or was all of it manufactured, knowing it would be playing out on camera for some future audience?

On the little screen, the smiles hold as Kendrick and Trent take a seat again, and Liam tries to recall what was said and when things changed. He struggles to remember the specifics, but knows the atmosphere soured when Kendrick mentioned the Lady Jane project, right before Trent sent Liam to get the drinks. He watches it play back in real time, Trent gesturing to the door, sees himself linger for a few seconds, unsure. Why hadn't he trusted his instinct and stayed in the room? Would things have played out differently? He wants to pause the video clip now, freeze himself in time, like it could somehow change the outcome. But he knows it's futile and watches on, having to ride it out to the bitter end.

In the video, Liam leaves. Trent looks back at the doorway several times, as if he's checking to make sure Liam has actually left the room. Once he's made sure they're alone, his face changes, the mask drops. No more pasted-on smile. His features are dark and he's pointing a finger at Kendrick, jabbing it a few inches from Kendrick's face, emphasising whatever it is he's trying to spell out. Liam tries to read Trent's lips and make out what's being said but he would need more time and both men seem to be talking over each other. Kendrick slaps away Trent's hand and the camera jerks in surprise. Liam loses sight of what's happening for a couple of seconds. There's another slice of darkness, a snatch of the garden outside the window before the phone returns to pick up on the action.

Kendrick is standing up. Trent stays seated, smirking as Kendrick leers over him. Liam feels a strange surge of hope flare in his chest. So Kendrick was the aggressor after all. Trent was only trying to protect himself. Will that at least relieve some of the guilt Liam currently feels? But before he can dwell on that, several things seem to happen in the video at once, so sudden that Liam almost throws the phone to the ground. There's a blur of movement as Trent springs upwards, while at the same time reaching inside his jacket pocket. There's something in Trent's hand. The phone camera lurches again. Flash of red brick wall and flowerbed, Titch, panicking at what she was witnessing. Now the phone is at some strange angle, everything tilted, as if the scene is playing out on a slope.

'I didn't know what to do,' Titch says now, her voice small as she stands beside him, watching.

In the footage, Kendrick and Trent come together. They're grappling, almost chest-to-chest. A glint of silver. A knife – Liam can see that now – in Trent's hand. Trent stabs three times in rapid succession into Kendrick's chest. Leaves it there and drives Kendrick back. Kendrick collides with the coffee table and falls. Glass top shatters as Kendrick lands heavily on his back. There's a moment – three, four seconds? – where Trent stands over him, panting, looking at the door-way, making a decision. He drops to the floor, on top of Kendrick and at the same moment, Titch must let go of the phone. It clatters to the ground – there's a weird upside down shot of Titch's trainer in the dirt. Over the wind and scuffing sound, Liam can hear Titch's voice, recorded in the clip.

'No, no, no,' she says, before bringing it back up to the window. If it was shaky before, now it's all over the place, but Liam watches as his past self re-enters the room and rushes to help Trent, who now seems to be lying beneath Kendrick.

'Fucking hell…' he mutters now. 'He must have rolled Ken on top of him. He made it look like Kendrick…'

He looks at Titch. Her bottom lip is trembling, yet still she doesn't cry. 'I told you. I fucking told you,' she says.

Liam looks back at the phone screen and sees himself – terrified and in shock – seemingly looking straight at the camera out of the window. Titch must have thought the same because that's where she stopped filming, and presumably made her escape.

The image is frozen on the last frame, the diagonal line of the wall outside, going from corner to corner. Half of the screen in grainy darkness, the other a blurred slice of the room. He stares at it a few more seconds, trying to think straight. He can't get anything clear in his mind. It's as blurred as the image he's looking at. Eventually, hand shaking, he holds the phone out for Titch to take back.

'Don't you want to copy it or something?' she asks.

Liam senses a change in her. It's like she can see the effect of the video on him and knows he's as angry and upset as her. There's a different vibe coming off her now, something closer to trust. The fact she's suggesting he makes a copy is proof of that, but something else occurs to him.

'Are you OK?' he asks. 'Are you worried something will happen to you?'

She takes a seat in an armchair, eyes suddenly weary. 'What do you think? You've just watched that and you don't think Trent is dangerous?'

His instinct is to disagree, but he swallows down the lie and instead gives a slow, grim nod.

'I know,' she says. 'I can see it in your eyes. So if I send it to you, or copy it over to your laptop or whatever, can I trust you to do the right thing, even if it means getting yourself in trouble?'

'I don't know, Titch. That's the honest answer. I don't know.'

'I think you do know. You just can't say it out loud yet.'

'Maybe. But best I can do right now is make a copy and promise you I won't tell Trent I have it, or that I even managed to find you. In fact, I'll give it a couple of days and tell him I found a support worker who told me you've gone to stay with some friends up North. Manchester, or somewhere.'

'You think he'll buy that?'

'Who knows? But maybe you should do that? Get out of here for a while. I can sort some money for you. It will probably take me a day or so because I—' He pulls up short, trying to find a better way of saying it, but Titch fills in the blanks.

'Because you'll need to make sure there isn't any trail. Nothing linking you back to me. It's why you started texting me from another number. A burner, and I'm guessing Trent told you to do that. Devious bastard.'

Liam looks at the floor.

'Don't worry about it. I get it. He's probably right.' She stares out of the window. 'Beginning to think I'm a curse.'

'Don't say that, Titch. You've just been caught up in something. We both have.'

'Yeah? So how do we get out of it? Because I can't walk away this time. I left Kendrick that night, but I won't do it again. I need to know what Trent did with him and then I want that fucker to pay for what he's done.'

Liam feels light-headed, sick. She's right, but how does that happen without him going down with Trent? He takes a deep breath, steadies himself on the arm of the chair. 'I just need time to think. I'll make a copy and keep it to myself while we work out what to do. Can you keep a low profile and stay out of sight? For just a day or two? I could get you a hotel room or something in the meantime?'

She's shaking her head, not buying it. So Liam tries again.

'Whatever happens, I promise I'll keep you safe. He won't get away with it, I'll somehow make sure of that. I just need time to process all this, you know?'

'I'll give you two days, tops, but then I'm going to put the footage out there, on Insta or whatever, and see what happens. Sorry, Liam. But he has to pay, one way or another. And forget the hotel. I'm not going back to the unit for a few days either. I think it's better for both of us if you don't know where I am. Text me when you've decided what you want to do.'

'OK. On a burner, yes?' He feels bad as soon as he says it, but they both know it wouldn't make sense to tie himself to her anymore than he already is. He thinks again about the chat with Bez and the chase through the streets. In truth, that horse has already bolted.

'Fair enough,' Titch says, grim-faced. 'But two days, tops.'

Ten minutes later and Liam is watching Titch walking up the drive and away from the house. He's sent the video to his laptop and given her some money for a taxi. He waits until she's out of sight, around the bend and invisible through the trees, then heads back inside to think.

Mickey is halfway down the stairs.

'What the fuck have you got yourself into, son?'

CHAPTER 40
MICKEY

GOT TO ADMIT, when I heard the girl shout, 'Let's do it,' I thought all my nightmares had come true, that Liam was indeed playing away. I was expecting to have to put my fingers in my ears for a while and go to my happy place to block out whatever they were about to get up to. But when those sounds didn't come and all I could hear was the low burble of serious conversation, I started to realise whatever this is, it might even be more serious than an affair. And the look on Liam's face when he saw me coming down the stairs was enough to tell me I was right.

'What did you hear?' he asks now. His back's to me as he looks out of the kitchen window and waits for the kettle to boil. You always know it's serious when someone needs to tell you something over a cup of tea. There's only one level up from that, and it's probably too early to crack open the whisky.

I tell him the truth, that I'd heard nothing that seemed to make any sense. A few fragments. Something about Trent being a bad man, a meeting, Kendrick.

I jerk a thumb over my shoulder. 'And whatever it was, it happened back there in that room.'

He slowly turns to face me. He's ashen-faced, bottom lip trembling, and I feel like I've gone back decades to when he was the emotional teen and I was the sometimes-too-strict dad. But he's nearly forty now and I'm certainly not the angry young man I was. It's unnerving. I want to go to him, put my arm around him, or at least give him a friendly hand on his shoulder, but I can't. I'm stuck, feeling like the six feet between us is more like six miles. A sadness pulls at me. I thought the time we spent together, nursing his mum in her last few weeks, would mend the bond we once had. It helped, and we're definitely closer than we were before that, but we both know there's still a lot of history neither of us is quite willing to let go of.

'What happened, Liam? Is it blackmail or something?'

A nervous laugh escapes his mouth, before he clamps down on it. 'Wish that's all it was, Dad. That's how it started, I suppose, in a way.'

He's staring at the red quarry kitchen tiles, unable or unwilling to continue yet. Rather than push it, I set about finishing the tea. He flinches when I drop the teaspoon into the sink, like it brings him out of whatever trance he was in.

'Come on,' I tell him. 'Let's sit down and chat it through.'

I take the drinks over to the small farmhouse-style kitchen table and take a seat. He eventually trudges over, but doesn't sit down. Instead, he leans on the back of the chair opposite and I can see he's trying to line everything up in his mind before he gets started. I give him the time he needs, run my thumb across the edge of my mug of tea, noticing for the first time that there's a tiny chip on the brim. The sharp edge pulls at a memory and after a few seconds it comes into focus; me sitting in Grandad's tiny shed at his allotment. I was probably twelve or thirteen years of age and complaining about a chipped tea cup. I told him mum always said never to drink from a chipped cup, because of germs or something. He'd scowled at me.

'That's because your mother still thinks life can be perfect. That everything has to be just-so before you can move on to the next thing. But that's bollocks, lad.'

I'd always got a bit of a thrill when grandad swore in front of me. Unlike my old man, who just swore *at* me, with grandad it was different. He always treated me like an adult, an equal, even when I was a kid.

He must've seen me trying to work out what he meant, because then he added, 'Sometimes – no – all the time, you've got to make the best of things, and get on with it. If you wait for everything to line up, you'll be dead before you ever start living.'

Maybe, I realise now, that's why he was so into picking locks and opening safes. Everything has to be lined up, manoeuvred into place before you can open a vault. Unlike me, grandad only ever did it for fun, his way of making the world make sense. He wasn't best pleased when I made it a profession.

I rotate the chipped mug and take a sip of the tea. Liam clears his throat and starts to lay it all out for me. Like the hot tea, it's difficult to swallow.

I keep my mouth shut as he tells me about Kendrick popping up after getting out of the nick, laying it on thick about implicating Liam in what went down to put him in prison in the first place. I can see it's killing Liam to tell me, like he's let me down or some shit, and maybe he has, but not in the way he thinks.

'Sounds to me like he was playing on how you felt about it, not what the actual crimes were, Liam,' I tell him. 'He blew it out of proportion. So you helped some of your showbiz clients get hold of the gear they wanted? Big deal. I'm not in your game but, even at my level, I've been around enough entertainers, singers and the like, who did a bit of Charlie or whatever. It's not like they were going to walk the streets trying to score.'

'I know but—'

'Did you do it? The drugs I mean?' He's about to answer, when I realise it's none of my business. He's a grown man. 'Actually, forget it. Doesn't matter.'

'Either way. The answer's no,' he says. He's still standing, ignoring his cup of tea going cold on the table. 'Other than smoking a bit with Claire on a city break to Amsterdam, that's not my bag.'

'Fair enough. But my point stands. It was no big deal. Maybe the police would have taken a look at it after the fact, but it's – what? – about three years ago now? They can't deal with the crime they've got now. Let alone that sort of nonsense.'

Liam looks hopeful. 'You reckon?'

'I know,' I tell him. 'And if you'd have talked to me about it in the first place, I'd have told you that. Instead, judging by your face now and whatever was going on with that young woman who was here, you've doubled-down on it and played along with whatever game Kendrick is playing.'

I'm trying to tone it down, but that's what I'm really let down by. The fact he couldn't talk to me about it in the first place.

'I tried to tell you about it, but you probably don't remember,' he says, his voice high-pitched and strained. 'Back in Skegness. Right after we got out of the casino.'

'Eh? Did you?'

'Yes!' He leans over the chair, firing the words at me. 'You kept telling me I was so much better than you, that you knew I'd never get mixed up in your world and all of the rest of it. And I tried to tell you, I really did. But you shut me down, like you always do, when it's something you don't want to hear.'

He waits, tense, like he's expecting me to blow up and come back at him, when all I'm trying to do is process what he's saying and try to remember the conversation back in

Skegness. I know I felt relief at getting us both through it, guilt for putting him through it in the first place. If he really did try to tell me anything, I can't remember.

'Well, if I did that, intentionally or otherwise,' I say, 'then I'm sorry. There was a lot going on. But I'm ready to listen now and clearly you have more to say. So I'll be quiet until you've told me all of it. Promise. So sit down, drink your tea, and tell me the rest.'

'It's bad, Dad. Really bad.' His voice cracks.

'Bad?' I ask him, forcing a smile on to my face. 'You think your old man hasn't had to deal with "bad" before? Come on, give it to me straight and we'll work it out.'

For the next twenty minutes, I don't interrupt, don't make any dramatic noises, don't let my face express what I'm feeling. It's tough, because what he tells me is gut-wrenching. It's like watching the innocent kid run into the scary house in a horror film. At every point, every bad decision Liam has made, I want to scream out, to tell him to turn back before it's too late. But just like a film, it's already been shot and edited and there's not a damn thing I can do to change the outcome.

As far as I can work out, Liam's made himself accessory to a murder, or best-case scenario, perverting the course of justice? Is that what they still call it? Or have I been watching too many cop shows? But helping that mad bastard, Trent, cover it up, isn't going to look good if and when he gets caught.

'I've fucked it, Dad,' he says now, crying, looking down at the table. 'I'm sorry.'

I reach out, put my hand on top of his and give it a squeeze. Something passes between us, I can feel it. It's like he's ten again and we're off together on one of our jaunts up to Leicester to see his great-grandad. Me driving, reaching out to pat his hand in the passenger seat, telling him we'll stop at the services for a burger or something soon. Seeing his little face light up, knowing how grown up he's feeling, sitting in the front with his old man. His dad, the one he still looked up to then. Before he found out the truth about who I was and what I did for a living. When he still looked at me with hope and something close to admiration.

Now, in the kitchen, Liam looks up at me again, that same hope there. Like I have all the answers and can make everything better.

'You've made a mistake, Liam, that's all,' I tell him. 'I've made plenty in my time. Still making them, actually.' I hold up my bandaged hand, which he seems to notice for the first time.

He frowns. 'What happened?'

'Doesn't matter,' I tell him. 'Just normal Mickey Blake stuff. Like I said, we all fuck up, son. We just need to work out how to deal with it.'

He sits up straight, sniffs and wipes away the residue of his tears. In a way, it hurts me just as much as the crying. Because now he has hope, and when I tell him what I think is the only way out of this, that hope is going to be destroyed. But it's the only realistic solution I can see.

CHAPTER 41
LIAM

'ARE YOU FUCKING JOKING?' Liam says, leaning back in his chair. 'The police? That's your big answer, is it?'

Mickey doesn't speak straight away. He mirrors Liam, leans back and lets out a slow breath. He raises his eyebrows in a gesture that says, 'Are you done?'. But Liam hasn't finished.

'Since when do people like you go to the police?' Liam gets a sadistic thrill from the way Mickey's face hardens at that. At least it's wiped that infuriating calm off his dad's face. 'Is that what you did when you got backed into a corner in Skegness?'

'No. And look how that turned out! I almost lost you by trying to sort it all myself.'

'I'm asking you for help now, aren't I?'

'Only because you have no choice.'

'Yes, because you're sneaking around my house like some kind of weirdo!'

Mickey seems to weigh this and shrugs. 'That's a fair comment. But I was doing it for the right reasons. Thought you were having an affair and was trying to get you to come to your senses.' He looks away and shakes his head. 'Wish that's all it was now.'

'Oh, I don't know,' Liam says, voice dripping in sarcasm. 'Maybe you could have called the police and had me arrested for adultery.' Mickey laughs, but Liam resists. 'I'm not fucking laughing, Dad. My life is being destroyed, I think Trent might be a psycho that's implicated me in murder and your answer is to turn me in.'

'Liam,' Mickey says, slowly getting to his feet, 'why don't you grow up? I'm not about to turn you in, so don't talk bollocks. I'm talking about getting ahead of the situation and bringing it to an end before it gets out of hand.'

'Out of hand? I think we're pretty fucking far past it being "out of hand". It's going to be my word against his and how do I explain not going to them sooner?'

'You tell them he threatened you and your family,' Mickey says, taking his mug to the sink and leaning against the kitchen unit.

Liam thinks he preferred the angry, reactive version of his dad. This calm, reasonable model is driving him mad. 'He hasn't threatened any of that.'

'Yet,' Mickey says. 'Just a matter of time. Trust me. I'm guessing he can already sense you're having doubts. Once he works out you're not on Team Trent, you and everything you care about will be in real danger.'

This finally pours water on Liam's anger bonfire, leaving only cold fear. 'It has crossed my mind why he didn't just kill me after what happened with Kendrick. Why not just make sure there were no witnesses?'

Mickey considers this for a moment. 'Because he must still need you in some way? Didn't you say he's in line for some big bonus when you get the buyout sorted?'

'Yeah, Flick managed to write it into the contract. Said he's one of our main assets,' Liam says, mildly surprised his dad had remembered this bit of small talk from one of their stilted phone conversations. Maybe he does listen to me sometimes, Liam thinks.

'But,' Mickey says, folding his arms, 'that could just be one reason. Another might be that it suits him to keep you around so that if and when the Kendrick situation comes to light—'

'He can pin it all on me,' Liam says, running a hand through his hair and feeling a damp nausea settling in the pit of his stomach.

Mickey nods, walks back to the table and sits down again. 'Yes. Any way you slice it, you're in danger, Liam.'

'Maybe we could…' Liam's words tail off and he looks at the table, shamefaced.

Mickey pats Liam's hand. 'No, son. That's not you and it's not me either. Trust me, we're not built to carry that kind of thing on our conscience, and I don't think either of us has the stomach for it. You think you'd be able to look Izzy and Grace in the face after killing a man?'

'But then what? If I go to the police, you know there's a good chance I'll go to prison. And both of us know I don't have the stomach for that.'

'I've got a good lawyer and I'm sure he'll give you the best chance. At least let me talk to him about it.'

'No. You can't tell anyone about any of this. Please, Dad.'

Mickey opens his hands. 'Well then what, Liam? Because right now, I can't see any other options.'

'Well. There might be something. Something that's been going around my head ever since Titch said it.'

'OK…' Mickey says.

Liam tells him about the safe in Kendrick's office and how Titch is convinced that whatever it was that Kendrick had over Trent is in there.

'Right. And?' Mickey asks.

'Come on, Dad. Don't pretend you don't know what I'm suggesting.'

'You want me to break into it. You want me to do something you've, rightly, looked down on since you were a kid. You want me to go back to being the thing you apparently hated all those years – a criminal – because now it suits you?'

'Absolutely,' Liam says and then cracks a smile of his own.

'Cheeky bastard,' Mickey says, laughing. 'But joking aside, there's a couple of things with that. Firstly, we'd have to get into the place without getting caught—'

'Come on, you're a locksmith—'

'But,' Mickey says, raising his bandaged hand, 'regardless, I won't be cracking any safes until this heals. So that plan is dead in the water for now.'

Elbows on the table, Liam puts a hand to his forehead, squeezes hard. He feels hopeless and confused and now even his dad is suggesting he's run out of options. Whatever Liam decides, the only thing he's certain of right now is he'll have to do it alone.

CHAPTER 42
TITCH

SHE HAD EXPECTED her two-day ultimatum to come and go and had already been considering her options, so it was a surprise when Liam's text had come through first thing this morning, less than twenty-four hours since their meeting at his house. On a burner, as he'd promised. She had wanted to feel more offended when he'd said that yesterday, but who was she trying to kid? Rejection was always there for her, like some half-arsed pet cat you live with – even when it wasn't sitting on your lap and asking for food, it was knocking about somewhere near by.

It's dark, most of the street-lighting reduced to a feeble glow at this time of the night, after eleven on a Tuesday. Lee Circle multi-storey car park squats there, a weird-shaped hunk of cracked grey concrete surrounded by a circular road. For some reason, it reminds Titch of a fat bullfrog sitting on a lily-pad in the middle of a swamp. The road itself is a hotch-potch of ethnic shops, run-down council flats and pricier luxury apartments. Titch approaches from the Charles Street side, walking past Epic House, where Radio Leicester was once based. It doesn't look so epic these days, run-down but just about clinging on, with a few random businesses in there.

Opposite is a derelict building Titch and the other street crew used to call Crack-atomi Plaza – after Nakatomi Plaza in *Die Hard* – because it was full to the brim with crackheads. Bruce Willis won't be saving the place anytime soon. Despite the signs warning of security patrols, it's surrounded by graffiti-covered boards and was abandoned to fend for itself a long time ago. Titch knows the feeling.

The roof of Lee Circle car park is a strange place for Liam to choose to meet and Titch is surprised he's even familiar with it. She knows he didn't grow up in Leicester, not prop-erly anyway. Even so, it's become one of the city's landmarks, no less historic than the Clock Tower or Jewry Wall. Mention it to any local over the age of fifty and they're likely to bore you with the only interesting fact about the place: apparently it was the first automated multi-storey car park in the country. She smiles briefly, remembering that even Kendrick trotted this out to her when she told him about the nights she spent sleeping in its stairwells. Halfway across the short-stay car park that borders the main building, Titch pauses. She stares at the two entrance doors which lead into those stairwells and up to the roof. She thinks about the piss-stinking steps and the flickering fluorescent lights and all the times she lay passed out on them, mindlessly drunk and searching for oblivion. There could be some of her old cronies in there now, maybe some new ones, waiting to welcome her back with a soggy cigarette or a battered can of Special Brew. She shivers at the thought and decides to use the main entrance, and wind her way up the spiralling car ramps instead. It will take longer, but will be safer. She's not sure Liam will fare well on the stairs either. Maybe he will drive in. Either way, that's his lookout, she thinks.

The car park is mostly empty, and with each level she trudges up, vehicles become more and more scarce. As she follows the road up and around, up and around, ever decreasing circles as she goes, she feels like she's making her way back up a helter-skelter, like the one they used to have at Loughborough Fair when she was a kid. She only ever got to ride it once, when she went along with the family of one of her friends. She remembers the anticipation as she'd climbed the last few steps, the greasy teenager handing her what looked like an old doormat to go down on. The way her stomach had dropped as she took the first bend, then the thrill as the mat slid beneath her. The delight was short-lived. Seconds later, her leg caught on a badly-fitted panel, tearing her favourite jeans and leaving a gash on her knee. She had sobbed so much that even the post-ride candyfloss couldn't console her. Still, it had taught her not to get her hopes up so high again. She had built up a level of expectation no big slide could fulfil, even without the injury to her leg. Nothing ever beats those first couple of seconds of a new experience, she thinks.

She finally reaches the fifth floor and eventually the roof, where there is only one car. It looks like it's been there forever, windscreen covered in dirt. She checks her phone. She's a few minutes early so heads to the far railing to look out over what she can see of the city and beyond at this time of night. She peers out towards the A50, the road that leads north towards the M1. During the daytime, when the sky is clear, she knows it's possible to see Bradgate Park on the horizon. In rare lucid moments, she has stood close to this very spot, looked out and imagined a different future. Now she stares into the darkness, remembers what happened to Kendrick and wishes she could go back to that night and change things. But she can't imagine how that might have played out any more than she can see past the city boundary in the dark.

Behind her the stairwell door creaks and a figure emerges. In the dim light and at this distance, all that stands out is Liam's bright white trainers. The rest of his outfit is dark – looks like a black or blue tracksuit, hoodie pulled up, face shrouded in the gloom. He's waiting, head bobbing as he peers towards her, probably trying to make sure he's not about to approach some random stranger. Even from here, she can see he's not one of the street people you're likely to find in these places at this time of night. Looks like he wisely dressed down, but she's still surprised he braved the stairwell. She doesn't call out – it seems somehow wrong to interrupt the background static of the late-night city. Instead, she gives a single wave of her hand and waits. Satisfied, Liam walks towards her. Except… something's off. It's in the walk. She's seen it before and something about it fizzes under her skin, makes it crawl. The way the right shoulder swings too much, hand low over the crotch. The way people outside her world assume bad men walk. Some do walk like that, true, but most of them don't make it so obvious. The pace is slow and sure and all the time Titch is trying to get a proper look of Liam's face. Is it Liam? She catches the glint of a light in one of the man's eyes but can't make out any of his features. She tries to take a step back and feels the hard concrete ledge in the small of her back. She brings up her hand and feels the rusty steel railing on her right. There's another to her left. She realises she's in a corner as the man strides towards her, closing off her angles of escape with each step.

Please be Liam. Please be Liam. Please be Liam. Her silent plea on repeat, hoping that the monster she thinks is coming out of the darkness is nothing more than a product of her frightened imagination. But when the man stops, now only a few feet away, and raises his bearded face, a small whimper escapes her. It's him. Deep down, she'd known it the moment he began to walk towards her. Maybe she knew it when he stepped through the stairwell door.

'Trent,' she says, taking a small victory from the fact her voice has a confidence she doesn't feel.

'Titch. How you been?'

'Did Liam send you?' she asks, wondering why she ever allowed herself to trust someone again.

'Nah. I think Liam's struggling with his conscience, bless him.' Trent's smile fades. 'He doesn't know I'm here.'

'Then how'd you get my number?'

'Ken gave it to me. Kind of.' His voice is soft, gentle almost. There's a sing-song quality that almost lulls her into feeling safe. Until she remembers what he did to Kendrick.

'You took it from his phone,' she says, through gritted teeth. 'You piece of shit.'

He takes a half-step forward. Titch flinches. He stops. 'Careful girl. You telling me Kendrick wouldn't have liked to have done the same to me?'

'He loved you, Trent.' When Trent pulls a face, fake-retches, Titch adds, 'No. Not like that. And you know it, as well. But you killed him anyway.'

'How much do you know?' he asks, taking another step towards her.

'Only that Ken had something on you, something you don't want anyone to know. But all he really wanted was to get close to you again. Work with you, you know?'

'Spare me.' He holds out a hand. 'Where's the video? Your phone. Give it to me.' His voice has changed in a way Titch can't quite work out. His accent is different somehow.

Thoughts tumble through her mind, decisions being made in less time than it takes to blink. The one skill she's learned from this shit life of hers: survival. He doesn't know I've given it to Liam, she thinks. On the one hand, she could try to use that to save herself, tell Trent killing her is a waste of time, the secret is already out. But she knows reasoning with him now won't make any difference. He will kill her, then he'll kill Liam. Then he will get away with killing Kendrick and this will all be for nothing. No. Let him think he has what he needs, but don't give it up easy.

'Fuck you. I wouldn't give it to Liam, so what makes you think I'd give it to you?'

He steps close now, looks down on her with cold, black eyes. Her defiance shrinks like plastic melting in a flame.

'I haven't got it,' she says, her voice now small and brittle. 'Not on me anyway. I can take you to it, though.'

He leans in, squinting into her face. 'Nope. You're fucking lying, Titch. You can't afford another phone and there's no way you're walking around without one now. So hand it over, or I'll just take it. And I won't be gentle.'

Titch knees him in the groin as hard as she can. He bends forward and she rakes her fingernails across his neck. He yelps and she tries to step around him, to run, sprint away and back down the helter-skelter to safety. He's prone, but his left arm springs out. She hits it hard. He slams her against the railing, pain shoots up her spine, breath leaves her lungs. She struggles to stay upright, almost collapses on the cold concrete. Trent hoists her back up, grips her jaw in a vice-like grip, turns her head towards him. With his free hand he touches his neck, which is bleeding onto the collar of his white T-shirt.

'Fucking dirty little bitch,' he says, before punching her in the stomach and rifling through her coat pockets until he finds the phone.

Titch wants to keep fighting, try to grab it back, but she's struggling to breathe. The railing behind her is all that's holding her up, as she drags in some air with a horrible death-rattle wheeze. She reaches out to push him away, make him stop and leave her alone, but it's pointless. He bats her arm away. She regards him, as if outside herself now, like watching a film or something. She wants to scream at herself to run, get away, keep fighting, anything. But she can't. There's nothing left.

Trent's face is lit by the ghostly blue light of Titch's phone screen. He frowns, scratches his beard.

'Passcode,' he says; an order not a request.

Titch takes in two more painful gasps of air. When she speaks, her voice is dark and rasping. 'Fuck. You.'

'Thought so,' Trent says. He nods and puts the phone in his pocket.

He takes a couple of deep breaths, like he's out for a pleasant evening stroll. Then, without warning, he crouches down, grabs Titch like he's picking up a child and throws her over the rail.

No, no, no, no, no… her hands flail, catch nothing but cold air. No time to scream, just a tiny half-gasp of white-hot fear. When Trent lets go, for a moment, Titch feels weightless. Back at the top of the helter-skelter that first time, let loose like she's flying, finally free, before she drops into the dark and hits the empty street below.

Trent pulls his hoodie tighter and walks quickly, but calmly, away and into the night.

CHAPTER 43
LIAM

THE DAY SEEMS to have slipped through Liam's fingers like melting ice cubes. It's late afternoon already. Dread has stalked him since he woke up at Twin Oaks this morning, sweating and edgy from some unremembered bad dream. All he wants to do is spend time applying logic to the problem, look at it from different angles and find a solution. But his mind is a frayed mess of ragged half-thoughts and paranoia. He feels like he's in a horror film, being chased down a corridor by some unseen monster, rattling locked doors and waiting for The Beast to lay a hand on his shoulder at any moment. And he's running out of time to tell Titch what he wants to do.

Work has been unavoidable today too. First, that tenacious old sod, Martin Chalmers, calling yet again to complain about the lack of work. Liam had promised to see if there was any theatre stuff going. Chalmers was talking about the new Pinter play, but Liam thinks he will be lucky if he can find him a panto with where his profile is right now.

Then came a stream of technical calls from Flick about the buyout, making sure everything is in place for Monday. She gave him shit for not being in the office and had even threatened to visit him at home until he'd talked her down. Apparently, there are some last-minute amendments to the contract, but Flick assures him it's all par-for-the-course in deals like this. She needs him to check over the latest version she's emailed and sign it, but every time he tries to focus on the endless paragraphs of legalese, his mind starts to drift. He knows that tomorrow and Friday will be even more fraught – the last working days to make the final arrangements before Monday's meeting. Even in his distracted state, he can see a few anomalies he needs to check with Flick, but it will have to wait until tomorrow. His brain is fried. And how much time will Titch give him? Will she really do what she said and tell the world what he and Trent have done? Has she done it already? The shortage of time, the phone calls, the contracts and consequences, all of it ramps up the pressure and minimises the time and brain power he needs to come up with a plan.

He's in the kitchen, taking his third pair of paracetamol for a now-raging headache, when yet another call comes. It's a number he doesn't recognise. He almost doesn't answer, but changes his mind at the last second.

'What did you do?' It's Bez, her voice is sharp and brittle. 'I trusted you.'

Liam swallows, the dry, bitter after-taste of the tablets still lingering at the back of his throat. Has Titch told Bez what's going on? His instinct is to lie. 'I went to the place you suggested,' he blurts out. 'Waited for a couple of hours around there but didn't see her.'

'Bullshit! It's too much of a coincidence.'

'I promised Kendrick I would spend some time on it, and I did. Wait. What's too much of a coincidence?' Liam walks out of the kitchen and into the hallway, trying to keep moving, to pace away the nervous energy that's now thrumming in his veins.

'You really don't know?' Bez asks.

Now he stops at the foot of the stairs and plonks himself onto one of the steps. 'Know what? Has something happened?'

Her tone softens, slightly. 'She's gone. Last night. It's been on the news. They haven't named her, but I just knew when they said it was Lee Circle. That's where she used to hang out. Before she got clean again. I called the team at Bright Futures and they're in bits. We all are.' The anger returns. 'What did you say to her? I swear to God, if you or Kendrick has got something to do with this, I'll—'

'I didn't find her!' Liam's voice is high and cracks, yet the lie slips out so easily, it makes him want to throw up. 'But what do you mean, she's gone?'

'She fell – or jumped – from the top of Lee Circle car park.'

'She... she's dead?'

Bez doesn't answer with words, but Liam can hear her crying.

'She jumped?' he asks.

She sniffs hard, composes herself. 'That's what they're saying, but Titch wasn't wired that way. Long as I knew her, she was a fighter. More likely she had a relapse with the drink and went on a binge. Maybe she was acting out, trying to impress her old crew that used to hang around there. I don't know.' She cries again.

He consoles her as much as he can and eventually manages to convince her that neither he, nor Kendrick, had anything to do with Titch's death. But Bez won't accept that Titch committed suicide and although Liam doesn't admit it to her, he won't either. The moment Bez gave him the news, he knew who was responsible. He doesn't know how Trent managed to find her, or how he managed to get her to meet him at that time of the night, but he knows that's what happened. Despite that, he's still shocked when he reads the local news report online. There is a CCTV photograph of

Titch, her usual pensive look of survival still visible on the grainy image.

Did you see this woman on Wednesday evening? Police are asking for information. Anyone who may have been in the Lee Circle area of the city between 11 p.m. and midnight should contact the hotline or email mispers@leicspolice.gov. Officers are also keen to speak to this individual, believed to be a white male, aged between 20 and 35 who may have information to assist their enquiries.

Another CCTV picture. Liam gasps. It's a man, head down, hood up, loose-fit nondescript jeans. But it's the trainers. Bright white Nikes, box fresh, just how Trent likes his shoes. Trent wouldn't usually be seen dead in that baggie unbranded hoodie and a cheap pair of jeans, but it's the trainers. His *sneaks*, as Trent sometimes half-jokingly calls them. When it came to the footwear, Trent couldn't bring himself to dress down. Maybe, Liam thinks, he doesn't even have any crap trainers in his closet.

Liam scan-reads the rest of the short article and everything suggests only a half-hearted investigation on the part of the police. Liam could be projecting, but there are no named officers mentioned, no caring relatives to quote and the phrase "tragic death" appears twice. There's even a statistic on the number of unhoused people currently thought to be in the city, alongside a link to a substance abuse charity. The tone of the piece is *another young homeless woman lost to the streets, probably a drug addict or an alcoholic. Oh dear, so sad. Now, read all about the new cycle lane being installed on London Road.*

He slams the laptop shut, takes out his phone and finds Trent's contact. He's angry. No, scratch that, he's raging. He stares at Trent's name, thumb poised and ready to hit the call button. He will have it out, right now, tell Trent he knows everything. Tell him he's seen the video of that night, that he knows the truth and that even if no one else has worked out who killed Titch, Liam knows and he will go to the police, go to the press, go to the top of Old John Tower, if needs be, to shout it out to whoever will listen. Damn the consequences. Fuck it. Trent has to be stopped. His thumb twitches again and he wills himself to do it, make the call and start the chain reaction.

A text message stops him.

Liam flinches, not from the vibration or the ping, but from the name of the sender. It's him, Trent. Liam swivels in the chair, looks around the room and out of the window. Is he here? Is Liam being watched. Has Trent come to finish things? After all, Liam realises, Trent was in Leicester last night. Did he hang around to tidy up the last loose end? Hand shaking, he opens the message.

LIAM, WHERE YOU AT? JUST DROPPED BY OFFICE BUT JEN SAID YOU'RE WORKING FROM HOME. YOU NEVER WORK FROM HOME. ALL COOL?

Liam releases the breath he was holding and stares at the message. His tired, adrenalin-filled brain takes a moment to process it. He reads it again, tries to think straight. *Just dropped by the office.* So, Liam realises, he's back in London. Up until now, Trent hasn't known Liam is back up here. If he did, he probably would have visited him last night. Liam sees flashes in his mind, Trent creeping into his bedroom, knife in hand. He thinks again of the dream and the monster.

No. Now is not the time to get paralysed by fear, he thinks. Deal in realities. Trent doesn't know you're here. Yet. And he doesn't know the extent of Liam's concerns about Titch and all the rest of it. Or does he? What, if anything, did he manage to get out of Titch before he chased her off that car park last night?

YOU NEVER WORK FROM HOME.

The subtext is obvious. Trent made a big deal about not doing anything out of the ordinary, not tipping anyone off that something might be wrong. The only person Liam is worried about tipping off right now is Trent. He taps out a reply, making sure he keeps his tone light and casual.

YOU NEED ME? BEEN SENT A TON OF SHIT TO TRAWL THROUGH FOR THE MEETING ON MONDAY. NEED PEACE AND QUIET TO GO THROUGH IT. TOLD JEN TO DEAL WITH ANYTHING THAT COMES UP TODAY AND TOMORROW. FREE FOR A CHAT IF YOU NEED SOME-THING THOUGH?

The three dots shimmer as Trent types his reply. Liam waits. Will he buy it?

NO DRAMAS. JUST CHECKING NO UPDATE ON WAINWRIGHT?

Liam goes straight back with a message he hopes will stop Trent deciding to turn up at the house. The kids are at school and Claire won't be there either, but he doesn't want to get caught in a lie.

NOTHING YET. SORRY. GOT TO GO TO A MEETING SOON. I'LL CALL HIS TEAM AGAIN BEFORE I LEAVE.

Trent replies.

EVERYTHING ELSE OK?

Now *there's* a loaded question, Liam thinks. Trent's testing the water. Liam knows he needs to answer quickly to avoid suspicion.

ALL QUIET. JUST FOCUSING ON NEXT WEEK NOW.

After a moment's hesitation, Liam adds a GIF to the message, a short video clip of an American gameshow host throwing wads of dollar bills into the air. Trent reacts with a laughing emoji and the conversation seems to be over. But is it?

CHAPTER 44

LIAM

LIAM FEELS SICK AGAIN, his tongue coated in a bitter film. He checks the time and remembers it's Wednesday, which means Claire is working late and the kids will be at Tora's house with her daughters. He needs to hear their voices, feel close to something pure and honest. He calls Tora, who eventually picks up. There's loud music in the background until it sounds like she steps out of the room and speaks.

'Hey Liam. Everything OK?'

For a moment, he's confused, like Tora can already sense his unease before he's even spoken a word, until he realises he's rarely – if ever – called Tora. He only has the number for emergencies.

'No, nothing wrong, Tora,' he says, trying to slow his breathing. 'I've just been super-busy and away from home the last couple of days so wondered if I could grab a word with the girls?'

'Sure. Izzy is playing Minecraft downstairs, but Grace is just next door. Hang on.'

The music returns and Tora shouts to get Grace's attention. The music drops a couple of notches and after a few seconds Grace gets on the call.

'Daddy? Is that you? Everything OK?'

He bites his lip, emotion threatening to overwhelm him. Does he really call so infrequently that when he does, everyone asks the same question: Is everything OK? He forces a smile into his voice and swallows down the guilt, like bad-tasting medicine.

'Hey, Gracie. I'm fine. Just missing you all and—'

'Where are you?' she asks.

'I'm up in Leicester, with your… Grandad Mickey.' Why does he still find it so hard to use that term?

'Oh. Why can't we come? Will he take us to see the deers again in the park?'

Liam smiles, for real this time. 'I'm sure he'll take you to see the deer. I'll ask him later and we can arrange another trip in a couple of weeks, when I get all this boring work stuff out of the way. How does that sound?'

'Cool. And an Eric's Ice Cream? Grandad says they do the best ice creams.' She leans away from the phone and responds to something one of Tora's kids has shouted. 'Yeah! Coming!'

'He's right. They're lovely.'

'Mm-hmm,' Grace says, distantly, and Liam can tell he's losing her.

'Grace,' he says, suddenly. 'You know I love you all very much, don't you? And I'll be home soon, I promise.' His voice goes all weird and high-pitched and he curses himself, clears his throat and tries to carry on, but it's too late.

'Daddy?' Grace asks, alarm creeping into her voice. 'Are you alright? You sound… funny.'

'I'm fine. Just got a bit of a cold. You go and play and I'll see you soon.'

'Alright,' she says, unsure. 'Bye daddy.' It sounds like she's handing the phone back to Tora, but Liam hangs up before she comes back on, knowing he can't hold it together much longer. He puts his head in his hands and quietly cries. It was a mistake to call. Now he's probably freaked out his daughter, but he had to hear one of their voices. His heart is fit to burst with the love he has for them all, Izzy, Grace and Claire, and he's on the verge of destroying everything they have.

Eventually, he regains his composure and scrolls through Kendrick's latest texts, looking for any clue he's on to Liam. He thinks about what his dad had said, about people like Trent being streetwise survivors who can smell when something isn't right. Is Trent just humouring him? Does he somehow know Liam has spoken to Titch? The more he thinks about it, the more he becomes convinced Trent knows everything. He opens the laptop again, scrolls down the news article and stares long and hard at the CCTV picture of the man in the hoodie. Can he say for certain it's Trent? The posture looks hunched, head down, face in shade, a contrast to how Trent usually carries himself, but then, wouldn't that be exactly how Trent would approach it? Taking on a role, disguising himself behind a character? Liam wonders if he's ever seen the real version of Trent. Yes, you have, he thinks. It was there in the clip from Titch's phone, the one that now resides on his laptop. Which reminds him – he needs to transfer it to a thumb drive. He takes one last look at the CCTV picture and decides to assume it's Trent. It all fits together, and the trainers clinch it.

All of which means, Trent killed Titch, or at least scared her enough to make her take her own life. And if he did that, Liam has to assume Titch gave him up before she died.

Liam opens his client calendar app and checks Trent's schedule. Tonight, he's doing a guest slot on a radio show. Tomorrow, he has a full day with a sponsor, an audio manufacturer in Kent, which includes a personal appearance at a club tomorrow night. It's worth a ton of money and equipment for Trent's studio. He's not going to miss it. Friday, his schedule's clear. If Trent decides to come for Liam before the meeting, that will be the day.

All that's keeping Liam safe at the minute is that Trent needs him to get the buyout over the line, so Trent can get his payday. That, and the fact that right now, Trent thinks Liam is somewhere in London. When either of those things change, Liam is a dead man. He has a day, tops, to turn things around.

He calls Mickey, who picks up, out of breath on the second ring.

'You OK?' Mickey asks.

'I'm alright. Are *you* OK?'

'Huh? Oh, the heavy breathing? Me and Warren have just had to carry a big reel of cable up two flights of stairs at some big house over in Swithland, and I was doing it pretty much one handed. Can't do any more for today though, because the alarm guys have been held up. You need me?'

'Yes,' Liam says, feeling weird admitting it. 'You know that job we talked about you doing?'

'The one I told you I couldn't do, you mean?'

'Things have changed, Dad. For the worst. It's my only chance.'

'I've told you what I think you should do.'

'That's a last resort. But can we at least try my way first?'

'Not unless you've got magic healing powers for my hand.'

'What about if I did it, under your guidance?'

There's a pause, then Mickey says, 'No. It's not the kind of thing you can just do straight off the bat.'

'Isn't it?' Liam asks. 'What about that day at the garage? Or did you trick me into thinking I could do it?'

'You remember that?' Mickey asks, surprised.

'You don't forget something like that.'

Mickey's breathing slows until all Liam can hear is the passing traffic outside wherever it is Mickey is standing. When he speaks, his voice is quiet. 'I promised your mum I'd never let you do it again.'

'She'd understand, Dad. You know she would.'

CHAPTER 45
MICKEY

IT'S bad enough Liam has talked me into this madness in the first place, but the fact he wants to rush the whole job as well, is giving me alarm bells. Which is exactly what we'll be getting if, when we break in there tonight, I can't disengage the security system. I pick him up outside the entrance to Twin Oaks. He's dressed as I suggested, black jeans, dark hoodie and a pair of black boots. When he gets in the car, I ask him if he's brought something for his face. He reaches into his pocket and pulls out a simple black medical face mask.

'Had it left over from the pandemic,' he tells me.

I suppose, with his hood up and that on, it should be enough if we do get caught on camera somewhere. We did a recce during the day, but it was broad daylight and difficult to get too near the place without sticking out like two parrots in a pigeon coop.

The studio is tucked away behind a snooker club in Syston. I don't know the area that well, but I've got a vague memory of the place being a social club back in the day. Looks like they've spent some money on it; big members-only place with a load of tables, according to Liam. Maybe one day, if we get through this, me and him can come back for a game. Relive his childhood, when we used to go with my grandad.

I park the van in a lay-by outside a deserted village hall about five minutes walk away from the studio. Liam opens his mouth to speak, but I silence him with a raise of my hand and we sit there, still and silent for a good two or three minutes. Liam isn't like Warren. He knows how to take a hint and doesn't fidget or give me funny looks while we wait. He knows I know what I'm doing. He mirrors me, both of us looking out of the windscreen, surveying the empty streets and checking for any signs of life or movement. I chose this spot away from any direct line of sight from the nearest houses. My window is open a crack, just so I can listen for anyone making their way back from a late-night lock-in somewhere or a worker on their way out for a night shift. But Syston's a small town, and we aren't close to its busy centre, full of pubs and takeaways.

Another minute of checking wing mirrors and waiting for any sign, any reason not to do this, but it doesn't come. No excuses now, Mickey. I grab my kit bag and straighten my black woollen hat. Liam leans into the back and pulls the suit bag out. There's no suit in it. It's concealing the telescopic collapsible ladder we'll need. We get out and close the doors as quietly as we can, then make the short walk in silence. Hardly any of the street lights are on, making it easier for shady bastards like us to go about our business. Last I heard, councils were calling this 'progress', saying it helps the environment. Total bollocks, of course. Saves them a shit load on their electricity bill and I doubt anyone's paying much attention to the rise in street crime in the meantime.

It's half-one in the morning. The club's been officially closed since ten-thirty and all the interior lights are off. The only illumination is a couple of security lights in the now-empty car park. The entrance to the studio is usually accessed from the snooker club car park. There's a camera over the club entrance. Without a proper recce and seeing the feed screens inside the place, I've got no idea how much of the car park is in view, but the camera looks like a HiLux Turret, so the field of view is pretty wide. We could go around the outside and try to climb over, but even without my dodgy hand I'd probably struggle these days. Not to mention two blokes clambering over a wall in the middle of the night looks a lot more conspicuous than us strolling, heads down, into an empty car park. Once we're inside the grounds, we step close to the wall, obscuring the view of any nosey neighbour who decides to look out of their window. Liam puts on his mask and I pull down the rolled-up balaclava that was doubling as a hat.

Liam flinches and whispers, 'Fucking hell. You look like you're in the IRA.'

Cheeky twat. I put a finger to my lips and we make our way towards the far corner of the small car park. Best we can do is stick close to the perimeter wall and hope the camera can't make out much. In the corner is a battered black metal gate, a fat Chubb padlock threaded through the catch plate. I pull my pick kit from my back pocket and hope that I've still got enough dexterity in my hands to open it. I gesture for Liam to hold the lock still, while I get to work. With my damaged right hand, it takes me a few goes to thread the first pick. There isn't a lot of sensation, but I've opened thousands of padlocks in my time and at this point, it's really a matter of muscle memory. The hardest bit is ignoring the pain of having to hold the pick in the same position for any amount of time.

Schlick! It pops open and Liam gives an appreciative grunt and raises his eyebrows. Yeah, I think, there's still life in the old dog yet. The gate screeches when Liam pushes it open but we step into the passageway as quickly as possible and close it again behind us. There's a few seconds of standing still, listening and waiting for our eyes to adjust to the dark. I can hear the distant intermittent wah-wah of cars and lorries on the A6, late-night travellers on their way home. The rustle of nearby trees and a garden gate banging in the breeze a few streets away. Using the torch on my phone, I shine a light on the alarm box mounted above the entrance to the studio, ten feet or so off the ground. I don't linger, holding the beam long enough to confirm what I already thought at first glance on our recce earlier today. It's an ancient CommScope. Liam's pretty sure it doesn't work anymore but we can't take any chances.

I nod for Liam to take out the telescopic ladder. He extends it enough to reach the alarm box, its rungs clicking into place with each level. He wedges it against the wall, as far into the shadowy bushes as he can. I take out the small power drill from my bag, along with the can of expanding insulation foam. I hand Liam the drill and lean against the bottom of the ladder. While we're down at ground-level, we're hidden behind the gate, but as soon as Liam climbs a few rungs, there's a chance he could be spotted so we need to be as quick as we can. I'd normally do it myself, but I'd struggle to climb the ladder one-handed, let alone drill the hole we need. I've shown Liam what needs to be done and, once he's got a solid purchase at the top of the ladder, he picks a spot on the bottom-left corner of the alarm box, waits a few seconds and then drills a small hole. The case is made of thin, rusting metal and it's mercifully quick, a satisfying little ping telling me he's through. He comes back down the ladder as quickly and quietly as he can, and we both stand still and listen for any signs someone might have heard anything. The drill is small, and I deliberately set it to the lowest power setting, so it's unlikely to have drawn too much attention, but you never know. We give it another minute, before I hand Liam the foam and he heads back up the ladder. He has a good look around as he goes up, checking we're still unobserved. He must be satisfied, because he continues back to the top, sticks the nozzle into the small hole and squirts the entire contents of the can into the alarm box. It will fill the space, quickly harden and – even if the old-fashioned hammer-action mechanism is still connected – the whole thing will be frozen in place and unable to sound. It's a quick and dirty way to deal with old alarm systems when you can't easily access the power source. Liam climbs down again and stashes the ladder back in the suit bag, while I pick the Yale lock on the front entrance. I get it open and hold my breath for any sign of the alarm kicking in.

Nothing. Not even a click from above. Still, always safe, never sorry and all that.

Once inside, we can use our torches without worrying too much about being spotted. There are no windows and we need to get the lay of the land. We're in a narrow passageway. The smell of damp laced with weed hangs in the air. I run my hand across the once-white woodchip wallpaper that brings memories of a childhood spent in council houses. I made a point of not going near the stuff when I got my own place. Doubt Liam has come across much of it in his life. Yet another reminder of our different upbringings. Even so, he still found a way into my world. I suppose some blokes would be pleased with that. I find it pretty fucking depressing.

'Down here,' Liam says and leads me along the corridor, past a tiny kitchen on the left – dripping tap and washed-up mugs stacked on the draining board – towards the studio at the far end of the building.

We go through two doors, heavy wooden jobs with rubber seals and Liam flicks the main light on to reveal the studio control room. Only studios I've seen are in music documentaries and films. This is a smaller, low-rent version of what I've seen before. The control room has a huge mixing desk that looks the part, dozens of faders and a strip of white tape running along the bottom. Words are scrawled on the tape in black marker pen. Stuff like 'KICK 1', 'OVERHEAD RIGHT' and 'MOOG MAIN'. Means nothing to me. In front of the mixer is a battered black desk chair on wheels. There's a big, double-glazed window that gives a view through to the main recording room, that's currently lit only by the control room light. I can just about make out a drum kit and what looks like a keyboard stand. The smell of weed is stronger in here and it's clear to see why. Remnants of blunts balanced on two overflowing ashtrays. An old reel-to-reel tape box juts out from a shelf under the mixing desk. There's a sorry-looking stained, red leather sofa up against the wall and wedged into the corner beside it, is the safe. It's a squat green Phillips & Son combination safe, proper vintage. Kendrick probably thought it looked cool. But it's a good safe. It's currently doubling as a stand for the small beer fridge balanced on top of it. I tell Liam to unplug the fridge so we can move it.

'Why do we need to do that?' he asks.

'Vibrations,' I tell him. 'It'll interfere with you getting it open.'

Liam freezes for a second – like he's only now realising it's him that's going to need to get the safe open – before he leans down to find the plug and we both lift the half-full fridge and put it on the floor in the middle of the room.

'Ready?' I ask him.

'As I'll ever be.'

In an ideal world, I'd have given him some practice this afternoon, but I haven't got access to any kind of safe at home, so the best I could do is talk him through it and try to get him into the right headspace. I watch him now, going through the motions and trying to get into the part. He touches his forefinger and thumb together on both hands and makes tiny circular movements, raising the sensitivity, bringing the skin to life. Like a runner might do stretches before a 10K. He spends a few seconds on the forefinger, before moving on to the next digit and then the next. He starts again, does the whole thing three or four times, all the while staring down the vault, trying to psyche it out. I say nothing, don't interrupt, don't move, but my chest swells with pride, watching him get into the zone. I know it's wrong, getting a kick out of this, but I can't help it. It's weird, yet satisfying, watching your kid show an aptitude for the only skill you've ever really had. Of course, it still remains to be seen whether he can actually do it.

He's breathing deeply now, synchronising it with the movements of his fingers, slowing down, looking calmer and more assured with each cycle of warm-ups. Eventually he gives the smallest of nods and steps up to the safe.

CHAPTER 46

LIAM

FAKE IT 'TIL *you make it*. That's what's really going through Liam's mind as he approaches the studio safe. He's always been a quick learner and likes to have a process he can follow, some technique he can put his faith in. He's used plenty of meditation apps over the years and even had a one-to-one session on some spa weekend Claire dragged him to years ago. He remembers being honest with the teacher, telling him he couldn't actually empty his mind and that, whilst he found it relaxing to do the breathing exercises and lie down for twenty minutes in the middle of the day, he never felt like he was achieving any kind of spiritual awakening. The teacher – a middle-aged man called Floyd – had just smiled and told him to keep turning up, following the process and one day he would be doing it without realising. Oh, Liam had thought, so it's just fake it 'til you make it. I can do that.

So now he does as his dad has shown him, goes through the motions and tries to attach logic and meaning to each action. The strange thing is, this already feels more natural to him than meditation. His fingers really are tingling and buzzing with sensitivity after a few minutes of the warm-up exercises. For the first time since what happened with

Kendrick, Liam feels calm and centred. None of which means he'll be able to get the safe open. But he has to try, so he stands in front of the little safe and lays his hands on the mottled steel surface.

Instinctively, he closes his eyes, like he's in some kind of holy communion with the cold hunk of metal beneath his fingertips. He splays the fingers of his left hand, resting them gently on an area close to the dial. He slowly moves his other hand into place, letting his fingers skate across the dimpled and cracked green paint, until he feels the ridges of the combination dial.

He's still. Locked into place. Is Mickey still in the room? Liam isn't sure, so focused is he on the task at hand. Which is why he flinches at the sound of his dad's voice, a few feet behind him.

'Keep breathing, deep as you can,' Mickey whispers. 'When you let it go, imagine the breath is forcing every other distraction away from you and out of the room. It's just you and the safe now.'

It would be, Liam thinks. If you hadn't just destroyed my concentration. He sighs.

Mickey says, 'Sorry, son. You were in the zone, weren't you. I'll shut up. Here if you need me.'

Liam doesn't answer, instead leaving his hands exactly where they were and doing as his dad suggested. He sucks in one long breath, holds it until it has to escape, releases it soft and slow until he gets to the end and is ready to start again. In. And out. In. And out. He recites the mantra his dad drilled into him this afternoon – left, right, left, right, four, three, two, one – but it seems slippery in his mind, hard to hold on to. It's there, a practical roadmap for what he has to do, the direction of turns and how many cycles the safe needs, but as a device to keep Liam centred? It just doesn't do it for him. Instead, he gravitates to something else, a memory from Izzy's childhood. She's sitting in her little plastic baby bath, wispy strands of golden hair sticking out on her almost bald head. She was an early talker, a proper chatterbox and always singing. He smiles, remembering her tiny voice as she tried to sing a nursery rhyme.

One, two, three-four-five. Once I caught a fish alive.

Except, when she sang it, the tune was the only recognisable thing about it. The words were just a series of sounds… bon, coo, pee-por-bibe… over and over again, splashing and laughing and waiting for Liam to give her a little cheer each time. Liam feels a smile, warm on his face. The memory should take him out of it, pull him away from what he needs to do, but as the same simple tune repeats in his mind, he becomes more in step with his breathing. Eventually, it feels like each of his fingertips is pulsing with energy. He's thrumming with it, like he's waiting for some unseen starter pistol to go off. He wills himself to begin.

He spins the dial, one, two, three times, just to see if there's any kind of sensation in his left hand. Nothing. He tries it again and noth—

No.

Wait.

There is something. But it's in his right hand, the one on the dial. He takes the dial around again, slower this time and feels it once more. It brings a jolt of surprise and joy so strong he almost giggles. It's surreal. He wonders, distantly, if this is the way his dad feels it too, but pushes away that thought, and any others that might pull him out of this feeling. He picks up the melody of the nursery rhyme again, its rhythm bringing him back to where he needs to be. He is more still than he has ever been in his life, more focused and honed than he thought was possible. He dare not move, for fear of losing the connection.

He resets the dial and starts again, moving in sequence now, working methodically. He and Mickey had already agreed Liam would simply call out the numbers as he found them, let them go and leave it to Mickey to remember them. Mickey said it would make it easier to work on the next part of the combination, and he was right. Liam sees the numbers going off like fireworks in his mind's eye, bursting with brilliance. Once he says the number out loud, it disappears, leaving the sky dark again for the next one to appear.

The first two come like that, as if he's catching a ball with his eyes closed – shooting a hand out and snatching it out of thin air. He's never felt a buzz like it. Is this how his dad experiences the world all the time? This heightened, almost ticklish sensation in his fingertips? Is this what kept him away from Liam and his mum for sometimes days at a time?

His mum. There it is.

The nursery rhyme stops, replaced by an image of her face, looking at him with sad, disappointed eyes. She had made his dad promise to keep Liam safe and away from the criminal side of his life, true. But she also made them both promise to try to rebuild their relationship and stay together no matter what. In a way, isn't that what they're doing now?

His right hand continues to turn the dial but it's mechanical now, forced. The sensitivity is fading like pins and needles in a numb limb.

Turn… turn… turn.

But all he's getting is static, no real signal, no nursery rhyme. Just the picture of his mum, lying on her deathbed, Mickey on one side and Liam on the other. Both of them holding one of her hands and swearing they will do their best to honour her wishes. Both of them probably believing it in the moment, too.

Turn… turn… turn.

Although he would never admit it to Claire, or anyone else, he knows it's his dad who's done all the running when it comes to trying to heal old wounds. So why hasn't Liam been able to fully reconcile their differences, put away the past and move on? Part of it, he now realises, is seeing the way Mickey is with Hazel. The way he looks at her when he thinks no one's looking. The way he lights up when she drops by, and even the way he smiles when he gets a text from her. Try as he might, Liam can't ever remember Mickey looking at his mum like that. He knows there were feelings there once, love of some kind, perhaps the bond they shared through him, their child. But compared to what he sees between Mickey and Hazel, it feels like his whole childhood, their relationship, was a sham. That's what it is, his life. A sham. Fake. Now he knows.

Turn... turn... turn...

CHAPTER 47
LIAM

'LIAM?' Mickey says.

It's like the plug being pulled from a TV, the picture shrinking to a small dot in Liam's mind. The safe is now nothing but dead metal beneath his fingers.

He turns. 'What?'

'I just asked if everything was OK, son, that's all. Could tell you were struggling. You've gone round the last number twenty-odd times.'

'Oh, sorry if I'm not perfect first time out,' Liam says, irritated and embarrassed at how angry he sounds, yet unable to do anything about it.

Mickey takes a few seconds to answer and Liam can see him making a conscious effort not to react to his tone.

'You've already done amazing to get *any* numbers. When grandad taught me, it took weeks to get my first one.'

'Fuck's sake,' Liam says. 'Where was this calm version of you when I was growing up? Huh? How come you can do it now, being all reasonable and shit? Why don't you say what you're thinking? I think I preferred the old you.'

Mickey clenches his jaw, shakes his head. 'No. You didn't.

And I don't blame you. I was a shit dad. I've known that for a long time. But I'm trying to make amends.'

'Oh, for Mum? Trying to honour her memory, are you?' He steps around his dad to stand in front of the control room window. He sees himself reflected in the dark glass and hates the childish, petulant look on his face. Mickey turns but doesn't come any closer. They hold their conversation in the reflection, like it's easier that way.

'Is that what this is about?' Mickey asks. 'Your mum?' When Liam doesn't answer, he continues, flicking his head back towards the vault. 'It's weird, working on a safe, sometimes, it opens *you* up. Takes you places in your mind. Sometimes, places you don't want to go. I know. I've been there. And I've been thinking a lot about your mum lately too. We both know how she'd feel about this.'

'If you're so bothered about keeping your promises to her, why didn't you give a shit when she was alive?' Liam's disgusted by what he sees in the reflection, the way he bares his teeth on the word 'shit'. The way he's staring at Mickey now, nothing but hate in his black eyes. But it's like he's watching someone else.

Now Mickey raises his good hand and points at Liam. 'You're under a lot of stress. But I'm not the enemy here. Remember that.'

Liam gets a perverse thrill at seeing Mickey's fuse slowly burn down.

'Aren't you?' Liam asks, finally turning around to face his dad. 'That why you wanted me to go to the police? So you can swoop in and play the good grandad with my kids? You and Hazel being the doting grandparents while I rot in prison. Where you should've spent the last few decades?'

'Fucking grow up, will you!' Mickey shouts. 'You're talking like you're in some fucking film or something. This shit is real and it's time you at least faced up to the fact it's your fault.' Liam is about to snap back, when Mickey steps close, and carries on, his voice now a low growl. 'Yeah, I got away with some stuff over the years, but I took responsibility for my actions and I accepted who and what I was. Have *you*?'

Liam blinks several times, feels tears prickling at the corner of his eyes.

Mickey goes on, his breath hot on Liam's face. 'Because from where I'm standing, I see someone who likes to play the working-class, son-of-a-criminal card when it suits him – like to get your bad boy clients and all the rest of it – but won't even use my surname above the door of his business and now looks down on me for trying to change. You want to have your fucking cake and eat it, don't you? *Son.*'

Mickey turns and walks away, back to the vault in the corner of the room. When he turns back, the calm mask is almost back in place, but Liam can see he's upset and disappointed.

'And as for the jibes you keep making about Hazel and your mum and the rest of it,' he says. 'You're right. I do feel something for Hazel that I may never have felt for your mum – or at least not since when we first got together – but is it so wrong I want to have that now? At my time of life? And don't think your mum was happy with our relationship either.' He pauses then, as if considering saying something else, then decides against it. 'Point is, you only get one go round, Liam, and I'm trying to be a better version of myself. Hazel's one of the things that helps me do that. Along with you, Claire and the grandkids. Maybe it's selfish, but can't some good come out of it as well?'

Liam rubs his eyes with his thumb and forefinger, turns away again to compose himself. He wants to stay angry, but it's fading away, like the sensation in his fingers had faded in front of the safe. Now he just feels exhausted, confused, empty.

Mickey lays a hand on Liam's shoulder, tentatively, like he

expects Liam to shrug it off, but Liam accepts it and doesn't move when Mickey gets close and turns it into an awkward side-hug.

'Come on, Liam. Maybe it's over? We gave it a go but—'

'No, Dad. Let me have one more go. We've got the first two numbers. We're halfway there. I reckon I can get back into the zone.'

'OK,' Mickey says, but Liam sees the look in his eyes. He doesn't think Liam can do it now. Maybe he's right. Mickey forces a smile. 'Yeah. Come on, then. One more go. I'm sure you can do it.'

Now Liam does shrug off his dad's arm and trudges back to the vault, but even he knows the time has past, the magic lost. His head is all over the place. Still, he thinks, it's this or the police. He begins the circular finger warm-ups again, takes in a deep breath, holds it and lets go. Tries to push away all the negativity and noise one more time.

'Liam?'

'Jesus, Dad. Can I at least have a couple of minutes.'

'You might not need it.'

Mickey's voice has changed, got lighter. Liam turns to see him holding up a battered-looking grey cardboard box with the word TASCAM printed on it in orange-red lettering. There's a discoloured printed catalogue sticker, stuck in one corner, with something scrawled on it in Kendrick's handwriting. Liam presumes it's the name of a track he was working on.

He shrugs. 'What is it? A reel-to-reel tape? Big deal.'

'Yeah,' Mickey says. 'A reel-to-reel tape, in what I'm guessing has to be a fully digital studio these days? You see a reel-to-reel tape machine in here?'

Liam glances around the room. 'Well, no, but—'

'Believe me,' Mickey says. 'I've watched enough episodes of *Classic Albums* to know one when I see one. They're massive and you'd know if there was one in here.'

'OK. And?' Liam feels his irritation building again now. 'Maybe Kendrick bought it because it looks cool.'

'You're probably right,' Mickey says, before tapping the sticker on the box. 'But he's also used it to make a note of the combination for the safe. He's tried to make it look like a timecode or something, but these are the first two numbers you found. There's two more written underneath. Can't be a coincidence.'

CHAPTER 48
MICKEY

IT'S BEEN a while since I've had that happen, but it *does* happen on jobs. I suppose it's no different to people writing down their computer password and putting it on a Post-it stuck to the monitor. Safe combinations aren't easy to remember, especially if you hardly ever use the safe in question. Bit different if it's a cash safe and you're in and out of it every day. The Kendrick lad had done time as well, so I'm guessing he wanted to make sure he could still access the safe when he got out.

Back in the day, I used to make it part of my routine to have a good look around the room before I got started on the safe. In the past I've found combinations written on calendars, in telephone books and once scrawled on to the side of a condom machine some sleazy nightclub owner had in his office. Long story. Point is, I should've checked. Would've saved us a lot of bother, not to mention that family therapy session I've just had to endure.

So, Hazel has been the real stone in Liam's shoe since I came back? Doesn't help that he still thinks his mum was always the perfect, dutiful wife and mother. For a second, I almost spilled the beans about her affair but that would just have been spiteful and what good would it do? No. I'm glad I kept my powder dry on that one and who knows? Now everything's out in the open, we might be able to eventually get past it.

That's if we can get past this first.

I tell Liam the last part of the combination and he yanks down on the handle and pulls the door open. It squeals but gives way. I step closer to try to see, but it doesn't look like there's much in there. A couple of hard drives, some documents and a brown envelope.

Liam picks up a small, black hard drive with the word '*Zebra*' written on it with a white chalk pen. 'That's the album he was working on. Guessing it's the stems and media.' When he looks up and sees my frown, he adds, 'The stuff he's recorded on the computer. Like you said, he wasn't the reel-to-reel type.'

'Is that valuable or something? Would Trent be after that?'

'I doubt it,' Liam says. 'Be risky for Trent to try to claim that as his own. Kendrick was working on *Zebra* even before he went inside. Too many people know about it.' He sighs, runs his thumb over the label. 'It's sad though. I need to make sure this gets out into the world at some point. Could be part of his legacy.'

Legacy? The way Liam's talking, you'd think it was some long-lost recording of Elvis or something.

'Maybe,' I say, managing to keep my voice neutral. 'Probably not a priority at the minute, though? What else is in there, then?'

He works his way through various documents, mainly insurance stuff, some probation paperwork and a printout of a real estate listing – some big country pile out in Nottinghamshire.

Liam scans the printout. 'Must have had some big plans, if he thought he was going to have the kind of money he'd need to buy somewhere like that. Offers over three million.'

He stacks it with the other paperwork and takes out a brown envelope, stuffed with a wedge of documents. It all seems to be from the Adoption Contact Register. He takes it over to the mixing desk and starts reading through it, handing each one of the documents to me as he finishes. First batch of stuff is something to do with Kendrick being accepted onto some kind of registry for people who want to trace their real parents.

'Thought you said he wasn't interested in knowing about his real mum?' I ask.

'He always told me he wasn't. In fact, I'm pretty sure he got contacted by the agency a few years ago, saying they had been approached by someone claiming to be her. He wasn't interested. Told them to pass on a message, something along the lines of that if she ever went public, he would make sure she was crucified in the press.'

'He wasn't keen on the idea then.'

Liam gives me a look, realises I'm being sarcastic. 'No. Even so, we thought she might try to approach him directly anyway. He told me to be on the lookout for it.'

'What could you have done about it?' I ask.

'Not a lot. But that doesn't stop clients asking, Dad. Thankfully, it was never an issue. Far as I know, I was the only one he told and it was pretty much a no-go subject after that.'

I glance at the request again. 'Obviously had a change of heart inside. Prison can do that to you. A lot of time to think.'

I only ever did one short stint inside, in my twenties, but it was enough to make me know I never wanted to go back. Didn't make me change careers, but it did make me more careful, which reminds me we've been messing about in here too long.

'Liam,' I say, pointing to the thick envelope he's still working through. 'If anyone saw us come in, there's been a long time for the coppers to get their lazy arses to the scene.

Check there's nothing else you want out of the safe, get it closed, and let's read through all this back at yours.' For a few seconds, it's like I haven't spoken. Liam's glued to whatever he's reading now, and his eyes seem to be getting wider with every new paragraph. 'What is it?' I ask.

Slack-jawed, he looks up from the paperwork. 'Fucking hell, Dad. Kendrick's real mum is Lady Jane Featherby.'

'OK,' I say. 'Am I supposed to know who that is?'

'Her husband was Lord Featherby, ex-Tory politician?' he says. 'Had a load of big jobs, failed his way to the top like most of them do.'

I shrug. 'Shit floats. Don't really pay much attention to politics. So what was all that stuff about Kendrick being abandoned by some alcoholic single mum or whatever?'

'No, I think all that's true. Big part of her backstory was she was a recovering alcoholic from a working-class background. Her and the lord met on one of the inner-city schemes he was heading up at the time. She had cleaned up her act and they fell in love, apparently. Tabloids went crazy for it when it eventually came out and I think he liked it because it made him out to be this sensitive man of the people. I don't ever remember there being any mention of her having a child before they got together though. He was nearly twenty years older than her. Creepy.'

'Was?' I ask. 'Popped his clogs, has he?'

'Yes. They both have. He went in 2015, and she passed end of last year. Liver disease. I guess she never fully recovered.'

'So Kendrick left it too late to meet her? That's rough.'

'No idea how he felt about that.' Liam continues to flick through the sheaf of paperwork. 'But I think I know why he called the meeting with Trent.' He meets my eyes. 'We've got him, Dad.'

We lock everything back up at the studio and get out of there as quickly, and quietly as we can, taking the wad of paperwork with us. After he's finished telling me what he's just found, I think he might be right about having some cards to play against Trent. But as we drive back home, and he starts laying out the bones of some scheme he has in mind to use the stuff and somehow get out clean himself, I start to worry he's losing it. It might make sense in theory, a good idea on paper, but it's nuts and involves far too many people and moving parts. I have another go at trying to convince him to throw himself on the mercy of the law – especially now he has the stuff from the safe – but he won't hear a word of it.

He's buzzing, leaning forward in the passenger seat, eyes sparkling as we pass each streetlight. 'Trust me, Dad. He'll go for it. He wants that part more than anything else right now. It's all about the call back – always is.'

Maybe I'm being defeatist in my old age, but if he's adamant about giving it a go, I have to try to help. We need to get home and get a few hours' shut-eye. Tomorrow – no, TODAY – is going to be a busy one.

CHAPTER 49
LIAM

LIAM CHECKS HIS WATCH AGAIN, waits another agonising two minutes or so and then turns his phone back on. It seems to take an age to come back to life, but he had to make sure it couldn't be reached for that small window of time. As soon as it finds the network, it buzzes three times in quick succession. All missed calls from Trent. One voicemail. He plays the message.

'Mate. Where are you?' Trent's voice is breathy, excited. 'Just had a call. Wainwright's PA, I think. They fucked up and called me by mistake. She wouldn't talk to me. I'm hoping you're on the phone to them right now and it's good news. Swear to God, if you've missed their call... well, let's just hope you haven't. Call me, soon as, yeah?'

Liam takes a few seconds to get into character and then returns the call.

Trent picks up on the first ring. 'Mate? What the fuck? Where are you? Was it them? What did they say?' There's no anger, just pure boyish excitement.

Liam puts a smile into his voice. 'Calm down. Let's not get ahead of ourselves, but... yes, it was his office. Did you say they originally called you directly? No idea how they even got your number, but then—'

'Whatever,' Trent interrupts. 'Like I give a fuck about that. What did they say? Have I got it?'

'Not yet. But, next best thing—'

'A call back?'

'Yep, but before you get all excited again, it's not going to be in person and it's got to be today, this afternoon if possible.'

'Sure. No worries. I'm ready for the call now. Whenever.'

'Hold your horses. They want me to be present and I'm still up in Leicester.'

'Why?'

'Oh, didn't I tell you? Had to come up last night. My dad's not been well.'

'Can't you just dial in?' Trent asks, ignoring the fact Liam's just said his dad is ill.

'Yes, but don't you think it would be better if we're in the same room? If we do it at Twin Oaks, I can give you a subtle heads up or ask for a break if things aren't going our way.' There's a pause, and for a moment, Liam gets the impression Trent is deferring to someone else. 'You on your own?' he asks.

'What? Yeah, but there's a lovely young lady here asking me if I want another chai latte.' He briefly takes his mouth away from the phone. 'No, I'm good, but thanks, yeah? And don't forget to ask me for that selfie before I go.'

Always looking for content for his socials, Liam thinks. He'll have some more soon. 'So, are you good to come up here? It's a zoom call, three o'clock.'

There's a pause, then Trent says, 'Liam, this better not be some kind of ambush again. I won't be as forgiving as last time.'

Liam tuts. 'Why would you even think that? I thought,

with everything we've been through… well, I thought we were past it. Anyway, you knew about it before I did.'

'Hmm. Suppose.'

'The alternative is I go back to them and see if we can schedule something over the weekend, when I can get back down to London. Up to you.'

'No fucking chance, mate. This is it. I can feel it. Sorry. Guess I'm already getting nervous. Your place is fine.'

'Good,' Liam says, managing to keep the sigh of relief out of his voice. 'I can pick you up from the station if you like?'

'No need. I'll drive. Might pop over to Notts, see my mum afterwards. Hopefully be able to give her the good news.'

More lies, Liam thinks. 'Good idea, but let's not jinx it, eh?'

'You're too superstitious. I'll be there at two. Your place, yeah?'

Liam finishes the call, checks the connection is definitely dead and nods at Mickey, who's been quietly sitting at the kitchen table listening. 'We're on.'

'Sounded touch and go for a minute. Obviously Hazel did a good job of the call. You sure he's not just playing along?'

'Positive. And even if he did think something was up, he can't know for sure and won't take the risk of blowing the whole thing. You heard how desperate he is. Careers have been made on the back of working with this eccentric old bastard.'

'Makes a good film, though,' Mickey says. 'I loved the one about the art heist—'

'Framed? Yeah, I bet you did.'

'Cheeky git. It had a great twist.' Mickey's smile fades. 'You still sure this is the way to go, son? Seems a bit over-engineered to me. Why don't we just show the stuff you found to the police, or my lawyer, and take our chances?'

'And how do we explain how we got hold of those documents?'

Mickey shrugs. 'Just don't like you putting your fate in the hands of so many other people – one of them being that dopey sod, Warren.'

'Thought you said he knows this stuff inside out?'

'I know he's got more of an aptitude for this than being a locksmith, but I've got no idea if he can actually pull it off. Not really my bag, Liam.'

'From what I've seen, he knows what he's doing and the documentary guy I know has got tons of experience. The kit looks top notch.'

'And what about the other bloke you're relying on? The one who's got the most pressure, apart from you?'

'Oh, he'll be great,' Liam says, clapping his hands together. 'Trust me. And that's why we've got the back-up, remember?'

But the confident gesture isn't fooling himself, let alone his dad, who stares back for a full ten seconds before eventually getting to his feet with a heavy sigh.

'Right. Well, I'm going to nip over to Hazel's place, make sure they're set-up properly, and then I'll get myself into position out front a good hour before he's due. Just in case. I'll let you know when he gets here.'

'Don't be late, Dad.'

'I won't,' Mickey says, stepping forward and giving Liam's bicep a squeeze. 'Stay safe, son. I'll be right outside if and when you need me. OK?'

'Thanks. Appreciate your help and I'm sorry I've let you down.' He swallows back the emotion he doesn't have time for right now.

'You haven't let me down. I'm a fine one to talk. We'll get through it together.' He holds Liam's stare, nods and walks away.

When he gets to the doorway, Liam asks, 'Dad?' then waits until Mickey turns around. 'Say hello to Hazel for me as well. I'm sorry about what I said last night.'

'Will do.' Mickey smiles warmly. 'See you later.'

CHAPTER 50
HAZEL

WHAT THE HELL is Mickey pulling her and Warren into now? He has assured her there's no danger and it's all to help Liam, who's in some serious trouble. Mickey had already put in the groundwork with Warren, knowing it would make it harder for Hazel to say no. So now Warren is upstairs setting up something he says is going to 'do mad numbers, yeah' on his streaming channel and Mickey is on his way round to properly explain what's going on.

He pulls up outside and she's waiting on the doorstep when he gets out of his van. She has her arms folded, ready to give him a hard time, when she sees the bandage on his hand and the black bags under his eyes and thinks better of it.

'What have you done now?' she asks, pointing at the bandage.

He gives her a peck on the cheek, his rough, unshaven face rubbing against hers, and steps into the hallway.

'I'll tell you all about it and what's going on, I promise. But can I just pop up and make sure everything's OK with Warren? Has he got it all sorted?'

'How would I know? I don't even know what it is that's

he's trying to sort.' She gestures to the stairs. 'But sure, be my guest.'

Mickey heads up and she goes into the kitchen to make the tea. She's putting milk into Mickey's drink, when she hears a car engine and looks out of the kitchen window. Shit. It's Craig. Why hadn't she been straight with him and told him it was over? Because, she realises in that instant, she still hadn't fully committed to the idea of trying to be with Mickey. But seeing Craig's scowl as he passes Mickey's van and marches up the path towards the door, she knows it was wrong to have kept stringing him along.

She rushes into the hallway to try to meet Craig on the doorstep, but he already has his key in the door and has stepped inside. He's wearing a slim-fitting tracksuit and smells of shower gel and freshly sprayed deodorant. He's on lates and usually squeezes in a morning gym session before his shift.

He stops and takes her in. 'Alright? You look guilty.'

OK, she thinks. It's going to be like that, is it? 'Not guilty,' she says. 'Just didn't expect you, that's all.'

He turns his head, motioning back in the direction of Mickey's van parked outside. 'Yeah. Can see that. Where is he?'

'If you mean Mickey, he's upstairs. Warren's showing him something on the computer.' She tries to speak as loudly as she can, without it being too obvious that she's trying to tip off Mickey and Warren that Craig has arrived.

He runs a hand through his short dark hair, still glistening and damp and snatches a glance at himself in the hallway mirror. 'Since when has that luddite been interested in computers?'

'Why are you here?' Hazel asks, inwardly cringing at how confrontational she sounds. But the last time she and Craig spoke had been a huge argument about the only thing they ever rowed about... Mickey Blake. Hazel had had the perfect opportunity to end it with Craig and she had changed her mind at the last minute. All because she hadn't wanted to give Craig the satisfaction of knowing it was because of Mickey. This, she thinks, is what happens when you put things off.

'Oh, that's nice,' Craig says.

'Well, it's clearly not to apologise.'

'Apologise? Me?' he asks. 'Thought you might have come to your senses.'

'I have come to my senses,' she says and folds her arms. 'And I do owe you an apology for not telling you sooner.'

'Tell me what?' His voice is quiet now but loaded with tension.

'You and me,' Hazel says, not quite believing this is happening. 'It's not working.'

'Oh, right,' Craig says, shouting past Hazel and up the stairs. 'That twat finally talked you round did he?'

There's movement upstairs, but Hazel calls back over her shoulder. 'Mickey. Stay where you are. That goes for you as well, Warren. I've got this.'

'Yeah,' Craig shouts again. 'Stay up there if you don't want to get hurt, you old bastard!'

More movement above them and when Craig smiles at something behind her, she knows Mickey is about to come down.

'No, Mickey! I mean it. Stay up there. I don't need you to fight my battles.' Craig tries to step past her and she uses both hands to push him back towards the front door. 'Grow up, Craig. Accept it. It's over. I don't want you.'

His voice cracks. 'But you want *that* instead?' He jabs a finger in the direction of the stairs.

'I don't know what I want right now,' she says, as sensitively as she can. 'But whatever it is, it won't be with you. I'm sorry. I should have told you sooner.'

Craig blinks, furiously trying to process it, trying not to

get emotional. He stares at Hazel, his lips a thin line. She feels like she should cry, to show him how sorry she is, but the tears won't come. All she feels is relief. Maybe Craig senses that and after a pause, he slams the side of his clenched fist into the picture hanging on the wall in hallway. It's a large, framed photograph, a black and white studio shot of them both taken last year.

'Hey!' Mickey shouts, but Hazel gestures for him to shut up and stay back and it seems to do the trick.

Craig leaves his hand there in the centre of the shattered glass, until a trickle of blood runs down to the frame. Hazel fights to hold back tears and Craig looks disgusted with himself.

Mickey comes down the stairs and Hazel flinches when he puts his hand in the small of her back and asks her if she's OK. Quietly, he says, 'I think it's time you were going, Craig. Don't you?'

Having lost the moral high ground, Craig seems to shrink, unable to look either Mickey or Hazel in the eyes. He turns and leaves, dripping blood on the beige carpet as he goes. He slams the door closed behind him and Hazel stares at the crimson blotches on the floor.

'It's OK, Haze,' Mickey says. 'I'll clean it up before it stains.'

It's already too late for that, Hazel thinks. Yet another blemish on her already patchy record of relationships and all because she tried to hedge her bets. She can see that now. Whatever she decides about Mickey, she needs to go 'all-in' or not at all. She still isn't sure what exactly is going on today, but she can sense it's serious. Seeing the blood on the carpet takes her mind back to Skegness. She knows life can change in a matter of seconds, everything you care about can be taken away in an instant. She might not get another chance. She needs to tell Mickey how she feels now. She turns around and opens her mouth to speak, but he pulls her in close, holds her tight to his chest and kisses the top of her head.

'It's OK,' he says. 'Don't say anything yet. Whatever it is can wait. Tell me when I get back.'

CHAPTER 51
CLAIRE

'SEE YOU LATER, MUMMY,' Izzy calls over her shoulder as she runs down the garden path, up the steps and into the house. Tora, Claire's best friend, is at the front door, holding a glass of Prosecco and laughing as Izzy squeezes past her.

'They're in the den downstairs, Izzy,' Tora says, but Izzy has disappeared out of sight, seeming to already know where her sister and Tora's daughter, Leah, will be.

'Thanks so much for this,' Claire says, handing over two backpacks with Izzy and Grace's things in. 'I owe you one.'

'Nah,' Tora says. 'Makes my life easier, to be honest. Leah was begging me to sit through *The Hunger Games*, again tonight, so having your two here means me and Paul can actually have a grown-up's Friday night for once.' She raises the glass of Prosecco. 'You got time for one before you hit the road? Think I've got some alcohol-free stuff somewhere.'

'Better not. Want to get on the road and beat some of the rush hour traffic. Hopefully be there by teatime.'

'Claire,' Tora blurts out, 'you're not doing this because of the call the other day are you? I feel like I shouldn't have said anything.'

'What?' Claire says, trying to put her at ease. 'No, no. I've known something hasn't been quite right for a few weeks now.'

It's only half-true. She had been shaken when Tora told her about Liam's call to the kids a couple of days ago. Even Izzy had been quite freaked out by it, despite Liam making light of it when Claire quizzed him.

'And you're sure about not telling Liam you're coming?' Tora asks. Her tone is light, but Claire knows what she's intimating: Shouldn't you warn him? You might not like what you find.

Claire raises a thin smile. 'It isn't that, Tora. I'm sure it isn't. Anyway, I'm not an idiot. I'm not going straight to the house. I owe Auntie Barbs a visit and Liam told me that's where he would be tonight with his dad. And if he isn't... well, I'll cross that bridge when I come to it.'

Even to her own ears, it sounds unconvincing. She's certain Liam is hiding something, knows he isn't being straight with her, but an affair? It can't be. Can it?

Tora steps down, puts an arm around Claire and gives her a squeeze. 'I'm sure you're right. Whatever it is, you'll sort it out. Probably business stuff, like you said.'

Claire had believed that, too. Until Liam had called again this morning and said he's spending one more night in Leicester and will drive back tomorrow. Something about Barbs wanting to cook for Liam and his dad. She hadn't challenged him at the time, but she knows he's holding something back. His voice had sounded strained, he was talking fast and couldn't wait to get off the phone. Claire sniffs away the tears, before they can get a foothold.

'Thanks mate,' she says. 'I think he's just stressed about the buyout on Monday. I've got a bottle of his favourite wine and then I'm going to—'

'Screw his brains out?' Tora asks, before cackling and covering her mouth.

Claire laughs for real now, gives Tora a playful slap on her arm. 'No more Prosecco for you!'

They say their goodbyes, hug one more time and Claire jogs back to the car. Keys in the ignition, she pauses. Should she go home, run a bath and have a night on her own? Give herself time to calm down, think straight? She instinctively feels like a grenade has been thrown into her life and knows she should be running in the opposite direction, grabbing her children and diving for cover. Instead, she's sprinting towards the imminent explosion, ready to throw herself on top of it and damn the consequences. Just wait, she tells herself now. Wait until Monday, when the buyout is signed off, and everything will go back to normal between you and Liam. Except it won't, she knows. It can't. Because he's lying to her again. She can feel it in her bones, as certain as the love she feels for Izzy and Grace. And by accepting lies and dishonesty from their father, what kind of example is she setting for them? No. For ill or good, this ends tonight.

She drives away before she can change her mind, heading for the motorway, for Leicester and the truth.

CHAPTER 52
LIAM

'I'VE SET up the laptop in the main room,' Liam says to Trent's back as they walk through the hallway.

Trent stops and turns. 'You sure you're okay with that, mate?' Trent has slipped back into the caring character Liam now knows he isn't. He even reaches out and puts a hand on Liam's shoulder, but Liam sees it in Trent's eyes – he's calculating, always trying to play the angles.

'Has the best light,' Liam says, 'and it's where the internet signal is strongest. And, as you've seen, the rest of the place looks like a mausoleum.'

'Good man,' Trent says before he continues on to the study.

Good man, Liam thinks. Yet another phrase he's never heard Trent use, or at least never noticed before. He wonders how many other clues he's missed.

In the room, Trent tosses his satchel onto the armchair, in front of which, Liam has positioned the laptop on the coffee table. The coffee table he had to bring in from another room, because the last one was destroyed when Kendrick and Trent fell on it.

Trent notices Liam staring at the table and seems to read his mind. 'You sure it's wise doing it in this room, mate? I know Wainwright's supposed to be a bit up himself, but I'm sure we can find a blank wall out there or upstairs or something.'

'No,' Liam says, too quickly, too loudly, and immediately regrets it. He takes a breath before adding, 'It's fine. And apart from the state of the rest of the place, this is closest to the Wi-Fi router. Last thing we need is losing the signal just as he's about to hand you the part.' He forces another smile.

Trent blinks a few times, looks around the room and takes on an air of sadness. The kid was born to act, Liam thinks.

'I do get it, mate,' Trent says, now taking a seat and putting his satchel on the floor beside the chair. 'I'm still trying to get over what happened that night, you know?'

'Really?' Liam asks, just about managing to keep the sarcasm from his voice. 'You seemed to have handled it pretty well. On the outside at least. It doesn't do you any good to keep these things bottled up.'

'Is that what you think I've been doing? No, mate. It's been on my mind every second of the day.'

'You've done a good job of hiding things then.'

'I'm not the only one,' Trent says.

'What d'you mean?' Liam's heart rate kicks up a notch.

'I think you know what I mean, mate.' Trent's face changes again. The hooded eyes are back.

'I really don't.' Before he spoke the words, Liam hoped they'd sound confident and resolute, but when they come out, they're brittle and unreliable.

Trent gives a tight-lipped smile and steeples his fingers. If Liam were directing him now, he'd tell him the gesture is clichéd and hackneyed.

'All this.' Trent opens his hands, looks around. 'Setting up the meeting back here. Your obvious nerves. You clearly know something I don't.'

Liam doesn't want to swallow, but can't help it. His mouth is drier than a box of talc. He's about to speak, but Trent cuts him off.

'Don't worry,' Trent says, grinning now. 'I know you get all uptight about keeping your word and all that. You can't tell me. Officially, that is. But I'm way ahead of you.'

'Are you?' Liam asks.

'Yeah. It's in the bag, isn't it? The part, I mean. This is just a formality. You're on edge in case I fuck it up.'

Liam allows himself an 'okay, you've got me' smile and says, 'You honestly think I'd tell you if that was the case? And anyway, nothing is in the bag until the contract is signed.' He pauses, nods. 'But, yes. If you can avoid any major faux pas, that would be great.'

'What do you take me for?' Trent says with a wink, now clearly struggling to contain his excitement. It almost makes Liam sad for what he hopes is about to happen. Then he remembers what lies behind Trent's good looks and charm. Remembers walking back into this room to find Kendrick's corpse on the floor. Thinks about Titch and what her last moments must have been like. It brings him back to the task at hand.

'Seriously, though, Trent,' he says now. 'You need to stay on it at all times. From the little bits and pieces I've been able to glean about Wainwright's process over the years, he's weird.'

'No shit,' Trent says. 'I heard he once asked Tom Cruise to eat a bar of soap to prove he was right for that sci-fi film he did with him.'

'Well, I don't know about that. But I do think he likes to throw curve balls. So stay on point.'

The Zoom call is due on Liam's laptop in ten minutes, but Liam needs to get Trent's phone from him. That won't be easy, especially when he's busy tapping away on it right now.

'Shouldn't you be getting in the zone?' Liam asks. 'Anything you want to run through with me? Possible questions? What's your pitch for the role?'

'Huh?' Trent says, looking up from his screen. 'Thought you said I should just be myself.'

'Definitely. But he still might want your thoughts on how you think this character should be played.'

'You think? I thought he was like Kubrick, or whatever? You know. Just tells you what he wants.'

Liam tries to affect casual nonchalance, but it's hard when his body is tight with nervous energy. He manages a shrug. 'Who knows? He hasn't even been seen in public since the last film, and that was, what? Eight years ago? I heard rumours he isn't in great health either.'

He hopes this comes out as a natural aside. He's heard no such thing about Wainwright's condition, but it may help him sell what's about to come.

'Great,' Trent says, edging forward in his seat. 'Don't want the old bastard dying before we get to make the film. That would be just my luck.'

Unbelievable, Liam thinks. Yes, a man dying would be a terrible blow to your career. He keeps his cynicism in check and feels a thrum of anticipation when Trent puts his phone on the coffee table. But he immediately picks it up again.

'Shit. Nearly forgot to finish my post.'

'What post?' Liam asks.

'Just teasing a big announcement.'

'Trent, I told you this had to be in total confidence. It's his main stipulation. Are you trying to lose the job before you even get it?'

'Alright, mate. Calm down. It's seriously cryptic and

worst comes to worst, I'll just come up with something else to feed the masses.'

'How cryptic? I'm telling you, he will walk if he thinks you've let the cat out of the bag. I had to sign an NDA before he would agree to the call.'

'Relax,' he says, then finishes typing and puts the phone on the arm of the chair. 'All I said was to look out for some big news coming soon.'

Liam sighs, pretending to be irritated. 'Even that could be dicey. Radio silence from now on, OK? In fact, I even had to promise there would be no phones in the room when the call comes through. You best hand yours over and I'll put them both in the kitchen and grab us a drink.'

Liam holds out his hand for the phone, but Trent doesn't move to give it to him. Instead, he leans back in the chair and gives Liam an appraising look.

'No phones in the room?' he asks, voice dripping with incredulity. 'No fucking way he said that.'

'That's what his PA told me. Said if they even got a hint of a mobile phone being nearby, Wainwright would terminate the call.'

'We can just turn them off and keep them in our pockets. Liam, what is this bullshit? What's going on.'

Fuck, thinks Liam. It feels like the room is tilting. Somehow, he holds his composure and turns the fear into anger.

'This bullshit, as you call it, is what it's like playing with the big boys. You know how mental these people can get and Wainwright is about as eccentric as they come. For the past few months, this is all you've talked about. Supposedly all you've wanted. And now I'm on the verge of delivering it, you're behaving like a rank amateur.'

The last two words cut into Trent like a couple of well-aimed fencing strikes. Trent flinches, before his face hardens again.

'Careful. Mate. I'm no amateur and you haven't delivered

anything until I get the part.' Trent gets louder, more animated. 'And if I do, it'll be because of what I've done. Not you. Not fucking Kendrick Locke… or any one else. Me. So get back in your fucking box.'

Now there's less than five minutes before the call comes in. Trent's got that look in his eye again, like the one he had that night, just after he'd stabbed Kendrick. Like the one he probably had when he threw Titch off the car park. Liam needs to tread carefully, but he also needs that phone.

'Sorry,' he says, nodding. 'You're right. That was out of order. But after everything we've been through, and with the final buyout meeting on Monday, I'm seriously stressed mate. I need this as much as you do.'

Trent narrows his eyes. 'Why? What difference does this make to the deal?'

Here goes, Liam thinks. He was hoping not to have to play this card. 'I wasn't going to say anything, but LimeLight have been making noises about trying to drive down the price, or maybe even getting cold feet.'

'I hadn't heard that.'

Why would you have heard that? Liam thinks. 'Don't get me wrong, I'm pretty sure it's just a negotiating tactic. They're playing hard ball to get the best price or whatever, but if I could get you attached to a project like this? No way they can fuck us around.'

Two minutes until the call. Trent picks up his phone, but still doesn't look like he's going to hand it over.

'He's going to call any second, Trent. Turn it off, please. And hand it over. It'll make me feel better knowing I've done what they've asked. As you're always telling me, I know I'm too honest for my own good. But I like to sleep at night.'

Trent sighs, nods and turns off the handset. 'Okay, I give in. Let's hope I get it after all this. Then you can sleep pretty easy, in a very expensive bed.'

'Yes,' Liam says, taking the phone and trying to keep his

hand steady. 'And you'll get a nice, fat bonus, which is the only reason you're giving in.'

Trent laughs and puts up his hands in mock surrender. 'You got me. Guilty as charged. Now grab me a cold Coke – or has Wainwright got a Pepsi fetish I don't know about?'

Liam heads to the kitchen to get the drink and sends the go signal, a text to Mickey.

CHAPTER 53
LIAM

AS ARRANGED, the video call comes through at three o'clock on the dot. Liam's laptop chimes with the repetitive jingle. Trent sits up in his chair and gives Liam the nod to connect. Liam crouches in front of the laptop and tries to ignore the sick feeling growing in his gut. What is he going to be greeted by? He clicks the connect button and tries to obscure as much of the screen from Trent as possible – in the hope he can quickly disconnect again if he doesn't like what he sees. But he knows that's futile too – at this point, what will be, will be.

After a second or two, a message appears saying the caller is connecting to video and audio and a moment after that the screen is filled with a figure sitting in front of a window, almost putting him in silhouette. But there is enough light to make out a man who appears to be in his sixties, wearing a baseball cap, a yellow silk scarf and a ratty-looking brown jacket. He's wearing large Jeff Lynne-style sunglasses and when he speaks it's with a strange transatlantic accent.

'Who are you?' the man on the screen asks. 'The agent? Ian or something, isn't it?'

'Liam, Mr Wainwright,' Liam says. 'And yes, I represent Trent Williams and—'

'Well put him on then, man.' Wainwright looks off camera, as if speaking to an unseen assistant and says, 'What is this shit? I thought you said you'd made the arrangements?'

'Apologies, Mr Wainwright,' Trent says, leaning forward and trying to peak over Liam's shoulder. 'I'm here.' He gives Liam the side-eye, clearly indicating he should get out of the way.

Liam nods and stands, taking a few steps off to the right, so that he can still observe the screen, without being in shot.

'Ah,' Wainwright says. 'There's the kid.'

Liam winces, hoping it isn't all a bit too much, but Trent seems so fully invested and focused on the job in hand that no amount of strange accents and eccentric behaviour can put him off.

'The kid,' Trent says now and smiles. 'I love it. Sounds like something from one of your westerns back in the day.'

'Indeed, indeed,' Wainwright says. 'But enough of this *Mr Wainwright* bullshit. Call me Larson for now. If things change, I'll let you know.'

Liam is convinced he heard a little Yorkshire in the way Wainwright said the word 'know', but Trent seems delighted with everything so far.

'Fair enough, Larson. Either way, this is a massive thrill for me. Can't believe I'm getting a chance to talk to the man who made *The Path Less Travelled*. And *Loose Morrows* is a work of genius, as far as I'm concerned.'

'Tell that to those assholes over at Paramount. They cut the marketing budget in half after the test showings. Pricks. Anyway, quit blowing smoke and tell me why I should give you this role.'

Trent flashes a look at Liam then takes a deep breath before diving into his pitch. He tells Wainwright about his early life on the street, the way he had to overcome a difficult start and being the product of a broken home. Really laying it on thick, just as Liam had assumed he would.

'Interesting,' Wainwright says, once Trent has finished. 'All interesting stuff. But I'm not sure I buy it.'

'You don't buy it?' Trent looks shocked. 'Which part?'

'How about any of it?'

'I know some inner cities in America are probably a bit tougher than over here, Larson, but I can assure you that—'

'You can't assure me shit!' Wainwright says, leaning forward, revealing more of his face. Liam's breath catches in his throat. He snatches a glimpse of Trent and tries to gauge his reaction.

Trent's jaw is set, eyes hard. 'Is that right, Mr Wainwright? And why might that be?'

Easy there, Larson, Liam thinks. Don't play all your cards at once. But Wainwright is in full 'Egocentric Director' mode and obviously isn't going to back down now.

'Let's have a little look-see, shall we?' he asks, and Liam is once again painfully aware of that northern English accent breaking through the American mid-west. Larson picks up a sheet of paper from the desk in front of him. 'I go deep on my research, Mr Williams, or should that be Mr Blythe?'

Liam frowns at Trent, feigning confusion. Trent's hooded eyes are back, composure has returned.

'So I use a stage name. What of it? Michael Caine was Maurice Micklewhite.'

A stage name you've never once shared with your agent, Liam thinks.

'Stage name, my ass!' Wainwright bellows. 'And I couldn't give a rat's ass about that. But the only reason you were even in the frame for this part was because I was told you were the real deal. Like your old pal, Kendrick Locke.' He pauses here to scratch his beard, lean back and generally chew some more scenery. 'How is Kendrick these days, by the way? I heard he's out of jail and trying to make another go of it? Now *him*?

I know he's what he says he is. My producer talked me out of asking him in for an audition. Says he's too much of a liability. He would've been my first choice.'

'You don't know what you're talking about!' Trent says, then jabs a finger at the screen. 'I'm superior to him in every department.'

Now it's Trent whose accent is slipping. It's in the way he says 'superior', a slight softening of the first R.

Wainwright leans forward again, a huge grin on his lips. Liam wills him to sit back and not give the game away, but it's too late. He sees something shift in the way Trent looks at the screen. Should Liam simply kill the call and say he's making an intervention to save Trent's career? Or let it play out and see what happens? While Liam's indecision simmers, Trent speaks again.

'Listen, Larson,' he says, and the anger of a few seconds ago seems to have been replaced by a calm assurance. 'I don't know what you think you've turned up in your "research" but regardless of my upbringing, I've dealt with my fair share of adversity and come out the other side. It's like the quote from Lafarge in your film *Broken Sound* – you know, from his big speech? What is it he says again?'

No, thinks Liam. Don't fall into the trap. He opens his mouth to stop Wainwright from answering, but it's too late.

'Trying to impress me by referencing my films won't work, I'm afraid.'

'I agree,' Trent says. 'Especially since *Broken Sound* isn't one of your films anyway. So who the fuck are you?' He looks up at Liam. 'And what is this bullshit?'

Liam tries his best to look as shocked as he can. 'I have no idea what's happening right now, but I think everyone just needs to calm down.'

'I'm chill,' Trent says, as his eyes burn with rage. 'Just want to know why some second-rate character actor is pretending to be Larson Wainwright.'

'Second rate? You cheeky young bastard. I was playing The Dane while you were still shitting green.' Wainwright, or rather Martin Chalmers playing Larson Wainwright, blurts out. His broad Yorkshire accent now running rampant, along with his temper. He leans into the light to jab one of his sausage-like fingers at the screen.

Trent squints. 'Knew it,' he says to Liam. 'It's that fucking dinosaur you've still got on the books, isn't it? Met him at a party years ago and he bored me about how women were taking over the industry. Chambers or something, isn't it?'

'It's Chalmers, you insufferable little cunt!'

'Martin!' Liam shouts. But it's too late, Chalmers' red mist has descended and nothing Liam can do or say now will change it. He watches on as Trent clutches the arms of the chair, like he's about to launch himself into the laptop.

'Why don't you fuck off back to Lord and Lady Blythe,' Chalmers spits now. 'Sorry, I forgot, they're both dead. Why don't you go and dry your tears on a few of the fifty-pound notes they must've left behind for you. You fucking posh twats, swanning in, lassoing all the best parts with your fucking school ties and—'

'Fuck you!' Trent screams, his face only inches from the laptop, before he looks up at Liam. 'And fuck YOU, as well. What is this? What are you doing?'

'Stop!' Liam pleads. 'Just wait, okay?'

Trent's eyes burn with rage. But he waits. For now.

Liam calls out, 'Play the video. Now!'

Trent frowns, confused, then looks to the laptop screen, where Chalmer's face is replaced by some wobbly handheld footage. It's dark and grainy but Trent's eyes widen when he realises what he's seeing. 'But... how? This... you can't have this. It's not possible. I...'

'Because you what?' Liam asks, as he backs away from Trent. 'Threw Titch off that car park? After you took her phone?'

Trent opens his mouth to answer, then glances back to the laptop and changes his mind. He smiles at the laptop camera. 'Ha. Good one, Liam. I have no idea what you're talking about or what that weird, ropey footage is. Can barely tell where it is, let alone who's in it.'

Trent squints again, making a show of examining the clip that's now playing on a loop. 'Is that supposed to be me? Nah. Presumably, you're recording this, but let me be very clear...' He adopts a rational, calm tone and speaks directly to the laptop. 'I have no idea what all this is about and I think my agent may be trying to implicate me in something very serious. He has been acting strangely of late and is perhaps suffering some kind of breakdown. That's all I have to say on the matter.'

He slams the laptop closed, killing the connection.

CHAPTER 54
MICKEY

I'M CROUCHING DOWN behind the boundary wall, to the right of the entrance. Hidden from the road and masked by the undergrowth and trees if anyone looks back from the house. I'm watching it all play out on a YouTube live stream, although Warren told me it's going out to Instagram and Facebook at the same time.

The live stream goes black for less than a couple of seconds, before it switches over to the hidden camera and microphones Liam got his documentary mate to rig up. There's a tiny camera above the window, giving a wide shot of the whole room. We positioned it close to the curtain rail, difficult to spot, unless you're close and really looking for it. Liam figured Trent might cotton on to the ruse with the laptop or that the silly old actor bloke would fuck things up. Give Liam his due, it was a smart move. Now Trent's closed the laptop, I'm hoping he's going to feel like he's got the upper hand, maybe even get more loose-lipped. Either that, or he'll lash out at Liam, hard to call. Either way, Liam had been adamant: do not follow Trent to the house. It's killing me, hanging back outside. I mean, technically speaking, I can keep an eye on what's going on, but there's bound to be a delay in this live stream and what am I supposed to do if something kicks off? Leg it down to the house? It'll probably already be too late anyway.

Who am I trying to kid? Even if I was there in that room with Liam and Trent right now, what could I realistically do if anything happens? I'm an old bloke with a dodgy hand.

Fuck that talk, Mickey.

He's your son. And you ain't that old.

You'll die protecting him if needs be.

But that's going to be tricky two or three hundred yards from the house. Maybe I should at least move a bit closer? No. Stick with the plan. It's like I can hear Liam saying it. I need to trust him and be ready to help if and when I can. Right now, that means paying attention to what's going on in that room.

'Was that it?' Trent is asking now. 'Your big play? Getting some washed up actor to pretend to be Larson Wainwright and hoping I'd confess to something?'

When Liam doesn't answer, Trent goes on.

'And what exactly is it you're accusing me of? Got to be honest mate, I'm really hurt and confused by all this. You saw for yourself what Kendrick tried to do to me.' He gestures to the laptop. 'I know what it might look like on that clip, but it was Kendrick who brought the knife to the meeting.'

'That's not what Titch told me. She said you took it out almost as soon as I'd left the room.'

'She was mistaken. If you think I'd deliberately attack Kendrick, without cause, you're deranged.'

'I think he gave you cause when he told you what he'd found out.'

'Which was what?'

'That you and he were brothers.'

It's hard to tell from this angle if Trent is shocked. 'No. I think you're getting confused mate. At one point, we were *like* brothers.'

'Un-unh,' Liam says. 'It was fresh news for Kendrick, but you've always known. Or at least, you knew before you turned up in Kendrick's life, trying to pretend you shared the same background as your idol.'

'Kendrick Locke was never my idol.'

Trent's street persona is starting to slip. The Midlands accent is still there somewhere, but there's nothing working-class about the way he speaks now.

He says, 'Maybe I just wanted to try to understand why he was being touted as the next Stormzy, when all I ever saw was a low-level thug who could rap a bit.'

'Ken was so much more than that.' Liam says, and I can tell he's getting angry now. Calm down, son. 'He was a great writer, a producer and was showing signs of being a good actor too. Yes, he struggled to put his upbringing behind him, but his talent and success was in spite of all that. Not because of it.'

'I've made my own way too!' Trent slaps a hand on the arm of the chair and comes off sounding like a self-pitying teenager.

'Bullshit!' Liam shouts, but he's got to be careful. No telling what this bloke might do. Especially if he thinks they're alone.

'Lady Jane,' Liam says now. Here we go. Game on. Tread carefully. 'It was right in front of me all the time. Here's me thinking it was some kind of coded message from Kendrick, when all he was doing was telling you he knew you both had the same mother. Although the version you got was a bit different, wasn't it? She got clean. Turned her life around and met your dad, Ken Blythe MP. Older man, very rich. The only estates you knew about were country estates in Notting-hamshire and the south of France.'

'We all have our own truth, Liam. We both know you weren't exactly the Oliver Twist character you like to make out. Pretty fucking middle-class now, aren't you?'

'Unlike you, I've never hidden my background.'

Trent gets to his feet and forces a sarcastic laugh. 'Ha! Total horse shit, mate. Total. Horse shit. And you fucking know it, as well.'

He's got you there, Liam, I think, as I try to stretch my back out and ignore the burning in my thighs from crouching so long.

Liam shrugs. 'There are levels, Trent. I didn't want to advertise who my dad was, or who he used to be. But what were your reasons? Why not just tell Kendrick everything when you met? And how did you find out in the first place?'

'Here's the thing, Liam,' Trent says as he walks up and down behind the chair. 'That shit you just tried to pull, recording me on the laptop, means you're trying to frame me for what happened to Kendrick.' Liam is about to say something else, but Trent waves him away. 'But, even if you had pulled that off, you seem to be forgetting the fact you're up to your neck in this too. If I go down, so do you. Your precious buyout will be dead in the water, you'll be disgraced with your family and you'll go to prison.'

'I didn't kill Kendrick,' Liam says. 'You did.'

'So you say.' Trent leans on the back of the armchair. 'But here are the facts. You lured me here under false pretences, just as you've done today, and you and Kendrick planned to kill me because I knew the truth about what went down between the two of you before Kendrick was arrested.'

Trent does make that sound plausible to anyone who's listening. Just have to hope they've seen enough to know it's bollocks. Why had Liam told Trent about what Kendrick had over him? I suppose because if he hadn't, he wouldn't have been able to persuade Trent to come to the meeting with Kendrick in the first place.

'I know, I know,' Trent says now. 'You'll say you didn't know anything about that and our lawyers will go back and forth, but let's be honest, I'll have the best counsel money can buy and—'

'Not so sure about that, Trent,' Liam says. 'About you having the best counsel money can buy, I mean. You've done OK with your career so far, but I also know you've welched on at least three business deals and you've ploughed most of your money into that vanity project you call a music studio. Again, trying to follow in the footsteps of your big brother.'

'There's that ruthless side you usually save for exec meetings and contract negotiations,' Trent says, with a lifeless smile. 'But I think you're forgetting, that due to the sad passing of mummy last year, I'm about to become very rich.'

'*Were* about to become rich. Past tense,' Liam says, with a smile of his own. When Trent only frowns, Liam adds, 'Until the will was contested by your mum's remaining blood relation, Kendrick Locke.'

Trent's rattled, but holds it together. 'Even if Kendrick was thinking of doing that, it would be a bit tricky now wouldn't it?'

'That's it, isn't it?' Liam says. 'That's why you killed him. He told you he was going to contest it. And you couldn't bear the thought of sharing it with him. Even though you grew up with all the privilege and everything else, you weren't prepared for him to have any of it.'

'Why the fuck should I?' Trent screams.

'Yes!' I hiss, punching the air and standing up to relieve the pressure in my back, stretching out some of the aches and pains. 'You've got the bastard now, Liam,' I say.

On the other side of the wall, someone clears their throat. There's a scuff of gravel and then a familiar voice.

'Any reason you're hiding behind a wall on private property?'

Fucking hell. Not again. Not now.

'Jeanette?' I ask, then stand on a log to give me the height to see over the wall. There, sure enough, is PC Crackers, hands on her hips looking up at me with a sour smile.

'When I'm in uniform, I'd prefer to be addressed as Officer, thank you.'

Aware my phone is turned up loud, Liam and Trent's voices tinny but audible, I try to subtly reduce the volume with my thumb. At first it gets even louder, before I adjust my grip and manage to mute it. I sneak a glance at the screen. Despite Jeanette arriving on the scene, I really don't want to kill the connection. I hold the phone down by my side.

'It's not private property,' I tell her. 'Well, it is. But it's my son's house.'

'Right,' she says, squinting up at me. 'Still doesn't explain why you're lurking in his woods, watching porn or whatever it is you've got there on your phone.'

Typical Jeanette. Always bringing it back to sex.

'It's just a meeting. Zoom thing he's having,' I say. 'Wanted me to dial in so I could give him some tips on…' I try to think of the right word. '…Negotiation and stuff.'

She sniffs, looks around. 'You smell that? Either the farmers have been muck spreading late this year, or it's total bullshit.' She jabs a finger at me. 'Stay where you are. I'm coming round.'

'This is harassment,' I call after her. 'You've clearly been following me. You were warned to back off.'

But she ignores me and strides off towards the main entrance. Fuck. Fuck, fuck, fuck. She's mental. I look back at the phone and turn the volume up again, just for the half a minute or so I've got before she's no doubt going to be trying to put the cuffs on me again.

It's great Liam has managed to get Trent to admit what he's done, but how's he going to get Trent out of there without him twigging what's happened? And if Trent comes out any time soon, he's going to see me hanging about the front garden with the psycho version of Juliet Bravo. Speaking of which…

'Come on,' she says, as she picks her way through the undergrowth. 'Hands up against that wall please. Spread your legs.'

'You've got a serious problem. You know that?'

'Yes,' she says as she reaches me. 'He's called Mickey Blake. And he keeps giving me legitimate reason to suspect he's up to no good.'

'What? By kissing someone outside and—'

'Adultery,' she snaps, without a hint of irony.

'Hazel isn't married and anyway, since when has adultery been a crime? And what's the charge this time? Gardening without a permit?'

'Oh, Mr Funny is back again, is he? With his little jokes. Now are you going to turn around and put your hands on that wall or am I going to have to assume you're resisting arrest again?'

I hold up my bandaged hand. 'Do I look up to resisting anything?'

'Probably fiddling with yourself too much. You'll go blind!' She cackles, like she's just come up with an absolute zinger. 'I say, you'll go blind! Because of all the wanking!'

'Yeah,' I say, stony-faced. 'I caught your drift.'

When I don't laugh, her hand drifts to her truncheon, or night stick or whatever it is they call it these days. 'Thought you were the one with the sense of humour? Or do you only laugh at your own jokes?'

I nod at the stick. 'You going to hit me if I don't laugh?'

'Don't tempt me. Now turn around and give me that phone.'

I try to pull the phone out of her reach but it's too late, she snatches it from me and takes a step back. When I move to follow her, she gives me one of her looks and I decide to stay put.

She squints at the screen. 'What's this then? A meeting, you said? Isn't that that musician lad? Trent what's-his-face?'

'Yeah. That's the one. My son's his agent.'

'And this is going on now, you say?' She tilts her head and watches for a few more seconds. 'Weird camera angle. And why are they standing up? Looks more like one of them hidden camera shows.' She looks up again. 'This is something dodgy, isn't it?'

CHAPTER 55
LIAM

'BEFORE HE FOUND out who she was, Kendrick didn't give a shit about knowing who his real mum was,' Trent says. It seems to Liam, the more Trent speaks, the more his real accent comes out. Maybe it's the emotion. 'Mum tried to reach out to him, through the proper channels, and he didn't want to know anything about her.'

'The adoption services wouldn't be able to put them in touch, unless Kendrick allowed it.'

Trent narrows his eyes. 'I fucking know that, Liam. But she knew who he was anyway. She could still have approached him directly. I told her to do that.'

'How did you find out about it?' Liam asks, now genuinely curious.

Trent sighs and plonks himself down on the arm of the Chesterfield. 'She told me, accidentally, while in one of her drunken stupors after dad passed. Blurted out everything. Crying and saying how proud she was of him. Said he'd made the most of a bad start. Unlike me, who she said was ungrateful, lazy. Of course, next day, she didn't remember a thing, so I let it drop.'

'Except you didn't let it drop. You became obsessed with Kendrick.'

'Stop trying to play Sigmund fucking Freud on me, Liam. I didn't become obsessed. I wasn't jealous. I just wanted to know more about my brother.'

'Rubbish,' Liam says, enjoying the way it lands like a slap on Trent's face. 'I saw what you were like when you arrived on the scene. Following him everywhere, spinning him the line about your similar upbringing and the rest of it. You wanted to be him. You always have. Killing him wasn't just about the money. It was about making sure he couldn't take back what you've stolen from him. I can see that now.'

Trent gets to his feet again. Liam flinches, but stands his ground. 'Swear to God, Liam, you keep saying shit like that and I'll end you.'

'There he is,' Liam says. 'The real Trent Williams. The ruthless little cunt who killed Kendrick Locke. Well guess what? Turns out Ken did contest the will after all.' He tenses, ready.

'The fuck you talking about? No. He didn't. You think I didn't check that afterwards? It's been two weeks and nothing. I've checked with my solicitors. The estate should be finalised in the next few weeks.'

'Turns out, he'd filled in the paperwork. Just hadn't got around to sending it.' Liam smiles at the way Trent's mouth drops open. 'But don't worry, I made sure it was posted first class today. It will be with your solicitor tomorrow.'

'You're bluffing.'

'Am I?' Liam asks, widening his smile. 'You sure?'

'Even if that were true, he'd need to be around to follow up and all the rest of it. And we both know that's not going to happen.'

'Well, at the very least, it's going to hold everything up. My understanding is now they know about him, they'll have to do everything they can to track him down.'

'But he's dead.'

'They don't know that. Could be years before they release the funds,' Liam says with a certainty he doesn't have.

Trent's breathing rapidly now, his eyes darting from Liam to the window, and back again. Liam prepares to grab the crowbar he's stashed beside the bookcase, and prays his dad is paying attention.

'Yes,' he says now. 'I've been busy. I had my doubts on the night, but I was in shock and felt partly to blame for putting your life in danger with Kendrick.' He shakes his head. 'Seems I got that the wrong way round. All I did was help Kendrick put his head in the lion's mouth.'

'He wasn't Snow White, Liam. What – you think he came here to have some nice family reunion? Claim the little brother he didn't know he had? No, mate. He saw a payday. That's all.'

'Can you blame him?' Liam asks. 'Maybe you could have gained a brother if you'd been straight with him from the start. Instead, he's lying God knows where, and all because you didn't want to give him a cut of what's rightfully his.'

There's a pause while Trent seems to process all of this. Eventually the tension seems to leave his shoulders, composure returns. 'You've been distracting me. Delay tactics. Trying to keep me talking. Who's coming? The police? Are they already outside? What makes you think they'll believe you anyway?'

'If the police were here, you'd already know about it. I don't want them involved. You were right. I know I'm tangled up in this, whether I like it or not. I also know you killed Kendrick in cold blood and did the same to Titch, which means you could do exactly the same to me as soon it becomes convenient.' Trent opens his mouth to object, but Liam waves it away. 'You are a threat to my family, my business and me. That's why I took action today. I wanted to get you back here, in this room and for you to admit what you've done. At least tell me the truth. Who did you call that night for advice? And where did you dump Ken's body? Tell me that, and I won't send Kendrick's claim on the estate.'

'I knew you were bullshitting!'

Liam shakes his head. Inside his pocket, his phone starts to vibrate with a call. He lets it ring out. 'It exists. I took it from his safe this morning. I haven't posted it. Yet. But the second anything happens to me or my family, it will be there the next day – as well as on the newsdesk of every red top in the country. Along with the full version of your riches-to-rags story. You'll be finished.'

Trent licks his lips. 'How do I know you've not done it already? And what about all that shit with Chalmers? Does *he* know everything?'

'Of course not,' Liam says. 'I told him you were from a posh background and that I wanted to bring you down a peg or two. He was more than glad to help. And as for telling anyone else – why would I do that? I've got as much to lose as you. Maybe more. My family are my number one priority. I want to keep them safe, get this buyout over the line and, to be honest, take a step back from the business for a while. Be there for Claire and the kids.'

Trent doesn't speak, but he's blinking, chest still rising and falling with adrenalin. This is it, Liam thinks. Be ready. He's going to reach into his pocket and pull out that knife, or run at you, full of anger and hate. But no... Ten seconds pass. Ten seconds more and still Trent hasn't moved. His breathing slows, jaw relaxes.

Sensing the change, Liam says, 'All I want is the truth about what happened that night. You owe me that. Was it really just about the money?'

CHAPTER 56
LIAM

TRENT STARES into his lap and sighs. 'When I first saw him here that night, I expected anger, bitterness, something. I know I felt all of those things when you told me it was him who had engineered the meeting. But then… I don't know. He embraced me, it seemed genuine and it all just… went away. Felt right, you know?'

Liam's phone begins to vibrate again in his pocket. He ignores it.

Trent goes on. 'So all of that stuff in the meeting, our chat, the laughs? It was all real, I meant it. For a few minutes I actually thought I could stick everything back together, come clean and that Kendrick and me could be a force together.'

'Then why didn't you?' Liam asks, trying and failing to keep the frustration from his voice.

'I wanted to!' Trent says and slaps the arm of the chair. 'When Ken dropped out the Lady Jane thing, I thought, right, this is my chance. He knows and I can finally shake off all the shit I've been carrying around for years, the lies and everything.'

Yes, Liam thinks. Something you could have done right at the beginning.

'I know, I know,' Trent says, 'I probably should have told Ken who I was – who *he* was – as soon as we became friends. But… it just never seemed right.'

'It never seemed right?' This is taking too long, Liam thinks and decides to up the ante, press a few buttons. 'Or were you jealous of what he had and didn't want to compete with him for your mum's affections too?'

'You piece of shit,' Trent says, eyes darkening.

'Am I wrong?' Liam asks, and almost flinches when his phone begins to vibrate again. Is it the same caller?

Trent stares up at Liam. 'Do you have any idea what it's like when your mother overlooks everything you've done, everything you've achieved, all the love you've given her, and puts this fucking… this fucking… gutter snipe on a pedestal?'

So much for all the brotherly love, Liam thinks. 'I doubt she was putting him on a pedestal, Trent. She was guilty for having to abandon him in the first place and was probably proud that he'd managed to make anything of his life. He was her son. Her firstborn.'

'And didn't I fucking know it!' Trent shouts. 'Even after he told the adoption agency he wasn't interested in knowing who she was, the silly bitch still couldn't stop going on about him. She made him out to be a saint, even when he went to prison. I wish she'd been alive just to see the look on his face that night. It wasn't love I saw in his eyes… it was pound signs. Greed. End of. You can take the boy out of the slums, but… well. You know the rest.'

'So that's why you killed him?' Liam asks. 'Because you didn't like the look on his face?'

'You weren't there! You didn't see it. He was laughing at me, mugging me off as usual. Thinking he can just waltz off with half of what doesn't belong to him. And with everything that's coming to me in the buyout.' He's trying not to cry. 'I told him he was a mercenary cunt and he slapped me – he actually slapped me! So, yeah. I took out my knife, just to warn him off. But he laughed. I had no choice. Just ran at him, we fell backwards, flattened the coffee table. You saw the rest.' He begins to cry.

Yeah, Liam thinks. I saw the rest of it, and the fact you rolled over on to your back, to make out Kendrick had attacked you. And then that you went on to kill Titch. You ruthless piece of shit.

'You called someone on the night, after it happened. You said they would know what to do. Who was that?'

Trent looks up, blinking away tears Liam now realises were never real anyway. Liam is so on edge he almost jumps out of his skin when his phone starts vibrating yet again in his jeans pocket. Even though there's no ringtone, it's so quiet in the room now, they can both hear it. He lets it ring out.

Trent's eyes darken and he gestures to Liam's pocket. 'You need to get that? Thought you put both our phones in the other room? Where is my phone, by the way?'

Liam says nothing and his phone rings again. He and Mickey had agreed no calls unless it was an emergency. Of course, it could just be the office or someone else, but the fact they keep trying, means something must be wrong. He has to take it, just in case. Keeping his eyes fixed on Trent, he digs into his pocket and pulls out the phone.

Aunty Barbs' landline. He thinks about rejecting the call again, but instinct takes over and he picks up.

'Liam,' Auntie Barbs says, 'don't speak. If you do, bad things will happen. She's already hurt Claire.' She sounds distant and scared. Her words crawl into Liam's ear like a tiny poisonous spider, ready to lay eggs. 'Someone else wants to talk to you.'

There's a pause while the phone is handed over.

'Barbs is right, partner.' It's Flick. She's calm, but there's a brittle, dangerous quality to her voice. 'Don't say anything. Especially my name, seeing as how you seem to be broadcasting this all over socials. First thing we need to do is close that shit down, don't we? Your auntie is being a bit over-dramatic about Claire. Had to subdue her with that ridiculous stun gun of mine you like to tease me about. Lovely old Barbs has behaved. So far. Not sure what happens when you Tase someone her age. Are you?' She says this in a sickeningly jolly tone. 'So, first things first, hand the phone over to Trent.'

Liam's mind is spinning and pitching up and down like a broken waltzer on the fairground. It feels like someone has replaced the bones in his legs with spaghetti. It's an effort to move, but as he takes the few steps across the room to give the mobile to Trent, he tries think of some way – any way – he can possibly sound the alarm.

He holds out the phone for Trent to take. 'Watch. My. Lips,' he says, pointing at his mouth. 'Don't say the name of the person on the other end.'

Trent frowns, but his face changes as he listens to whatever Flick is now telling him. He glances up towards a spot above the window and the colour drains from his cheeks. His face shows shock and anger, before settling on a determined expression that chills Liam to his core. After a few more seconds, he nods and hangs up. Liam optimistically holds out his hand for the phone.

'I don't think so, do you,' Trent whispers. He smiles and begins to speak like he's on stage, annunciating to the back row. 'Wow. Apparently, this has done amazing numbers on the socials, Liam!' He looks towards the camera. 'And from what I hear, most of you lot thought it was real? Ha! Job done.' Trent gets to his feet and bows to the camera. He puts a hand on Liam's shoulder. Liam is frozen, unable to shake off the hot and heavy hand, as Trent continues his little speech. 'Credit to my manager, Liam here, as this was his brainchild. I thought he was nuts! But it worked. I've been trying to land a massive part I haven't been able to talk about yet, but that call we just received means our little audition has worked. And you lot helped with that as well. So thanks. Look out for a full update later.'

Trent gives a mock salute to the camera then marches over to the Wi-Fi router in the corner of the room and yanks out the cable. He waits a few seconds, holding up the phone. He nods, and Liam realises he's checking the internet is dead.

He points at Liam. 'Stay where you are. You know what will happen.'

He steps up to the window, dragging a foot stool with him so that he can reach up to pull down the tiny black camera. He drops it and crushes it beneath his shoe.

'Showtime's over, you sneaky little fucker.'

CHAPTER 57
MICKEY

JEANETTE'S EYES light up like the first night I met her, looking at me the same way a hungry drunk looks at a doner kebab. It's the scent of danger that clearly gets her going. I always assumed people became coppers to stop crime, but maybe for Jeanette it's just because she's got a thing for criminals.

'Well?' she asks now, holding up the phone and waving it around like it's the knife in the OJ trial.

I need to make a decision. My gut tells me Liam is going to need help very soon – that's assuming things haven't already gone pear-shaped in there. I could try to make a run for it, but I wouldn't fancy my chances against Jeanette. The crazy pervert would have me down on the ground, trying to do a strip-search before I could say 'inappropriate touching'. No. There's nothing for it. Maybe I should just give her what she wants – the danger part, that is.

'Depends what you mean by dodgy,' I begin. 'But, yes, my son has been dragged into something by Trent.' I point towards the house. 'They're in there now. There will be a bit of a delay on that feed, but for the past twenty minutes or so, we've been live streaming Trent's confession out on social media.'

'Confessing to what? And does he know it's being streamed?'

'Obviously not,' I say, trying to quell the sarcasm. 'But he's very dangerous. Killed at least one person, maybe another and to be honest, Jeanette, I'm terrified he's going to do the same to my son in there.'

She slowly shakes her head. 'What a let-down you turned out to be. You can't even make up convincing lies. You must think I'm really stupid.'

'I know it sounds mad. I wouldn't believe it either, but if you let me go to the house and check on him – come with me if you like – then you'll see for yourself.'

'Oh yeah, I'll let you just stroll down there and—'

'Shh!' I shut her up, realising there's a sound coming from the direction of the house.

'Hey! Who do you think you're talking—'

'Be quiet, woman!'

She takes a step towards me then stops when she hears the car speeding up the drive behind her. It's Trent's black BMW, Trent behind the wheel. I can't see Liam, or anyone else in the car and Trent doesn't seem to spot me and Jeanette in the undergrowth off to his right. He barely slows down at the entrance, takes a left as fast as he can, and he's gone.

'He was on his own!' I shout, before running towards the house whether Jeanette likes it or not.

She's clearly taken by surprise and doesn't move for a few seconds but it's not long before I can hear her crashing through the bracken behind me. She's swearing and it sounds like she trips at least once, but I'm away, heart pounding. I reach the stony, uneven drive and run as fast as I can back to the house. If that fucker has touched my son…

Jeanette more or less catches me as I reach the front of the house, but I ignore her, take the steps two at a time and head in through the already-open door.

'Wait!' Jeanette shouts. 'You run away like that from me again and I'll…'

But her voice fades away as I charge into the study. The light is weird in here and I realise the curtains are half-closed. One of the tie-backs is missing. What looks like the hidden camera is in bits on the floor, but the room is empty.

Jeanette's in the doorway, but her expression and demeanour has changed now. The cockiness and edge softened. I must look like I've lost my mind.

'Hey,' she says. 'Slow down, will you. Doesn't look like there's anyone here, not downstairs anyway.'

Sighing, she lets me push past her to run up the stairs. The whole time I'm shouting Liam's name over and over again. I go from one room to the next, but nothing.

'Where the fuck is he?' I ask Jeanette when I come back down the stairs.

She's standing in the hallway, taking everything in, checking the front door for signs of forced entry and all the rest of it. First time I've actually seen her look like she knows what she's doing.

'Outside,' I say, suddenly realising it's the only place we haven't checked.

'Hang on. Stop, will you? This could be a crime scene and you're charging around like a madman. I know you want to find him, but let's take one step at a time.'

She sounds so reasonable and calm, it shocks me into taking her seriously. 'OK,' I say.

'Right. You said this was being streamed or whatever. If that's true, we should be able to see what happened. Yes?'

Fucking hell, she's right. So obvious, even Jeanette can see it.

'My phone.' I hold out a hand and she gives it to me. I open YouTube again, trying to find the link. 'Fuck. It's gone.'

'Give it here,' she says, and I hand it back. 'It'll still be on there, up to the point it finished. Look, here it is.' She plays it and holds it up, while I step close to watch.

I tell her to scoot forward and to keep going until we get to the end. Images whizz past, Liam standing, Trent sitting, then standing, then sitting. Both of them moving their arms about, faces changing at rapid speed as she drags the playhead along the bottom of the screen.

'Stop there,' I tell her. Something has changed. Liam is on the phone. Why did he answer it? We agreed the only person who would call would be me, if there was some kind of emergency. Whoever it is on there, it shakes him up. He hands the phone to Trent. His lips move, and he makes a familiar gesture, but there's no sound and I remember I turned the volume down. 'Wait. What did he say?'

Jeanette drags it back a few seconds and turns it up. On the recording, as Liam hands over the phone to Trent, he points at his mouth and says, 'Watch my lips. Don't say the name of the person on the other end.'

It's some kind of message. There's only one reason he would say it in that way, because there's only one person I know who uses that phrase.

'Trent's got help,' I say out loud. 'I need to go home. Now!'

She grabs my arm, pulls hard. 'Hey. You're going nowhere... not without me. But first, I want to check the garden. I saw something out of the window I need to check.'

CHAPTER 58
LIAM

LIAM IS face down on the back seat of Trent's car. His hands bound together behind his back with the torn curtain ties from the study.

'I can't believe I didn't see it,' he says, as he tries to roll over onto his side, but when Trent turns left out of Twin Oaks, he's thrown back into the seat again. 'I've always wondered how you managed to wheedle your way into the agency and Kendrick's circle and somehow bypass me. It was Flick. She was the one who was championing you back then. I put it down to her being slightly younger than me and more in touch with the music scene, but of course she'd know who you are. Who you *really* are, I mean.'

'No, it was nothing to do with that. I was gigging regularly around the scene and—'

'Oh, so it wasn't anything to do with the fact you went to the same school as Flick's younger brother? Or that Flick knew your mum and dad were Lord and Lady Blythe? It's why you grew that stupid beard as well, isn't it? Hiding from all your old crowd.'

'Just shut the fuck up, will you!' Trent screams. 'I need to think.'

They only drive for a minute or so. They're supposed to be going to Barbs' house, but now it feels like Trent takes a right at the bottom of Hunt's Hill. In the past, Liam vaguely remembers seeing a lay-by a few hundred yards up whatever road this is, where it feels like they're parked right now. Liam can't be sure. Not without looking out of the window, but it's impossible with his hands tied so tightly and his legs bent awkwardly against the car door. What will happen to poor Auntie Barbs, if he doesn't show up? Or his dad, if he decides to go steaming in there? He curses the day he once took Flick to meet Barbs on a visit up here, otherwise she would have no idea where she lived. This is it, Liam thinks. This is where I die, stabbed and dumped by the side of the road.

But Trent isn't showing any signs of getting out.

Isn't showing any signs of doing anything, in fact. He's still and silent in the driver's seat. His phone has rung multiple times and he's ignored it. From Liam's vantage point, all he can see is the side of Trent's head, him twitching every couple of seconds like a hunted animal on high alert.

'Why aren't we going to Barbs' house?' Liam asks now. 'Your boss was clear about that. She wants me to sign that dodgy paperwork. It's all she cares about.'

'She's not my fucking boss, Liam. She's…' He tails off.

Oh Christ, Liam thinks. They're fucking. So it wasn't just harmless flirting after all. He's running out of time. What has Flick done to Claire? *Subdued.* That was the word she'd used. What does that even mean? Before that call this afternoon, Liam couldn't imagine Flick hurting anyone, but she's clearly desperate now. Everything is unravelling for her. She's clearly implicated in all this. Right now, it's time to make his pitch.

'She's using you, Trent. Can't you see that? You think she made that intervention back there to save you from incriminating yourself? No. She was worried you were going to mention her.'

He shakes his head. 'No. It's not like that. Flick's always

had my back. She just wants to make sure this deal goes through, that's all. And you're fucking it all up.'

'That's who you called, isn't it?' Liam continues. 'On the night it happened. When you said you knew people who could help with stuff like this. I thought you meant some bad people from your days on the street. Course not. You lot are always the same.' Liam's raging now, squirming on the seat and trying to loosen the ties on his hands. But he also knows he has to be careful not to alienate Trent. In a negotiation, no one likes to feel stupid.

He forces some calm into his voice and tries again. 'All she cares about is getting this buyout over the line and now I know why. Yesterday, I found what I thought was a mistake in the final paperwork, that the lawyers had accidentally got mine and Flick's shareholding mixed up. I'm an idiot. She's using the buyout to steal my company from me.'

The look Trent gives Liam now isn't shock or surprise. He's known about it all along. In fact, Liam now realises, that's why a bonus for Trent was written into the contract in the first place. It had nothing to do with a stipulation from LimeLight. It was Flick's doing, to keep Trent onside until the deal was done.

'So you're doing her bidding because she's thrown you some money into the deal?'

'You think I'm fucking stupid? That I can be bought off for a few quid?' Trent says, spittle settling in his beard. He wipes it off. 'She's written in that I get my own production company out of it.'

'You seriously believe that? Have you actually seen the contract? Because I have. And there's no mention of anything like that.' Liam can see he's making a dent. Trent is frowning now, looking at down at him and trying to work out if he's telling the truth. 'You know I'm right, Trent. She's added one of her dad's businesses in there. With hers and his shares, she'd have a controlling interest and I'm guessing the plan was to just steal the company out from under me.'

Trent nods, like none of this is news, then asks, 'But there's no mention of Hombre Productions?'

'Nope,' Liam says. 'Still think she's going to help you out of all this? She's going to get the contract signed and then throw you under the bus.'

'She can't,' he says. 'Not with what I know about her. She helped me deal with Ken, for fuck's sake!'

'Deal with him?' Liam asks. 'You mean, his body? Where is he?'

Trent, grim-faced, ignores the question and starts the car.

'Where are we going?' Liam asks.

'To ask that bitch what she thinks she's doing and to see if you're telling me the truth.'

CHAPTER 59
MICKEY

'WE HAVEN'T GOT TIME, JEANETTE,' I say. 'We need to go. Now.'

But when we round the corner into the back garden, there's a swarming sound that only gets louder as we head down the path towards the ancient well. Flies. Thousands of fat bluebottles, zigzagging around the heavy wooden lid. Once we're close, there's a faint smell of rotting meat, acrid and claggy in the back of my throat. I put my arm over my mouth. Jeanette motions for me to stay back and I'm glad to oblige. Nothing good is going to be down that well. Whilst trying to wave away the flies, she peers into what must be a hole in the splintered wood, near a heavy rusted padlock.

She shakes her head and comes back up the path towards me, speaking into the radio on her lapel. Mostly jargon, but I pick out the word SOCO – scene of crime officers. Looks like Trent didn't spend much time trying to find a good place to get rid of Kendrick.

'You know Liam has nothing to do with this, right?' I say. 'This just proves he's in real danger. You've got to let me go there now. He needs help.' I try my luck and touch her arm. She gives me a look but doesn't shake me off.

I suppose any other copper would arrest me, wait for the forensics team and all the rest of it and send backup to Barbs. Fortunately, this is PC Crackers and she doesn't do anything by the book.

'I told you before,' she says. 'You're going nowhere… without me.'

We race out of the garden and up the drive, back towards her patrol car.

Hazel has texted me. Seems she worked out Liam's coded cry for help as well – she lived with Barbs for months and recognised the exaggerated 'Watch my lips' clue Liam gave. I've told her to stay home and wait for my call. I can't have her getting caught up in this. As me and Jeanette approach Barbs' house, I tell Jeanette to park up on the road outside. I don't want to drive straight into the courtyard and announce our arrival to whoever's in there. We don't know what we're going to face yet. To my surprise, she does as she's told. I jog down to the courtyard entrance and take a quick look to see what vehicles are parked there. Shit. Trent's car is parked closest to us, and I can see Barbs' Volvo in her usual spot off to the left, which means she's in there. If anyone has touched her, I'll fucking kill them – dodgy hand or not. There's a sporty Mercedes I don't recognise next to that and, even though I've got no idea why, I'm pretty sure the other remaining car – a Toyota SUV – belongs to Claire. What the fuck is she doing here? No wonder Liam looked so shaken on the video.

'What's going on?' Jeanette hisses into my ear and I almost soil myself.

'We can't use the front door,' I tell her before explaining who might be in there and why we need to get the lay of the land first.

'You're teaching your grandma to suck eggs. I'm a police officer.'

I decide to skip the sarcastic comeback and lead her round the perimeter wall, through a side gate. We make our way as quietly as possible along a narrow alley that runs down the side of the house. There's a door I'm hoping Barbs hasn't locked that leads into a small utility room. It's usually open in the day so Barbs can hang out the washing in the back yard. I've got my keys, but if Barbs' keys are in the other side of the door, we're fucked.

I gently test the handle. It squeaks but opens and we step into the narrow utility room. Washer, dryer and sink line the right-hand wall, coat hooks and muddy boots on the other. There are raised but muffled voices coming from another part of the house. I put my finger to my lips for Jeanette's benefit, but she rolls her eyes and shakes her head, as if to tell me she's not an idiot. I take her to the other end of the room, where there's a door off to our left which leads into the rest of the house. She's creeping towards it, when I put a hand on her arm and point to the ventilation grate, seven or eight feet up on the end wall of the utility room; Barbs' Nosey Grate. It has a perforated tin cover and a small sliding mechanism underneath it. It's currently closed. It's stiff and makes a tiny scraping noise as I force it open, but as soon as I do, we can hear more or less exactly what's being said in the living room, the other side of the wall. Jeanette's eyes widen in surprise and we try to tune in to what's happening and who else might be in the house.

CHAPTER 60
LIAM

'JUST FUCKING LET HER OUT, will you!' Liam shouts, flicking his head towards the pantry door where Claire is currently locked inside. There's a kitchen chair wedged under the handle. Liam's in front of the fireplace, plonked into another wooden chair, hands tied painfully behind his back. Trent stands close, brandishing what looks to Liam like the same knife he killed Kendrick with.

They're in the living room, door to the kitchen open. Flick stands next to the sofa, where Barbs sits, stoically pretending that Flick isn't holding the garish red Violator stun gun a couple of inches from her head. So far, Barbs looks unharmed. Flick, on the other hand, is dishevelled. Her cream blouse is torn at the neck and the side of her face is puffy and swollen.

'I'm not letting her out, Liam. No. Fucking. Way,' Flick says and gestures to her red cheek. 'She punched me!'

Claire kicks the pantry door. 'There's more where that came from, as well. You stuck-up bitch.'

Liam struggles not to smile. At least it sounds like she's recovered from the stun gun.

'I didn't want to hurt her, Liam,' Flick says now. 'But I had no choice. I didn't know she'd be here.'

Neither did Liam. 'So it was just the little old lady you were going to threaten, then. That makes everything OK.' Barbs raises her eyebrows but, out of character, decides not to comment.

Trent steps forward, into the middle of the room. 'Flick, what the fuck is going on?'

'I told you, babe. This deal is massive for us. I couldn't let him destroy it.'

'Massive for *us*?' he asks. 'Or massive for *you*? Where's the paperwork? I want to see it?'

'It's in my bag over there,' she says, flicking her head towards a black business satchel. 'But the only person who needs to see that is Liam. And he needs to sign it. No more stalling.'

'And what's the plan then, Flick?' Liam asks. 'If I sign it under duress, I'll just say so. Not to mention going public with the fact you were involved in Kendrick's death.'

Before she can control it, she glares at Trent, then tries to change her expression. 'Don't know what you're talking about. All that was news to me when I saw it on the stream earlier.'

'The stream that must've been seen by every man and his dog by now,' Liam says. 'The genie's out of the bottle, Flick. You're finished. You must know this is all futile? It makes no sense. The deal is dead.'

'No, see,' she says, stepping away from the sofa and getting animated, 'I've thought about this and if you sign it, now, I can get it ratified at the meeting on Monday and, and—'

'And what?' Liam asks. 'Then you'll kill me? And Barbs? And Claire?'

'What? No. I think once it's going through, you'll realise it's a great deal for you and—'

'You've cut me out. That other company you said was a subsidiary of LimeLight, it's one of your dad's businesses isn't it? You're so desperate to get back into his affections, you've lost your mind.'

'What about Hombre?' Trent says, referring to his supposed production company. He takes another step towards Flick and uses the knife to make his point. 'Liam says there's no mention of it in the contract. That true?'

'Of course it's not in the contract,' Flick says, smoothly. She closes the gap between them and touches his cheek. 'I told you. That's one of the first orders of business, once everything goes through. Daddy's promised me.'

Trent pulls away from her and looks back at Liam. He doesn't speak, but Liam can read the question there: Is she telling the truth?

Liam slowly shakes his head. 'Even if that were the case – and we all know Flick's dad is one of the most ruthless people on the planet – do you really think that little pantomime you added to the end of the live stream earlier is going to stop people from asking where Kendrick Locke is? The police and journalists and a couple of dozen paparazzi will be searching for him as we speak. Even if Flick doesn't give you up, within hours, her dad will. You think he's going to hand you a production company after this? She wants me to sign the paperwork and pin Kendrick on both of us, so even if I wanted to dispute the contract, who's going to believe the accomplice to a murder?'

Trent is sweating, and wipes his face with the palm of his hand. 'But she… she's the accomplice!' he shouts. 'She helped me hide the body, for fuck's sake!'

'Even if that were true,' Flick says now, looking from me to Barbs and Trent, like she's trying to convince a jury, 'no one would believe you and why would I do such a thing?'

Trent whirls around to face her. 'Because you said we needed insurance. Said it was there if we ever needed to take Liam off the board.'

'And was I wrong?' she asks.

Take me off the board, Liam thinks. One of Flick's favourite sayings. Has he always just been a chess piece to her?

'It was stupid,' Trent says. 'I said we should've found a place miles away. Not in his fucking back garden. When they find him in that well, I'm fucked. Especially after what I said on the live stream.'

Liam's reeling, a distant sound ringing in his ears. The well? Kendrick has been there this whole time? He remembers looking out of the window earlier, seeing the bees buzzing around there, except, he now realises, they weren't bees at all.

'Liam's right,' Trent says through gritted teeth and shakes his knife, inches from Flick's face. 'You're going to throw me to the wolves. You ruthless fucking bitch. It was your idea to get rid of Titch. I still think we could've paid her off.'

Trent's hand is shaking with rage. Flick looks scared but holds her ground. 'Listen, Trent. Babe. It's not like that at all. Why do you think I called you earlier? To protect you from saying anything else to incriminate yourself. I—'

'Lies! You thought I was going to mention you, that's all. And you needed him—' He points at me. 'To sign your fucking contract. He's right. You've lost the fucking plot.' He lurches towards her, stops short. She yelps, takes a step back and raises her stun gun.

Trent laughs. 'You won't fucking use that on me. And if you do, so what? It'll hurt but then I'll fucking kill you, understand? Same goes for anyone else who gets in my way now. Thanks to you and him—' He jabs the knife at Liam, 'I've got nothing to lose.'

CHAPTER 61

MICKEY

WE'VE WAITED LONG ENOUGH. It's hard to know exactly what's going on in there, but Trent sounds like he's on the verge of losing it. We need to intervene before it's too late. I try to push past Jeanette, to get the door open and charge up the corridor, but she slams her forearm hard into my chest, glares at me and goes first. As she reaches the door that leads from the hallway into the kitchen, she pulls her nightstick and gives me a look that says *here we go*. I nod and she charges in, me following. Straight through the kitchen to the lounge. There's a kitchen chair wedged under the handle to the pantry door, presumably where Claire has been locked in. In the lounge, Liam is tied up and, off to my left, I'm relieved to see Barbs sitting on the sofa, looking scared but unharmed. Trent stands between Flick and Liam, his knife close to Liam's face. As me and Jeanette enter the room, he's distracted and turns to look at us. Flick sees her chance and jabs what looks like some kind of stun gun into the back of Trent's neck. He screams and drops to the floor, writhing in agony. Flick steps over Trent and goes for Liam. She manages a couple of steps before Barbs – bless her – sticks out a leg. Flick falls, smacking her head on the corner of the stone hearth. She's dazed, blood running down the side of her face, but still tries to get back to her feet.

Jeanette tells everyone to stop what they're doing, but Trent is recovering from the stun gun and scrabbling around on the floor for his knife. Liam desperately shuffles forward in the chair and kicks the knife across the floor, where it clatters against the skirting board. I move past Jeanette. Trent is on his knees and reaching for Liam. I kick him hard in the ribs and he crumples next to Flick in front of the fireplace.

'I said STOP!' Jeanette shouts so loud and fierce that everyone is shocked into silence and does as she says.

Trent is still eyeing his knife that came to rest a few feet away beside the dresser.

'I wouldn't, if I were you,' I tell him.

He's breathing heavy, wheezing and holding his side. He's got a burn on the back of his neck and two puncture wounds as well. He closes his eyes and goes limp, looking relieved to give in. A single tear leaks out. Only crying for himself, the selfish, posh prick.

Jeanette squeezes past me, letting her hand linger a little too long in the small of my back and giving me those hungry eyes again. The woman is tapped. But to be fair to her, she quickly turns to business and slaps the cuffs on Trent. She reads him his rights and makes him shuffle across the floor until his back is against the wall, then calls for backup.

Flick tries to use the mantel piece to drag herself up to her feet. Her top is ripped, her head's bleeding and one side of her face is red and puffy.

'You look like shit, lady,' Jeanette says. 'You gonna give me any trouble?'

Flick raises her chin, purses her lips and says, 'Who the fuck do you think you're speaking to?'

'A plummy little rich girl who's about to get nicked for aggravated assault and conspiracy to pervert the course of justice? Am I wrong?'

There's a commotion behind me. Barbs has let Claire out of the pantry, who stalks into the room ready to kick Flick's arse, but when she sees Liam tied up in the chair, she runs to him instead. She has a fierce-looking burn on her bicep and her hair is a mess but she seems to be OK. She unties Liam and they hug. Enjoy it while you can, son. When the relief fades, I think Claire's going to have a few things to say to you. I just hope they can put things right.

My phone buzzes with a text from Hazel.

I'M OUTSIDE x

I let her in and we stand in the hallway, our voices low. I tell her what's gone down, all of it, and by the end of it, her jaw is almost on the floor.

'Anyway,' I say now. 'I specifically told you not to come here. It was dangerous.'

'And you should know by now, that I never do as I'm told.'

'I know,' I say, laughing. 'It's one of the reasons I love you.' It comes out without me thinking about it and she seems shocked. 'No. Wait,' I say, panicking. 'Can't believe I've said that at a time like this.'

'What, at the end of a hostage siege?' she says, eyebrows raised and arms folded. 'Luckily for you, your lack of tact is one of the things I... *like* about you.'

'Oh, that's nice!' I say. 'Wouldn't even say it back to me.'

She laughs, leans in and kisses me, keeping her eyes open so she can fully enjoy my surprise.

'Does that mean we're courting now?' I ask.

'Courting? How old?!'

SIX WEEKS LATER

CHAPTER 62
JOSH SANDERS

TODAY IS GOING to be a good one. End of a good week, now Josh comes to think of it. For once, he's actually made a few legit sales – full fascias job in Aylestone and windows and doors at some rich twat's house in Woodhouse. Now, to top it off, he's had some old dear get in touch from one of his flyers and if the phone call's anything to go by, she's going to be gullible as fuck. Apparently, she's disabled and recently widowed. Silly cow even mentioned she's just had a load of money off her premium bonds and wanted to know if he'll take cash. Oh yes, he thinks now. I'll take your cash, no bother.

He pulls up at the address she's given, a nice three-bed semi in Groby. He gets out, clipboard in hand – got to have the clipboard, makes you look professional – and makes a show of appraising the house. *Appraising*. Josh likes that word. Got it from his Uncle Ripper, who told him you've got to sound like you know what you're doing. Clever bastard, is his Uncle. And Josh still needs to make amends after all that shit with the old locksmith. That's why Josh has been chasing down every lead and bringing home the bacon – another one of Ripper's sayings – these past few weeks. Got to show

Ripper he's more than some poxy salesman. He's *management material*.

After ticking a few boxes, even though the windows and the fascias look like they've only been in a few years, he heads up the drive and is about to ring the doorbell when he sees the front door is actually open a couple of inches.

He looks over both shoulders – force of habit – and is about to push it open when a voice comes from somewhere upstairs, making him flinch.

'Hello? Is that the window man?'

The woman's voice is so comically frail, Josh almost laughs thinking about how easy this is going to be.

'Yes, it's me, Mrs Crane. You OK?' He steps inside and closes the door behind him. 'Shouldn't leave your door open, you know. Not everyone's as trustworthy as me.'

'Bless you, love. I'm fine. Saw you pull up and just remembered one of these window locks in the bedroom is broken. Was just looking for the key and wondered if you do repairs? My eyesight's terrible though and I'm struggling to see it. Could you have a look for me?'

Josh smiles. 'Of course. Shall I take my shoes off?'

'If you could, love, yes. Just had the carpets cleaned.'

He unties his brogues, noticing the antique oak table in the hallway and what looks like a top of the range fitted kitchen beyond. This woman's got some dough, no doubt about it. He heads upstairs with a smirk on his face.

'Through here, love,' the old woman says.

He follows her voice to what must be the main bedroom. The door's open but he hasn't caught sight of her yet. The second he crosses the threshold, the door is slammed shut behind him. From where she was lurking, behind the door, a woman copper steps forward grabs his arm and twists it up his back. Shoves him hard against the fitted wardrobe, jerks his other arm around and before he knows anything about it, she's cuffed him.

'What you doing? What you doing?' he keeps asking, over and over again.

He's squirming, but the copper kicks the back of his legs and forces him to his knees, his nose still pressed against the wardrobe door.

'Stay down there, or I'll do you for resisting arrest.'

'Arrest? What you arresting me for? I ain't done owt!'

'Apart from stealing from vulnerable old people? That what you thought you'd be doing today? Shafting some poor old dear?'

'N-no.'

She rests something on Josh's shoulder. He turns his head to see it's her night stick.

'Well today, you're going to get some of your own medicine.' She pulls him away from the wardrobe and throws him, face down, on to the floor. With his hands behind his back, there's nothing to break the fall and his head takes most of the impact. Dazed and confused, he watches as the copper goes to the window. She looks out and seems to blow a kiss to someone, before giving a little wave and drawing the curtains.

She tosses her hat on to the bed. 'This is going to be fun.'

Outside, Mickey stares at Jeanette's bedroom window for another few seconds, shudders and almost feels sorry for Josh. Almost. But it passes quickly, and he starts the car, drives away and tries to decide what he's going to have for dinner. Oh yeah, he thinks. It's Friday. Time for a chippy tea.

CHAPTER 63

LIAM

LIAM AND CLAIRE sit on a bench in Bradgate Park. They're close to the ruins, the red-brick remnants of the house where Lady Jane Grey once lived. Izzy and Grace are clambering up and down the small outcrop of rocks nearby. It's early morning and their last day of a week-long break up here. They've been staying at Barbs' house, what with Twin Oaks being a crime scene. From out of sight, somewhere in the grounds of the ruins, comes the sorrowful-sounding call of a peacock. The morning mist lingers on the bracken, but Old John is still visible at the top of the hill in the distance. They sit in silence, both staring up the hill, Liam thinking how hard the climb is from this direction. Long and steep, over difficult terrain, but what a view when you get there.

Not for the first time since the events at Barbs' house, he reaches out to Claire, his hand finding hers. Every other time, Claire has pulled away, folded her arms, turned her back. This time she doesn't flinch, allowing Liam to gently stroke the back of her hand. She doesn't reciprocate, or show any other reaction but, he supposes, it's a start.

He's trying to make other amends too, for Kendrick, Titch and their legacy. He has put Kendrick's *Zebra* music project into the hands of a prominent producer. Kendrick doesn't have any living relatives, but the whole project and any money it makes, will go towards supporting and promoting rehousing and youth projects in Leicester. After seeing Trent's now infamous live-streamed confession, Bez has agreed to facilitate it. She wants to set up something in Titch's name – a new facility called Titchener House. Liam isn't sure he will ever come to terms with what happened to Kendrick and Titch, but he can at least try to create some good out of their deaths.

A cyclist rolls past and gives Liam and Claire a cheerful morning greeting. They both break out of their sombre personas to smile and wave, before slipping back into their own thoughts. Right now, Liam is just grateful Claire is still around. For a while it was touch and go. It was the secrets again. That's what Claire had told him. The fact he had kept everything from her, including that his heart had never really been in the buyout. He had been doing it because he thought it was what Claire wanted, what she expected even. It was a lot of money after all, and it meant Claire could finally build something for herself, in the same way Liam had built his agency.

Of course, the deal is dead in the water now. No chance of LimeLight or anyone else wanting to buy into the aftermath of all this. Liam is lucky to currently have his freedom, although that may change when all this goes to trial. Mickey's lawyer was as good as Mickey had been making out. Liam has been charged with conspiracy to pervert the course of justice, but with his lack of record and everything else, he at least made bail. Given the mitigating circumstances and the fact that Liam felt his and his family's lives were at risk from Trent, the lawyer says there's a chance any sentence Liam is given will be suspended. Right now, it's the best he can hope for.

'I'm sorry,' he says again, for what seems like the hundredth time.

Claire sighs and looks at him, really looks at him. There are tears in her eyes and Liam can sense this is it, finally the moment she tells him it's over. Kendrick, Trent, the betrayal of Flick, being arrested, all of it had seemed like it was the worst thing in the world that could happen. But looking into Claire's sad eyes, having seen the hurt and pain there these past few weeks has enabled him to put all of that into perspective. None of it matters, unless he has Claire by his side.

'Listen,' she says now. 'I told you what would happen if you weren't open with me again and—'

Liam tries to interrupt, to plead his case again but Claire, shakes her head.

'No,' she says. 'Let me finish. I told you that and still you kept those secrets, but I also know that you thought you were doing it to protect us. The way you fought to make things right…' She breaks off here and allows herself a small smile. 'Even if it was the most stupid over-engineered plan I've ever heard of. But I know you were fighting for me, for us. Our family.' She looks over to Izzy and Grace. Izzy is standing on top of the rocks, reaching down to her sister and helping her climb up.

'It's the same reason you've worked yourself into the ground these past few years, for something I now realise you didn't even want,' Claire says. 'You thought it was what we wanted. But Liam, all we want is you. Your time. Your smile. Not the fake one you give us when you're tired or thinking about work, your actual real smile.'

Liam doesn't deserve this woman, he knows that. His throat closes and the tears start, yet he finds himself smiling at her, his heart fit to burst.

'Yes,' she says now and touches his cheek with a soft, cold hand. 'That's the one. That's all me and the girls want. Family is everything. Why do you think I've been pushing so hard for you to patch things up with your dad?'

Liam thinks about Mickey. The way he came to his aid at Barbs' house, bringing that crazy policewoman with him. He thinks back to their conversation in Kendrick's office. He feels guilty, remembering what he said to Mickey about Hazel. Especially having seen again how happy he has been since he and Hazel officially became an item. He thought he would be angry when Mickey had jokingly told the kids to call Hazel 'Granny Haze'. Liam's pretty sure Mickey was only saying it to annoy Hazel, but the kids loved it and why shouldn't they get to enjoy a real grandparent relationship while they can?

Claire seems to read his thoughts. 'It's been great seeing the kids with him, hasn't it? They already have a bit of a bond.'

'It has.'

'Which is why I'm not leaving. For now.' Liam leans in for a hug, but Claire leans back. 'Hang on. I'm not finished. The condition is we quit London and move up here. Obviously not Twin Oaks, not now. But somewhere close by. You can still run the agency, or some form of it, from up here if that's what you want, and we can use the money from the sale of the house down there to get me started with my business.'

He doesn't have to answer and couldn't get the words out even if he wanted to. Instead, he pulls her into an embrace and squeezes hard. She hugs him back and it's the first time in months he has felt safe, strong, ready to face whatever comes next.

Eventually, Claire gently separates herself and calls to the kids.

'Izzy, Grace! Come on.'

'Why?' Grace shouts back. 'Are we going home?'

'Yes,' Claire says and then points towards Old John in the distance. 'But first, we're all going to climb that hill together.'

ENJOYED THE CALL BACK?

Scan the QR code to leave a quick Amazon rating and review or discover other books in The Mickey Blake series.

ACKNOWLEDGMENTS

My first thanks always go to you, my readers, for reading and supporting my books. If you've enjoyed *The Call Back*, please take a moment to leave an Amazon rating and review – it makes a huge difference to new authors. The feedback and encouragement you gave me after my debut, *Safe Hands*, came out into the world was humbling. It also gave me the belief to think I could do it all over again, and within a much shorter timeframe. A belief which at many times during the past year seemed, at best, misguided and at worst, deluded. As with any book, I could not have completed it without the help and support of some amazing people.

Bead Roberts, thank you for your continued 'tough love', especially your anger and disappointment when I considered taking a break from this book when things got difficult. Without your justified rage, I doubt I would have hit my deadline.

Dan 'The Man' Howarth. An excellent writer, friend and support who has to suffer my daily rants about self-doubt, the state of the publishing industry and Leicester City's relegation battle. He always listens, never complains and somehow manages to write loads of great books and stories while he's doing it. Thanks a million, buddy.

Speaking of productive and enthusiastic writers, Lauren North is one of the best. Despite being one of the busiest authors I know, she finds the time to read early drafts of my work and gives me the feedback I need to elevate the books and keep my readers turning the pages. I really appreciate your input, Lauren. Thank you.

Jackie Kabler. You may not realise it, but allowing me to whinge and moan at you for several hours at Harrogate Crime Fest, really helped me to finish this book. You encouraged me to lay out my story, asked the right questions and, ultimately told me to 'just get on with it'. You were, of course, right. So thanks again for your continued support.

Support networks are everything to creatives and I'm blessed with another one – Indie Write Place – my small cabal of talented writers which includes Angela C Nurse, Victoria Goldman, Neil J Hart and, of course, Dan Howarth. Thanks for sharing your ups and downs, sage advice and realising that a high tide lifts all boats.

Thanks to Debra Newhouse, a talented and patient editor who allowed me to move the goalpost several times with this novel. She is a pleasure to work with and will always improve your book.

Now, my family. Mum, Dad, Liam, Sean, Kerry, Sam and all my lovely nieces and nephews – I draw on your love and support more than you realise.

Meg, not only the best daughter anyone could have, but an early reader and champion of my books. Having you by my side at book events has been one of the best things about being a published author. Thank you. Aly, my long-suffering wife, you are always there for me and accept that half the time I'm 'away with the fairies', thinking about my books and characters. I'm sorry you have to repeat yourself so much and I hope you realise how important you are to me and our family. Love you loads.

ABOUT THE AUTHOR

Wayne Kelly is a writing coach, mentor and producer of the award-winning feature length documentary, NO FARE: The Sian Green Story. In addition to novels and short stories, he's written and directed several short films including INKLING, which was an official selection at the International Horror-Hound Film Festival in Ohio.

Since 2014 he's hosted The Write Place Podcast (formerly known as The Joined Up Writing Podcast), where he interviews successful authors about their books, writing and journeys to publication.

He is passionate about helping and inspiring other writers and produces educational courses and content. Take a look at waynekellywrites.com for more information.

With his limited spare time, he's a singer-songwriter with The Wry Dogs and devoted cat father to Milo. He loves to cycle around the beautiful Leicestershire countryside, where he lives with his wife and daughter.

To find out more and to download a free eBook with two brand new crime stories, go to waynekellywrites.com

Please take a moment to leave a rating and review. It really does help new authors reach a wider audience.

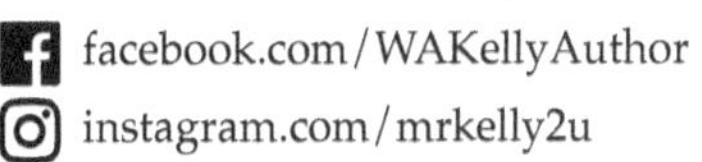
facebook.com/WAKellyAuthor
instagram.com/mrkelly2u